Isobel Kelly is 8[...] , Scotland, she now lives
in England. A long life with many experi[...] enhanced her imagination
and her gift for telling stories. Together with her love of words she set
out to create a series of books that pleased her readers, and surprised her
when they were sold in countries around the world.

Once an artist and restorer of oils and wat[...] colours, she owned a
picture gallery until retirement and was also a consultant in art and
interior design to major UK businesses. Laying brushes down and taking
up writing, her poetry was published in several anthologies. She was
asked to write for the 50th anniversary of The Lelant Village Produce
Association in Cornwall. She decided a magazine would be appropriate,
so with contributions from villagers and local advertisements she filled
it with interesting wartime memorabilia, composed poetry and found
pictures of the village. It sold at annual flower shows, and copies have
gone all over the world via tourists and villagers sending them to friends.

An accident laid her low for a while during which time a computer
became her best friend and from these small beginnings she launched into
novel writing.

On her own now, the widow of a lovely man she adored, she has four
adult children and four grandchildren. However, writing fills her life and
the intensive research required for every book keeps her mind active and
enthralled with the discoveries she makes. She wants to continue writing
for the enjoyment of her many readers from all over the world. To that
end the ninth book is already taking shape.

Read more about the author and her work at www.isobel-kelly.co.uk.

The Runaway

Isobel Kelly

SilverWood

Published in 2013 by the author
using SilverWood Books Empowered Publishing®

SilverWood Books
30 Queen Charlotte Street, Bristol, BS1 4HJ
www.silverwoodbooks.co.uk

ISBN 978-1-78132-165-2 (paperback)
ISBN 978-1-78132-166-9 (ebook)

British Library Cataloguing in Publication Data
A CIP catalogue record for this book is available from the British Library

Set in Sabon by SilverWood Books
Printed on responsibly sourced paper

To my dear friend Carol, a lady I much admire
as she is never at a loss for a word or two!

Book One

Cornwall – Spring 1833

Chapter One

"Charis! Where the hell are you? It's almost twelve and Baron Whaley is due at noon. Damnation, you bloody girl! You'll feel the weight of my cane if you're late." Thomas Tenby stood seething with rage in the main hall of the old Carwinnion Manor in Durgan, a small hamlet close to the Helford River in Cornwall, waiting impatiently for the arrival of his stepdaughter.

"Fenton!" he roared after a long, silent pause. "Where is Charis?"

Mrs Fenton, Tenby's housekeeper, wiped her hands on a kitchen cloth, straightened her apron and, having heard her employer's initial yelling, stood expectant for his next call which she knew would be for her.

"Katie, get up them back stairs to Chary's bedroom and warn her that the master's guest is expected any time now and he wants her down here soon as possible. Move it, girl, before worse happens. Heaven help us if he can't find her." She shooed the maid out of the kitchen and waited for his summons. When it came, she unhurriedly made her way to the hall; then, reaching it, curtsied to Tenby who was frowning angrily, tapping a stout, flexible cane against his thigh.

"Where is my stepdaughter, Fenton? Baron Whaley will be here shortly to settle the betrothal with her. It will not do for her to be late. I presume luncheon is prepared?"

"Yes, sir, the dining room is ready and the food on the way."

"You know most things that go on here. Where is the chit?"

"Some things maybe, sir, but I've no idea where Charis is now. She could be walking on the beach and has forgotten the time. Or maybe she has gone to the village. She was concerned about old Sam Trevarris. He's still ailing from the rheumatics—"

"Blast Trevariss! You both had your orders she was to be here to attend her betrothal. You'd better find her double quick! She will attend or rue the consequences." He waved his hand in dismissal.

Back in the kitchen, Katie shrugged her shoulders. "Bedroom's empty. I don't think the bed's been slept in. I changed sheets yesterday and the bed's still how I left it. Looks like she washed in cold water and has gone out early."

"Hmm. Well, get on with finishing them greens. The men will still want their bellies filled even if the betrothal is cancelled."

"Reckon that'll be the way of it? Will he make her marry him? Charis wasn't keen, was she? Nor would I be." Katie shuddered at the thought. "He's an ugly, smelly old man even if he is a baron with money."

"Pity she's still a month away from her majority or old Tenby couldn't do a thing about it. At least, I don't think so," she added.

"And I don't hold with gossip neither;" said Daisy Fenton, "so get on about your work. And let me remind you, girl, she is Lady Charis. She's quality, which is more than can be said for him out there or Whaley, come to that, even if he is thought to be a baron."

Just then, the knocker on the front door pounded a summons.

Baron Josiah Whaley had arrived.

Earlier that morning, some miles away, a ketch from the Helford River approached Falmouth Docks bound for the fish market with its load of crab, oysters and mackerel for sale in the city. Hidden between the fish boxes on deck was a small stable boy. Clad in riding breeches, boots, an enveloping coat filched from Barnaby, their man-of-all-work, with a large cap hiding the abundance of golden curls that would give her away, Lady Charis Landon prayed she could elude the deckhands and leave the boat when it docked in the same way she had managed to board it undetected. She also prayed that no one would guess her route of escape and make for Falmouth to cut her off. She was desperate to travel across country up to Bath to seek safety with her grandmother, for she was the only one who could guarantee protection from her stepfather and this dire unwanted betrothal. If she could stay out of reach of Tenby until she reached twenty-one years of age, she would be out of his control.

Secure for the moment from discovery and sheltered from the brisk sea breeze, Charis relaxed and let her mind review the kind of life she had endured under the hated rule of her stepfather after her mother died.

Naturally high-spirited, she had resented his dominance in her life and showed it. Her defiance cost her dearly as he would lash out with the cane that he always carried unless she was quick enough to dodge, and often she had been confined to her room on reduced rations until she agreed to behave.

Daisy Fenton was her good friend and saviour while she was growing up; always ready to protect her until she reached an age when she could act with guile.

The order to marry Baron Whaley had been the final reason to escape from her stepfather's clutches and gain her freedom.

She felt a shudder go through her as she thought of the recent encounter she'd had to endure with the baron. He had waylaid her in the hall on one of his visits to see Tenby, and caught hold of her arm with claw-like fingers to stop her getting away. She had immediately flinched and tried to evade him, but he had grinned, showing broken teeth between slobbering lips that exuded a sour odour that made her want to retch.

"You're a pretty 'un to have around. You'll do me nicely, I reckon, in not too long a time. Hope you're a good breeder. I need me an heir or two to inherit me wealth. In due time of course, after I've had me fun."

Charis had wrenched her arm away and fled to the safety of her room, but his blatant actions gave notice of his intentions, and she knew the time had come to escape. To achieve that, it was imperative to leave Cornwall and reach the safety of her grandmother, who lived in Somerset, before she was recaptured and made to comply with Tenby's wishes. While she thought she could refuse, she did not put it past him to drug her into compliance. Also, the last blows she had suffered from the wielding of his cane had hurt abominably, and she knew she was too fragile to take a bad beating, which would happen if she refused to marry the baron.

Left a widow with a young child after the death of her husband at the Battle of Waterloo, Cecile, her French-born mother, giving way to Tenby's blandishments, had married him and allowed him to take over as master of Carwinnion, but thereafter deeply regretted it. He was a cruel man and treated her badly until eventually she had succumbed to illness then death. Charis knew her mother had left her money in her will as well as the manor but Tenby had never allowed her to claim either it or the house. He had said that, being her stepfather, he had a right to manage her affairs and, although she had argued, nothing she could say would alter his mind. To defy him would be useless if she remained at

Carwinnion. Her only hope was to flee and put enough distance between them to hold out until Tenby could no longer rule her life.

Landing proved easy: she was just one of many deckhands around to unload the fishing boat and soon, when no one was looking, she sidled away and reached the town centre to hover in the vicinity of the Seaview Inn, a regular coaching establishment that had a good reputation for service. Indeed, the place was constantly busy with travellers from near and far seeking refreshment or a change of horses or setting off after a night's stay to break a journey.

She had already eaten the bread and cheese she filched from the pantry so she munched on an apple as she waited and watched the traffic come and go. Although she had a little money with her, she had not been able to save much. Most was earned from selling packets of herbs to the villagers. Tenby was the meanest person she knew unless it was for himself, for he denied her everything he could get away with.

Charis watched closely as a carriage was driven into the yard from the stables behind the inn. The groom descended and handed the reins to an ostler. He went into the inn and, almost immediately, a servant came out carrying baggage that he placed in the luggage trunk at the rear. Then a stagecoach drove in, and for several minutes there was chaos as passengers crowded the courtyard and the smaller carriage was backed to make room. Seizing her chance, Charis lifted the lid of the luggage trunk and, sliding quickly inside, closed it. Luckily, there was ample room, and she hoped it wouldn't be opened again before they set off. She had no idea where the carriage would be going; she only wanted to put enough miles between her and her stepfather.

Moments later, she heard a deep resonant voice giving orders to his groom, his accents clearly that of a nobleman, so she was not surprised to hear a confirming reply, "Yes, milord, all is ready for us to leave."

"I'd like to get home by tomorrow latest, if practicable, without changing the cattle. We'll give them a breather at St Austell and possibly over the moor, but we need to get to Launceston before nightfall. However, better not spring them, Roger. They are not what I would call prime quality though they should last till we reach home." Viscount Tristan Amery Fortesque, of Castle House near South Molton in Devon, sighed. "I've had ample travelling to last me a lifetime. This time, I'll let others do the journeys and rest on my laurels. I'll have enough to do running the estate now Henry has gone and Father is ailing. I don't need to hanker after more adventures. What say you, Roger? Is it time to make a new and far different life?"

"As you know, sir, whatever makes you happy suits me. Yes, I'll be glad to take it easy for a while. Maybe find me a good woman to warm my bed. Anyhow, there's a back road to St Cleer that I seem to remember. It cuts quite a few miles off the journey, milord."

"As you think best, Roger. I've got enough papers and accounts to read to keep me occupied. I can use the time to get through them. Let's have to it then. The roads should be clear this early in the morning."

Charis felt the carriage tip as His Lordship, whoever he was, climbed in and sat down with a thump. She realised he was sitting directly over her as she lay curled around his portmanteau in the luggage trunk and grinned happily to herself. Going up-country would suit her admirably.

She would be able to go on from wherever his home was. Wriggling to get as comfortable as conditions allowed, she closed her eyes intending to catch up on her sleepless night. Creeping out of the manor had been easy; she knew every creak on the stairs and had taken the precaution of oiling the back door hinges, but racing across fields at night to reach the fishing boat had been fraught. Not that she was scared of the dark, but she knew she must make all speed to get to the dock well before daylight.

Yet all had gone well: no one saw her as she crept aboard the fishing boat and hid between the crates already filling the deck. Luck was on her side for once, and an escape which she had once thought impossible seemed to be feasible now she was safely hidden in a carriage that was going up-country far away from the perilous situation she had previously endured. She was determined to reach her grandmother and finally rid herself of her stepfather's cruel dominance. All she had to do now was evade being found and sent back to face a dreadful future, so although her mode of transport was unusual and highly irregular for such as herself, no one would have the slightest idea where she had gone or how she had achieved her disappearance. With a thankful sigh, she settled to catch up on her lost sleep.

Sometime later, still hidden in the trunk of the coach, she was not feeling quite so cheerful. The bouncing of the carriage was causing real distress to her stomach which she thought unusual as she did not suffer from seasickness. More than that, she found she had to cling on to the man's baggage to avoid being tossed around. Biting her lips to avoid groaning did not help, except she knew she had to remain quiet at all costs. Even the short respite at St Austell gave no relief except for a quick foray out to drink water from a pump behind the stables and see to her needs while the two men enjoyed a tankard of ale. Back in the trunk once more, she pushed the baggage to one side then used the small bag she had brought with her that contained a dress, toilet things, a change of underwear and the little money she possessed to lay her head on. Sadly, there was no more food so she would have to do without for a good while longer.

Unfortunately, the jouncing grew far worse. Tristan had purchased the carriage and pair in Falmouth when his ship had docked. His overseer at the harbour had obtained the vehicle, and so far Tristan was pleased with the matched team of horses, and Roger, as ever, was a skilled driver.

Roger also felt the beasts worked well in tandem and, happy to be back in England on this lovely morning, quietly whistled a cheery tune to express his satisfaction with their response and the way they handled. His Lordship would attend Tattersall's Sales, once he had seen what his father had in the stables, and buy fresh, but for now these would do.

However, the route they were passing over had not been attended to since the last winter's snows and consequently was in a bad state of repair. Potholes and debris littered the way forward, and Roger, a careful and most experienced driver, was easing back on the reins to slow the team to a walk when, without warning, disaster struck their progress. One wheel went high over a boulder, and it took every effort of his strong arms to hold the plunging horses steady on the reins and to swing the carriage sideways to avoid a ditch and stop it turning over. Expecting his master's loud imprecations once he had brought the carriage to a halt, he was surprised to find him climbing silently out of the vehicle and making his way to the back.

"I'm sorry, milord…" Roger began as he joined him on the ground.

The upraised hand silenced him, and he stared as Tristan held a finger to his lips as he looked at the trunk. "I think we have a stowaway," he whispered quietly.

A thump from beneath the seat was not surprising given the force of the jolt, but a following groan certainly was. Tristan, having bent to rescue his papers that had gone flying, had no doubt that it emanated from human lips and the baggage trunk. He intended to give the trespasser hell.

Raising the compartment lid showed him who he had to contend with, which did not please at all. It was obvious that what initially looked to be a young stable boy judging from his clothing was not the case, for his cap had come off with the abrupt stop. Losing his disguise and displaying a wealth of golden curls which lay strewn around what was a female head, Tristan could not in all conscience deal out the anger that was on the tip of his tongue. Furthermore, the girl's eyes were closed, a sooty array of dense lashes lying on whitened cheeks. A very large, purpling bruise that seemed to be spreading quickly on her forehead as he watched accounted for the silence. Tristan picked up her hand and stared at the neatly kept fingernails and the fine skin. This was no stable hand, or peasant. He would lay odds she was gently bred. What the hell was she doing dressed like that in his trunk?

He shook her gently with no result. That bruise could turn out to be more serious than just a simple bang on the head.

Carefully, he wedged his arms under her slight frame and, lifting her out of the trunk, carried her round to slide her onto the back seat. There was no sign of her gaining consciousness. This could be grave. His mind ranged over all the possibilities, and the only answer seemed to be to get her to a doctor as soon as possible.

"Roger, fetch that bag that was under her head. She might have some identification in there."

Searching in the bag proved futile save for a letter from someone who appeared to be a relative addressing her as 'Dearest Charis' and ending only with 'Your loving grandmother, Caroline'. The heading was an address in Bath.

The enclosed sentiments gave no indication of anyone else; not even a surname. The toilet gear and underwear was a sign that she intended to revert to her normal gender at some point, and thankfully Tristan found the dress and other undergarments.

It had already struck him that an explanation for the strange attire the girl was presently wearing would be called for from any doctor summoned to see to her, plus a reason for her being in his carriage and likely badly injured. Reflecting on all the possible scenarios filled him with exasperation. Damned female! Why did she have to choose his carriage to cause problems?

"Considering the circumstances, Roger, I believe I should effect a change of the young lady's costume. Thankfully, she has brought a dress with her. She cannot hide any longer as a youth, though why she should do so is a mystery. Hopefully, one we shall discover. In the meantime, I shall change her back to being a female. It's bad enough as it is. I do not fancy having to invent a story about the strange stable garments. Keep a watchful eye on the road, and I shall be as quick as I can. With that head injury, she needs a doctor soon as possible so plot your course to the nearest inn."

"Thinking the same thing about the clothes, sir, and I reckon we should head for Liskeard. I recall a number of inns around there, to be sure. Anyone we stop at will be sure to know a local doctor. Though she could recover before we get there and save us the trouble."

"Choose a discreet one, until we know more about the lady. I'll be as quick as I can, and hopefully she'll come to in the meantime."

Chapter Two

Tristan was no stranger to undressing females. Well experienced in encountering many delicious inamoratas in his rakish career; even, over the years, keeping a mistress for a time, preferring to know that the woman was clean and free from disease, until, at the age of thirty-two, he considered he was most accomplished in the art. So, he was not unduly concerned to take on the task of disrobing then dressing a young girl. Though never before now, he thought, had he dealt with an unconscious one. Getting back in the carriage, he knelt on the floor and started by removing her boots and socks. Then off came her jacket, which smelt of tobacco. He had already guessed from its size and style that she had borrowed it from a man. Removing her breeches took careful handling, and when finally he took off her large man's shirt and the wrapping that flattened her breasts, he gazed with awe at the form he had revealed.

Clad only in her flimsy chemise, and though small in height, she hadn't the figure of a girl but was a grown and beautifully nubile young woman with skin like silken ivory. Her pink-tipped breasts were beautifully formed, while curved hips below a slender waist drew his eyes to... His lips dried while a wave of heat washed through him as he stared at her loveliness barely hidden by the chemise. Taking a deep breath, he reined in his immediate ardour and, glancing hastily out of the carriage door, hoped that Roger was not looking over his shoulder. However, his groom was standing by the horses holding them still. Returning to his task, Tristan slid her dress over her head. Despite his actions, there was still no sign of her rousing, so he gently turned her on her side to do up her dress laces.

Raking in her bag, he found a pair of stockings and two garters, and a light pair of slippers. By the time he had fastened the final garter and put on the slippers, he was sweating with rampant desire. Her long, silken, shapely legs seem to go on forever, and smoothing the stockings in place left him wondering why he was so affected to touch her skin. He was no stranger to a female body but never before had he dressed someone like her. With a deep, thankful sigh, he made sure she was comfortable and would not roll off the seat then went outside.

"Has she come round, milord?" Roger asked as he saw Tristan appear. He pursed his lips as he saw Tristan shake his head. "Wind's getting up and looks like rain on the way. We best stir ourselves. Don't fancy them potholes filled up with mud and water. Get stuck here and the Lord knows when we'd get out."

"Yes, up with you and head for Liskeard. I don't want to be marooned out here either if the weather catches us. I'll hold the girl still. Use your best speed, but with great care, Roger. Tipping us over will very likely see us all dead, and certainly the girl. She has enough to contend with as it is with that bang on the head. "

"Yes, milord, I'll be right careful."

Two hours later, they arrived at the outskirts of Liskeard and pulled into the courtyard of a small but clean-looking tavern. At once, the landlord bustled out and immediately bowed to Tristan as he descended from the coach.

"Have you two rooms, landlord?" Tristan, tired and concerned, was terse with his request. Thankfully, the woman had roused from her torpor, but she was showing signs of confusion, had no idea where or who she was, and was obviously in a great deal of pain.

"A large bedroom is available. Our only free one, Your Lordship. My wife will arrange a private parlour. It has a sofa—"

Tristan had plenty of time to think over all the eventualities during the journey to Liskeard, and his able mind saw a way of countering too many questions as to the propriety that both he and the stranger might have to face, so he was ready with his answer.

"Good. My groom will have that. My wife and I will occupy the bedroom. Can you fetch a doctor? We sustained an accident going over the moor and my wife needs urgent attention—"

Desperate not to lose a guest and obviously a wealthy one, the landlord bowed obsequiously. "At once, milord, I will send for him directly. If you would like to follow me, I will show you to your room."

Sliding into the coach once more, Tristan picked up Charis and, easing out of the door, carried her carefully up to a bedroom. Glancing around, he saw it was clean and adequate though not in the first stare, but he had slept in far worse. Placing Charis on the bed, he examined her face carefully. The bruise on her forehead had darkened and was now spreading downwards to her temple. His concern increased even more. Taking a towel, he wet it from a jug of cold water that he found on a side table then laid the cloth over her forehead. She at once gave a groan of relief and appeared to relax.

Tristan turned to the landlord who was hovering nearby anxiously wondering just how ill his patron's wife was. "The doctor? At once you said! Hurry, man, I do not like to be kept waiting, and my wife needs his services as quickly as possible. She is in a lot of pain. My man will see to my horses and bring up our things."

"I've sent my boy off to fetch him. He'll come directly, I'm sure."

"We shall need dinner. I shall have mine up here."

"And Her Ladyship?"

"The doctor first, obviously, before we know what she can eat!"

A short while later, the doctor, a local man called Charnley, having finished his examination of Charis turned to Tristan who was seated by the window. "Apart from that unlucky blow to her forehead when she tumbled against the coach window," the doctor had taken in Tristan's account of the accident, "Her Ladyship is otherwise in good health. However, a severe blow like that gives cause for concern, so I recommend she is kept in bed for the next three days with light meals. I shall leave an opiate for the pain and shall call tomorrow to see how she is."

"Three days? I can't stay here three days." Tristan was dismayed.

"I'm sure you have a care for your wife, sir. Her senses are strained, and she appears unaware of what has happened to her. She is also in a great deal of pain and is bound to have the headache and will likely have a concussion as well. I feel it unwise for her to travel tomorrow. In any case, if you look out of the window, you will see the weather has changed and is not advantageous. I fear the roads will be treacherous tomorrow which does not make my life easy. However, a night's rest will undoubtedly mark an improvement in your wife. I hope for your sake this is so. I will call in tomorrow and we will see how she is. Good day, milord. Jasper Burney keeps a capital inn and his wife is an excellent cook. I trust you will enjoy your dinner."

The doctor bowed and, not waiting for an answer, left the room, closing the door firmly behind him.

Tristan gave a muttered curse then strode over to the bed to see how his make-believe wife was faring. Matters had escalated beyond his control. Despite wanting to be on his way, he could not leave the girl on her own especially if she was confused. Although it was her own fault she had climbed into his carriage trunk, she was not responsible for the accident, and he had further compounded things by owning her as his wife. He had to take responsibility for her from now on. So, come what may, he must make sure she was recovered before he moved on.

As he stared down at her face, her eyes fluttered open and he saw for the first time that they were a dark periwinkle blue and amazingly lovely. They were also looking deeply puzzled.

"How are you feeling, Charis?" If she was confused, he could not question her, so a great deal depended on whether she answered to the name in the letter.

"My head is aching, but not quite so badly as before. I gather I've had an accident. Am I called Charis? It feels right but I can't remember anything else or who you might be. I heard the doctor say wife but..." Tears gathered in her eyes almost ready to spill. "I'm so sorry. I cannot recall marrying you or even your name. In fact, I cannot remember anything at all about you. Where are we, sir, and who are you?"

Suddenly the tears overflowed and ran down her cheeks. He smiled gently, fetched out his handkerchief, and mopped the flow. Poor thing. Despite her unfortunate action to hide in his carriage, he would not wish her harm. Here was a right coil indeed. Should he confess to the subterfuge or continue with the fiction of their marriage? She could well be incensed with his deception and give the game away before they left. Better to leave things as they were and confess later.

"Rest easy, my darling. You've been hurt, and it isn't surprising you are confused. You usually call me Tristan and it's not so remarkable you cannot remember as we are but lately wed. Sleep and before long you will be composed again. I shall be here should you need me." He wet the cloth once more and laid it across her forehead.

With a sigh of pleasure, she relaxed and murmured her thanks. "Oh, how comforting that feels, Tristan. How kind you are."

"I'll leave you for a moment and let you rest. I need to check on the carriage and Roger, our groom. I'll be back soon, so don't worry."

He eventually found Roger in the stable area where the coach had been pushed under a lean-to. He was busy examining the undercarriage and wheels.

"No great harm done, milord. We shall be fine to travel when you are ready. Though, once home, I think we should have a new set of wheels. They are a bit gouged here and there."

Tristan grunted his assent then frowned as Roger looked up perceptively at him. Roger Maberly had been with the viscount for many years and in many situations. They knew each other well, and Tristan appreciated that, if necessary, each would lay his life down for the other.

"How's the young miss? Has she recovered yet? Though I did overhear the doctor say to the innkeeper's wife her mind was likely in the rafters as she was so confused and didn't know what had happened. Not surprising with the nasty blow she had to her head."

"True. She has also become my wife, for the sake of expediency. At least it has saved further explanations. I don't know whether that was wise in the event but at the time..."

"Yes, I heard that too. No great harm, sir. It's a quiet inn. You are not known here, so it should be safe enough. Trouble is, what do we do with her when we leave? Taking her back home...well...?"

"I'll cope with that if necessary. Meanwhile, I hope she recovers and we find out who she is. I can't imagine what made her hide in my boot, especially as she is not a servant. Running away from something is my guess. I expect we'll know soon enough when she recovers her senses."

Chapter Three

In the end, Tristan dined downstairs in the parlour with Roger while a maid helped Charis to take off her dress and robe her in a wispy silk nightgown that Charis had inherited from her mother, and was all she had room for in her small case. The maid also helped her take some soup and then produced the draught the doctor had left.

"It will help your headache and let you sleep," she persuaded, as Charis demurred about taking it. "Doctor Charnley is a fine doctor and we are lucky to have him hereabouts. He wouldn't leave anything harmful."

"Very well, if it will help." Obediently, Charis swallowed a spoonful then made a face. "Oh dear, laudanum! I never take it as a rule…" Then she paused as she realised what she had said. How did she know she never took the wretched stuff if she couldn't remember anything else? Her mind was totally blank, like a dark hole that ached fiercely when she tried to pierce the fog.

The maid took her leave, and soon Charis, overcome with the potent drug, fell asleep. Downstairs, the maid knocked at the parlour door and, with a curtsey to the viscount, reported that his wife had eaten a little food and was now settled for the night. He thanked her and tossed her a coin which she gratefully received.

Once gone, he looked at his groom who had a faint smile on his face. "For appearances' sake, I shall have to go upstairs though I'd as lief take the settee and have a restful sleep. However, for once, you are lucky not to sleep in the stables. I hope you are suitably gratified? As for me, I daresay a chair is all I'll have tonight." He gave a *humph* at the smirk on Roger's face.

"Don't come it, man! Don't dare come it. A little respect is due from you unless you wish to be sacked forthwith."

His glare emphasised his order but Roger, knowing him so well, just bowed and said, "Your pleasure, milord. If you wish it, the sofa is yours."

"I'll see. Meanwhile, the doctor comes tomorrow, and we shall make arrangements after he has been. See you tomorrow."

At that last remark, Roger presumed his master was staying with the young woman whatever the reason. He wasn't surprised. The swift look he had given into the coach as his master was dressing the girl was quite enlightening, and he knew the earl well enough to know his tastes. It would be interesting, he thought, to see what happened next. As the next heir to the earldom, and in view of the news they had received about his father ailing, it was time Tristan married and started his nursery. So far, a bride had not been sought or even thought of. Perceptive about his master's moods, Roger had scanned his face as they were about to resume the journey to Liskeard. He had noticed a strange expression, almost a startled one. He would have given a lot to know how the viscount's thoughts ran.

Back in the room, Tristan found Charis fast asleep, the candle burning low, and then he surveyed the chair that he had sat in earlier. He felt there was no choice. He wasn't as forgiving as all that. She had, after all, stowed away in his carriage. And, fortunately, she was fast asleep. He sat down and removed his boots then divested the rest of his clothes. Blowing the candle out, he slid carefully into the bed and lay still on his back. So far, so good. With a brief thought that he was very lucky to have a comfortable bed to sleep in instead of a chair, he closed his eyes and fell asleep. Sometime later in the night, he aroused to find he was lying on his side and the woman had come to his part of the bed and was lying spoon-like cuddled close to his warmth. Her exquisite derrière was pressed close to his groin which was reacting with a full and needful urgency.

Hell's teeth! Was she awake? Did she realise? Then the deep, even breathing of his sleeping companion made him aware that her proximity was innocent, and he would be the world's worst rake to take advantage of the situation much as his body was clamouring to do otherwise. Thinking that he would wake her if he moved, he stayed where he was, but the light nightgown against his flesh was tempting, and slowly and carefully he slid his arm round her waist and let his hand lie under her breasts. With a sigh of contentment, she wriggled a little closer to his heat, and he held his breath in case she roused completely and screamed at his touch. Much as

23

he desired more contact, he knew that daring to fondle her as he wished would not be wise. Painfully but adamantly, he reined in his rampant flesh, closed his eyes once more and settled to sleep.

A distant rooster woke him as daylight lightened the window, and he found that, in his sleep, his hand had moved up and was holding one tempting handful of warm breast, albeit covered with her nightgown, that instantly set fire to his demons with a vengeance. Her breasts were not large yet still filled his big hand with a softness that set his senses afire. Feeling the nipple pebble under his fingertips, he gently stroked then, unable to resist, closed his fingers over the bud.

Immediately, there was a squawk of fright and Charis wrenched around, sat up and angrily cried out, "What on earth are you doing? Unhand me, sir, get out of my bed! My God...!" She shrieked, "How dare you! You are naked!"

Pulling up against the pillows, Tristan stared down at the irate face glaring up at his bare chest; then his eyes moved further down to gaze at outline of her breasts barely covered by the silken nightdress.

"Of course, my dear, I never go to bed fully dressed. Nor do you as far as I can see," he said, deciding to face things out.

At once, a blush turned her cheeks to rose, and she pulled up the sheet to cover her nakedness. "This is quite impossible. You have no right to be in my bed!"

Here it comes, trouble in spades! Had her memory come back? How do I deal with this? Then the thought struck him as he had stared at her lightly concealed body that he wished she was truly his wife. Lust? No. It was more than that. Something deep within him felt there was a connection that was stronger than merely wanting the woman beside him. She was lovely, true, but far more than that he wanted to get to know her and find out why she had disguised herself and hidden in the luggage boot. Incredibly, much as he felt he could charm her into allowing him access into her life, he actually wanted to protect her.

Well, here goes my reputation if I fail to convince her.

"Gently, my dear, I do have a right—"

"Then tell me, please, where were we married?"

He had to think quickly to answer and inspiration struck. "Surely you haven't forgotten already. We met and married in France."

"*Dites-vous je suis français...?*" She paused at his startled look.

Hell's teeth! She is well educated. Her French is faultless.

"*Mais non!*" Adding, "No, you are English despite your brilliant ability to speak French like a native." From the purity of her speech and the general impression he had got as she yelled at him, he felt confident in stating she was of the English nobility. "However, I will say no more. You must try to remember on your own. Your recall will come back, believe me. It was just a bump on the head that has upset your memory. Give your brain time to recover from the accident."

"But I don't feel married. Surely I would know you as a husband? Am I supposed to love you?"

He grinned. "That was the idea why we married."

"Oh." She gave that some thought. "Then kiss me."

"What?"

"Kiss me. If I love you then I should know with your kiss."

The reality that this journey home was turning into the strangest of ventures unlike any he had encountered before filled him with unease. Used as he was to coping with any problems, how on earth had he ended up naked in bed with this lightly clad female trying to convince her she had married him? It was crazy! He was crazy! Nevertheless, he had got himself into this tangle, and there was only one way out that he could see at present. Do what the lady asks and take the consequences. Turning towards her, he cradled her head between his hands and gently feathered his lips across hers. She lay still, staring up at him anxiously as though trying to call to mind his face.

He raised his head and quirked his lips in a reassuring smile then bent again to deepen his kiss. Her lips tasted soft, sweet and hot like sunshine on honey as he coaxed her to open her mouth to his, and she gasped and shivered as he touched her lower lip with the tip of his tongue as though she had never known the like before. The instant that happened, Tristan knew it was wrong.

Not only was he playing a dire, despicable game with someone he felt sure was an innocent, his instinct was screaming stop before you do something you will regret. It was completely at odds with his integrity, the way he had been brought up to treat a woman as a gentleman should. Then, before he could draw another breath and retreat from the game, all at once the spark of fire that raged through him as he touched her, and inhaled the flowery scent of her skin, exploded in his mind and ruined him for life. No woman hereafter would do for him unless it was Charis. He had read and at once scoffed, that for each person there was a soul mate, the other side of a coin, an alter ego that cleaved with one's spirit until they were as one. God help him, he felt it was true. He didn't care who she was, or where she had come from, he only wanted her to stay and be his for always. Slowly, her hands reached up to his shoulders, and then he felt them sliding into his hair to keep him from pulling away. No chance in hell of that happening. Nothing would drag him away or make him stop.

A tremor shook his hand as he held the exquisite line of her jaw, gently angling her face upward as he sought the warmth between her lips again, fuelling a hunger that threatened to rage out of control. He lifted his head, and she sighed and pressed closer almost tipping him over the edge. His hand dropped down to encase a warm breast and fondle the nipple through the fine silk nightgown. He felt her shiver as her body betrayed her awakening feelings, and her eyes flew open in surprise. That was when he knew beyond doubt that he really was playing with disaster.

She was no courtesan. His long experience with women told him so. He held a virgin in his hands and, when her memory came back and she discovered he had taken her without her knowledge, she would count him the lowest cur on earth. Pulling away from her was the hardest thing he had to do, but oh so necessary. Seeking to assuage her pride, he kept his cursing to himself then aloud said, "Much as I would like to linger, my darling, I must get dressed. The doctor will be here early and we have to be ready for him." So saying, he swung his legs out of the bed and reached for his breeches.

"Oh!" He heard her startled cry of disappointment. "I rather liked your kiss though I still can't decide why. Perhaps we can do it again after the doctor has been?"

And fill me with more pain than I presently suffer? No, I don't think so, my darling. Not until we have your memory restored and I can take you with more honour than these circumstances allow.

"Charis, you seem better this morning. How do you feel?" He decided not to answer her request but pose one of his own. "The doctor will want to keep you here in bed, but I am eager to get home. It is up to you to let us know what you wish. If you still feel unwell then say so. I will, of course, make sure you have all the medical attention you need once we are in residence, so if you can manage the journey I would be most grateful."

"Yes, although my head is tender, my headache has eased. I am happy to do as you wish, Tristan. I shall tell the doctor I am better."

"Thank you, Charis. I shall make it up to you in every way I can."

"And kiss me when we are home?" Her eyes twinkled gaily.

"Yes, anything you wish." He bowed gracefully before turning to the door. "I'll see a maid is sent up with breakfast. Let her help you to get dressed, and I'll be with you when Doctor Charnley comes."

To Tristan's relief, the day stayed clear and bright, and Charis played her part admirably. Then, with blankets provided from the inn, she curled up in a corner of the carriage and they were on their way to Launceston. After they arrived, he settled her in an inn then left Roger in charge to order dinner and headed into the town. Making discreet inquiries, he found a small, select dress shop and, judging sizes, bought a number of dresses and garments that he thought would suit. The owner was overwhelmed with her customer and could not do enough to please.

When he asked for suitable cases for the garments she said she would make sure to get them from a nearby leather shop and pack them for transport. Where would the gentleman like them delivered?

"Send them to the Rose and Crown and ask for Roger Maberly. They will be taken in by the landlord. Thank you for your help." So saying, he paid for the goods and departed. Back at the inn, he left directions for the cases to be taken to his wife's room then joined Roger in the parlour.

"I sent her to bed, milord. She has a maid to help her settle. She's having a light supper and will try and sleep. She looked very poorly and the bruise has spread even more, so I have the feeling her headache has returned and she is not very well."

"We can do nothing until we are home. An early meal and bed I deem wise. We shall leave as soon as possible come morning." Tristan frowned. This journey was proving difficult in more ways than one.

"Once we are back I shall summon our doctor and make sure she is well cared for. Hopefully her memory will soon return and we can decide what to do then. I have reasonable experience with wounds and fevers, but the mind is a closed book to me and needs an experienced doctor. I hope my father has an available one to consult."

Once again, Tristan found Charis sound asleep, and slid gently into bed alongside her. She didn't stir, and he composed himself to rest as well except for a lengthy time his thoughts kept him awake thinking of the past and the future that lay before him now so unexpectedly changed.

Tristan had been absent for many years from Castle House, a Palladian mansion of great beauty. Originally, it was an Elizabethan manor before being knocked down then rebuilt in stone, finally, in another generation, enlarged into a palatial house filled with treasures from many eras. Tristan spent his youth there, and then joined the army, later working for the Foreign Office for a time. Gaining a great deal of experience in many areas, he decided to put it to use and left the service to make his fortune in the Far East where he began to engage in shipping and trade. Secretly, he still worked for the government: passing on information acquired from mixing and advising nobles and ministers in the countries where his trade took place. Soon his ability and knowledge ensured his fortune increased impressively, and he became well content with his lot. The sudden death of his older brother Henry without leaving an heir meant he was now in line to inherit the earldom after his father was gone.

When he received the news of Henry's demise, Tristan was not only distressed at the loss of his brother but was at first reluctant to accept the duty believing his life still lay in foreign parts. Subsequently, after thinking things over, he realised he was homesick for England and green fields and, strangely, his father.

The earl had been a remote figure when Tristan was younger, little given to showing emotion. Losing his wife when she was about to bear his third child, a daughter, was a tragedy he had borne in isolation, never allowing his family see how much he grieved. Knowing he had his heir with Henry, he hadn't been unduly concerned when Tristan left home and joined the army. But fate never works out as one wants and, as they approached the long drive leading to the elegant house where he had once lived, Tristan knew he had never forgotten the many aspects of his childhood before his career had claimed him. He was filled with a strange nostalgia as he eyed the beautiful stonework of the Arcadian facade which he could see was glowing pale and golden in the faint moonlight. Long and large, the mansion comprised two storeys with dormers atop; the facade was classical in design with twin columns supporting a central portico. However, it was not straight, but shallowly curved; the middle containing the main house, with the east and west wings angled forward as though to shelter the portico and favourably claim their own view of the valley that fronted ahead.

About the house stretched the darker green of trees now appearing black in the darkness of night. In the distance would be the fields of home farm, the stables and barns, while behind the house he would see tomorrow the formal lawns and gardens. He felt a rush of joy fill his heart as he remembered every stick and stone of his boyhood home. At last, for good or ill, he was back.

Chapter Four

Three days had passed since Carwinnion Manor was in an uproar with Thomas Tenby almost speechless with rage and embarrassment over the disappearance of his stepdaughter. Particularly so after Josiah Whaley said scathingly, "I trust you realise your gambling debts will no longer be paid, Tenby, nor will you be given the extra money we agreed on once I married the girl. No bride – no contract! And I *will* collect the debts, count on it."

"I'll search for her, milord. She can't be far, I'm sure. A moment of natural timidity, I expect, has caused her to delay her appearance. All young virgins are the same before marriage. Take sustenance with us and I'll set my people to search straightaway. I promise you this will be put right as soon as the chit is found."

"Very well," Whaley agreed, "but this bodes ill for my future plans. You will recollect I stipulated a docile maiden and one who is virtuous. Should this not be the case, and if the matter is delayed beyond her majority and I lose the dowry that you say she is due to inherit not to mention the possibility that she declines my suit, then there will be unfavourable consequence. Just call to mind I make a bad and ferocious enemy, Tenby."

The search took place but Charis could not be found anywhere. Baron Whaley had driven away in his coach, replete from luncheon but adamant in his decision. No bride – no money!

The mood at Carwinnion had been dire from then on with all the staff walking on eggshells as Tenby's temper rose to boiling point especially as the search grew wider into the local countryside but produced no result. By the end of that week, tidings of her disappearance had spread round the district as had a rumour of a reward that could be gained if anyone had news or even the slightest clue that could be followed up.

Barney was slumped on a chair before the kitchen table early one morning slurping his tea and frowning as Daisy Fenton set a piled breakfast plate in front of him.

"What's matter with ye this morning? Sore head from beering it last night? Get yer food down and maybe the day will brighten for ye."

"My coat's missing." His tone was surly. "I reckon Charis took it to disguise herself. Happen you know if anything else has gone?"

Daisy Fenton did know; not that she would let on to Barney. Food missing from the larder, and Charis's riding breeches and boots were also gone. "You likely lost it a week or so back when you came in sozzled that night you were celebrating with village lads," came her sharp retort. "I heard you stumbling on stairs. Weather's warm lately so no wonder you forgot where you put it."

"Drunk or not, I allus knows where I'm at," he growled. "Coat's gone and I got my suspicions. I reckon I ought to tell the master."

"You tell him anything of the sort and you'll get your vittles laced with hemlock. 'Tain't none of our business where she's gone or why. Changed your tune, ain't you? Bent my ears for ages after the missus died, didn't ye? You were grieved long enough and rightly so. We knew the cause and couldn't say owt! I'll find ye an old coat to wear. Still got some of Harry's stuff, I daresay. God rest his soul."

She thought of her husband who had passed away some two years ago from a heart attack. He had maintained the land which lay around the estate. Tenby had not replaced him, and the area was beginning to suffer badly from neglect. Daisy was relieved that Tenby had not turned her off as well in an effort to save money. She was too useful as a cook for him to go to that length although he had protested loud and long when she said she wouldn't stay unless Katie was kept on too. No way was she going to manage the house without help. For the sake of his comfort and stomach, Tenby had given way.

"What do I say if the master notices and asks me?" Barney grunted.

"God give me patience! Use your head, man. Say it'd got too old and was past repair. Clothes don't last forever. Anyway, Tenby's got more'n your clobber to worry him. His gambling's gonna be his ruin lessen he stops it. You ought to have heard Whaley go on about it. First time I realised the baron had been staking master in order to marry our girl. Dirty dogs, the pair of 'em! Up to no good, I'll be bound. They are villains and if'n she's got away then I says good luck to her. So mind you keep your mouth closed tight. An' say nowt to Katie. If she thinks there's a reward in the wind, she'll blab to high heaven. She ain't got one shred of conscience when it comes to money in her pocket." Daisy scowled in disgust. "Takes me all my time keeping watch on that filly. She's at the age when she'll open her mouth without a second's thought if it concerns something for nowt. Or her legs, I don't doubt. She'll catch a bairn, mark my words, if she's not careful."

Daisy tossed a saucepan into the sink with a clatter, irritated beyond measure at the problems that surrounded her. Much as she was pleased Charis had escaped from the betrothal, coping with the other two resident staff was a nightmare. "You need keep your eyes peeled too. You know what those lads from the village get up to. A heavy hand round t'ear of some of 'em might not come amiss to save the lass. She gets with child; Tenby'll throw her out without thinking twice. She's only got an ailing mum to go back to, and no hope of another job if she can't work. It's up to us to see her right even if she drives me daft at times."

Barney had eaten his breakfast then had gone out to resume the chores that he'd put to one side during the searches for Charis. Daisy's words had hit hard in reminding him of Lady Langdon, as she once was, and her tall, good-looking husband, Lord David Langdon, who was also a major in Wellington's army. Barney had been a young farm boy working for the major's grandfather, Lord Alastair Langdon, when the couple took over the estate after the death of the old man. Lord Alastair's son, Alain, who was David's father, had been lost at sea during a bad storm off the Cornish coast. David, once he left school, had become an undercover agent for the Crown and, during his time in France, had met Cecile, fallen in love with her, and brought her back to England. Then, once the property in Cornwall became his, he worked hard to bring the estate up to scratch. All too soon, with trouble escalating in France, his expertise was again called for and he decided his country needed him. Promising he would only be away a short time to do a job for Wellington, he had bidden his wife and young daughter farewell. David had lost his life at Waterloo. Cecile, far from her family in France and scarcely knowing much of English customs, had fallen for Tenby's courtship and married him.

Barney had watched Cecile's slow decline at the hands of Thomas

Tenby and mourned her passing. He kept an eye on her daughter and watched her grow up to be a lovely young woman with a spirit that, no matter how he tried, Tenby could not quench in the same way he had treated her mother. Now Barney was concerned that, in running away, Charis was lost in the countryside and in peril of starving or had come to grief from another danger. If she had disguised herself, where would she go? Who would take her in and look after her? Torn between telling Tenby what he suspected and keeping his mouth shut, Barney thought he had better follow the latter course in view of coping with the housekeeper's wrath. Daisy Fenton would play merry hell with him if he said anything amiss.

Tenby, although an uncouth bully, nevertheless possessed an able if Machiavellian brain, so he sat in his study night after night consuming brandy, his mind continuing to work at solving the whereabouts of his stepdaughter. Unlike Barney, he did not think she had come to grief. He also felt sure she was far too clever to make off without a plan. No, he mused, she had been working on leaving for some time. At least, ever since he had told her she was to marry Whaley. Her reaction was as expected, and he had his cane ready though she had fought him off and fled from the room. He had yelled to her retreating figure that she would obey him and to be ready one week hence for the betrothal.

Strange, an excellent rider, she had not taken her horse; therefore she was on foot. Inquiries at the coach office brought nothing, so how could she leave the district without a trace? And, without funds, where would she go? Getting to his feet, he went upstairs to her bedroom and searched round the room and in the cupboards. Clothing had been disarranged probably from the last cursory search he had done, but again he found nothing – except – he looked down at her shoes. Slippers, walking shoes, dancing pumps, boots? No boots! He looked for her riding breeches which she was fond of wearing. Gone! Yet she had not stolen her horse. Why not? Where was she going with riding gear but no horse?

Not on a coach, that was certain. It cost to go far even on an ordinary stage. Besides, a maiden by herself would have been noted, and no news had reached him from the village. But where could she go? Then he thought of a ship. They sailed from the Helford River every day. To have boarded as a woman it would have been reported back to him days ago. He knew many of the men around the river. So, his mind progressed rapidly. She had boarded disguised as what or whom? As a boy, almost certainly; she was small enough and young-looking enough to pass as one.

Next question: where would she go then? Likely to Falmouth; then more than possible head up-country out of Cornwall.

Then where? London? Who would she find there? She knew no one outside of Cornwall. Except, his mind leapt ahead, if she was alive then Charis had a grandmother. If she was still living, where was she now? All letters were delivered to him and always had been. Charis had never had one from the dowager to his knowledge so how would she try to reach her if she did not know her whereabouts. Had she been given a letter by someone who hated him?

Possible. In fact, more than probable. He knew he was hated by all who lived at Carwinnion. Thinking back, he knew his wife had exchanged letters with her husband's mother; at least until he had confiscated them and flung them in the fire. He also knew she had stayed with Cecile and her first husband when they were first married.

After her son's death, she moved away and never returned to Cornwall. Still, he had papers galore in the study desk that he'd never cleared out. Chances were that Cecile had left her address in a diary. If he could find it quickly, he would head there at once. He may not be right, but he couldn't think of anything else to try. He was under no illusion that Whaley meant to keep his promise. He had to get his stepdaughter back as he had no desire to face the man's wrath and end up in a debtor's jail. And time was short. After she gained her majority, he would not be able to coerce her. Or could he? If she was drugged to the eyeballs then he would have his way and she would have no choice but to marry. First, he had to find her, and that meant finding her grandmother's address. Heading back to the study, he began to search.

Chapter Five

By the time they reached Castle House, Charis was exhausted and asleep, so it was only Tristan and Roger who saw the house in its gorgeous setting as they approached the entrance.

As the carriage came to a stop, Roger jumped down and opened the door. Nodding towards Charis, he said, "Your directions, milord?"

"Announce her as Lady Charis and try not to say more. I want to speak to my father first. She looks poorly again. Rather than wait for tomorrow, I'll tell the butler to arrange for the doctor to see her tonight. Ah, here's help coming. Settle yourself, Roger. I'll see you later." Tristan stepped down from the carriage.

"Well, bless me, if it isn't Harwood. Don't tell me you are still running the show?" He smiled at the ancient white-haired retainer who was the butler when he was young; then shook his hand. "How are you and how nice to see you."

"I'm tolerable, milord, tolerable. I only work for your father nowadays. The main house is taken care of by Arthur Maxwell."

He gestured to a man by his side who bowed deeply. "Your father has moved to a suite in the west wing. When we heard you were coming we made your quarters ready for you in the master suite. They were decorated for Master Henry but—"

"Quite. I'm sure they will suffice. Is the countess's room in order? Only I have Lady Charis in the coach and need her established close by me. She has suffered an accident and I need you to arrange for a doctor to come."

"Oh, dear me, how unfortunate. I'll do that and we'll get the room ready at once. Maxwell," Harwood turned to the other butler, "will you deal with it?" He called to a speedily retreating back as the other butler, realising what was required, immediately took the stairs two at a time and went inside the hall to relay orders.

Confident that all was in hand, Tristan bobbed back into the carriage, carefully took Charis up in his arms and brought her out. She moaned quietly but did not open her eyes as he gazed down at her. His heart lurched with concern as he stared at her ashen face. Then he turned, carried her up the stone steps to the main door and entered. As he was walking across the huge chequered marble floor, Maxwell came forward and said, "Can we help you, milord? The footmen can carry Her Ladyship."

"Thank you, no, she is not heavy. I prefer to handle her myself and will see her safe to her bedroom. Send for the housekeeper, please. I will give her instructions."

Once at the top of the stairs, Tristan paused then, calling down to Maxwell, said, "Let me know when the doctor comes. I wish to see him first. I presume the grooms are seeing to the horses? Concerning Roger Maberly, he will need good accommodation. He is also my personal aide so he will stay in the house and not above the stables. I shall dine after I have bathed and changed. I think that is all for now."

Maxwell bowed. "All shall be as you wish, milord. Oh, one more thing. Your father, the earl, left a message for you to visit him when it is convenient."

"I shall see him when I have bathed and after the doctor's visit."

"Yes, milord. May I pass this message on?"

"You may."

Maxwell bowed again as Tristan continued further up the carved oaken staircase to the next floor and down a corridor to the master's suite of rooms. All was at a bustle in the next room. Bed-making was swiftly taking place; a maid standing by to take charge, another maid unpacking suitcases which a footman had brought up. Tristan surveyed the scene before walking forward and laying Charis gently on the sheets. Turning to the waiting maid, he said, "A cool cloth for her head and undress her with care. The doctor is being fetched now. I will speak with him before he sees her. He will need her history."

In his bedroom, he found a strange man already busily sorting out his own luggage. "Your pardon, milord. I was told to see to your comfort. Your bath is about to be run, and I will have your evening suit pressed by the time you are ready to dress."

Tristan smiled at him. What luxury to have a valet again. He felt he had been travelling for years instead of merely returning from the Far East. He had left his former servants behind, except for Roger. He had felt it was not fair to remove a man from his natural habitat and bring him to a cold climate just because he was a good servant. He reminded himself that he too would have to acclimatise.

"Your name?"

"Edwin, milord," the valet said and bowed.

"Then, Edwin, I look forward to your ministrations. My clothes are in an appalling mess especially those which have yet to arrive, but time will put things right. Don't fuss for now. I merely need a simple suit for this evening. The bath will be most welcome to relieve me of my travel dirt. I look forward to changing to clean clothes."

"Yes, milord."

A moment later, Maxwell appeared with the doctor. "Milord, may I present Dr Marshall? He is your father's physician."

Tristan nodded, raising his hand to stop the doctor before he entered the other room. "A word if you please, Doctor, before you see Lady Charis."

Aware that servants had long ears, he walked the doctor to the end of the corridor and quietly explained that she had hit her head while travelling. "It was diagnosed as concussion, though permission was given to bring her home. However, as she is still in pain and unwell, your consultation is necessary. It has affected her memory, so events for her are vague. She does not recall anything."

"Do you mean she does not know who she is?"

"Precisely. Naturally, I could tell her, but I wanted her to remember of her own accord."

"Do you have medical knowledge, milord?" Marshall asked.

"No, only a smattering of field surgery and, I suppose, common sense. I was in the army for a considerable while, and one learns to make do when one is out of touch with medical facilities."

"Your common sense is excellent. I wish some of my patients had as much. You are quite right. We will not frighten the lady with too many questions. I will give you my verdict after I have seen her."

"In that case, I will leave you to examine her. Take your time. Let my valet know when you have finished. I am about to have a bath and refresh myself for the evening. Join me in the study later and we'll enjoy a drink together."

Tristan was already dressed and waiting in his study when at last the butler brought Dr Marshall into the room. "Doctor." Tristan came forward and offered his hand. "Come sit. I believe you are a regular attendant here for my father?"

"Yes, that's so. I quite thought I was being summoned to attend him tonight. He is not in the best of health, and I have been concerned about him especially after the unfortunate death of your brother. It was a shock he did not need. Indeed, it has been a bad time for him, particularly as you were so far away." Marshall sat down, took the glass of sherry the butler offered, and toasted his host before taking a sip. Leaving the decanter near Tristan, Maxwell bowed and left the room.

"So I gathered from the messages I was receiving from various people in England. Hence my urgent return from abroad. I would have come in any case concerning my brother's demise. I gathered it was unexpected, but know no more than that."

"I scarcely know more, milord. He had a habit of early morning riding and was found in the far meadows with a broken neck. It was presumed his horse had thrown him. The horse returned sweating and lathered to the stables, and the grooms immediately organised a search party. Your brother was found and brought back." Marshall's voice held a strange note that intrigued Tristan.

"So you did not attend him in the meadows?"

"No, I was called in after the event."

"And your findings?" Tristan's senses were already alert.

The doctor paused, assembling his words. "Well, he definitely had a broken neck which is consistent with a fall." Again, he hesitated. "With so many to bear witness...well, I'm afraid I lacked courage to disagree that he died from *falling* from his horse."

Tristan was silent as he sat staring at the doctor who now wore a crestfallen look on his face. It must have taken courage to confess this to another person, particularly to someone he had not met before. Should he trust the man? He had Charis in his care. Was she safe? Deciding to go with his gut instincts, he said, "Who else did you tell?"

Marshall looked surprised. "How did you know?"

"I make a guess your conscience bothered you. Essential tutoring and education in the army, and working in different countries has taught me there is no shame in having second thoughts. In fact, as the brain mulls over experiences, there are always doubts as to whether one has made the right decisions. Pronouncing on the dead is never easy, no matter how many times it happens, and even when a death is obvious."

"I told your father," Marshall answered abruptly.

"Interesting. And what did he say?"

"He said to wait and tell you. That you would sort things out."

"Good God! How on earth could he make that judgement? I haven't seen him in years." Tristan blinked in astonishment. "In fact, I was just thinking that I would have to start over afresh to get to know him after such a long time away."

"That may be so, but that is what he said, and he was firm with it. I have to say I agree having met you." Marshall grinned. "I also have to add I am pleased you are back. Your father has missed you."

"I don't know that I would agree with you. However, to change the subject, Lady Charis? What are your findings with her?" Tristan felt it was well time to direct attention to the patient and return to what most concerned him.

"The injury to the forehead was severe and, while the bruise will heal, hopefully without a scar, trauma to the brain is cause for concern. You are correct in thinking she has lost her memory. She has no idea where she is now or even who she is. Your wife..." Marshall halted as he saw Tristan start. "Is she your wife?" He paused, and steepling his fingers stared over them at Tristan. "She appeared puzzled to find out that she was married and that the staff thought so. Judging her surprise when I mentioned that you, as her husband, were most concerned about her health, she was even more so."

Tristan stared back, marshalling his thoughts and forming an opinion on the type of man he was dealing with.

"To be sure, I was careful to question her more when the maids were not around. Oddly, I have a strong feeling that it was only as if it was something she'd heard rather than knowing it was right. I even went as far as checking whether she was pregnant as sometimes the fright of having to bear a child will trigger a mental problem. She is not pregnant. Forgive me if I am treading on delicate ground...but she is still a virgin as far as I can tell."

"No." Tristan waved his hand in dismissal. "I believe it's time to salvage *my* conscience. This is in confidence, of course, though I am aware of your Hippocratic oath, but I would appreciate your advice."

He then related all that had taken place since he had found Charis. "All I know about her is the letter from the grandmother. I feel she is a gentlewoman, and the manners, actions and speech that I have noticed since finding her bear this out. She also answers to Charis quite naturally, so I assume that is her name and even accepts my putting Lady in front of it causes no denial. When one is ill, I believe nature has a way of disclosing one's natural habits."

"Yes, my examinations agree with this. I studied in London and Berlin before my finals with some eminent doctors working with the brain, and though I am just an ordinary practitioner and it suits my style of life, I have never lost the interest. So, was she running scared?"

Dr Marshall sipped his sherry then said, "I believe she was. No woman of her calibre dons such garments and hides in trunks unless she is forced by circumstances. Usually I disclose nothing further, particularly if you were actually her husband and might be responsible, but I could see she has been physically mistreated. They were old bruises, not consistent with any she might have acquired in the carriage. Possibly with a cane or stick and across her back and hips. Someone recently sought to beat her quite violently. I think she was escaping from a villain."

"In God's name, who would do such a thing?" Tristan gasped.

"Who knows? It could account for her flight, and possibly adds to the trauma of the head injury. And you seek my advice? Hmm, not the easiest thing to offer. You must be aware she may never regain her memory. Equally you have, I perceive, a desire to marry her. In the circumstances, a rather sudden desire, though she is a beautiful woman. How interesting. Forgive me, milord. Interesting for me, damned annoying for you. I take your point that should her memory suddenly recover...hmm." He cradled his fingers round the glass and stared at them as though willing inspiration before continuing, "I will vouch after what you have told me she has never known the married state. I checked as well as I could in view of her modesty. I believe she is a virgin; therefore, one would guess, free to marry. If you assume to all and sundry you are wed and she gets with child then any offspring would be illegitimate. Not the best thing to happen with your status here as the next earl. Equally, the picture you

40

envisage if she regains her memory and finds her position a sham would be, at the very least, disastrous. She would truly call you a knave. I think you are right to want to keep her safe if she is running from danger. If she is your wife in actuality then you could guarantee it."

The doctor paused again, turning the glass in his hand as he sought for the right advice. He nodded as though satisfied he had reached a conclusion he was happy with. "If it could be contrived, I think you should have a small wedding ceremony that we can pretend is for the lady's benefit so that in the present time she has something to remember. I recall you gave her the impression that you met and married in France?"

Tristan nodded.

Marshall flashed a wide smile at him. "Have you thought your father might have liked to attend that wedding? He is family after all. You could always say it is for his benefit as well as for your staff. Everyone adores a party, even a small one, and I'm sure no one would question your reasons, especially your father."

Thunderstruck, Tristan stared back at the doctor in amazement. Then he grinned. "Doctor Marshall, you are a genius! This can solve many problems and keep her safe from harm."

"I don't know about genius." Marshall grinned again. "Simple common sense. Though it does not answer questions about the lady's past life and why she ran away. As far as protection is concerned, it will give you that right, but Lady Charis must be told what she is agreeing to before you marry again. If that is done then I'll be pleased to help in any way I can. Do please call me Richard for in taking a presumptuous liberty, milord, if I am to stand as your best man...?"

"Couldn't think of better!" Tristan stood and held out his hand. "We will talk of this later. Will you join me for dinner?"

"Much as I would enjoy it, duty calls. Two of your parishioners are unwell so, as I am already out, I shall visit to check on their progress. Think things over and let me know tomorrow when I return to see Her Ladyship."

Chapter Six

Dinner can wait, Tristan decided. *I have dallied long enough. I can no longer delay seeing him.*

Swiftly, he took the stairs down to the first floor and walked the lengthy corridor to the west wing where his father had his suite. A soft knock on the door and Melrose, his father's valet, answered immediately.

"Good Lord Almighty! Melly! I thought he would have killed you off long before this! How are you?"

"Surviving, Master Tristan. Lost most of me nine lives, though."

"Stop whispering, you two!" thundered a strident bellow. "Melrose, get the hell out of here. I'll ring when I want you. Tristan! Don't skulk by the door. I don't intend to conduct a conversation from here. I have a chair waiting."

Tristan shrugged at Melrose then grinned. "Forgot the book in my pants," he whispered.

"Hard luck! I'll get the embrocation ready." Then Melrose was gone.

Tristan walked nearer the fire to where his father sat, a blanket draped over his knees, and gracefully bowed. "Good evening, sire. I trust I find you in reasonable health?"

"Took you long enough to find me, healthy or otherwise."

"You did have Henry, of course."

"Not for long, it seems."

"No," agreed Tristan, a note of sadness in his voice. "I came as soon as I could after I received the news. It's a mighty long way from the other side of the world, and travel conditions are not of the best. It has been a long, weary journey, and I am glad to be home."

"And I see you have brought a wife with you?"

"Yes." Tristan had made up his mind. Marshall's suggestion for a small wedding ceremony to take place would solve the problem if he could only get Charis to agree.

"I've heard she is sickly. Hardly suitable for breeding, I'll wager. No sooner here and Marshall called. Bad enough your brother couldn't manage an heir, but according to your earlier prowess, I assumed you could do better."

"As far as I am aware, I have never left any woman with a child. I do have a conscience, sir. I will breed an heir for the dynasty when I am ready." His voice turned chill as iced water.

"Oh, for God's sake, Tristan, sit down. I know you haven't left any illegitimate brats around. Forgive an old man for his petulance. I feel as if I've been waiting forever for your return. It seems you kept me till last. Still, you are here, and I'm glad to see you looking so well."

"Have you eaten, sir? Perhaps we could dine together?"

The olive branch came out without thinking. His father was right. He *had* left him until last instead of immediately greeting him after such a long time away. Had he sought to pay him back for his strict childhood? Belatedly, it occurred to him, not that strict, for he had been happy and worshipped his brother Henry dearly, looking up to him with respect. In truth, his father had only behaved like any parent would: determined to instil the ways of behaviour and loyalty befitting his class. As indeed he would himself, when he fathered a child. Thinking of that, his mind visualised Charis as his bride and mother of his children, and determined what he dreamed of would come to pass.

"I have eaten, but would be happy to join you and have a pick at this and that, and maybe enjoy cheese and a glass of port. Ring for Melrose to fetch my chair."

"No need for that. I could carry you if you wish, but why don't we eat here? I only wish to eat lightly, and the food can be fetched without too much trouble. We can talk and be comfortable rather than endure a formal setting." Tristan sat down gracefully in the opposite chair.

His father stared back at him then smiled. "Good gracious, lad, have you become a human being?"

"I trust so. Have you become the father I have always wished for? I was a very poor second to Henry."

"That I deny. Henry was his mother's boy and soft. You had far too much of my nature in you to get close, and I decided it would stand you in good stead when you went out in the world. Mollycoddling would not have been good. Events have proved I was right. You are a man of principle and I am proud of you."

"But you don't know me. I've been away years…a lifetime of adventures…" Tristan began to protest.

"I have followed your every change with interest. Surely you recall the FO is no stranger to me, especially as it concerned my son. Don't be fooled that, because I was distant, I could not keep pace with you. I was kept informed of all your movements. Your exploits do you great credit and have filled me with enormous pride. On top of your army record, I gather you have become a wealthy man and are greatly respected in the Far East. Not an easy accomplishment, I collect. Most foreigners have little regard for our ways."

Tristan took in the meaning of his father's words at first with annoyance; then with a wry feeling of being guarded and held safe.

"Every movement?" he retorted.

"Excepting this last one of getting married."

"Ah yes, that one. We shall eat then talk of that one."

The preliminary conversation set a convivial tone for what followed, and the meal was filled with reminiscences of past times and tales from Tristan's adventures and what had changed with the estate.

"Excellent! Here comes the cheese." Amery Fortesque rubbed his hands in delight. "And the port, of course. You remembered to decant the '87 early as I instructed, Harwood?"

"Certainly, milord. I also remember Doctor Marshall leaving word that cheese was only to be eaten lightly, and you have already had your portion this evening, and port is never to be served."

Tristan watched his father's face fall in dismay. "Harwood," he interjected. "I don't recall you being cruel."

"Cruel! Why no, sir!" Harwood looked embarrassed.

"Then leave the cheese and the port. I must confess the '87 is far too good to reject. And two glasses, if you please."

Harwood hesitated momentarily then said weakly, "It's the nightmares, you see, milord."

"Which we will cope with if they arise, but I think the earl will sleep soundly tonight. Don't you agree, Father?"

The wide grin was all he could ask for, and he nodded to the butler to withdraw. Pouring a small glass of port from the decanter, he handed it to Amery with a caution. "A taster only, Father. I have no wish to further your demise. I wish you good health and a long life."

He toasted his sire and watched his father taste the ancient port with relish. The bottle had been cellared a long time and was much prized. Sampling the liquor himself, he appreciated the age of the port and that the intense sweetness of early years had gone leaving a dry finish that clung to the tongue like nectar. He hoped there were a few more bottles like it in the wine cellars.

"Having met Richard Marshall, I'm pleased you are in his capable hands. He is not only likeable but seems extremely sensible."

"Yes, despite the fact I deplore the need of a doctor, I like him as a friend as well. He does not try to mollycoddle me and his ability as a doctor is the best we have had in years in this area. I trust you were satisfied with him regarding your wife?"

"Yes, this brings me to Lady Charis. Her condition has sadly been caused by an accident in the coach travelling over a rough road. The wheel hit a boulder and lurched. She lost her balance and hit her head against the window ledge; so hard and swiftly she suffered a concussion. According to the doctor in Liskeard, we should have stayed longer at the inn, but I was selfishly eager to get home and persuaded her to travel so perhaps have worsened her condition. Unfortunately, the shock of the blow has caused her to lose her memory, and Richard and I were earlier discussing means of restoring it which, I'm sorry to say, caused the delay in seeing you."

The earl waved his hand in dismissal. "No matter, I understand now what kept you. Poor girl, how dreadfully regrettable. I trust the housekeeper has seen to all that was needed and made her comfortable."

"Yes, indeed. I will see how she is tomorrow. Then hopefully after her rest, she will visit you. She is gentle and passing fair."

"Excellent, I already have presumed, at this stage in your life, you have developed good taste in your choice of women and a pleasing wife is so much easier to live with. I look forward to seeing her."

"Now I shall say goodnight." Tristan smiled at his father. "The hour is past your retirement, and I am weary as well. It has been a long day. Sleep well, Father. I am glad to be home at last and know that you are safe. As far as Henry is concerned, we have much to talk over. An unhappy end considering he was a champion rider. I would have wagered a great deal against such a strange accident. You told Richard I would sort things when I came home. Thank you for your faith in me, however premature. You may be sure I shall be most vigilant in gaining all the facts, and we can compare notes. However, it will keep until tomorrow, as will a great many other things we have to discuss."

Tristan rose and, with a light comforting stroke across the gnarled hand of the old man as it rested on the arm of his chair, bowed and left the room. Once outside, he breathed a sigh of relief. The visit had gone well, and further disclosures could wait until another time. As he walked along the corridor, he met Melrose coming towards him.

"All's well, milord. You have no need of embrocation?"

"Nary a drop, Melly. Luckily, I have grown too big for a beating. Thank you for looking after him. It was good to see him. I think he will rest well tonight."

"In his mind, yes. I don't know about the rheumatics."

"True, no getting away from old age and its infirmities. See him to bed and I hope the port will soothe the pain." Tristan gave a swift nod and headed for his own bed.

Chapter Seven

Edwin was waiting to help Tristan disrobe. Then, donning a dressing gown, he dismissed the valet after informing him he would ride early and just to leave his clothes in the dressing room. He needed no help.

"I have already anticipated your wishes, milord. Roger was kind enough to give me direction of your habits until I become used to your ways. Just let me know what you require and I'll do my best to please you, milord."

"I'm sure you will. Goodnight, Edwin, and thank you."

Tristan waited until his valet left before going to the adjoining door between his room and the bedroom normally used by a countess where Charis presently lay at rest. He opened it quietly and saw a maid sitting drowsing near the bedside of Charis who appeared to be asleep. Obviously, the doctor had ordered a watch kept on her.

As he advanced into the room, the maid stirred and hastily began to rise. He laid a finger to his lips and motioned her to sit again; then approached the bed and looked down at the tumbled array of fair curls surrounding the lovely pixie-like features of the woman he was determined to marry. As he did so, Charis opened her eyes and stared back.

"Hush, my dear, go back to sleep. I just came to make sure you were comfortable."

"I am happy to be away from that rocking coach, but I missed you. There are so many people I don't know here…"

"Don't be concerned, my dear. They are here to help you recover. It is so long since I've been home that I too feel adrift. You will soon get used to your staff and be at ease in your surroundings. Now, doctor's orders say you will rest and mend your health and resume a full life once more—"

"My staff! Are you talking about the servants here? Why do you say they are mine?" Charis cried in astonishment, seizing on the only words that made no sense to her troubled mind. "You talk in riddles, sir. You know they are not mine!"

Immediately, Tristan turned to the maid. "Leave us. I will ring if I need you later. For now, I will stay with my wife."

At once, the maid rose, curtsied then left the room. When the door had closed, Tristan perched beside her on the bed.

"Charis, the accident has left you confused, and I understand you only see a blur. I believe it better to remember the present rather than the past, and establish new memories allowing the old ones time to recover, return when they are ready." He stroked a curl off her face. "You cannot recall our marriage so we will have another simple ceremony that you will remember."

Her eyes suddenly filled with tears as she said, "You were going to kiss me again. Have you forgotten?"

"No, my sweetheart, I haven't forgotten, but you were not, shall we say, *comme il fait*. And I have been with my father."

"Oh, then we have arrived at your home. How is he?"

"Not as fit as I would like, but pleased I have returned. He is eager to meet you as soon as you are able."

"I'll not disappoint you, My Lord. I will attend him tomorrow."

"Only if you feel able. Now, sleep and regain your strength. I am close by and will hear you if you need me."

"My kiss?" she begged, her eyes luminous in the candlelight. "I will sleep if you kiss me goodnight."

"Minx!" He sat closer on the bed and, bending over her, gazed at her lips before pressing lightly against their softness. At once, her arms went round his neck, and she allowed him to press deeper until he lost himself in the joy of tasting the sweetness she offered him. His arms went round her body lifting her up against his chest, and still the kiss went on until he drew his mouth away allowing her a breath and him a chance to subdue his need to join with her.

"Tristan, am I so terribly disloyal that I do not remember our wedding or where it was? You are as devoted as I would wish any husband to be, yet still my mind is a blank over what should be the most important thing in my life. It is terribly frightening that I cannot remember."

"Charis, forget your fears. I am here to keep you safe. I care not if you don't remember. We will make new memories in the days to come. For now, darling, sleep, and tomorrow you will begin your new life with people who will be devoted to you as I am." He laid her down in the bed again and, drawing the covers over, gently kissed her forehead. Turning down the lamp, he said, "I am only next door. Call me if you need me."

Back in his own bed, he reviewed the events of the previous days. What was it about her that he was so arrogantly determined to want her for his wife, and so suddenly? What had drawn him to want her? Who was she? Did she belong to a family who would turn down his suit?

Hardly, he thought. His lineage and rank of viscount would never be spurned. He also felt she had been reared by someone with gentle manners and education. A family of quality? It had to be. Except, could she be promised to another man? Yet, she had escaped in such a strange fashion. Not just running away but hiding her identity as a woman. Someone trying to trace her would be hard put to it to track her down. Hardly the action of a girl of her breeding, unless scared. From whom or what was she escaping? To go to those lengths, it showed courage and a determination not to be found.

He judged he had been asleep for some time when he awoke to the sound of terrified screams. At once, he leapt out of bed and raced into the next room.

Charis was twisting and turning to rid herself of the sheet that was wound about her, and crying frantically not to be beaten. "I won't marry him. He is too old! You can't make me – I'll tell everyone you beat me! You always beat me—"

"Charis! For pity's sake, calm down!"

Tristan tugged on the sheet to free her and tried to take her in his arms, but she screamed out again, "No, no, go away, I don't know you. I want my grandmama—"

"Charis! Wake up! You are having a nightmare. It's me, Tristan. You do know me, and you are safe."

"T-Tristan?" She pulled herself up in the bed as he gave up trying to hold her and turned up the light.

"Yes, it's me. You were having a nightmare…"

"Oh!" She stared at him, her eyes wide, and suddenly he realised he was stark naked. At once, he turned about and, racing back to his bedroom, flung his robe about him before returning.

"My apologies. I came quickly as I didn't want you to wake the household. Now, tell me what scared you." He sat on the edge of the bed but made no attempt to touch her.

"All I can remember is shouting at someone, and I knew I had to run away. Was this in France?" she asked, her face still pale with fear.

Truth or fiction? Decision time. Playing with someone's mind was not ethical and could possibly be dangerous.

"No, Charis, I believe you ran away from something that frightened you. It was here in England. Falmouth or near there, to be exact. You hid in my coach – in the luggage trunk. Much later on our way here, we were travelling over a rough road and hit a rock which caused you to slam your head against the side of the carriage. I heard your groan and found you unconscious and knew you needed a doctor. The nearest inn only had one room so I pretended you were my wife to protect your respectability. I also needed to keep an eye on you with that serious bang on the head and acted as I thought best at the time – I'm sorry if I misled you."

"Then..." her face flamed red with embarrassment as she thought of his appearance a moment ago and recalled his nakedness in her bed at the inn, "you slept with me—"

"Charis, for my sins, yes, I did but I did not touch you. I promise on whatever honour I have left, I did not take you to wife. I was tired, you were already asleep, and the bed was better than a chair."

"Oh." She did not know whether to be glad or sorry. "Then we are not married. I am not your wife. In fact, you don't know who I am. Worst of all, neither do I remember anything of my past. I just feel blankness where I should have memories..."

"Can't you remember anything more?"

She shook her head. "Only shadowy things. The sea and a beach I loved. I must have gone there often as I even recall the rocks that surrounded it. Oh, and herbs. I think I had a garden where they grew. I recall the smell when I cut them, for drying, I think."

"Did you cook with them?"

"No, I don't cook, at least not much. Oh dear, I sound stupid. How do I know I don't cook when I don't know who I am?"

"Not at all. It is as I said: your memory is coming back. Maybe in bits and pieces, perhaps a little at a time. Soon you will know it all and be comfortable again. Charis, I truly mean what I say: you are free to choose what you do when you recover. However, in getting to know you I would like to marry you, if you will have me."

"Oh, good gracious!" She stared at him in dismay. "The staff – your staff – think we are already married! When they get to hear how we have behaved, it will not be with approval. What shall we do?"

"Hmm, I don't have a problem with that. Would it go against your principles to continue with the pretence? We can let a measure of time go by and, if you want to leave after you have found out your past, then the parting can be arranged. Quietly and amicably, I assure you. In the meantime, have I leave to court you? If you decide in my favour, the marriage can be equally quiet."

"How do I pretend to be a wife when I am not? Do you share my bed? And your father? It is not fair to deceive him. It would distress me very much to cause him pain."

I wish I could share your bed now, but I'll be patient. "No. People in our station of life need not share a room. In fact, I believe not many do. Don't fear that I will pester you. As for my father, he is different from what I remember as a youth: far more approachable."

Tristan smiled, thinking of the time he had spent with his father. "I'd like to think he is happy to have us home, and we could be a family again."

Charis blushed again. "I don't fear. I merely wished to know how we go on. My duties to your household, for instance? How do I go on with that? I presume your father has a housekeeper as well as butler."

"And how do you know that, madam?" He grinned.

"Well, I do know how a house is run!" she said haughtily.

"Ho! Do you, by Jove! Then I suggest you confer with the housekeeper and begin to run the house as you wish. Father won't mind, and I certainly don't mind what you do. Have things how you want. I'm sure we will like them too. As for the staff, they always work well for a mistress who involves herself in the household, especially one they like. I have the oddest feeling they like you very much." His eyes sparkled humorously. "Have fun and make us all smile. Now, if you don't mind, we'll save all that for tomorrow. No more nightmares. Get some sleep and awaken tomorrow refreshed for a new day. Doctor Marshall will be along to check you over, but say nothing of our talk. I shall be pleased to see you dressed later in the morning, and we'll tour the house and visit my father. Sleep well." He kissed her forehead and retired to his own bed to lie awake once more thinking of the future.

Chapter Eight

Mid morning arrived, and Charis was roused from a deep sleep as the curtains were pulled back to reveal bright sunshine.

"Good day, My Lady. I'm Kate if you please, ma'am. I've been sent to maid you, which is a great honour, to be sure. I've taken the liberty of bringing chocolate, but can fetch tea if you prefer. Doctor Marshall is with the earl. His Lordship asked me to see if you were awake and to prepare for doctor's visit, if you would be so kind. I shall run your bath. Then, after Dr Marshall has seen you, His Lordship would be pleased to meet you in the breakfast room unless you prefer to have your breakfast sent up here?"

The maid sounded bright and cheerful. Charis sat up in bed and smiled happily. Despite being awake in the early hours, she felt rested.

Kate? The name sounded some way familiar. Had she heard that name before, or something like it? Sadly, the memory would not come to mind; there was still a dark blankness whenever she tried. She decided to concentrate on the here and now. "Thank you, Kate. I'm sure I'll be happy with your help, and the chocolate is most acceptable. Tell Doctor Marshall I'll see him when he is ready."

Kate bobbed a curtsey then said, "I've started to lay your clothes out. The blue morning dress looks suitable, if you are happy with it?"

Blue morning dress! The only dress she remembered was the green one she had worn for travelling, and that was as shabby as could be. Where had the blue one come from? "Er – yes, that will do nicely." And very nicely it did, too.

After she had bathed and Marshall had pronounced her well enough to go downstairs and resume a normal life, she had dressed and had her hair brushed and pinned up in so pleasing a stylish manner she felt she had changed beyond all recognition.

Tristan rose as Maxwell showed her into the breakfast room, and his eyes glowed at the sight of her. She looked truly exquisite. The bruise on her forehead was fading to yellow and had been further disguised by a dusting of face powder that the maid had found, but apart from that the colour of the dress emphasised the blue of her eyes.

"Good morning, milord." She greeted him as Maxwell seated her in a chair alongside. She helped herself to toast and shook her head as Maxwell gestured at the laden sideboard. "Just coffee with my toast I think today, thank you. My morning chocolate was enough to fill me."

Maxwell bowed and, picking up Tristan's empty plates, left the room. Charis took the opportunity to murmur in a low voice, "Dresses? Underwear? Are you a magician? How did you know my size?"

Tristan laughed. "Hardly! Practical, yes, and I guessed your size. Your bag was scarcely filled with clothing." He eyed the butler who had returned and was standing by the sideboard, trying to hear their quietly spoken voices. "Thank you, Maxwell, that will be all. I'll wait on Her Ladyship; then we'll tour the house."

"Very good, milord. Will you take luncheon at the usual time?"

"Charis?"

"Whatever is convenient for you, Tristan?"

"Yes, usual time. We hope the earl might join us, but we will let you know later."

The butler bowed and left the room.

"I know it might take getting used to, my dear, but softly does it in front of the servants if we are to maintain our roles. I have always felt they know exactly what is going on in the household even before we do. Most irritating." He smiled at her. "Although I have finished my breakfast, there is no hurry. Have some more toast."

"No, thank you, this is ample. You mentioned a bag. What else did it have in it?"

"Just toilet things, a change of underwear. You will find it with your other things."

"Where did you get the clothes? What made you buy them?"

"Launceston." He shrugged. "Your luggage was a little sparse."

"Hmm, you knew what a woman needed for her wardrobe. You are a man that needs watching. Too clever by half, I collect."

"Do you like them?"

"Need you ask? They are luxurious." *Another clue. She is not used to expensive dresses and finery.* "I'll have a couturier brought from London as soon as possible. You must have an adequate trousseau. Those clothes are merely a stopgap to tide you over."

"But, Tristan," she stared round-eyed, "you don't have to purchase anything more. They are expensive and enough for me—"

"I have ample funds to dress you in the best. Now, if you please, madam, no arguing. If you are ready, let us explore the house."

With a glare of exasperation, she rose to her feet and followed him into the hall. Once there, he placed her hand on his arm and they set off on a tour of the house. Charis was introduced to the principal staff they met as they went round. She particularly enjoyed the North Gallery where portraits of the family had hung for many years.

"You and your brother were adorable when you were young," she cooed. "Just fancy, you both had blonde curls! Quite a change now." She glanced at his dark hair cut short in the current fashion.

"Oh hell! That was painted years ago. Trust you to pick it out! Adorable? Not on your life. Couple of reprobates, more like."

She laughed at his discomfiture. "Only being boys, I expect."

"Let's go meet Father. It's not far." He glanced at his watch. "It's nearly time for luncheon. I'd like him to join us, if possible."

Melrose opened the door to his father's sitting room and bowed to Charis. "Welcome to Castle House, My Lady, please to come in."

The earl was sitting in his usual chair reading, and looked up in surprise as they entered. He went to stand up, and at once a spasm of pain hit him and he grabbed hold of the armchair trying to recover. Before Tristan could stop her, Charis flew across the room and, putting an arm around Amery's shoulder, helped him to sit down again.

"Please, My Lord, you do not need to stand on ceremony for us." She knelt at his feet. "We are family after all."

Tristan and Melrose held their breath waiting for the blast of invective that would undoubtedly come. Instead, there was silence as the earl settled back into his chair and gazed down at Charis. "He said you were fair. An understatement, I feel. You are charming, my child, as is your kind heart. Thank you for your forbearance. A mere faltering of an old man, but much better now. Melrose, where are you, damn you! Fetch the sherry. I can't have my guests go wanting! Come sit, both of you. Tell me how you are and what you have been about this morning."

Charis perched herself close by the earl on a low stool that Tristan fetched and, gazing up at him, said, "We have been in the long gallery looking at your family portraits. It seems your family has a prize history of adventurers, I've been told. Pirates and all sorts of wicked ancestors if I am to believe your son, milord." Her mouth quirked and a dimple appeared.

Amery laughed. "It's got you wondering what sort of family you have tied yourself to, no doubt. Well, pirates were some time ago, but I seem to recall my grandfather was engaged in the smuggling trade. We owe a good cellar of brandy to his expertise, so I don't complain. How say you, Tristan? Will she put up with us?"

"She's probably still making up her mind, but with luck and a fair wind we might come through and she'll stay." Tristan glanced at the clock on the mantel over the fire. "It's nearly time for luncheon. Will you join us, sir? We would like your company, wouldn't we, Charis?"

"Oh yes, if you can come, that would be splendid. I want to hear more of your family; the nice ones as well as the others."

Amery nodded, and soon he was carried downstairs and helped to his seat at the head of the table with Tristan and Charis on either side.

Tristan was delighted with the outcome. He listened, almost in surprise, to his father talking at length on all manner of subjects in order to entertain Charis. That she enjoyed the discourse was in no doubt. There was no pretence, no dissembling to please the earl's ego; she genuinely enjoyed listening to him as indeed he enjoyed listening to his father as well. When they rose at the end of the lunch, Amery bowed his head to the woman he thought was his daughter-in-law and smiled. "That was agreeable, my dear, most pleasing. I hope you young people can amuse yourselves this afternoon. I must go to rest, but I trust we shall meet at dinner."

He reached out, took her hand, and pressed a kiss to her knuckle. "I shall look forward to your company again, my dear." He waved his hand to the footmen and they wheeled him out of the room.

Tristan held his arm out to Charis and said, "A walk in the garden might please you, my sweet. Shall we?"

She nodded as Tristan said to another footman, "Tell a maid to fetch a shawl for My Lady." Then to her: "It might be cool outside; a wrap will be in order."

As they walked across the dining room to the glass doors opening to the terrace, Charis stopped to look at the large portrait above the marble fireplace. "Tristan, she is beautiful. Who is she?"

"Oh yes, I wondered where the picture had gone. She used to be in the gallery. Father must have had her brought down here. She was our mother. She died not long after that was painted. In childbirth, I was told. I was about five at the time, so I only knew I had lost someone I adored. I might have had a sister, and perhaps my life would have been different and I would have stayed here. Who knows? I suppose we go where fate leads us. Ah, here is your shawl. We will walk our lunch down and see the view." He led Charis on to a wide stone terrace edged with an ornate balustrade. He gestured with an out-flung arm. "Behold my former playground! Can you imagine the antics that two small boys got up to in all that space?" He smiled down at her.

She stared at the green sward running down from below the terrace to a lush valley filled with flowering trees and shrubs; then rising to the edge of a forest with a huge open grassed ride between the trees which ended in a stone archway on the horizon. "It's beautiful. You must have had so much fun."

"Not quite," he said wryly. "Plaguing the gardeners earned us many beatings; then father brought in tutors who were equally strict. We seldom saw him or, if we did, it was to gain a lecture on our shortcomings, me particularly. Then I was shipped off to school."

She glanced up at his frown and guessed his memories were not always pleasant. "But surely your father loved you?"

"No. I can't remember if he did. Children were never regarded until they became of age. The first emotion I have ever seen from him has been displayed since I've returned home; especially towards you."

He saw her start in shocked surprise. "Please don't think I am jealous, Charis. On the contrary, I am delighted you have cheered him. I believe he must have loved my mother very deeply as he never married again."

He frowned wistfully. "Maybe as children we reminded him too much of his loss."

"How very sad for him. Yet now you are home, you can begin a new life and comfort each other."

"My only desire is to begin a new life with you. I've no doubt the earl will show his true colours before long and blast us all in sight. Come, before the afternoon sun deserts us, I have much to show you."

The next hour passed in a pleasing manner as Tristan led Charis through the landscaped gardens ablaze with colour and scents. He was aware that she was no stranger to the names and varieties of the plants. Wherever she had been brought up, she had obviously appreciated her surroundings and gained a great deal of knowledge of gardening.

Eventually, he said, "I think we will go back and enjoy some tea. I have very nearly walked those dainty shoes you are wearing to ribbons. Next time, I will suggest stout boots and hiking sticks for you!"

"Not quite in ribbons," she laughed, "but tea would be splendid."

They had walked in a half circle so, after reaching the back of the house, he led her through a garden door into the rear of the main hall. "We'll use the small parlour. It is cosy there and looks over the garden. You may like to have it for your own use."

Tristan pointed to one of the doors as they walked through the hall. "That is the study. My den from now on. A necessary place to deal with all the estate functions. Father hasn't used it for some time. He's conducted the affairs of the estate from his sitting room to avoid going downstairs. And here's the library."

He opened a door further on and stood aside for Charis to walk into a vast room furnished with comfortable chairs and side tables and filled with books. Shelves built floor to the ceiling filled two walls. Huge windows dominated one side of the room and a large granite fireplace took pride of place at one end.

Charis stood for a moment gazing round at the countless volumes in amazement then sniffed. "You can tell it is a library. Books have a smell all of their own. In fact, I could be back in Carwinnion..." Abruptly, she swung back to Tristan and, with widened eyes, stared at him as the colour fled from her face leaving her ashen white. Her mouth dropped open but nothing emerged for a moment then she croaked, "Carwinnion..."

The next second she dropped at his feet like a stone.

"Charis!" Tristan yelled. "For God's sake! What's wrong?" He knelt beside her and taking one of her hands rubbed it hard to try and rouse her. She did not stir so, raising his voice, he shouted for the butler. "Get Marshall! Quick as you can. Tell him it's Lady Charis!"

Picking her up, he headed for the stairs. "Fetch her maid, Maxwell, on the double!"

Chapter Nine

Daisy was heading for the dining room to check whether Katie had completed the tasks she had been given when she heard muttering coming from the study together with the banging of drawers. Pausing outside the door but ready to run if Tenby suddenly decided to emerge, she listened to him cursing and realised that he was busily searching for something that eluded him. All at once, the noise ceased and there was silence.

Immediately, Daisy scampered across the hall and was about to enter the dining room when a loud voice exclaimed, "Fenton! A moment, if you please."

She turned around as though startled. "Yes, sir? Oh, you gave me a turn. Thought you was in the stables. Supper's nearly ready—"

"Never mind that. Pay attention. Where did Cecile's mother-in-law go to live? That's if she is still alive. Must be a good age now, I dare say. What's her name? Of course, I never met the woman."

What's the old goat up to now? Bloody ignorant swine. Never has the decency to address me as Mrs Fenton as he should. All that swearing and ruckus. And what's he want with the dowager? He's too crafty by far. I reckon he's guessed Charis is heading for her grandmother's place in Bath.

"That's a time or two back. I think it was something like Arabella or was it Isabella? She was very young when she married Alain Langdon and had a son straightaway. I don't rightly remember all the details. I only came here when she left after her husband got drowned. I heard tell she fell out with the old lord because he had insisted on his son sailing to Falmouth to collect something he'd wanted urgently. The seas were already rough and they worsened. The boat and all the crew went down in the storm. She left after that and took her son with her. They came

60

back when the old man died but she didn't stay long, though she loved the Lady Cecile. Carwinnion was too quiet for her, I expect. I think she was more used to a social life. Anyhow, she went back to her own home."

"Which is where? I need her name and her whereabouts."

"Well, my memory ain't so good these days; don't rightly know if I can bring it to mind. Is it important?"

"Mind your own business, woman. Get thinking!" Tenby growled before returning to the study and continuing his search. Damn woman! He thought of his wife. Just the same. Never could please him.

Daisy went outside hoping to see Barney close to the house getting ready to finish work and have his supper. It was urgent: she had to warn him not to say he had passed that letter to her for Charis. She had been hanging the washing outside when he had come back from the village with the mail one day, had held up the letter and said, "That's a surprise. Old Lady Langdon's never written in a long time, far as I recall. And this one's to Charis."

"Give it here!" Reacting swiftly, Daisy snatched it off him. "You know he'll never hand it over to her. It'll go in the fire after he's read it, same as the others to her mother. Bloody man! Now, don't you go saying a word. Hear me? Less he knows the better, I'm thinking. Best thing that could happen for Charis to be in touch with her grandma. It'd put his nose out of joint straightaway."

It had immediately struck her when he had asked her about Lady Caroline Langdon that he was thinking the same thing she was: that Charis was heading for her grandmother's place in Bath. Oh yes, she knew where the old lady was if not the actual address. Cecile had cried many a tear because her mother-in-law never replied to her letters. It wasn't until near the end when she was failing that she realised that her husband intercepted any letters that came for her and destroyed them. She had secretly managed one last attempt but, as far as Daisy was aware, if any letters had come from Bath after that they too had gone the way of the others before reaching Charis. Except for this one, and if she hung for it she would make sure Charis got it.

It was the following late morning before Tenby found what he was looking for. A small address book tucked in between some cards of solace after David had been killed. In it, he found the address of Lady Caroline Langdon who, at the time his wife was alive, was residing in

Bath. Excellent; so much for Fenton's memory, daft bitch that she was. Or was she? He wouldn't put it past her to try and mislead him. Still, he'd got there by his own efforts. Now to travel to Bath, and beard the old dowager and hopefully find his stepdaughter. He rubbed his hands together in glee. No one bested him for long. He'd lived by his wits for too long to be overridden by a chit of a woman. He would have her back in no time. Pleas wouldn't save her.

He had the law on his side for a change which hadn't been always so in the past. In fact, he could remember…no…he did not need to remember anything. Sins were better forgotten and never resurrected.

He had done very well for himself in the past few years. A cosy berth and, up until the last few weeks, plenty of money to indulge in gambling. He just had to keep his mind on the objective: that of securing his safety from the debtor's court. Tucking the address book into his pocket, he went outside and yelled for Barney. When he eventually appeared, Tenby gave him orders to have the carriage ready for early the next morning. He was going to Bath.

"Bath?" exclaimed Barney. "That's a mighty long way to go. Don't know if the old thing will get that far."

"That's why I'm telling you now. Make sure it's fit to travel. And you'd best borrow a pair of decent nags from Tredegar's farm."

"He'll want paying first, sir. You know how he was last time when you hired the horses. Said he'd never do it again, you took so long to settle the bill."

Tenby frowned. "Yes, well, them nags he gave me last time were rubbish. No stamina. Weren't worth the money he asked. I need good enough cattle to get me up-country to Somerset."

"Mind telling me why we are going?"

"We are going up there to fetch my stepdaughter back. Seems she's lost her way and needs a bit of guidance." He gave a throaty chuckle. "Can't have her wandering the countryside, now, can we? Women need control in their lives, and I'm well practised at controlling. As for you, here's the money." He fished in his pocket for a couple of sovereigns. "Get up to Tredegar's and fetch the nags and make sure they are worth paying for. Then, if it takes all night, you get that carriage ready for tomorrow sharp or look for another job, understand!"

The next morning, Barney was on time but there was no sign of

Tenby. Eventually, Daisy went upstairs to see where he was, and found him abed groaning and sick as a dog.

She stood at the bottom of the bed and looked down on her employer with dislike. "Barney's ready, Mr Tenby."

"Barney can wait. My stomach's giving me hell. Gotta be something I ate…what the hell are you at, woman? 'Tain't what I pay you for…" He groaned again and vomited into a pot.

"Nothing wrong with my food. Rest of us is all right and you had the same as us. You went out late last night, and if it was to the grog shop then maybe it was bad beer."

She turned away so he didn't see her smirk. "On the other hand, I reckon it's all that dust you bin swallowing last two days."

"Dust! Don't be daft, woman, dust doesn't give you bellyache."

"Those in the village know they get bellyache every year when they spring clean. You ask 'em! That study is in such a mess with dirt and goodness knows what that it'll be a sennight before we get it clean and tidied up. You stopped me going in to clean regular like, and look what's happened. Belly ache, that's what."

She heard him groan again and mutter, "Get the hell out." She smiled inwardly. *That herb sure was effective. If it gives Charis a bit more time to escape, it's worth clearing up his sick!*

It was two days before Tenby felt well enough to endure the trip to Bath, and even then his passage was slow. By now, Barney was under no illusions that he meant harm to the Lady Charis, and he was determined to prevent that if he could.

Chapter Ten

Charis slowly recovered from her faint to find she was lying on her bed. She could hear two male voices talking close by. For some strange reason, she didn't alert them to her revival but peered between half-closed lashes and saw Tristan and Dr Marshall standing at the foot of the bed intent on discussing her. She lay quiet and listened.

"It's possible that her memory or maybe some of it came back and caused her to swoon. Perhaps the library stimulated it. You say she spoke of a smell? Smells are evocative and can often bring back memories of places one has been to. As to the name she cried out, Carwinnion, it doesn't ring bells with me. Do you know of any place called that?" Marshall said quietly.

"Not that I can recall," said Tristan, "but then I have only recently returned to this country. Even when I was young, I don't think I went to Cornwall. In fact, until I joined the army, my life was either here or at school. Perhaps I can make some inquiries in the Falmouth area. I'm due to contact my steward who deals with the shipping concerns I have put in place as I've instructions for further trading. He has lived in the area all his life so would know the name or its whereabouts."

"I am reluctant to bring her awake with smelling salts. She needs to recover quietly on her own. It could be that she has remembered something horrific, and we need to guard her mind from retreating into oblivion. By all means, make your inquiry. It will give us a further clue when she comes round. If she remembers everything, so well and good we can deal with that, but my feeling is the past might still be shadowed, so don't be surprised if she remains unaware of what she uttered."

"I have to confess I'd like her to stay without a memory so that we may marry and have a life together," Tristan replied.

"Despite the fact I was willing to help, I've had second thoughts with this new relapse, and I'm sure, milord, you don't really mean that. Both of you would always be wondering what had happened in the past, and it could possibly affect your relationship in the future. It is better to resolve the problem rather than leaving a trap. I don't believe her amnesia is so deep that she will never regain her mind."

"I can't believe she can have a better life elsewhere. I'm sure wherever she was running to can't offer her more than I can," Tristan said grumpily. "A future earl's wife is no mean ambition."

"However, My Lord, I still advise you to allow her memories to recover naturally. Marriage is a serious business, at least in my book it is. You've left taking that step for long enough that a few more weeks will make little difference. It might make a big difference to Lady Charis if she gets to choose with a healthy mind."

Memories or nightmares? Leaping from a state of blankness to recalling her whole previous existence as she stood in the library made Charis wish to go back to the blankness. The shock of remembering had obviously caused her to faint. The jubilation she'd felt on escaping from her stepfather was swept away as she realised she had tumbled into a strange misadventure with the accident to the coach. Her lucky escape in gaining the passage to Falmouth, pleased she could hide in the luggage trunk and travel out of Cornwall, had incredibly ended up in a situation that seemed uncanny. Despite her efforts had she come round in a circle, and would she be sent back to Carwinnion and Tenby?

She stole a swift look at the man who wanted to marry her. For goodness' sake, what had happened since her senses left her? No one in their right mind, certainly not a peer of the realm, professed a willingness to marry a total stranger. Nor would he once he knew her story. He didn't look simple-minded. In fact, he was the handsomest man she had ever come across; though, in truth, her lonely life apart from neighbours had never brought her in contact with many from the *ton*. His eyes looked clear and honest, and his demeanour with her since her recovery from the accident had been all she could have wished for, but it didn't make sense, or was it simply the male ego that always clung on to what they possessed? Did he think he owned her just because he had found her? She would soon disabuse him of that conception. Nobody from now on would own her. She would fight tooth and nail to be free of male domination.

In running away from her stepfather, she'd found pride in becoming her own woman at last and able to act as she thought best. Nobody was going to take that away from her, certainly not someone who was almost a complete stranger. While she liked him, she was wary. He had lied to her even though he had explained it was to help at the time. Now, there was the added problem that the staff thought they were actually married. The idea of pretence did not sit well with the moral code her mother had taught her.

Nevertheless, if she *secretly* became his wife then she would be back under someone's control again. His control would be absolute. Already she knew him for a person who wanted his own way. No! Impossible! She couldn't – wouldn't give up her freedom! She switched her attention back to the men. Dr Marshall was carrying on a reasonable conversation, and he, at least, sounded sensible and on her side. However, she decided, in the same way she was not going to marry Whaley, this viscount was not going to intimidate or persuade her into marrying him.

What to do now? Her mind quickly raced through all the various possibilities but eventually settled on the most obvious. Time was swiftly passing, and she had lost days with the accident. For all she knew, Tenby could be at her heels and might have traced her to Castle House. He could call any time and take her back to Carwinnion and Whaley.

So, did she confess her background, trust the men would see things from her point of view, and save her from her stepfather, or were they like most men and believed that, as she was only a woman and her needs did not count, they must abide by the law? She could not take a chance on them helping her. She must make her escape and reach her grandmother in Bath.

But how? Hmm, first things first. Somehow she must pretend she still knew nothing of her past history then must plan her way to freedom. It was a great pity that they would think badly of her as they had treated her well. Sadly, she would have nothing more to do with the earl whom she had enjoyed meeting and conversing with. He would retain a disgust of her after she left. And Tristan? His kisses had been intriguing and, she had to confess, rather more than merely nice. They had thrilled her to the core, but she still had to escape. The only way was with subterfuge. Pretence was not her style but, with so much at stake, her conscience would have to be subdued.

She made a slight murmur and fluttered her eyelashes. At once, the men moved swiftly to the head of the bed.

Dr Marshall lifted her wrist and felt her pulse. "How are you feeling, my dear?"

"All right, I think. What happened? Why am I on my bed?"

"You don't remember?" He studied her closely.

She turned her head and looked up at Tristan. *Careful now, you must act the part to succeed. Don't let them know you remember.* "What do I have to remember, milord? Have I done something wrong? Oh dear, I am sorry..."

"No, certainly not. I'm at fault for tiring you out." He smiled at her. "We stayed too long in the garden and you swooned. I should have been more careful of your health."

"And you mentioned tea, I remember. I must confess to being thirsty so may we take it now? The rest has done me good. Dr Marshall, shall you join us for tea?" She swung her legs round and sat up. "The parlour, I believe you said, Tristan? You'll have to show me where it is. Gentlemen, shall we go down to the parlour?"

She caught the quick look the men gave each other from the corner of her eye, but neither said another word, and she placed a hand on Tristan's arm as he led her downstairs to a pleasant room where soon tea, scones and fruit cake were served. The conversation after that was general, and though she knew the doctor's eye was on her quite a few times she also felt that she had successfully passed a test and they had no idea she had regained her full memory.

Dr Marshall rose to his feet and bowed to Charis. "The tea was most pleasant, My Lady, but duty calls and I must take leave of you. If you need me, don't hesitate to call. Perhaps we can talk later this week if you can spare the time?"

"Yes, I would like that." She smiled and offered her hand in farewell. "I will see you when you visit the earl, I expect."

"I'll see you out, Richard. I need to talk to you about one of the gardeners...I'll be back shortly, Charis."

"Don't hurry. I need to confer with cook about dinner tonight. Your father is dining with us, and we must have his favourite food."

Outside on the portico, Tristan scratched his head. "What do you make of all that? All remembered except that visit to the library. It's almost as though I made it up."

"You didn't make up the unconsciousness. No one can fake a genuine fainting fit, though society ladies have a swoon off to a fine art. Something happened in the library, I think, but vanished so quickly she can't remember. We can only wait and see if it will happen again. I have every confidence it eventually will."

The hour was early the next morning when Tristan crept into the next room and dangled a stocking he had found on a chair across the face of the sleeping Charis to rouse her. He laughed as she woke and sat up with a surprised frown on her face, and he tried not to look at her low-cut nightgown covering her bare shoulders and the sweetly jutting breasts that he ached to hold in his hands and press his lips to.

"You did say to wake you early. You wanted to ride. It's my time for riding. Coming or not?"

Her face cleared. "Yes, I'll be pleased to come. Give me a few minutes. I'll meet you at the stables. But you didn't say you rode in the early hours, milord?"

"It's past six o'clock. Hardly early; the day is racing by." He grinned. "Right, see you at the stables. By the way, can you ride? Or do I pick a mild 'un?"

"Don't you dare! I want a horse, not a donkey!"

Charis found the new habit which Tristan had bought her and her old boots which she had told her maid to leave out. Instead of ringing for Kate to help, she dressed quickly and went down to the stables in less time than Tristan expected. He was still talking with the head groom and surveying the horses when she arrived. Glancing at her attire filled him with deep pleasure. The rich green habit, fastened with gold buttons, suited her perfectly, and once again desire flooded his mind. He smiled as she joined him and he bid her a good morning.

"Come, let's see what you fancy." He led her along the stalls somewhat surprised that she inspected each horse carefully with a discerning eye until she stopped before one and smoothed her hand over the enquiring nose that poked over the gate.

"I like this one," she said. "What's her name?"

Sykes pursed his lips. "Butterfly Beauty, milady. She's a mite frisky, lives up to her name she does, dances about like a butterfly when she has a mind to. She has plenty of spirit and a tendency to go her own way, especially when she hasn't been exercised. She was due to go out today with one of the grooms but we've yet to get around to it. Now I've a calmer one here." He moved on to the next stall.

"Butterfly will suit me well. She looks to have a good spirit. Saddle her up, if you please, Mr Sykes. As My Lord was saying, the day is racing by. We need to take full advantage of it."

Sykes glanced at Tristan who shrugged and said, "Saddle the horse up. Milady has chosen her ride and we shall exercise her."

Soon they were both mounted and, though Tristan was keeping a watchful eye on Charis, he soon saw she was so much at home in the saddle he had no need to worry. She kept the horse well in control until it had confidence in her and there was never a sign of jibbing at the bit; then let the mare move easily at her own pace. Once they reached more open country, she loosed the reins a trifle more and set off, first in a canter then into a full gallop with a joyous whoop.

Tristan was taken by surprise but his huge black hunter soon caught up with her, and the two steeds pounded alongside each other up the open ride to the Triumphal Arch on the top of the hill. Once at the top, they had a marvellous view over all the countryside and, as Charis gazed around in wonder, Tristan stared at her glowing cheeks, bright eyes and obvious delight in the surroundings.

"That was amazing! I haven't ridden like that in ages. And the view! Oh, Tristan, you are so lucky to live here and have this wonderful place to ride in."

"Yes, I am fortunate. You could be too, if you will accept my proposal to marry me. As I have said, it would be a quiet wedding but I will do full justice to the occasion."

"Yes, I'm sure you would." Her voice changed and became subdued. "Can you give me time to think? I must know where I come from. Unlock my mind from the darkness. It is only fair to you, My Lord," she pleaded. "Otherwise, you are marrying a stranger who might be anyone or at least someone who is not suitable for your rank."

"I'd lay odds that you are, Charis. But, yes, I will give you time to make up your mind. Don't delay too long. I want you for my wife."

The ride back to the house was quiet and restrained as each had a great deal to think about.

Chapter Eleven

Charis allowed one more day to pass before she made her move. One more day to get used to the horse, the surroundings of the stables and the house, as well as a swift visit to the library when Tristan was out touring the estate with his steward, to seek the maps and directions she would need to find her way to Bath. A rummage through the books and atlases proved very useful.

That night, after Kate had finished getting her ready for bed and left the room, she made sure the door between the two bedrooms was closed, and quietly she turned the key to make sure he could not come through. Swiftly, she donned her undergarments with a nightdress over and retired to bed just in case Tristan took it into his head to visit, likely coming through her main door into the corridor. Later, she heard him talking to his valet, and soon the light went out under the connecting door and she knew he had retired for the night. They had spent some time with his father, and she had encouraged Tristan to drink deeply and had even pretended to imbibe herself though she thought a plant nearby her chair would die of alcohol the amount that she had drained into it.

She heard a distant clock strike one as she rose, donned her breeches, shirt and jacket, the original garments she had worn from Cornwall which she found in a cupboard. She picked up her boots and the small bag from a wardrobe where it was hidden, that held a dress and the sundries she had brought with her from home. Adding the unexpected money which Tristan had persuaded her to accept in case she had a fancy to buy something from the village, she was ready. With fresh experience from her last escape, she had packed everything she thought suitable. *Deja vu, history repeating itself*, she murmured to herself.

Silently leaving her room and tiptoeing downstairs to a dark, silent hall, donning boots and going to the stables was easy. Saddling a horse and getting out was not. When she eventually rode clear of the estate, she could not believe she had accomplished her escape without rousing the grooms who slept over the stables. Yet she had and, losing no time, she took the road north to Somerset and Bath.

Tristan woke much later than usual and cursed as his headache reminded him he had drunk to excess the night before. Rising, he went to his dressing room and poured cold water over his head to soothe the pain. All was quiet in the room next door, and he presumed that Charis was still asleep. He recalled that she too had drunk more wine than normal as they listened to some of his father's tales, and he hoped she would not wake up with the same kind of headache he had.

Maybe it would be better to give riding a miss this morning and yet, looking at the sky, it was going to be a fine day. A gallop over the hills in the early morning freshness and a return to a good breakfast would surely chase away the megrims. He dressed and went over to her door and quietly eased the handle. Strangely, it was locked. Ah, a headache for sure. She must have woken early; decided she would not ride, and did not want disturbing. He would be riding on his own this morning. A pity, as he enjoyed her company, but so be it.

Down at the stables there was unexpected consternation. "Milord, a horse is missing."

"Which horse?"

"Butterfly Beauty, the one milady rides."

"I am later than usual. Did she come down earlier?"

"No, milord," said Sykes as he stood at his elbow, his brow lined in dismay. "I was one of the first up, and I never saw hide nor hair of anyone else. It wasn't until we did the water rounds that we spotted the horse had gone. I swear to God I never heard a thing and me a light sleeper—"

"Get the others mounted and we'll get ready to search the estate. I'll check upstairs to see if Her Ladyship is still asleep; then we'll be off."

Damn it to hell, he thought as his head pounded with pain, *I could have done without this.*

Somehow, he wasn't surprised to find her bed empty. He thought of the locked door and turned the key back to open on her side. She had not wanted to him to come in unexpectedly, had she? Oh, very clever!

So where the hell had Charis gone? Out riding, of course, but what was she up to now? On her own and not waiting for him. Why?

He went back to the stables to fetch his horse intending to go out with the others when Sykes met him in the doorway.

"Milord? Did you find Her Ladyship?"

Tristan shook his head. "No, she is probably out riding."

"I don't think so. I've just discovered that a saddle is missing."

"Well, it would be, wouldn't it? It's on the damned horse!" he replied tersely, his head aching worse than ever. *By God, I'll kill her when I find her!*

"It's not the side saddle milady uses. Looks like a stranger has the horse, though I've not seen any men lurking about here."

Tristan stood silent as he weighed up the situation. The thought that came in his mind as he'd searched the bedroom hardened. Charis had been intent on going somewhere out of Cornwall when she had stowed away in the carriage boot. Somehow in the library, he felt sure her memory had returned. Yet she had concealed it from him and Richard. Whatever she had to do or wherever she had to get to must be so important she had to escape from a place of safety without asking for help, which she must have known would have been given freely.

His lips tightened. Unless it concerned a crime she was involved in. *Charis, what the hell are you up to?*

As for the saddle, no need to question that. She would be riding astride and probably dressed as he had found her in the carriage. He hadn't a clue as to the disposal of the clothes he had taken off her, had just slung them in the carriage trunk. It seemed likely now they had ended up in one of her cupboards. Too late to regret that mistake even if he had ever given it any thought. What was far more important was figuring out where she had gone.

"Milord?" Sykes fidgeted beside him. "Hyperion is saddled and ready for you."

"What!" Tristan came to with a start. "I'm not going after all. I believe I know what has happened. I'll speak to you later and let you know what I intend. Stand the men down. There will be no search." He turned on his heel and walked briskly back to the house knowing it would be useless to pursue her at that moment. She would have left in the early hours if his guess was right and would be miles away by now. He headed for the breakfast room. It was time to get rid of his headache and plan what he should do next.

Maxwell, noting the scowl on the viscount's face as well as being aware of the liquor consumed the previous evening, placed a concoction in a glass in front of him before he poured out the coffee. Knowing what it was, Tristan made a face as he picked up the glass, nodded his thanks to his butler, and drank the lot down. Reaching for his coffee, he took a long swallow to take away the taste then concentrated on eating if not entirely enjoying his breakfast.

However, by the time he had finished, the magical brew had done its work, his headache was just a memory, and he felt able to concentrate on the problem of the missing woman.

Looking back to the event in the library, he recalled the look of fright on her face just before she fell to the ground. Why did she look so scared? Being found out? Possibly this would be the case if she had committed an offence. Yet he couldn't believe she was running away from a crime. Christ Almighty, he knew villains and their devious ways. His experience had been honed in the Far East where villainy was a way of life. He would lay his life on the line that she was an innocent probably running scared from who knew what or whom.

All at once, another thought came into his head. She had been equally distraught the night she had the nightmare. Intent on soothing her distress and his mind filled with the problem of confessing that he had contrived a falsehood of their marriage, he had ignored her mumbled words about her grandmother. At last, they made sense. She was running away from a forced marriage that was obviously abhorrent to her. The blame rested with him. He had been more intent on his sexual desire of her than investigating the cause of the nightmare. If he had taken more notice of her misery then she might not have fled, and she might have got her memory back sooner.

With breakfast over, he went to his study still racking his brains for any clue of that night and how it might help him to understand where she might have gone. Then he remembered her pushing him away and wanting her grandmother. That thought led to the letter he had read when he had delved in her bag. Of course! He berated his stupidity. She was heading for her grandmother's.

With a swiftness that surprised Maxwell, who was about to knock on the study door, he pulled it open intent on going to the library. He came to a stop and listened as the butler told him that Dr Marshall was visiting the earl and did he wish to see him? It didn't take a genius to realise that news of Charis leaving the house so suddenly had flown through the household. In view of her recent accident and the relapse, it was only natural that his butler felt Tristan would discuss things with the doctor. And not only him, his father must be told too. He gave an inward groan of exasperation. That was one job he was not looking forward to. His deception of a marriage was coming back to bite him with a vengeance.

"Thank you, Maxwell, I'll go upstairs."

The look on his father's face was not reassuring as he entered the sitting room. Richard also looked sombre, and it did not take a moment to perceive that Charis was the subject of the conversation.

Tristan marvelled at the spy network his father had in place. It was hardly more than an hour since he had heard, yet his father's frown said it all. However, it wasn't surprising. Harwood had always been an excellent butler. He knew everything that went on in the estate.

"It seems we have more to discuss than my damned rheumatics." Amery was abrupt. "I've had time to wonder about things these last few days and think about the conversations we have had. Charis, I suspect, has a fine mind. In fact, she's a rare intelligent woman allowing her to interact with whoever she is talking to but cleverly, I now realise, avoid divulging anything of her past. Naturally, we accepted that she had amnesia, and that was probably true at the beginning, but now and again, as I recall, many of her recent answers did not fit the part. So I think it time you two came up with the truth. I might be getting old but I haven't yet reached senseless dotage. No one runs away unless they have something to hide. Out with it, boy! Where did you meet the girl?"

Chapter Twelve

An hour later, after coffee had been served and all revealed to the earl, he sat back in his chair, his eyes half closed as he pondered on the recent events. Other than his first demand to his son, the earl had not uttered a word of reproach, which made Tristan feel even worse, but had listened quietly to the discussion only now and then interceding with a question, the answer to which he did not further comment on.

All of a sudden, he raised his head. "That letter from her grandmother – what address did she give?"

"Already thought of that, but blessed if I can remember. I knew it was up-country somewhere, not London or anywhere south." Once again, Tristan tried to visualise the tiny writing at the top of the letter. He had the feeling it was a short name. It also occurred to him that she had answered quite happily to Charis. Nor had she demurred at being called Lady Charis. Could her gentility include her coming from a noble family? In that case, there was one town up-country that catered for the *ton* and that was Bath. Her grandmother could well be there.

"I've got an idea it could be Bath. I'm going down to the library to look at Burke's Peerage. If she is part of a notable family in Cornwall, it might give us a clue."

"Regretfully, milord, I have to leave too," said Richard. "I like unravelling mysteries, and this one has me intrigued. Alas, I have other patients to see and must get on. Keep me posted, please?"

"Will do. I'll send one of the grooms with a message if I find anything important but, in any case, I'll be heading off shortly to Bath. I have the feeling I might find her there."

"Do you need my help, Tristan?" his father asked.

"Not at present, but if I find anything in the book I'll be straight back.

I expect you know pretty much all that Burke's can offer."

He smiled at his sire feeling pleased that things were right between them.

Once in the library, he sought and found the big tome that held all the histories and lineages of the British peerage, and settled down to leaf through it, concentrating on a Cornish link.

It was nearing mid morning before he found a connection with the name Carwinnion. Faced with the number of family names and at a loss where to begin searching, it struck him that he had yet to discover the whereabouts of the word Charis had exclaimed before she fainted.

Going to the map shelf, he saw it had already been disturbed and a folder was open depicting Somerset. Just as he thought! Bath was in Somerset. Eureka!

Branching out in an ever-widening circle from Falmouth, he found the name in an old outline map showing districts and enclosed lands belonging to estates. Carwinnion lay close to the sea not far from the Helford River. Back he went to Burke's, and this time his task was easier. Unearthing the name Langdon and a Lord Alastair, a son named Alain and wife Caroline gave him a clue, for although Alain had been drowned they had a son called David who was a major in the army. He had married a French lady called Cecile. The next words solved everything: they'd had a daughter called Charis. No wonder she excelled in French. She had learned it as a young child.

Picking up the peerage book and the map, he went upstairs.

"Langdon?" Amery mused for several minutes before saying, "Only one I recall was a surly individual I encountered once in a debate in the Lords. Come to think of it, I believe a scandal caused by his daughter-in-law occurred about that time. She took off with his grandson accusing him of causing her husband's death. Apparently, the son had drowned in a storm off the coast obeying his father. She went back to her family with the boy and, like all scandals, it was a ten-day wonder, and we heard no more. Incredibly, Langdon must have let her go without a protest. Guilty conscience, no doubt. Don't think they went back to the manor until the boy was past his majority. Caroline must have returned to Somerset after he married and took over the estate. Hmm, he wed a French girl?" He closed his eyes and pursed his lips. "Met him once in the service. Nice chap. Worked for Adderbury undercover in France for a bit. Damned shame; we lost him at Waterloo among so many others who died. If his wife was French, she could have had a hard time of it after that débâcle. Feelings ran high with the loss of so many men even if we did win the war. No clues from thereon?"

"Not a thing. I'll have to go back to my steward in Falmouth to get more information. At least I've some names to work on now."

"Bring her back, Tristan. I've taken a liking to the girl whatever she may have done or been involved in. She has a kind heart, and I'd lay odds she hasn't a shred of wickedness in her."

Tristan blinked in surprise. "My thoughts entirely. I'm very glad we agree. Your wish is my command, sir."

Back in his study once more, Tristan sent for Roger Maberly. "Pack a bag, Roger. We leave for Bath as soon as we've eaten. Tell Edwin to pack for me, and he is to come too."

"You think Lady Charis has gone to Bath, milord?"

"It seems a likely destination. We'll take the greys. They are the most suitable for town travel yet have the stamina for distance. Have our carriage wheels been replaced?"

"Ordered but not yet arrived. I suggest we take His Lordship's coach if he approves. It's big enough and most comfortable. Lady Charis will approve, I think, when you bring her back home."

"If I do." Tristan did not feel entirely confident of achieving that result after all the happenings since he'd come across her.

"I think you will. I've never known you overset since you first took me on, milord. I'd back you against all comers."

"We'll see. There's always a first time. Now, get to it. I want to be in Bath as soon as possible. We shall stay at the duke's. I've sent Stevens ahead to make arrangements. He'll be on hand to see to the cattle. That will leave you free to help me search. With luck, we may arrive ahead of milady. But if not then one can only hope she will be safe with her grandmother. Off you go. I'll see you in half an hour.

"No! Wait a moment!" He paused, feeling suddenly indecisive, which was most unlike him. He had always in the past carried out his affairs without hesitation, not vacillating as he was now; often acting on intuition, but never at a loss. In fact, he could not recall a significant time it had happened before. Was it the thought of Charis in danger that had brought this on?

"Change of plan, Roger. We'll take our mounts. My patience won't cope with sitting for days in a coach and delays on the road. The coach can follow behind us at its best speed. It can include her maid and all the baggage necessary for both of us for a longer stay in Bath. Thinking about my brother's death has raised some questions in my mind. My father still has connections in the city, so I can make use of the time I shall be there. I need some family history."

He started back to the house then stopped in his tracks again, his mind still busily thinking about the strange situation he found himself in. He ran his fingers through his hair feeling desperately troubled about the lady he was about to hunt down. Where was she and, more importantly, why had she vanished? What secrets would he uncover when he found her? Was she guilty of a crime or an unfortunate victim running away from a forced marriage? The only way he would find out was the path he had determined on. Once he had Charis again, he would never let her go.

Finally deciding, Tristan followed Roger to the stables. "Have Everton do the driving. He has safe hands especially with those greys. He'll need good hands, especially in the city."

Turning at His Lordship's words, Roger bowed, a faint smile flashing across his face. "As I said, milord, I've never known you overset. I will await you in the stables."

"Oh, get on with it, you scoundrel! Stop plumping me up. You are delighted to be riding instead of being in a coach. You enjoy speed much as I do," growled Tristan, cheering up at the thought of another adventure. Not that delving into the death of his brother was an adventure. His subconscious mind was prodding him to investigate. He owed it to his father to find out if Henry's death really was an accident.

As far as finding Charis was concerned, he thought that the least of his troubles. If his able brain couldn't manage that after all he had learned in the years he had been away then he would count himself the worst of duffers. Was managing the Castle House estate going to be too tame for him? Could he settle down and be happy? He thought of Charis, of marriage and having a family if all went well. Whatever happened, he would cope, but the dream of having her by his side filled his mind with a tantalising future. Meanwhile, a visit to Bath beckoned.

Chapter Thirteen

The forest was dark and silent except for a faint burbling of water from a stream close by. Charis slid from her mount still holding onto her saddle until she felt her trembling legs could hold her up. She tried to think of a deprecatory word that would adequately describe what she had just gone through, but all she could remember and mutter was *Merde!* It was a word her mother had whispered to herself many times after Tenby had used her badly. She hadn't been meant to hear, but her knowledge of French stood her in good stead. *Shit!* Yes, it conveyed just the right meaning of the man that had grabbed hold of her reins and tried to steal her horse.

The four days on the road since she had left Castle House had been gruelling to say the least. One had been spent in the shelter of an abandoned haystack, which meant a virtually sleepless night as she could hear the squeaks and burrowing of rats or mice. The second was in a deserted half-ruined cottage where she had left Butterfly on a long enough tether so that the horse could graze on knee-high grass. She was so tired she had just flung the saddle down in an empty room and herself after it. Rats or not, she had to sleep. The rough billets, she felt, were absolutely necessary. She did not know who might come after her, but inquiries along the road could easily ascertain if she had sought a night's lodging at an inn. Knowing that, she had avoided villages along the way and kept to the open country where dwellings were few and far between. This course of action put a further burden on her as she had eaten the last of her food and knew if she was to maintain her strength she must find more provisions.

Late in the afternoon of the third day, she came across a priory not far from Taunton where she was able to pay for a night's lodging and also food. Best of all, the place had few guests, and she was able to use the washroom and the accommodation without anyone realising she was a female. The washing water was cold, but she didn't mind. The previous wash had been in a stream, so this one was luxury.

Though the food was plain, she ate her fill and fell asleep feeling safe and far more cheerful. Confirming directions the next day showed her en route to Langport and the road to Glastonbury and Wells. Still keeping to the open countryside, she followed the road alongside as best as she could so that she could escape if she felt threatened.

Bad luck struck just short of Langport when her horse threw a shoe. It was market day in the village and the area was crowded. She found the forge, but would have to wait her turn for the shoeing. While she waited, she decided to buy adequate provisions for the next stage of her journey. Who knew what lay ahead? The nearer she got to Bath, the more care she knew she ought to take. Until she actually knocked at her grandmother's door, she was at risk. It had been some time since the letter had come, and Lady Langdon might be away visiting, in which case her staff would never let her stay.

She wandered down the High Street and filled her saddlebag with bread, cheese and fruit and a flask of milk which she hoped would suffice for the next couple of days before returning to the smithy and leading Butterfly inside.

The blacksmith smiled at her then waved his apprentice away. "I reckon as you should hold her head. 'Spects she trusts you better'n anyone," he said as he bent to inspect each hoof. "I dursent recall this mare, lad. You ain't from round here or I'd know you and this fine horse. Where you come from, if I may ask?"

"Oh, just passing through. Master's staying at the Cock and Pheasant (*she had noted the most prestigious-looking inn in Langport for this very reason in case she was asked*) so I got the job. Horse belongs to his wife and she dotes on her. I'm along to guard the mare, you might say. More'n my skin's worth to make a hash of things."

"Don't 'ee worry young 'un. I'm worth my weight in gold. You won't find a better smithy this side of England, and that's the truth." His huge beer belly shook with mirth and made Charis stare in awe. "She'll be well shod time I've finished."

Charis knew enough about the craft to know the job was well done and did not haggle the price.

Heading along the road past the market traders to leave the town, she felt pleased all had gone well until a rough-clad man stopped her by grabbing hold of the reins. "'Ere you, boy! Watcher doing with that there bit of horseflesh. Tell ye what I'll give 'ee a guinea for her. Or a stick to yer back if you don't agree!" He brought up a cudgel he had hidden behind his back.

It seemed a lifetime but was only seconds as Charis stared at the man; then, loosening her foot swiftly from the stirrup, she lashed out at his face. The toe of her boot caught him under his chin and he went down to lie spreadeagled in the road. Quickly regaining her stirrup, she kicked Butterfly to action. The horse immediately took off heading for the open country as though all the devils in hell were on her tail.

Behind her, she could hear the yells of "Stop thief! Catch the varmint – bloody boy near killed me!" Heaven help her if anyone gave chase and caught her. She would end up in the local jail without a soul to vouch for her. As soon as she could, she left the road and, still travelling at speed, surveyed the land around for a hiding place; then headed towards an outcrop covered in gorse and shrub trees. She was just in time. As she slid into the bushes, she heard the sound of galloping horses and a carriage of some sorts on the road. The sounds disappeared up the road and, as soon as she felt safe, she took off eastwards across the moorland and did not ease up until she reached much higher ground covered with trees.

At the moment she was lost but did not care, for at last she could breathe a sigh of relief and know for a little while at least she was out of danger. Catching hold of the bridle, she led Butterfly towards the sound of water and came across a small stream where she allowed the horse to drink. Scooping up water for herself, she drank her fill then rubbed her face with her wet hand to refresh herself. Getting to her feet, she stared around to see if there was a reasonable place to spend the next few hours. She would stay here overnight until dawn to give them both a chance to rest and recover before moving on and picking up the trail again. Now, more than ever, she knew she had to avoid villages or places of habitation. A stable boy riding a prime bit of horseflesh was inconsistent with the norm. Only someone of standing would be abroad with a horse like hers. A stable boy would be where he was meant to be – in the stables.

On the evening of the following day, Charis reached the outskirts of

Wells as darkness fell. She had lain up in surrounding woodland outside the town for several hours intending to ride through during the night and be in Bath early the next day. It would be another hard ride, but at least she and her horse were rested and able. Leaving Butterfly hobbled in a safe place, she decided to reconnoitre the lanes to choose the easiest and quietest way through the town without attracting attention.

She was making her way along an alley when a hand grasped her collar, and she was yanked round to face her captor. With a frightened gasp, she thought her nemesis in the shape of Thomas Tenby had caught her at last.

"So that's where my bloody coat disappeared," growled an irate voice. "Charis Langdon, you are a thief!"

"Barney! Jesus, man, you scared me half to death!"

"And so I ought!" Barney released his hold. "Where have you been these past weeks? Daisy's been out of her mind with worry."

"Oh dear, I'm sorry, but there was no other way. Marrying Whaley would have been a nightmare." She glanced around as they spoke, eyeing her surroundings warily.

From the snatches of conversation he had picked up from Tenby and Daisy, Barney guessed where the girl was heading, but he only said, "Don't worry, Charis. He's booked into the Swan and is probably well into his dinner by now. I get a shilling or two for whatever meal I can scrounge, and told to bed down in the coach. I tell you straight, after the journey here, even murder's a damn sight too good for such as him. I'd hang him up live in a deserted place and let the crows finish him off in their own sweet time. Begging your pardon, little 'un, but it's how I feel."

"Oh, Barney," she reached out and hugged him, "you haven't called me that in a long time."

"Well, I've known you long enough. A chubby babe and a young nipper who plagued me to death to help her catch frog's spawn." He chuckled at the memory. "In spite of Daisy nagging me to be polite and call you Lady Charis now you've all grown up, I still remember the old days. As for now, where are you headed?"

"My grandmother's in Bath. If I can reach her, she will hide me and keep me safe."

"Daisy guessed you'd try and get to her. Say no more then I won't have to lie to his nibs. Daisy always says my face is like an open book. Best thing

I can do is to give you time to find your grandma. I'll nobble the coach. It's on its last legs anyway, so Tenby will have to accept another delay while it gets fixed. Though it will be a miracle if it can. A godforsaken rattletrap, that's all it is. Even the horses were scared with the noises that came from it. They tried to bolt now and then to get away. It's all I can do, I'm afraid, to delay things. If Daisy were here now, she might have some other ideas but she's not, so we'll just have to muddle along without her."

Charis stared at him in the gloom perceptively hearing something in his voice. Was it a longing? "Why don't you marry her, Barney? You know you love her."

"She wouldn't have an old codger like me," he growled back.

"You don't know till you ask her. Think it over. You may be surprised. Meanwhile, now it is dark, I must get a move on. Tenby's sure to have Grandmother's address. I must get to her soon as possible. See if you can leave a message with her butler or a servant to let me know where you will be and when we can meet again. Of course my grandmother may not be in Bath; she might be travelling elsewhere. God willing, she is still alive and well. However, I am not banking on anything but a hope. If all else fails, I must seek a place to hide until I am of age. Don't give me away, Barney. I have hated my stepfather as long as I have known him, and even more after he was so cruel to my mother. I will kill myself rather than go back and marry that dreadful man, but I hope it won't come to that. So let me know what is happening, and I'll try and contact you the same way. God willing, we will come out of this affair with my freedom and yours as well. Once I have my majority, I plan to sue him and get my property back. Then you and Daisy will have a home with me forever."

"Oh, little 'un, I have missed you so much, and here you are with your kind heart thinking of Daisy and me. Bless you, child, I will do what I can to help, though I fear it won't be much. Tenby has always been a mean brute and he won't change his nature now, that's for damn sure. Yet, he probably still needs me to back him up even if the coach is useless." Barney rubbed his whiskery chin. "Don't know how he plans to go on, but I'll try to let you know. Take care, Charis. I hope we meet in better times."

Awkwardly, he gave her a hug which she returned in good measure then wiped a tear from her eye as she turned away to find her horse and take the road to Bath. What a dear soul he was and how much had she missed him and Daisy now, she thought. They could almost have been like parents during her growing years.

In a short time, she was through the town and on her way again with a prayer in her heart that she could find her grandmother and feel safe once again.

Chapter Fourteen

Lady Caroline Langdon read the card again, still at a loss to guess why Viscount Fortesque should pay her a call. Thinking back over the years to her youth, she remembered his father. A dashing rake of a man that all the young debs sighed over, not least her, but he had fallen for Aurelia Elwood, a particularly beautiful damsel and the daughter of the Earl of Pembroke. Out of her league and both of them too high in the insteps to even notice her. She had to be content with a mere lord and, though Alain had cherished her and she him, moving down to Cornwall had put an end to her social round in London, obliging her to get used to the parochial ways of the neighbourhood. Sadly, her marriage had been cut short with the death of Alain. In a flash, she had seized the opportunity and escaped. Choosing to settle in Bath near her family had been the wisest course, and David was brought up with his cousins in the style she had always wanted and could never have achieved down in Cornwall.

Much later, after mourning David's loss at Waterloo and staying for a while as she liked his wife and her granddaughter, Caroline knew Carwinnion was not a good place for her. It was far too isolated and away from the social scene that was her joy, so she left, resuming her former life in Bath where she was happiest. Hoping to entice Cecile to join her, she had written quite a few times but had no reply to her letters. Then one arrived telling her the reason why. Immediately, Caroline had replied but there was no further communication, and eventually she heard through a friend of a friend that Cecile was dead. Quite a long time passed after that until she thought of her granddaughter and wondered how she fared. The girl would be grown to adulthood by now and be of marriageable age. Perhaps she could sponsor Charis in Bath society and achieve a better marriage for her than the one she might have in Cornwall. So Caroline wrote again, but did not know that letter was fortunately intercepted by Daisy. Charis had received it and was at that moment on her way to see her grandmother.

"Tell His Lordship I will be with him shortly."

Bedford bowed low. "Very good, milady. He is awaiting you in the best parlour. Do I offer sherry or Madeira?"

"Madeira, of course. And, Bedford, a freshly opened bottle into a decanter, if you please. I should hate him to think we are parvenus."

"Of course, milady. Already thought of it." He bowed and left.

Lady Langdon spent a moment or two making sure she was tidy before going downstairs to the parlour. She found Tristan nursing a glass and staring up at a portrait over the mantel. At the sound of her voice as she dismissed her butler, he turned, placed his glass on a table, and bowed before coming over and taking her outstretched hand.

"Your Ladyship, please forgive my calling on you without notice. It is kind of you to see me."

"It is somewhat of a surprise, milord, as I don't recall meeting you in person before, though I have met your father many years ago. However, I'm sure you will enlighten me now you are here. Please take a seat."

She waved him to a chaise and took the one opposite before raising her brow in puzzled inquiry.

"Before I explain, may I ask if your granddaughter is with you?"

"Charis? Here? Why no, she lives in Cornwall." She watched a frown of concern wash over his face. "Why do you ask?"

Where the hell is she? Nigh on a week since she took off from Castle House. Is she in trouble? How do I explain what's happened? What will Charis tell her grandmother when she arrives here?

"I think you should tell me how you know my granddaughter and what brings you here. You obviously expected her to be with me, but I have had no notice of this whatsoever. Your hesitation worries me."

"I met your daughter entirely by accident and coincidentally through an accident, and took her to my home in Devon to recover. Don't worry, My Lady, she was well chaperoned. The doctor believed she had lost her memory, and you can imagine my concern when she left us unexpectedly overnight a week ago on horseback. From the small clues I gathered while she was with us, I suspected she was kin to you and would head here. Naturally, I wanted to make sure that she had arrived safely. Hence this unexpected visit."

"I see. Did you get to know why she left Cornwall?"

"Guesswork only. I believe she was being coerced to marry someone she did not care for."

"Tenby! Of course, that explains it! A villain if there ever was one. He killed my daughter and, as stepfather to Charis, is still plotting his evilness. God help the poor child, I should have gone down to Cornwall to see how she was. Unfortunately, my health precluded me from travelling, and I have selfishly avoided the long journey. You say she left your home on horseback? One of yours?"

Tristan nodded.

"I trust we shall not add thievery to her misdeeds?"

"Certainly not. The horse is hers if she wants her."

"You are generous, milord." Lady Langdon raised her brows and stared at him with piercing eyes. "Perhaps you will enlighten me with the rest of the tale for I warrant there is a great deal more to tell. While we talk, will you join me in partaking of coffee?" At his nod, she rang the bell.

Before either of them could say a further word, a loud disturbance in the hall heralded the door swinging open, and a small figure dressed in what seemed to Caroline as outlandish clothes burst in and flung herself down at her feet. "Oh, Grandmama, thank God you are here!"

Bedford, close behind, was totally unnerved with the sudden appearance of whom he had taken to be an urchin at the back entrance. The abrupt questions: "Lady Langdon? Where is she?" had made him stutter, "The parlour – hey, wait a minute, you can't go in there…

"Milady, I couldn't stop him…" He wrung his hands wildly.

Two voices drowned his words as Caroline cried, "Good God!"

And Tristan, recognising the figure, said, "Charis!"

Charis rose to her feet, flung off her hat and a scarf that bound her hair, and started to explain when something made her turn and she saw Tristan. For a moment, she was utterly unable to accept the evidence of her own eyes. When she had run from him, she'd never expected to see him again. Yet here he was, no phantom but a living human being whose eyes were filled with a fierce intensity that set her blood racing as never before. How had he known where she was going? How had he got here ahead of her? What had he told her grandmother? Would they send her back to Cornwall? Oh, dear God, no! Never that! Her face paled to a chalky white, and she swayed on her feet.

At once, Tristan leapt to hold her up. "No, you are not to faint again. Everything is all right. Come sit, drink this." He grabbed his half drained glass of Madeira and almost forced the rest past her lips. She choked but obediently swallowed, and gradually her face warmed.

He stared down at her attire and grinned. "You do favour the tomboy, don't you? I'll have to make sure you have more elegant breeches made for you. You could have told us, you know. I would have brought you here in rather more comfort."

He turned to Caroline and gracefully waved his hand at Charis. "My Lady, may I introduce your granddaughter. I collect it is a while since you last saw her and you may be forgiven for not recognising her as quickly as I. Where is Butterfly, Charis?"

"In the mews." She waved a hand to the rear of the house.

He glanced at Caroline who promptly said to her butler, "Tell Dave to stable and feed the mare. Have Mrs Noakes prepare a room and bath, and I think tea as well as coffee and something to eat for my granddaughter. We are out to all other visitors. Thank you, Bedford."

She looked over at Charis and smiled. "Your visit is rather unexpected, my dearest, but most welcome. I suspect you have come to be rescued, and you could not choose a better place."

Her eyes took in the apparel Charis was wearing, and then moved to Tristan's as she lifted a handkerchief to her nose.

"Perhaps you'd prefer a bath first, my dear, before you tell us your tale. I'm sure His Lordship and I can contain our curiosity for a while longer, is that not so, Your Lordship?"

"The scent of horse does not repel me and, as Lady Charis has had a long journey and is likely more hungry and thirsty than concerned with niceties, I leave it up to her to make a choice."

Charis glanced at Tristan and grimaced. "I expect prudence will serve me better than concern with hunger. I'll find Mrs Noakes and see you both soon." With that, she rose and went rapidly out of the door.

Once she was gone, Caroline turned to Tristan. "While she is bathing, I will listen to what you know of this affair. Running away is one thing, but I perceive this is a more serious event than Charis escaping a marriage she had no taste for. Whilst I am aware in our present society young girls have to be guided in their choice of husband, to be coerced is not my idea of a happy marriage. Please, My Lord, you obviously know a great deal of recent happenings."

"Knowing a little and merely guessing others, I fear. I think Charis should give you her story first," Tristan replied, wary about going into details of the sojourn at the inn and him claiming Charis for his wife. If Charis mentioned it, so well and good. He had an explanation, but he was still intent on finding out how much of her memory had come back and how it related to him. Lady Langdon did not appear to be a slow top and was quite able to piece things together if their stories did not match. Not that he was guilty of anything base, but Caroline's instant voicing of someone called Tenby made him aware that he knew virtually nothing of the background of the woman he wanted to marry, and despite his desires he knew his father would want her history.

"Your reticence does you credit, Lord Fortesque. I collect you are not a blabbermouth, which is as well. Gossip in Bath is meat and drink to many people, and servants are the worst culprits however loyal they are to the families they serve. I can only hope that my granddaughter's abrupt descent on this household will not be bruited abroad and will take the necessary precautions, but I fear the inevitable problem."

Chapter Fifteen

It was a vastly different vision that appeared in the salon a short while later. Charis, her hair still damp and drawn back in a ponytail, soft tendrils escaping and winding round her face in curls, was dressed in a pale blue dimity gown with matching slippers. Tristan recalled it was one of his dresses bought in Launceston, and commended his good taste to buy something that suited her so well. He was on his feet in a flash to bow, and led her to a table set with a late breakfast. Her eyes lit with pleasure as she sat and took up the teapot.

"When did you last eat?" Tristan smiled at her enthusiasm.

"I can't remember. Perhaps two days ago. Grandmama, may I eat before we talk?"

"Certainly, my child, milord and I will enjoy our coffee and converse of other things until you feel ready to disclose what I suspect will pain me dreadfully. You are so like your mother, it is uncanny. I still cannot believe she is gone. Later, we will talk of her. Enjoy your meal and relax. Thankfully, you are home and safe with me."

An hour later, the table cleared, Tristan ensconced with a brandy, the three of them sat comfortably and Charis began to tell of all that had happened before she ran from Carwinnion. She told of Thomas Tenby's treatment of her mother and her death; of a letter that her mother had bade her hide and take to the vicar to post on. Sadly, there had been no reply nor any letters after that until the one that had been rescued before her stepfather had got his hands on it.

"I took the influenza that winter," interrupted Caroline. "It was ages before I recovered. I was too poorly to read the letter which I received from your mother at that time, nor did I know until much later that your mother was dead. I was quite a time in recovering, and though I should have come to see you instead could only write. Receiving no reply, I felt I was being ignored. However I made one last attempt so it must have been the last letter I sent that you eventually received."

"I began to make plans after reading it," Charis began. "Mama had often spoken of you but I had no idea where you lived; only that it was in Somerset. Knowing I had family somewhere made all the difference. I did not feel so alone. As for my stepfather, he was not a kind man to either me or our staff. We all hated him for his cruelty. I knew I had to keep your letter secret and try and save some funds to reach Bath. But money was hard to come by even though I scrimped and saved."

Tristan watched as her hand stole along her ribs, knowing full well that the area still felt bruised. Bruises would heal, he thought, but not his intention to do the utmost harm to Thomas Tenby. Come what may, he intended paying back the man for his cruelty.

"When I found out that my stepfather planned to marry me to an old man, I knew I had to escape from Carwinnion immediately until I reached my majority and could deny him," Charis continued.

She rubbed her hand over her forehead and grimaced. "Although hiding in His Lordship's luggage boot might have been a mistake, at least I got away even though it took me a while to remember why."

"It was the library back at the house that made you remember, wasn't it," Tristan said. "Why didn't you tell me?" He watched a slow blush cover her cheeks.

"Yes, it was the smell of the books. Was it there I fainted?"

He nodded.

"Probably the shock of getting my memory back. When I roused, you were talking with the doctor, and I thought you'd send me back to Tenby."

"What the hell gave you that idea? Sorry, ma'am." He bent his head to Caroline. "There's no way I'd—"

"I think, milord that is a subject we will discuss later. For now, we must concentrate on what Thomas Tenby will do and how we can protect Charis. As he is legally her guardian and I am not sure how the law will regard my relationship, I suspect my wishes will count for little until Charis reaches twenty-one in a few weeks' time. Of course, if we are lucky, he may have given her up for lost and we shall hear no more."

"Unfortunately not, Grandmama. He has already reached Wells and could be here in Bath as we speak. I bumped into Barney as I passed through the town. He recognised the coat I was wearing..."

Tristan raised his eyebrows. "He must have been pleased to see an old friend, if not discern its original odour."

She blushed again as Caroline looked mystified. "Barney is our handyman and farm worker. He also drives the coach when necessary. I stole his coat. He said he would delay Tenby as long as he is able, but couldn't guarantee how long."

"I believe, milady, I can protect Charis better than you. If she returns with me to my father's home, no one will be able to get at her.

"It will leave you free to say Charis is not with you, and you do not know where she is," Tristan added impatiently.

"What is your interest in all of this, Lord Fortesque? We are strangers, despite your benevolence in helping my granddaughter. To cope with a man who is intent on causing trouble is not, may I be frank, your affair. The help you have given so far is beyond kindness."

"I asked your granddaughter to marry me." The words came out before Tristan could guard his tongue. At once, he realised his mistake. Except time was passing, he wanted Charis away before this Cornish fellow, whoever he was, came to put his oar in and demand her return.

Lady Langdon was no fool as he watched her eyes blink in surprise then narrow. She frowned as she stared at him. "You are of the *ton*, milord, a viscount, and awaiting earldom. An ancient lineage with a heritage to keep up. According to your stories, I have gathered you had no idea where Charis originated from. Her background is not to be despised, but she is hardly the choice for an earl and his future family. Yet you offered for a stranger?"

"Well, you see, Grandmama, we had to keep up the pretence..."

Jesus! Now the fat is truly in the fire! Tristan held his breath and, sure enough, her grandmother turned and looked at each of them with ice in her eyes. "Pretence? Pretence of what, may I ask?"

Wordlessly, Tristan waited to see what direction Charis would take so he could back her up, but Charis looked discomfited at his silence until she could bear the suspense no longer so she said, "The inn was crowded and there was only one room. His Lordship was protecting my honour, I believe. He said I was his wife."

"So you shared a room?" The intense atmosphere grew deadlier.

Shrugging her shoulders as though it was no great deal, she continued, "I was unconscious most of the time, or at least unaware of what had happened or who I was. Then, w-when we got to His Lordship's home..."

Tristan decided it was his turn to intercede, suspecting that what was revealed or however they tried to explain was not going to alter the knowledgeable look that Her Ladyship was now casting upon him, or that it would mitigate his actions in her eyes.

"My Lady," he began, "your granddaughter is untouched. It is as she said, and I was protecting her honour—"

"And at Castle House? Does your father know of these events?"

He swallowed hard, dimly wondering where his wits had gone. "Well, things are not exactly—"

"Exactly! My Lord Fortesque, exactly what is the position now?"

"He has been told of the situation and was in agreement of me coming to Bath to make sure Charis is safe. Although on our arrival at Castle House, the housekeeping servants were led to believe that Charis is my wife. There was no other way to protect her honour—"

"So eventually your staff and soon the whole neighbourhood will get to know there have been dubious goings-on. It will not stop there, as you may allow. Because of your status, the *ton* will be delighted to have something to gossip about, and meanwhile my granddaughter's reputation will be torn to shreds. I am not unaware of your position in society. Unmarried, you could be classed as a rake of the first order. Avoiding marriage becomes a fine art for people of your sort. Not so for Charis. Henceforth, with this scandal, she will be unable to contract a marriage suitable to her station...you will have to marry her—"

"But that's what I want to do—" he interrupted.

"If I may be allowed to speak..." Charis broke in to what she could see was becoming an angry quarrel, and feeling she had more right than anyone to feel furious. Her temper rose as she stared at the two people fighting over her future. "I ran away from Cornwall to get away from a marriage to a man more than twice my age. No way will I agree to a forced marriage with His Lordship to please a society I have never been a part of in my life. My reputation is my own to decide. I will live my life from here on as I choose. Even if I have to work for my living. Both of you, please understand I am not marrying anyone! I will not be forced into any alliance at a moment's notice. I have had to obey my stepfather's wishes for so long it has sickened me. Now you wish to take over and do the same. I am not having it! I want to be free and not marry anyone." She stared at them defiantly. Then she stood and went to the door.

"Grandmama, if you will excuse me, I am retiring to my bedroom to sleep. I feel I have been awake for days, and I dislike arguments. I shall see you later after I have rested." She glanced at Tristan. "Thank you for your help, milord. I presume you will sort the whole affair out to your satisfaction and resume your bachelor ways. Please tell your father I am truly sorry he was misled, and that I appreciated his stories. He seemed like the father I sadly lost before I could get to know him." She curtsied to them both and left the room.

Caroline shook her head in dismay. "David's daughter, without doubt. When he felt the bite of the rein he always took off like a stallion out of control avoiding all my attempts to reason with him. I should have remembered that persuasion works far better than coercion. And, talking of that, we have Thomas Tenby to sort out. He will arrive and will demand the return of Charis."

Caroline rose to her feet, walked over to the window, and stood for several moments gazing out at the street. She turned at last and looked wryly at Tristan. "I think we have more to argue about than my granddaughter's wishes about marriage, whether it be with you, anyone or not at all." She walked back to the chaise and sat down. "My concern is Thomas Tenby. I deem him an utter scoundrel, an evil being that had no regard for my daughter-in-law, and still less it seems for Charis. However, I lack the proof to confound him with it. Hearsay does not convict, no matter if one wished it were so. He has gained the legal right to affix a betrothal even if Charis says no. I believe the courts would uphold that right and compel her to obey. If he turns up here, have I legally the right to stop his entry and deny him access to Charis? My servants are loyal to a point though I've never had to put them to the test. I wouldn't put it past that rogue to offer them a bribe to reveal her whereabouts, much as I trust them. That is the problem we are facing. How do you suggest we resolve it?"

Chapter Sixteen

Tristan gazed thoughtfully at Caroline, aware that his intention to marry Charis could ultimately rest with her approval. He decided not to press the urgency of his suit, particularly as Charis had spurned him outright together with this baron whoever he might be. His immediate task after safeguarding Charis would be to investigate both men from Cornwall and persuade them otherwise. Painfully, if necessary. He also knew he needed more information on the legal rights of women, even after they had obtained their majority. Did the courts uphold the will of a guardian to espouse a female, no matter if she disagreed, if they felt it was in her interest?

Aware of his lengthy pause and Caroline's scowl, he bowed his head and smiled at her. "A tough problem indeed, milady. I also feel we have more to think about than just keeping Thomas Tenby away from your granddaughter. I think you need to be kept safe as well."

Caroline blinked in surprise. "Me? He can't do much to me!"

"You could make a deal of trouble for him if you contest his right to dispose of his stepdaughter. I believe he is handy with a cane. My doctor disclosed Charis had been beaten. Whilst your butler would no doubt come to your aid, a man in a temper could do a lot of harm in a short while. I would be amiss not to point out the danger, and I beg you to take care. As far as Charis is concerned, I'm sure she will agree to us hiding her until her birthday. It is, after all, why she escaped. How we do it is another problem. Although I have the means to solve it, I suspect neither of you will agree with my proposal to take you both back to my home where I can keep you safe until the matter is settled. Regarding Tenby's likely visit here, I do feel you shouldn't let him know you are aware of the recent events regarding Charis. If you pretend ignorance of her whereabouts, he may neither realise nor accuse you of hiding Charis. I can't prejudge the meeting with this man, but I believe you will more than hold your own if it comes to a battle of words. You strike me as a lady who knows her own mind and who will give as good as she gets in exchange. At least for now, until we get to know the extent of his plans."

Caroline laughed at his sally, displaying, despite the advancing years, the charm and beauty she had been blessed with. "You, My Lord, are an outrageous flatterer! Although I have to say your suggestion holds merit. As far as hiding Charis is concerned, my cousin Leticia Manville, who lives on the outskirts of Bath, would willingly lend her aid and have Charis stay with her until this trouble is dealt with. Her family and mine were much involved during my son's youth. He grew up with her children, and I know that, though he has sadly gone now, he would approve of his daughter being with her. With your help, Charis can be smuggled away into her keeping. I can then truthfully say that she is not with me."

Despite his disappointment at not being allowed to take Charis into his own protection, Tristan decided not to argue the merits of where she went. He only cared that she would be safe. "Very well, Lady Langdon, we will try it your way first, and I will arrange with my men to deliver her to your cousin. I will also, if I may, leave one of them discreetly on guard. Should this not be sufficient to protect her then I take leave to arrange a more suitable place. I'll send word as soon as arrangements are readied. Be assured also that your house will be watched and we have a care for you as well. Any strangers will be noted and I will be alerted."

"My goodness, how many men did you bring with you?" Caroline asked in surprise, noting that he did not request her permission but merely stated firmly what he would do. She rather liked his manner. He would make a good husband for her impetuous granddaughter if she consented to marry him. Caroline could hardly achieve a better offer from a nobleman in the social circle that she moved in now.

"Enough to use for the present, but I am sending for more to help out. I suggest you send word at once to warn your cousin to expect your granddaughter. Give Charis a couple of hours to rest then wake her and let her know she will be collected soon after. I took the precaution of bringing her maid and ample clothes with me, so she will not feel at a loss in the company of your cousin. Not knowing of this stepfather and that she will have to hide for the present, I guessed she might enjoy visiting Bath and catered for that event. Are you agreeable with these arrangements?"

"Gracious, My Lord! I can hardly disagree. You appear to have gone beyond all that is necessary to keep Charis safe. I, in turn, will do my best to confound Tenby. I can pretend ignorance of her flight from Carwinnion, and try and discover why it is so important for her to marry this baron that sends him chasing her all the way to Bath."

"It is as I said." Tristan gave Caroline a wide smile. "You are one clever lady, and I'd back you against anyone. I perceive only one main reason for Tenby's efforts: it is probably money. If the baron is elderly, he will know he can only get a young bride by paying for her. Tenby has probably made arrangements to gain that reward."

"There is more, Your Lordship." Caroline gave a sudden gasp as if she had only just realised then continued, "Charis has a dowry to claim if she reaches twenty-one and has not married. It was bequeathed her by my son just before he returned to France where he met his end. He, of course, thought he would still be alive and could arrange a marriage for her and the subsequent handing over of that dowry to a husband. He also took the precaution of naming her to inherit Carwinnion at the same time if anything happened to her mother. I have the original will stating this, although a copy was sent to my daughter-in-law. Tenby will be aware of it. It has the usual provisions that one puts in place in time of war. The dowry money was placed in the Funds, and I would imagine it has gained considerably over the years. Carwinnion is not all that large but was extremely profitable in my son's day. It may not be the same now, but it still belongs to Charis as sole legatee, and we can send that rogue packing."

"Hmm. Significantly more money than I thought. I believe she is an heiress of considerable wealth and it gives her stepfather every incentive to find her—"

"Or indeed any prospective bridegroom!" Caroline's interjection was sudden and unthinking, meeting a scowl of extreme ferocity.

"If you are thinking of me then guard your tongue, milady! When I marry Charis, any dowry or ownership of an estate is hers to keep. I have ample funds of my own to content me. I care for Charis and want her to make a good marriage with me. How it has come about I know not, but if I don't marry her then I will marry no one."

"Your pardon, milord. I spoke without thinking and intend no condemnation of your ambition to marry my granddaughter. My mind simply leapt to her future and how best to advise her. She must be overwhelmed at the moment. Running from one hated marriage then meeting you. If you'll further pardon me for saying, you are such a strong and most determined man that possibly she will take fright again and run from you. That I can only conceive as being disastrous. She may not feel entirely confident staying with me but will run off into the unknown. I think we have much to fear with Charis."

"One step at a time, milady. Charis will have had a hard time reaching you. A long enough journey at the best of times, but she has been battling with fright through most of it. I think it wise to take her to your cousin and let her settle down in safety. Once she is fully rested, we can talk with her again and put her mind at ease. Let her know that no way will she be coerced into anything she does not want. Between us, we will handle Tenby and prevent him from harming her. I am content to wait until she comes to me of her own accord though, with your permission, I will court her." He grinned at Caroline.

Her answering smile reassured him she would have no objection to his courtship so, standing to take his leave, he took her hand and bowed his farewell. "I shall see you shortly when I have arranged all that is necessary. I wish you luck with your meeting with Tenby."

He turned on his heel and was swiftly gone, leaving her to ponder on the extraordinary morning and all the goings-on that had preceded their meeting. Despite her criticism of him as a rake, he had behaved as well, if not better, than any gentleman she had ever known. That he would make a fine husband for Charis seemed in no doubt, but what the next day or two would bring seemed too dreadful to contemplate.

Chapter Seventeen

Despite Charis's disappointment in leaving her grandmother's home so soon, she readily obeyed when Caroline woke her; then sat down and explained the problem of keeping her safe and the help that Lord Fortesque was rendering. "My dear girl, he is a good man and seems to have a great regard for you. He has also said that no one will coerce you into marriage if that is not your will. I value his help in getting you to my cousin Leticia. She is very dear to me, and was of enormous help when your grandfather was drowned and I had your father to rear. He would be so pleased that you are going to a place he respected when he was only a young boy. I need you to be safe, my dearest. Please understand that we are not trying to force you into anything you don't want. It is only to stop Tenby getting his hands on you."

Charis listened quietly to all her grandmother had to say and realised the sense of it. Equally, knowing Tenby's partiality for bullying, she reiterated Tristan's warning to take care. "He has a very nasty temper when he is thwarted. Even when I defied him, I always planned my escape or suffered the consequences. You must take the greatest care, Grandmama. He has a devious brain. He uses violence without regard."

"His Lordship said you had been subjected to ill-treatment. I feel devastated I did not investigate how you fared before this. Even so, could I have prevented Tenby from deciding to marry you off to this baron if you hadn't escaped? I doubt it, so from now on we will make the best of how we deal with that dastardly villain."

Consequently, after Charis had left in Tristan's carriage, Caroline told her butler that he must stay close by whenever she received a stranger to the salon. "Leave the door ajar and keep alert, Bedford. The man who might call is after my granddaughter, and we must not allow him to know where she is. Warn the rest of the staff there must be no talking or gossiping out of the house. No one is here or has been here. We are as usual, understand? We have no visitors."

"I understand perfectly, milady. We've gathered what is amiss and, although delighted for you that your granddaughter has come to see you, we will guard her when she returns as we guard you. This has always been a happy home, and I hope she will soon be back with us to enjoy it."

His kind words brought tears to her eyes as she reflected how long Bedford had been with her and how, lacking a man of her own, she had come to rely on him. Always polite, never overstepping the role of servant, he had nevertheless been a pillar of strength.

A further day passed before Bedford knocked on the door of her study where she was penning a letter and informed her she had a visitor. "He is a Mr Thomas Tenby, milady. He insists on seeing you so I have taken him to the salon. I have given leave for milord's man to wait in the kitchen. I'll be on hand as agreed."

Caroline dusted off her letter and stood. "Well, I'd better see what Mr Tenby's come about. Thank you, Bedford. Stay close."

Bedford showed his mistress into the salon, and pulling the door closed left a crack of it open as he stood on guard outside.

Caroline advanced into the room but stood waiting for the man who was once the second husband of her daughter-in-law to rise. He was slow to do so as the arms of the chair he had chosen to sit in held onto his bulk with an unforgiving pressure. Eventually, he stood and, somewhat embarrassed with the inelegance of his movements and further abashed by her silence, bowed. "Lady Langdon."

"Mr Tenby. You wished to speak to me." Her voice was cool.

"You recall who I am?"

"Yes, I know who you are."

"I've come about your granddaughter."

"Oh. How is she? Is she not here with you?"

He fidgeted, wishing she would ask him to sit down again. He had eventually taken lodgings on the outskirts of town leaving Barnaby back in Wells coping with a broken carriage that looked as though it had come to its end. Hiring a nag in order to obtain a saddled horse and riding into Bath had taken some time, and finding a cheap lodging even more time.

Eventually, he had found the address he required, but he was tired with walking the streets, needed a drink, and was fed up with the whole affair. By God, he would kill Charis when he found her.

"No. I presumed she would be here. Look, could we sit down only my feet are killing me. I've had to come some way to find you."

Raising her eyebrows at his abrupt tone, Lady Langdon nodded and seated herself on the chaise arranging her gown around her before looking up. "Why on earth would you think Charis is here? I have not set eyes on her for years, much to my disappointment. When her mother died, I asked her to visit me. I heard nothing more. I presume you would have known of the invitation?"

"Well, it was up to Charis to say, and I heard no word."

"I see. Why do you think she would be here now?"

"Maybe took a bit of fright. You know what these young girls are like just before they marry."

"Marry? You didn't inform me that Charis intended to marry."

"Inform you? Why should I do that? I have the say-so to agree her marriage, not you. I'm her stepfather, don't ye know?"

"If you have ever read the will that her father left, you will see that I have been named as co-guardian who also has to give permission for her to marry. Failing that permission, she cannot wed."

"Bloody hell!"

"Mr Tenby, I already have a dislike for you considering how I believe you treated my daughter-in-law. Coming into my house and swearing does not further your interests. Either desist or leave. But before you do, tell me where Charis is. I may not have seen my granddaughter for some time, but I still have a care for her. If she has run away then you will undoubtedly know why. Plain speaking, Mr Tenby, if you please. Who was she going to marry?"

"Someone entirely suitable for her rank, believe me. Baron Whaley holds the utmost respect in the district."

"Describe him."

"Er – how do you mean?" Tenby's cravat suddenly felt tight.

"His appearance. How old is he?"

"Perhaps a little older than her. Maybe middle-aged."

"Too old, I venture! A little seniority is acceptable, but older than that is not right for a young maiden. How long has the man courted her?

Was she agreeable with his visits? I presume you took her wishes into consideration?" Caroline paused, awaiting his answer which was slow in coming as he decided his tactics. "Come, Tenby, are your wits lacking that you cannot answer these questions?"

"Certainly not! I object to being cross-examined," he growled.

"Do you indeed! I wonder why? Answer me this, sir. Has my granddaughter run away because she did not wish to marry this man? Have you proposed someone she is not happy to marry?"

"Whether or not isn't up to her. I know what's best for the chit, and I'll have no one say me nay. Now, is she here or isn't she? If not, I'll soon find her, and you can forget giving permission. The law is on my side to make provision for her, and I stand by that."

"Not after she reaches her majority, Mr Tenby." Caroline's voice was soft yet held all the menace she could command.

Tenby at once stood up and, for a moment, he stroked the cane in his hand. "Interfere with me, Your Ladyship, and you'll wish you hadn't. I am not one that takes to provocation."

His cane flashed out and made her flinch, but thankfully it wasn't directed at her. Instead, it fished from beneath a chair the scarf that Charis had wound round her hair. "Her scarf! I'd know it anywhere. She's already been here and is probably hidden close by. Don't think you'll keep me from her. I'll have the law on you if you try. She's coming back with me to Cornwall, and she'll do as I say!"

He marched across to the door and flung it open. Seeing Bedford standing outside, he grabbed the front of his frockcoat almost throttling the man then threw him to one side before heading for the front door. "Don't any of you get in my way or I'll have you, just see if I don't. Cross me and you'll regret it." He shouted the words as he flung open the door and then slammed it behind him.

Everton emerged from the kitchen stairs and helped Bedford to stand up. "So sorry, I couldn't get to you in time. Are you hurt?"

"Only my feelings. Strewth! That man is a bloody villain!"

Another figure appeared behind him. It was Tristan. Everton had sent word to Roger when Tenby had appeared, who at once had alerted his master, luckily remaining close by anticipating Tenby's visit.

"Everton, Roger is tracking Tenby. See if you can pick them up and work with Roger. Turn and turnabout should do it. Get moving!

"Bedford! Let's see how Her Ladyship is, and serve us brandies. She will undoubtedly need sustaining after that conversation." He went into the salon and across to where Caroline sat white-faced on the chaise. "My dear lady, I sincerely regret you had to endure such a tirade. I heard most of your conversation from the dining room, but felt it wiser not to show my face and alert him just yet. Of course, I would have had he threatened you with violence. Unfortunately, Bedford got the rough end of his anger, didn't you, old chap?" Tristan looked up as the butler came in with a decanter and two glasses on a silver tray.

"Good man! Just what is needed. I trust you'll medic yourself by and by?" His eyes held a twinkle as he looked at the manservant.

"Already done, Your Lordship. Finest medicine ever." Bedford bowed and left them to discuss the awful happenings.

Caroline silently sipped her brandy until eventually her shivers stilled and colour came back into her face. Tristan sat quietly alongside her watching her recover her usual composure.

"What a truly abominable man. I am saddened to realise my daughter-in-law had to deal with such as he. No wonder she died before her time."

"I regret you had to endure such a horrible experience even though you handled it well. Unfortunately, it was the only way of finding out just how arrogantly evil he is, and also how determined he is to get Charis back. I suspect there is more to it than him merely cashing in on her marriage. Can he get his hands on her dowry?"

"No. That will go to her husband and he would only get some money if there is an arrangement between him and the man he wants her to marry. Charis did tell me before she left to stay with my cousin that she thought Tenby would refuse to hand over Carwinnion and that he would continue to live there. She was afraid for her housekeeper and the manservant who have to put up with his bullying."

"I would have accompanied Charis, but I thought it more important to guard you and get a look at the man. I sent trusted people with her, and they reported that she was received with great kindness and welcome. One of my men fetched a letter back for you from Lady Manville to confirm this. Charis also has her maid with her, so she is not entirely alone."

"I can't thank you enough for all you've done. I feel despair that I left my daughter-in-law to die in the care of this dreadful man. As for Charis, thank heavens she was able to escape his villainy. I tremble to imagine what she has had to endure already. I saw his cane. He kept it in his hand all the time."

"Oh yes, she spoke of a rigid cane. He may yet regret keeping it with him. However, I have to point out we are not out of the woods yet. Charis still has to reach her majority, and I have to confirm with my solicitor that, when that happens, she will be safe. It will be supremely ironic if Tenby can still keep a hold of her. It may be that she will have no alternative but marriage to get free from his clutches. I tell you plainly I will not tolerate anyone else marrying her. I'm derelict in not asking your permission before, and I apologise for that but I deem the situation is grave and we must protect her with every means at hand."

"I think, milord, that you need not worry about my feelings in this matter. You have my permission to marry her if she agrees. I have already made up my mind you are suitable, but I need to think carefully about persuading Charis to wed you. As you have already experienced, she has a mind of her own and maybe plans of her own. However, if I can influence her direction in life, I will."

At once Tristan reached out and put his arm around Caroline and hugged her. "Not perhaps the most elegant way of expressing my deep gratitude but, damn it all, woman, I truly wish I'd had you for my grandmother when I was growing up. God bless you, ma'am, for your gift. I promise I will always take care of your granddaughter."

"I know you will, Tristan, if you have a chance to do so. There, I think we can be comfortable with our first names, don't you agree? I trust you will stay for dinner. I have yet to hear the rest of your plans. Here I was, settling into comfortable old age with every day marked out for me and, suddenly, I'm pitched into putting right the dreadful wrongs that were done to my daughter-in-law and see my granddaughter safe in a better future. I can't think of a better reason to go on living and achieve that end."

"Amen to that sentiment, milady, and yes, I shall be pleased to stay and join you for dinner. If I may, I'll send a note to my valet that I won't be back for some time, so any messages that come in from my men can be directed here. I want to know what this Tenby is up to from now on. The sooner he can be persuaded back to Cornwall the better. As for ongoing plans, I fear we must take each day as it comes to try and anticipate how we must act. I have learned never to have things cut and dried as fate will always confound one. So we will watch and wait and do our best to keep Charis safe."

As this scheme was entirely agreeable with Caroline, she was content to spend the time before dinner talking of events in Bath, titbits of scandal, and the doings of the *ton* in general, and finally getting round to talking about Tristan and his life abroad.

He was happy to give her some facts, but in view of her curiosity about his travels abroad he was careful to keep a veil over most of his life. Relatives were all very well but they were a confounded nuisance when they interfered.

Chapter Eighteen

Keeping well out of sight, Roger and Everton followed Tenby until he went into the local posting office. After a moment's thought, Roger instructed Everton to run 'hell for leather' and fetch his horse. "I've the feeling he will be going further than the streets of Bath when he is finished in there. In any case, it's better to be prepared. If he moves before you get back, follow these chalk marks. I am a good runner. I'll try and keep up with him until I see the road he takes." He pulled out a piece of white chalk from a pocket and drew a small arrowhead on a nearby wall. "I'll try to make them easy to find. Now, hop to it!"

Everton did. Luckily, as the stables were close by, he was soon back with Roger's mount, and one for himself, to find him still waiting patiently outside the office.

"Skate round the back, lad, and see if they have a rear door. He's taking his time whatever he's doing, but we'll make sure he hasn't skedaddled out back."

Everton came back a moment later to report that Tenby was still inside but arguing with a postal man. "He wanted his letter sent right quick, but Royal Mail's left and there won't be another till morning. It could go on a slower coach, but they wanted him to pay more for that service so he is having a curse at all and sundry. They're not giving in to him, so the letter won't go till tomorrow."

"I reckon he wants to let that Whaley know that Lady Charis is in the area, so likely we'll have more visitors," Roger said. "I'll see where he goes next, and you let His Lordship know what's happening then get back to guarding the house. I've a feeling he will head back to Wells to check on his coach and wait for Whaley there. Tell His Lordship I'll send word soon as I know where he is staying."

A moment or two later, Tenby appeared and headed off in the direction of the livery stable. Waiting close by, Roger heard the sounds of another altercation as Tenby disputed the bill before emerging on the sorriest nag Roger had seen in a long time. He followed Tenby to the start of the Bath to Wells road then sent a young lad back to the hotel with a message for Tristan saying he would return as soon as he had gleaned more information, but the likelihood was that Tenby was returning to where he had left his carriage.

Riding easy, he tracked Tenby from then on.

Chapter Nineteen

After leaving Caroline's and receiving all the news of his men, Tristan Fortesque couldn't settle so he went to a nearby club to play cards. Even that palled after a while, so he was soon back at his hotel leaving orders for an early call as he had determined, with the absence of the Cornishman from Bath, he would call on Charis and make sure all was well and she was happy staying with the Manvilles.

Baron Manville was in the stables talking with a groom when Tristan arrived the next morning. He greeted the viscount with a firm handshake and a discerning look that took in more than just the style of Tristan's appearance, elegantly clad in buff breeches, a dark green coat of fine tweed, a cream silk cravat, and well-polished, tall black riding boots.

Tristan removed his high-crowned hat and bowed to the baron. "Tristan Fortesque at your service, milord. I collect you are Baron Manville?"

The baron nodded.

"I'm pleased to make your acquaintance, milord. Forgive me for not sending a prior message to warn you of my visit, but as you can guess in these unusual circumstances discretion is important."

"Nothing to forgive. I'm pleased you have called. Join me for a drink while you wait. Leticia and Charis have gone to the village, but I am expecting them back shortly." Ellis Manville turned to his groom. "Continue with the poultice today, Jarvis. We'll see how the mare is in the morning. In the meantime, let me know if the swelling goes down."

Walking back to Tristan, he gestured with his hand. "Come in the study, milord. We can chat there." He led the way round to the main door and through a large hall to his study as he explained his problem with his mare. "She was out on exercise yesterday and put a foot down a rabbit hole. She has an inflamed hock, but with a bit of treatment it should recover quickly. Now sit, sir, and be comfortable. Brandy?" he added, going to his decanter.

Tristan nodded, taking a seat and looking round the large study. It was pleasantly comfortable with two large windows letting in the light, and one shelved wall filled with books of all descriptions. A log fire gently burned in an iron brazier giving off a pleasing scent of apple wood and warming the room to an equitable temperature.

Ellis took a seat behind his desk and gave a sigh. "My place of refuge when the ladies get too much for me." He laughed and shook his head. "Seriously, they rarely do. I am very much a family man so your efforts are warmly appreciated by my wife and me. Knowing and loving David, the father of Charis, has helped, but she is a delightful person in her own right and has become dear to us as well. The efforts of this dastardly man Tenby to destroy her life need to be stopped with all haste. Whilst we keep her hidden for now, it won't avail if he brings the law to bear on us."

"You are quite correct, Manville," said Tristan. "I suspect the man is wily enough to know he can invoke the law before Charis is twenty-one. Whether he can after that time, I don't know. I have an appointment with my legal man later today to ascertain that problem and what else we might face with keeping Lady Charis from Tenby's clutches. I gather her birthday is barely two weeks away. But that may not be the answer. The right of a parent or someone standing as a guardian is always upheld in law."

He sipped his brandy as he considered his next words. "Tenby is a villain. One very smart villain, I collect. He seemed confident when he spoke to Caroline that nothing she could do would prevent him from dictating his stepdaughter's future. He may be whistling in the dark, but experience tells me never to underestimate an enemy."

"Well, I'm doing my best," said Ellis Manville. "She never goes anywhere off this estate unless she is accompanied by two grooms, your man and one of mine. She doesn't like it, but recognises that it is sensible until the danger is past. She adores riding, especially on that superb mare you gave her, and of course prefers her own company as she was used to having in Cornwall but..." Ellis shrugged, tightening his lips with a frown. "It has been quite difficult persuading her to obey my dictates. I've never cared to bring on the heavy hand even to my own children before they left home to get married. I've always let Leticia rule the roost in that respect. She is a more able sergeant major than me." He grinned and fetched the decanter to refill the glasses. "Besides, knowing and loving her father I care greatly for his child."

"Having had a little taste of the obstinacy that Charis can bring to bear, you have my sympathy. Despite that, we must guard her even if she pulls at the bit. I intend to marry her when this trouble is over, but I suspect I shall have my work cut out to achieve that aim even though her grandmother is on my side. You, of course, will say nothing for the moment. And I will keep as firm a hand on events."

"Hmm, I understand completely. I'm glad we have had this talk and just in time, for I hear the carriage now. The ladies are back."

The sound of female voices in the hall echoed through the study door. Then it was thrust open, and Charis stood in the entrance looking a trifle mussed and windblown from her ride in the open carriage.

"Uncle Ellis…" she began then stopped as Tristan rose to his feet and bowed. "Oh, I'm sorry. I didn't know you had company."

A blush turned her face pink as she realised who the company was. She at once curtsied. "My Lord, I did not expect to see you."

"Why ever not?" Tristan raised his eyebrows as he stared at her, feeling his body clench with longing as he surveyed the woman he had planned to make his wife.

"Charis," Ellis Manville's voice displayed a hint of disapproval, "His Lordship is still taking care of you. You must be aware that we all have to be discreet until we know for sure what your stepfather is capable of. Whilst for the present you are safe with us, it may not continue. Then other arrangements will have to be made. You will be kept fully informed if that is so. Now, I would suggest you escort milord Fortesque for a brief stroll in the gardens as no doubt he has a message for you from your grandmama." His eyes went to Tristan who gave a brief nod of thanks for Ellis's manoeuvres. "Will you stay to lunch with us?"

Tristan glanced at the clock and shook his head regretfully. "I only have time for a quick chat with Lady Charis. Then I must return to Bath. The appointment I have later must not be delayed, but I will come back again soon to give you the result of my meeting. In the meantime, it was pleasing to meet you, Manville, and know we are of one accord."

He bowed to Ellis then held his arm out to Charis. "Please do show me the gardens, my dear. You must continue educating me on all the plant names you know." He grinned at her as she wrinkled her nose. "I have to confess I have been so long abroad I have forgotten what an English flower looks like."

"And that, if I may say so, is quite a humbug of a tall story. I can't imagine you forgetting anything, at least nothing important." Charis placed her hand on his arm and led him out of the door. "I shall test you on your first lesson, so pay attention, milord."

He laughed. "Tristan, if you please. We have been on first names for quite a while, Charis, as I'm sure you remember."

Ellis smiled happily as their voices faded. He liked the viscount and was sure that he would be good for Charis to marry. It would be an important role for her to fill as his wife, but he had the measure of her and was sure she was up to it. She would have to gain a little Town bronze and maybe lose her country ways, but he had no doubt her intelligence would soon accept the ways of the *ton*. As for Tristan, it was obvious he was determined to marry her and that it would be a love match as far as he was concerned. So many *ton* marriages were made for hereditary or money reasons, and he was thankful that if Charis accepted Tristan in marriage he would make her love him before long.

Chapter Twenty

"How fares my grandmama?" Charis said, leading Tristan along a gravelled path that wound its way between flowerbeds. "I was with her for such a short time I scarce had a chance to know her, but I feel she is on my side and willing to do all she can to help."

"Without doubt, Charis. She is a brave lady. Already she's had a run in with Tenby, and he did not get the better of her. I was close by, in case, and I fully understand why you ran from home. A nastier piece of work I've not seen in a long while, and it's vital he is stopped in his tracks and prevented from harming you."

"I'm safe here, aren't I?" She glanced swiftly at him, and a frown of concern creased her brow. "How can he possibly find me? I'm sure he doesn't have a great deal of knowledge of my family or people that my grandmama knows."

"If someone has tenacity then nothing is impossible." Tristan slid a warm hand over hers which still rested on his sleeve. "I did offer to make you secure," he reminded her. "Your safety is important to me, and I can ensure that more easily at Castle House."

"Except that comes with a kind of obligation to your father; to the staff of Castle House as they know me as your wife; and to you who rescued me and are still looking after me. I feel I am being pushed along a path where *my* wishes count for nothing. I don't want to sound ungrateful but from Cornwall to here I've been told what to do. I was being forced to marry Whaley; I was apparently married to you; then sent here under the nicest possible guardianship but nevertheless a guard. No one has asked me what I want to do!" Her breath caught in a sob with her last words, and Tristan could see her eyes glistening with the tears she was desperately trying to hold back.

"Oh, my dear, please don't get upset. The present circumstances are only in place to keep you safe. You have people who love you and want to protect you from harm. This is only for a short time until the danger is past; then you will be free to choose what you want. You are not a prisoner, but you must allow those that can help a free hand."

Tristan took out his handkerchief and handed it to Charis. "Dry your eyes, my dear, and then take me to that charming summerhouse down by the lake. Baron Manville has cultivated an enchanting garden. Quite the nicest prison I have ever perceived!"

His lips quirked up in a smile and Charis laughed as she mopped her eyes. "You are quite right to scold me. I am being tiresome, I know. Let's change the subject. I think we have enough time to walk to the lake before you leave and I promise to try to behave better."

A few minutes later, they reached an elegant summerhouse overlooking a fair-sized expanse of water with a small island near the far side where waterfowl were nesting. It was a tranquil scene that was meant to fill the heart with peace, and they both stood silently on the porch enjoying the ambience until Tristan became aware of the fragrant perfume drifting from the girl in front of him. He gazed down at the fair curls lying loose on the curve of her neck where he longed to kiss. He held back a groan, wanting her in a way he'd never wanted any other woman, and with an intensity that left him breathless.

Charis must have sensed his desire because suddenly she turned her head to look up into his face, catching the strange, sensual look that gleamed hotly in his eyes. Without a protest, almost hypnotically, she stayed where she was, ignoring an instinctive urge to flee. Slowly, he put his hands on her arms turning her towards him.

Sensation, unnervingly powerful, shot through her as she felt his strong grip. She gasped, managed to draw in a breath, felt her heart thudding as she struggled to steady her senses as he briefly paused to look down at her. Then his firm lips closed over hers, and he slid a questing tongue along the seam of her mouth moving and coaxing until her lips parted and, letting him in, trembled at his touch. With the encouraging though involuntary response, he pressed deeper, tasting, learning her texture, his tongue probing gently into her inner recess, exploring. All at once, she was tumbling headlong into his kiss, myriad sensations pouring through her from the magic of his mouth. In that instant, she felt a strange feeling pooling and blossoming within the depths of her body arousing an extraordinary ache inside, and a shiver of desire urged her to close the gap between them. Sliding her hand up to his shoulders, she leaned against him and his arms folded around her and tightened their hold, and a soft whimper lodged in her throat as he continued to kiss her.

At the sound, Tristan drew her even closer, her breasts against his chest, and her thighs against his sinewed ones. Her body reacted helplessly: her spine arched and her limbs weakened as his tongue continued to stroke, tangling, mating with hers in a bewitching rhythm. A prime rake in earlier days, with his experience in many parts of the world, Tristan's ability to seduce was second to none.

When his kisses grew more passionate and his hand rose to cup her breast making her flinch with surprise, he knew he had to rein back before losing control and ravishing her on a nearby couch. It took all his strength to master his lustful ardour, pull back from her swollen lips, and withdraw his arms from her body.

Startled by his sudden withdrawal, she gazed silently back at him, her eyes still slumberous with the feelings he had raised.

"I believe, my dear, this kiss confirms I truly have strong feelings for you. Give it some thought and decide whether a marriage with me will be filled with pleasure and happiness. I have to leave now to go back to Bath. There I will confirm with my solicitor whether your majority date will put you safely out of reach of Tenby."

Taking her hand, he guided her down the steps of the summerhouse. Then, walking quickly, they returned to the stables. Mounting his horse, Tristan gazed down at her. "I don't know when I can return. It will depend on how safe I think things are. Please be patient, Charis. I'll not delay longer than necessary. Manville will get word to me if you have need."

With a wave of his hand, he went trotting quickly from the yard and, after a nod to the groom, she returned to the house and the baron's study. Knocking on the door, she entered and found Leticia and Ellis deep in conversation.

"Oh, I'm sorry to disturb you. It was only to say His Lordship has gone, and I am going to change for luncheon. And also..." She paused as they both stared at her, trying to find the words. "I think I understand more of your kindness in trying to help me. I have been a nuisance and probably stubborn..."

Leticia laughed. "Stubbornness we can cope with! It is your happiness that is more at stake here. Uncle Ellis tells me he likes the cut of your viscount, whatever that means." She rolled her eyes. "Men have a weird way of assessing a person. However, we have decided, with your grandmother's approval of course, that you are entitled to a London Season. Once we are sure Tenby is no longer a threat, we shall go to London and introduce you to the *ton*. I have no doubt, once you are accepted, you will have your pick of suitors and make a good marriage with the man you prefer. Our children have done well for themselves and will welcome you into our family and make it easy for you to be accepted into society."

"A London Season! Oh, Aunt Leticia, it will cost too much! I couldn't possibly agree to the expense."

"I think between your grandmother and our family we shall manage very nicely. Your viscount is a fine man and you may well marry him, but you need experience to mix in the society that is second nature to men of his class. You must learn to be a *hostess par excellence* and run his estates with finesse. Then again, you may decide that someone else is more suitable. Marriage means a lifetime of caring for one's partner." She glanced affectionately at Ellis, and they smiled at each other. "With the wrong partner, it is a lifetime of sorrow and dislike. I feel you should have the opportunity to choose. Now, run along and get changed. We shall join you in the dining room shortly."

Charis bobbed a respectful curtsey and went upstairs to her bedroom where her maid was waiting to help her dress. She had much more to think about now than hiding from Tenby. For heaven's sake, she thought, what was wrong with everyone? They were all seeking to get her married! To a man of her choice, she supposed, but nevertheless shackled to someone who would control her for evermore. Couldn't they see she desired freedom; not a guardian for the rest of her life? And Tristan? What about him? He had professed to care for her but had never mentioned love. Once he settled her in his home, he would be off about his affairs, maybe travelling abroad, not in the least concerned she was left behind. Safe? Yes, of course; with child, most likely. While he could indulge himself in London with his mistresses.

Now where had that thought come from? Ah yes, she had overheard two of the Castle House maids gossiping about Tristan while they made the beds.

"*What wouldn't I give to be his mistress, 'stead of slogging here,*" one said.

"*You wouldn't, would you?*" said the other. "*How do you know he's got one?*"

"*Stands to reason, don't it. I got to know them boys when I worked in the London house for a time before me ma took ill and I came back here to be near my family. He and his brother were the talk of the town at one stage. Then the younger one joined the army and left. Henry came back here as he was the heir. Shame him popping his clogs. No wonder his brother had to return. Still, mark my words; he'll be off soon as he's got his wife pregnant. Once a rake, always a rake, I says.*"

Charis hadn't given much thought to the conversation beyond noting that a watch should be kept on Ellen as she was obviously a scandal bearer with an eye to the main chance. As for Tristan, what he had done in his youth was none of her business. Although, ages ago, she recalled her mother once talking about faithfulness in marriage, and being close and loving. Certainly, she would love a child or children if she was blessed to have them, but there had to be more to marriage than procreation. She wanted a meeting of minds, companionship, someone to share thoughts and feelings with.

Now it seemed everyone was dictating what she should do and maybe, despite her plan to avoid having to make a choice, deciding on whom she *ought* to marry and making it happen, pushing her into a marriage she did not want. She was trapped. Totally and utterly trapped. Yes indeed, she had much to think about.

Chapter Twenty-One

The small parlour at the back of the Fountain Pub in Wells felt airless to Tenby as he sat facing the growing fury of Baron Whaley. He tried to ease his cravat loose as it seemed about to choke him.

"What do ye mean, you've found her but you don't know where she is now? You stupidly lost her back in Cornwall and now assure me you've found her here. So where is my bride? After searching most of Cornwall, I don't take kindly to being hauled up here. It's your job to fetch her back to Carwinnion where I have the priest waiting to marry us."

"Well, Your Lordship, her grandmother has put her oar in and says she has to give her permission as well. It's down in the will the chit's father left, so she says. I think she's lying, so I'm not heeding her. It's up to me to give permission as I told you. Trouble is, the chit has been hid so well I have to search again. Me coach is wrecked beyond repair into the bargain, and I ain't got the blunt to replace it."

"I hope you are not looking to me to help you out? You're already deep in the shit with your gambling debts. Don't expect me to provide a carriage for you. Change of plan, I think, Tenby. You tell me where the girl is and *I'll* take her back to Cornwall. I've had enough of your stupid blunders. From here on, I'll deal with things. All I need from you is your signature of permission to marry. Course, it'll make a difference to what you owe me—"

"What d'ye mean? You're never going back on your given word, are you? You was going to clear what I owe you. And you're getting a prize filly into the bargain if I sign the marriage agreement. Supposing I don't sign the agreement?" Tenby scowled at the baron.

"An interesting thought, I perceive. I lose a bride and a dowry. However, you gain greatly in the process." Whaley smiled back at Tenby, a smile so evil Tenby felt a shudder of ice down his spine. "You gain a second mouth. A bit lower and a lot bloodier than the one you have now. A permanent feature, I fear."

At once, Tenby's face blanched with fright. Christ, the man was going to cut his throat if he didn't get Charis and her dowry! What the hell was he to do? No bloody choice, it seemed. He had to get the girl!

"I ain't about to let you down, milord. I've a lot to lose too in the scheme of things. It's just a smidgeon of bad luck that's set me back a bit, but I'm never down for long and I'll get your bride for you if you give me time. Course, it would help if I could borrow a bit of blunt to get me a decent horse. It's all that's stopping me from success. I've had me feelers out and I've an idea where the chit's hidden. Once I get me hands on her, I won't let go, milord, I assure you. A slip of a girl is no match for me. One cut of me cane and she'll come like a lamb." Tenby followed his remarks with a similar evil grin.

"If you mark my bride then expect the same marks tenfold! I don't want damaged goods. If she doesn't come up to expectations in my hands then I'll deal with her my way. Just get her and hand her over quick as you can. Just remember..." Whaley's eyes glinted maliciously as he scowled at Tenby, "...I'm not and never have been a patient or forgiving man. In fact, your demise might well suit me. I'd gain Carwinnion in lieu of your debts and the girl into the bargain." He rubbed his hands together at the thought. "Yes, that path would suit me well. However..." He thrust a hand into his pocket and pulled out a purse. Extracting a few sovereigns, he gave them to Tenby. "I'll give you a last chance to make good. See you don't mess up this time. Now, get moving. I want this finished. My business won't wait on the likes of you dawdling around." He waved his hand in dismissal and, reluctantly, Tenby, who was expecting to join Whaley in a meal, took his leave. Cursing fate, he made his way back to the stables where lay his ruined coach and patiently waiting servant, Barney.

With a sigh of relief, Barney rose to his feet from the straw bale he had been sitting on. "Ah, you're back, thank goodness, guv." Then anxious as to what was going to happen next, he burst out unhappily, "What's to be done now? How do we get back home? My belly's near forgotten what a meal is like. They do say travel broadens the mind, but I say it shrinks the stomach." His grumbles were loud, his mind filled with worry about Tenby's next actions and the whereabouts of Charis.

Despite his hunger, he knew he had to do all he could to stop Tenby from hurting her, and he could tell from the scowling determination in his face that Tenby, far from heading back to Cornwall, was still embarking on his pursuit of Charis.

Barney wasn't surprised when Tenby rehired the old nag for him and a better steed for himself then said, "Make haste. We are bound for Bath and an end to this affair. So stop your whining. You ain't the only hungry one, so we'll stop for a pie and a mug of ale shortly. Come on, get your arse in the saddle and let's be off. I've wasted too much time already on this matter, but I'll see an end to it, damn me, if I don't. That brat won't get the better of me. No, by God, she won't."

Chapter Twenty-Two

Tristan was cantering down a quiet tree-lined lane heading back to town when he felt a waft of air alongside his cheek and a tug at his collar. A second later, he heard the roar of a gun and instinctively dug his heels into the flanks of his startled horse as it jumped sideways at the sound of the shot. A few moments later, he had galloped a hundred yards up the lane and out of reach of the shooter's chance to reload or use a second gun.

What the hell was that about? Tristan fingered the cut in his coat collar as he drew to a halt. *Hellfire! Too close by far.* Was it Tenby? Had he discovered where Charis was and that she had a protector, namely himself? Bloody clever if he had. In fact, as far as he knew, Tenby was still in Wells. Roger would have warned him if he had come back to Bath. If not him then who? His mind went back to the strange and sudden death of his brother. Was someone out to get both of them?

Looking back, he could see the wooded area where the shooter had probably hidden. There was no sign of him now. The decision to get out of the area and back to Bath was increasingly important. So he urged the horse into another gallop and was soon in the crowded streets of Bath. A little later, he was sitting in the offices of his father's solicitors, Cranby, Peters & Cranby.

Charles Cranby, the son of the founder, was at his desk ready to begin. "I followed your instructions to the letter, milord, and investigated thoroughly. I have to say that I think it extremely likely that if a court of law was asked for a judgement for Lady Charis they would come down on the side of Thomas Tenby. Times are changing for women's rights, but not nearly quickly enough. A great deal of work has been done by Harriet Taylor, an advocate of the rights of women and a follower of the suffrage movement. She is also closely allied to the Unitarians who embrace gender equality more readily than the Protestant groups, but even she admits it is an uphill fight. The fact that Lady Caroline could withdraw her consent to the marriage would mean little. She is a woman, and therefore not qualified to have enough intelligence to override Tenby's wishes."

Cranby shook his head and frowned. "I'm so sorry. I consulted with the best advocates but they said the same. Not the greatest of news I fear, milord."

"No, Charles, it certainly isn't. But consider this course of action: What if I marry Charis before Tenby gets his hands on her?"

"*Fait accompli*, I believe you mean?"

"Precisely."

"The baron would naturally be exceedingly annoyed, yet even in that case the marriage still could not be annulled. His hopes, as I understand it, of having a virgin wife would be shattered. Tenby might want to sue, but again there would be little point as we would counter with quoting extreme duress towards a minor."

Tristan began to look more hopeful. "That seems to be the way."

"Milord, I beg you, don't tell me your plans. I must stay outside of any illegal actions if I am to remain your advisor. You must be quite sure you want to enter into a marriage with Lady Charis in this underhand way. Equally, you must gain her full consent or you are just following in the footsteps of Tenby. Despite my rigid following of the law, I do have a leaning towards equality, and I sympathize but cannot condone. What actions you take are yours alone."

"Thank you, Charles. I understand. Now we will talk of the other matter I asked you about. You will be aware of Henry's demise? A strange and unexpected death, considering what a good rider he was. I almost joined him a short while ago on my way here." He pulled his coat collar forward to show the burned groove that creased it. "A little too close for comfort, I have to say. Luckily, it missed. However, it does throw up a dubious cause for Henry's death borne out, I recently discovered, by the doctor who viewed him shortly afterwards."

"Oh. Why did he not say at the time?"

"Circumstances were not convenient at that time which I have taken into account. The doctor was not to blame."

"Hmm, I see." He sounded doubtful but Tristan did not explain any further so Cranby continued, "I've spent some time researching your family's records over the last hundred years and have found quite a few offshoots; by that I mean offspring of relatives who married and moved away from the main family for one reason or another. Your father was explicit in rendering a legal will, but if for any reason the three of you die then the whole estate passes on to a distant cousin: Reginald Mountford. Do you know him?"

"Mountford? No, never heard of him. Though, wait a moment, I believe the youngest sister of my grandfather married beneath her. It caused a bit of a scandal at the time as she was reckoned to be an old maid and suddenly eloped. We boys only got to hear about it from the maids as it was all hushed up at the time. It was meaningless gossip as far as we were concerned, though I recall it was connected to some of the family. Though, God knows, that was years and years ago."

"You have a good memory, milord. You are correct. That is the family connection I was referring to."

"Where is this Mountford now? He must be an old man if he is the son of my grandfather's sister?"

"Reginald Mountford is her grandson and probably about your age. His family does not appear to have prospered well over the years. Alicia Fortesque, as she was, married a carpenter, a Harold Mountford. They had a son called Albert, who carried on in his father's trade. He died some while ago. Reginald, his son, went to sea, merchant navy, I believe. I have no idea where he is now or if he ever married."

"Good God! And he is an heir, you say?"

"According to the Legal Rights of Inheritance, yes."

"Does my father know this?"

"It was spoken of some time ago when your father dealt with his affairs. With two sons and the possibility of grandchildren, he totally ignored the danger. However, that danger seems to be alive and well. It needs to be taken into account, and preventative measures put in place."

"Preventative measures?"

"Certainly, sir! Guard your back!" Cranby boomed. "I also have to add that, if you marry, you must guard your wife's back as well. A son would put any succession out of reach for Mountford if he's the one who threatens your lives? The trouble is proving he may be involved. Hiring a Bow Street Runner might help to locate him, unless he is hiring someone else to do the dirty work. In that case, the whole thing is impossible."

"That word is not in my vocabulary. Nothing is impossible if one sets one's mind to it. At least one thing is confirmed. My instincts have never let me down. Proof or no proof, my brother did not die through riding carelessly. He was murdered!"

"In view of the recent happenings, you are probably right. Can you recall any other times you have escaped injury? Something you thought was merely an accident?"

Tristan sat silently for several moments as he took his mind back to the past and thought of events that had puzzled him at the time. "Yes, once when I was ambushed by a gang of thieves. My tiger helped me defeat them, but it was close. It wasn't the best of places, I submit. I had been delayed and it was a short cut to save time. I took it for granted they were only trying to rob me, but there could have been any reason, and I question the motive for that delay now. Two men would have sufficed, but the fact there was four makes me think in hindsight that they had murder in mind. However, I was able to escape relatively unharmed except for bruises. Another incident happened when aboard one of my ships newly docked in port. I was standing on deck chatting with the captain..." Tristan rubbed his chin as he recalled the crate coming out of the netting and falling from a great height as it was being unloaded. It hit the deck where he had been standing. Had the captain not pushed him out of the way, he would not be talking with Charles Cranby now.

"...A crate fell out of a sling and nearly decimated me. I took it for just an accident, but again I must wonder."

"Hmm, interesting. And Mountford joined the merchant navy? A coincidence that gives one thought."

"Yes, too many thoughts, I fear." Tristan rose to his feet and held out a hand to Cranby. "Thank you, Charles, for seeing me. I'll be in touch after I decide what to do."

A few moments later, Tristan was walking back to his hotel, every sense he possessed aware of his surroundings: noting who was walking close by, the traffic on the street, what lay ahead, totally alert and ready for a sudden assault. *But hellfire! What a way to live,* he thought. Something had to be done about the killer lurking to murder him, or Charis, or indeed his father.

Chapter Twenty-Three

Tristan was not best pleased when he discovered that Caroline planned to take Charis to London for the Season in order to present her to the *ton*, display her to those looking for an heiress, and possibly find a husband for her. While she truly sympathized with Tristan, Caroline was resolute in her purpose to do what she felt was the right thing for her granddaughter, and allow her a chance to decide who she would like to marry.

Although she thought Tristan the ideal man, she was wise enough to give Charis a choice. If Charis became more drawn towards his company than anyone else and there was a definite attraction then Caroline would happily agree to a marriage between them. She was also pleased that Leticia and Ellis were in agreement with this plan, and were lending their considerable aid to make it happen. Equally, she was delighted with it for herself. She was no stranger to taking part in a London Season or mixing socially with many long-time friends. And, although she was getting on in years, she still felt a thrill for the forthcoming adventure.

"I trust you realise that this visit will present a serious problem of safety for Charis. Although I have men to guard her and we will all do our best, there is still the mischance that can occur," Tristan said grimly as he sat taking coffee with Caroline the morning after his visit to his lawyer. "I've told you the bad news from Cranby and my suggestion to safeguard Charis from kidnap by making her my wife. A quiet wedding followed by a later larger gathering to celebrate it would be sensible. Her protection is all that matters to me," he added.

"But what matters to Charis? She has been hidden away all these years in Cornwall, putting up with dreadful abuse from that villain. She has no real idea of what life with you would be like. The social mores, the ability to become a fully-fledged hostess, to govern staff – oh, a hundred things you are not aware of that it takes to manage a household. Have pity, Tristan. You've been a part of that life forever so you are not aware of the pitfalls. She has to take it on afresh, and if she fails so will your marriage. Believe me, milord, it would cast a shadow over what should be a loving and beautiful partnership."

Tristan gazed back at Caroline as he reflected on the short visit to his home that Charis had coped with. An urge to argue with her filled him although sensibly he knew the words must remain unspoken. Charis had not only charmed his father but had been accepted happily and honoured by the staff at Castle House. He had no concern about her ability to be a graceful and welcoming hostess, or doubts about her success in everything she chose to do. As for himself, he could imagine no other woman filling her place by his side, and eventually becoming the mother of his children. How could he bear to watch her attend balls and tea parties, and stay quiet knowing every rake in London would be chasing after her?

"I'd like to see her once more before she leaves for London. I too have to make a trip back to my home as estate business demands my presence. I'll be gone a few days so will miss her departure. I'd like to explain how my men will keep her safe."

"Yes, of course. Send a note to say when you are visiting. I'm sure she will be happy to see you. I presume you will visit the capital after your stay at home?" He nodded. "I look forward to seeing you, milord. You will be most welcome to call on us."

"Tenby has not returned again, my men tell me. If he does while I am gone then I beg you not to see him. He is at present in Wells, so it might not be likely. Still, I don't want to give him the chance to upset you again. Once you leave for London, we shall put other plans in place. From then on, it will be guesswork, I'm afraid. I beg you once again to give more thought to my marriage to Charis. We know her birthday will not solve matters. She will be entitled to her trust fund then, and if she is forced to marry this Cornishman then he will claim it as is his right. Can't you see the risks we are running?"

"Yes, I hear what you say, but my cousin and her husband agree with me that Charis should have a chance to enjoy life before she is swept into marriage. If she wants to marry you after the Season is over, I have no objection."

Tristan rose and, making his bow to Caroline, thanked her for seeing him. It was no use trying to persuade any more. She'd made up her mind, and he had no desire to waste more time. Returning to his hotel, he called Everton to his rooms and began to issue a new set of instructions. It was all very well for Caroline to make these wonderful plans for her granddaughter, but he felt that Charis must say what she wanted.

In fact, he was sure that she'd not been given all the facts to make a choice. He realised it was her grandmother who was more eager to go to London and enjoy the social whirl of a Season, ignoring what Charis truly wanted. However, if Charis agreed then he would abide by it, even if it meant them running into danger.

Rather than sending a note to announce his arrival, Tristan determined he would set out immediately to visit Charis. If he caught her unprepared, maybe he had a better chance to persuade her not to go. With his men dispersed about the city and Roger down in Wells, there was no one to watch his back except for a ragged individual who had followed him from the Langdon House back to his hotel then, on a decrepit old donkey, shadowed him until he saw the route Tristan took out of the town.

Having either done odd jobs or begged his way through life in Bath, the old tramp had spotted Tenby and thought he was on the search for someone. His instincts told him there might be money in it for him so he had talked Tenby not only into buying him a glass of ale but also accepting his services. Luck was on Old Ben's side as he trailed the nobleman to the edge of town. Ben knew where the road led, and a good idea of the people who resided in that part of the country. When, two hours later, he spotted the viscount returning, he was aware he had news which should earn him a good sum; that's if he could prize it out of the meanest miser he had ever come across. He sent word to Tenby who wasted no time in returning to Bath with Barney. That evening, after making sure of his money, little though it was, Ben gave Tenby his report.

Tenby was jubilant when he met Barney a little later in a local tavern. "I knew the old bitch had help from someone. She was too cocksure," he crowed. "But a viscount? She has powerful friends to be sure. Still, she ain't got the law on her side, and I have. Tomorrow, we hike ourselves out to this estate and reconnoitre the land. We ought to have Charis out of there and back to Whaley before anyone realises she's gone."

Tenby rubbed his hands together. Then, as a thought struck him, he scowled at Barnaby. "Don't you go blabbing to anyone, you hear? It'll be the worse for you if you do. We ain't dealing with the kindest of men with Whaley. He's a real villain. Cut your throat soon as look at you. Even had the gall to threaten me. He don't appreciate I'm wearing out me boots working on his behalf. I've had enough of this affair so I aim to turn Charis over damn quick to Whaley, clear me debts, and be done with the whole ruddy business. Might even sell Carwinnion and move elsewhere. Had enough of the place anyway. Now, I suppose you're hungry again? Well, it's a pie and ale again, and you'll just have to sleep in the snug or the stable. I ain't got the wherewithal to lash out for the two of us. So, you'll have to take pot luck."

Barney didn't reply. He hadn't expected a bed anyway. He wasn't concerned about that. He was more troubled about Tenby's plans to kidnap Charis, and what he could do about it. A bare few pence in his pocket and Tenby watching his every move. Hell's teeth, why wasn't Daisy around when he needed her?

Chapter Twenty-Four

Hitchens hastily smoothed down his black coat and adjusted his collar before opening the front door to the caller. He was surprised to hear the bell as no one was expected to call that day. Lord and Lady Manville were visiting friends, and Lady Charis was out riding. The rest of the servants were going about their tasks quietly, so the house was silent and he had taken advantage of the peace to relax and rest.

"My Lord." He bowed low to the visitor.

"Good day. I've come to see Lady Charis if she is at home," Tristan said, wondering if his journey was in vain.

"Lord and Lady Manville are out at present, and Lady Charis is also out riding. I'm sure she won't be long. Do you wish to wait?"

"Does she go far on her rides?"

"Not today, only as far as the meadows by the river. She is allowed by herself without a groom there." Hitchens was an astute butler. He recognised that Lord Fortesque was a favoured guest, having overheard Ellis Manville praise him to his wife. He also knew that Charis had been allowed to spend some time in the garden with the viscount although unescorted. He assumed an understanding was in place between the couple so did not hesitate to reveal Charis's whereabouts. Noting Tristan's riding gear and the horse tethered close by, he said, "If you ride past the orchards and down the lane towards the river, you will see her coming back. Refreshments will be waiting on your return."

"Thank you, er…?"

"Hitchens, milord. You are most welcome. Lord Manville, I'm sure, would not have it otherwise for an honoured guest."

"Excellent, I will find Lady Charis and see you shortly."

Tristan was delighted at the way things had turned out. He would not have to make excuses to get Charis by herself. The way was clear to speak of that proposal again and try to persuade her that he would not deny her a London visit, but she needed his protection even if it meant opposing her grandmother's wishes. The old lady might think she was wise, but she did not know the danger as he did.

Mounting his horse, he set off down a stony lane, past orchards filled with May blossom, and then out into the countryside.

He recognised Butterfly grazing on some lush grass before he caught sight of Charis seated on a fallen log gazing into the distance. Dismounting, he led his horse towards Butterfly and, loosing the reins, walked quietly towards the girl.

"Dreaming of the delights of London, Charis?" he said softly.

"Oh!" She jumped round with fright. "I didn't hear you coming. What a surprise, My Lord! Were you expected today? I wasn't told."

"No, Charis, and, as always, the name is Tristan." He laughed as she blushed. "You'll have to get used to it sometime, so don't forget. I had expected to see a groom with you but, as to my visit, yes, it is unexpected but hopefully not unwelcome. I have a great deal to discuss with you and sooner rather than later when it might be too late."

"I've promised never go far on my own, only to the river, but when I ride further I make sure I am accompanied. You sound grave. What do you mean 'it might be too late'? Have you had news from your lawyer?"

"Yes. Not good news, I'm afraid. Becoming twenty-one doesn't mean a thing. Your stepfather can still dictate whom you marry."

"Then I will leave the country and hide abroad somewhere. I cannot and will not marry that horrible man!" She snorted angrily as her face tightened in a stubborn frown. "Surely if I refuse…"

He shook his head as he searched her eyes, her face…put himself in her place and accepted that she wasn't exaggerating how affected she would be. Probably so incensed she might do something drastic.

"I can give you an alternative. Will you marry me, Charis? You know I will guarantee your safety, provide a loving home, and yet leave you free to follow whatever path you choose. You've had a taste of my house and have endeared yourself to my father. His instruction to me before I left was to find you and bring you back to him as he missed you very much. It seems he has grown fond of you"

"Oh dear!" As Charis turned to him, her eyes filled with tears and she forced back an emotional sob as she cried, "Oh, the dear, sweet man! I was so afraid I had disappointed him dreadfully when I left. He is like the father I never knew. Mama used to speak of Papa in the early days before she married my stepfather, and it was so strange when I met your father. It was almost as though I knew him already and also esteemed him like I would have done my own father."

In spite of his determination never to lose control, Tristan's reply was instant. "Charis, my darling girl, don't get upset. Please marry me so Tenby cannot dictate to you again. I've already obtained a licence, and if we get married quietly in a small church I know of then later you can have a bigger party to celebrate."

He caught up her hand and rubbed a thumb over her knuckles trying to convey how he felt. "Once we are joined in matrimony, my dear, Tenby will have no legal right to dictate your future. You will be free. Do you understand?"

The gentle stroking caused a wave of anticipation to glow in her body as she gazed at the tall, wide-shouldered, athletic figure, superbly attired in garments made by eminent tailors, his hessian boots reflecting the efforts of his valet. Charis thought how fine-looking he was, quite the most handsome man she had ever seen. Any other woman would think she was crazy to deny him. Yet that spark of obstinacy was still with her and, in spite of her gratitude for him rescuing her, she nonetheless felt she must hold to her previous plans. Inwardly cringing at her temerity, she swallowed bravely and said, "My Lord, er, Tristan, my decision not to marry anyone still holds true, which was why I ran away from Cornwall. I was sick of being ruled, of others dictating what I should or shouldn't do even though the compensation was the country and the sea around Carwinnion. I was happy with that life – at least between times – when I was able to dodge Tenby. Thinking of it now, I'd no idea how much I'd miss Daisy, our housekeeper, and even Barney, our gardener. But the fact remains, I want to be my own mistress. I've been thinking about London and the crowds and strange people I'll have to endure. I don't want to disappoint my grandmother or the Manvilles who say they are acting for my own good. Nevertheless, even as nice as they are, it seems I still have no choice but to do as they say."

"So you'll run away again?" Tristan said sternly.

Charis stared back at him, her eyes wide with the realisation of how her life could change for the worse if she left the safety of her present situation. Tenby would still pursue her. She had no means of earning a living unless she could get hold of her inheritance, and even then she supposed she would be unable to live on her own. Could she rely on Tristan to help her? Her stance was both a demand and a plea. She waited, her eyes on his, clearly hoping for some hint.

He watched her carefully, accurately guessing the course of her thoughts. Which way would she decide? He had a very good idea what she was feeling: the disconcerting uncertainty, the nervous confusion, a natural stubbornness that was a part of her upbringing. She was so open, so trusting, that she thought nothing of showing her vulnerability to him; didn't even realise he could read her like an open book. He knew all the questions crowding her mind – the questions she couldn't begin to formulate. He knew the answers, too.

Chapter Twenty-Five

"No, I won't run again, but Tristan, I really don't want a big event."

Oh, heaven be praised! Had he at last persuaded her?

"You can have what you want and more if you will only say yes! Carwinnion, Daisy and Barney. The sea, the countryside and freedom. Anything you want."

Her face was tilted up to him; her tapered chin was firm; her full lips tinted delicate rose. The soft green of her eyes was clouded, displaying the anxiety that troubled her. She gazed up at him, seeing the emotion glinting in his eyes, and realised he was speaking from the heart. Even if she found another man she liked, she would not discover his true nature until after she was wed when it would be too late to change her mind. Whereas Tristan had saved her from Tenby's clutches and was more than generous with help. She thought of the passionate kiss he had given her and the feelings it engendered. Strange heated sensations she'd never felt before. Did that mean she was in love with him?

Charis hardly knew what the word meant except for some vague idea garnered from a romantic novel and a strong feeling that she should only marry someone if she loved them. Maybe a memory of being told of her parents' happiness inspired that wish. Hitherto, she had run from Carwinnion to avoid marrying anyone, and she had thought herself capable of managing her life on her own. The experiences she had gone through since then had taught her that she was living a fool's dream. Even if she depended on her grandmother to support her, she knew Caroline's eventual aim was to see her wed and, though hardly similar to Tenby, still might persuade her to accept someone her grandmother thought suitable but one she could never truly like. Reaching her majority was useless, it seemed: others had the power to dictate her life even if they couched it in the nicest possible way. So, no, she wasn't in love with Tristan, but she enjoyed his friendship, the security he offered. He made her laugh and, more than anything else, she felt safe in his company.

"How do we make this happen? My grandmother will be furious. She won't allow it. Does this mean I sneak away from the house and not tell anyone?"

"No your grandmother won't be furious. She gave me leave to court you, but wanted you to enjoy the London Season, without realising that it might be a trial for you. When one's life revolves round a society, especially the *ton*, that person can never visualise another not wanting the same thing. Rather than argue with her, it might be better if you slipped quietly away and did as you wished instead. Believe me, Charis, I would not take this path unless it was absolutely necessary to keep you protected. Despite my close watch, you are still at risk."

Suddenly, the thought of Tenby still on her trail and maybe closer than she realised was horrifying. He was still at large and able to kidnap her. On top of that was the problem of coping with the people she would meet in London and must be pleasant to whether she liked them or not. It was not as though she was untrained in the graces of society, her mother had been strict with her tuition, it was just the thought of strangers that was so overwhelming. The quietness of Cornwall and living among simple people had not taught her to deal with the sophisticates she would meet. Even if she did not love Tristan, anything was better than marriage to Whaley, or making her go to London.

Faced with the barest possible chance of being allowed the freedom to run her life as she wished, she realised she actually had no choice at all but to consent. At least she would be safe and cared for. Yet this was not part of her long dreamt of plan to be free to please herself, buy a small house, engage a companion if only to allow the social considerations of respectability. She had been certain her funds would afford that, not that she was truly aware of the size of her inheritance, but what of the future? Would she make friends? Would there be an opportunity to meet someone she could love? And if she didn't, would she remain single, grow an old maid, deprived of a family, children?

She was silent for several moments as she decided on her next words. Perhaps there was still the chance of an alternative path.

"My Lord, I have to be honest with you. I left Cornwall not intending to marry anyone. From what I have seen of that situation, I did not want to be beholden to any man or give him the power to rule my life. My mother was desperately miserable in the end, and she told me never give a man that kind of hold over me or I would rue the day."

Tristan frowned. This was a dilemma he hadn't anticipated. "Yet you agreed to the pretence of being my wife at Castle House."

"Did I have a choice? Everyone assumed I was your wife, and my mind was totally blank so how could I disagree? Yet you know when I recovered my senses, I escaped to find my grandmother."

"And now she is taking you to London to find you a husband. How do you propose to overcome that?"

"Quite simply. It will be a pity, of course for her efforts, but I shall merely not find anyone to suit. I am sure there must be many women in town who will be more desirable and more in need of a husband than I, and I can be most obnoxious when I choose." Her chin rose defiantly, and her eyes lit at the thought of the battle to come. It would be difficult but, once she took charge of the legacy her father had left, maybe she could live her life as she wanted.

Tristan's eyes narrowed as he thought of her strategy. Stubborn minx that she was, it could well work in her favour.

"I trust you realise that either Tenby or your grandmother will have a great deal to say about how you intend to exist from now on. You cannot hope to escape from them both. They will fight to rule your future, and you will be caught in the middle. I am offering you freedom from their dictates, and I promise never to misuse you as your stepfather did your mother. The only thing I ask is that you comport yourself as befits your rank as my wife."

"But marriage means more than that, doesn't it?" A blush coloured her cheeks, and her eyes dropped to where her fingers were twisting a wisp of a handkerchief.

It took him only an instant to comprehend the significance of her question. Tenby had much to answer for, if he was still alive. What she might have seen as a young child probably frightened her badly. He tried to think of any action he might have made since he'd found her and knew he was not entirely blameless. He had set out to seduce her from the beginning. He had not sought to hide his desire or his feelings in any way since the time he had slept with her, albeit chastely, at the inn.

The experience he'd gained over past years proved valuable. Quietly, yet adamantly, he had kept up the pressure to coax her to agree to marry him. Damn! He still had to find answers.

His kisses had been full of the passion that now filled his every waking moment. He had to conquer his demons and treat her gently. Her total innocence, which shone like a beacon, forced him to draw back. Almost certainly, she was terrified of him, and trying to hide it bravely and prove she could manage her own life.

"Yes, marriage is more than merely two people living together if it is to be long-lasting and successful. I strongly believe that trust is important as well as liking, if not loving one's partner. Children also are important if one is to carry on one's family legacy. Are you concerned about any of this?"

"No, I like children," she said slowly.

"Do you like me?" His voice was deep and serious.

"Yes, of course. You've been very kind."

Hmm, she is agreeable to liking but not loving, at least not yet.

"If, for example, we marry, and remain just friends so that I can keep you safe but you are free to decide how you want to live your life and can make up your mind if you want more, would that suit you?"

As her eyes widened again and met his with a surprised but joyful look, his dreams of immediately making her his true wife crashed in flames. How he kept his face from showing his shattered feelings was only due to the experience he had gained in the Far East where dignity and self-esteem held pride of place. 'Losing face' was not to be borne. *One step at a time*, he told himself, *first marry her. Then you will have the freedom to court her.*

"Yes, I think that a good idea. As my grandmother says, I have a lot to learn and I would hate to embarrass you."

She was silent for several moments as she contemplated all his suggestions. He *was* honourable and kind, and she felt she could trust him, certainly a great deal more than any stranger introduced to her in London. She raised her head and looked back at him proudly. "In that case, I'll marry you but *you'll* have to tell my grandmother! I do not know her well enough to find the words. And I hate to disappoint her."

"Oh, I will! Never fear, it will be alright. She is a reasonable person and she knows what is at stake. As I said, she has already given me permission to court you." *Not only me*, he mused ruefully, *but all the young ne'er-do-wells looking for a beautiful heiress.* Then guilt overcame him once more so he said, "Charis, my dear, I am delighted you've agreed, but do you truly want to be my wife? I am aware I am interfering with plans for London. I'm rushing you into a marriage before you've had time to think or even, the gods forbid, find someone you like better. My only excuse for not waiting is lest Tenby has his way and kidnaps you. Since I met you, I want only to protect you from harm and make sure you are safe."

"Oh, Tristan, you've protected me from the moment we met." Charis spoke softly. She repressed a shiver at the thought that, despite all her plans, she would be a possession, owned and subjected to an unknown future. Well, so be it, he wanted her answer now. At least she would have a chance to see if she liked being married, and if it didn't suit she could always leave. Naively unaware that once they wed he would never let her go, she took a deep breath and smiled. "I've made up my mind. The answer is yes, and I will marry you."

For an instant, Tristan gazed heavenwards as he wondered what benevolent god was on his side. Then his mind turned to how he could achieve his heart's desire and sneak her away.

"Excellent. Right, now we must plan how you'll slip out of the house without alerting anyone. We need enough time to get out of the area before you are missed, though we shall leave a note to explain. As I said, I have a licence, and finding a priest will be no trouble. We will return to Castle House for a short visit then go to London afterwards so that you can have a taste of life in the city. You know you will be safe and can enjoy the delights of the Season for as long as you wish. Have you planned anything over the next few days?"

"Not that I know of, apart from the packing of personal things I need. I believe the dressmakers attend us when we reach London, but I've not been told of anything else."

"I heard from your grandmother that you won't be leaving for at least ten days. That should give us time to marry and control our arrangements afterwards. Thus I don't see a problem with our trip to London which will not disappoint your grandmother. I collect she was rather looking forward to a time there so she can visit with friends. We can accommodate her wishes in that respect. As for the Manvilles, they will choose when they want to go so she may well stay with them."

He gazed at her lips once more and, unable to help himself, slid his arm around her saying, "This is goodbye for the present, so how about an engagement kiss, sweetheart? Do I deserve one?"

Relieved she had made up her mind and the future seemed less scary, her natural humour came to the fore. She grinned at him. "Have you been very, very good?"

He smiled at her words and nodded. "But of course!"

"In that case..." She offered her mouth. In seconds, her breath was snatched from her as he covered her lips with a scorching kiss that left her in no doubt of his deep feelings. For a moment, a shred of anxiety smote her. Was she doing the right thing by agreeing to marry him? Would her feelings for him grow stronger? Perhaps many a promised bride felt as she did: unsure of what lay ahead. At least one thing she *was* sure about. Never would she give herself to Whaley. She'd rather die!

Chapter Twenty-Six

Barney dug his heels again into the old nag he was riding hoping to get more speed out of the sorry beast and avoid another angry shout to 'get a move on' from Tenby who led the way on a far better horse. He managed to urge it to a canter, but knew it would not last long and the pace would dwindle to an unwilling trot which played havoc with his aching back. His thoughts fairly steamed with the vengeance he vowed, if ever given the chance, he would inflict on the man in front of him, who was turning into more of a villain than he had thought possible. He had known him a long time for a mean, surly employer, and many times had thought of leaving and finding another job. Except it would have meant he had to leave Daisy behind. Charis was right: he had a fondness for the woman. It would have been unfair to ask her to leave her home and job especially as he had no future prospects, nor could he foresee any in the future.

Glumly, he pondered the next problem: that of preventing Tenby from kidnapping Charis. If luck was with him, they might not find Charis where Tenby thought she was, but Barney no longer believed in luck. She'd be there all right, hidden out of reach, hopefully safe from those that meant her harm. How the devil could he save Charis and also save himself from retribution? For if it wasn't Tenby then it'd surely be Whaley who would kill him.

And where did this viscount fit in? Barney pretended deafness as Tenby had recounted the news earlier. "Viscount? Who's a viscount?"

"A Lord Fortesque, so my contact said." Tenby's answer was irritable and surly. "Supposed to be helping the grandmother, the stupid interfering fool. Not that it's any of his business."

"Oh. Never heard of him." Barney displayed indifference but tucked the name away for future reference. His next thoughts took in the possibility of getting word to this viscount that Charis was in danger. However, if the man lived in Bath, they were already riding out of the city and the chance of finding him was gone. Or was it? Spying a small alehouse up ahead, Barney had an idea, and he dug his heels viciously into the flanks of his steed which, surprised out of its lethargy, sprang into a gallop and drew alongside Tenby.

"Well, bugger me! What set you alight? Getting a move on for once?" Tenby grinned sarcastically at Barney.

"I'm stopping here, guv, for a privy. My insides are giving me gyp. Them pies ain't fit for eating, I vow." With that, Barney dismounted quickly, tied his horse to a rail, and headed for the back of the inn.

Taken unawares, Tenby could not deny Barney ease, so he yelled out that he would wait in the bar and to get a move on.

Once out of sight, Barney headed for the kitchen door and, peering inside, saw a man hauling a barrel up from a cellar.

"Excuse me, good sir," he began politely, "could you do me a favour? I'll pay, of course."

"Yeah? What you want doing?" said the innkeeper.

"Fetch me a scrap of paper and a pen without letting the man in the bar see you; then take the message to the man I name. It's urgent; might save someone's life. I'll go to the bog when I've written it. If the man wants to know where I am, tell him. Fill him up with ale to keep him quiet. And don't breathe a word or you'll get me hung!"

Within a short time, Barney had written his note and passed it over to the innkeeper with some coins:

C in danger. Come quick.

"Get this to a Lord Fortesque in Bath quick as you can. He'll be staying somewhere like a special hotel. He'll likely reward you as well. Tell him Barney sent it." Hopefully, Charis had mentioned his name.

Walking round to the front of the alehouse a bit later, Barney stuck his head in the door. "Ready when you are, guv."

"Took your time, didn't you? No ale for you. I ain't stopping any longer." Tenby drank the last of the ale, threw a coin on the bar, and stomped out. "I hope you can keep up now. Daylight's wasting. We've a lot to spy out before it gets dark."

Barney didn't reply. He had done what he could to help Charis. He just hoped His Lordship was good at figuring out cryptic messages.

Chapter Twenty-Seven

Tristan was finishing lunch when the waiter gave him a message that one of his men was waiting to see him. Glancing through the glass door that closed off the dining room from the reception hall, he spotted him standing by the desk. Immediately, he rose and went outside to find Roger looking unusually dishevelled and weary.

"What's up, Roger? Is our man on the move?"

"Yes, milord. He gave me the slip yesterday morning and is not only on the move but I believe is on his way to the Manvilles'. I almost ran my horse into the ground once I discovered he'd vanished after meeting Baron Whaley. The news here in Bath this morning is that he met with an old man then took the north road out of town. He had a companion with him riding a swayback horse that surely must hold them up. He's not been gone long so we'll be able to track him. I suspect he'll have to reconnoitre the estate before he makes any plans."

"How the hell did he discover we have her out there?"

"Probably same way we have: informers. Float the odd bit of cash around and someone will always keep their eyes open. I expect you've been watched since you've been here."

"I thought I'd been careful not to be followed. If I'm to blame, I hold myself responsible. I'll change to riding gear then call briefly on Lady Langdon to let her know we are still guarding her granddaughter and not to worry no matter what she hears. I'm determined that villain will not have his way. Get some food while I'm gone. When you are done, tell Everton and Stevens to saddle up. They are coming with us."

"Right, milord. I'll expect you in, say, forty-five minutes. I don't think we should delay too long. He's a sly one, and there's no telling what he'll get up to. Apart from catching him, we need to be in the house to guard milady Charis."

"A bit like old times, Roger, when we were chasing bandits, eh?"

"And killing them as well. I don't think we can do that here in England. It'll have to be a capture, I expect?"

"More's the pity. I have good reason to exchange the pain he has doled out to others with a good helping for himself, but, yes, he must be dealt with by the law."

Tristan was in the stables about to mount his horse when a groom came running from the hotel followed by a young boy.

"Message for you, milord. This here lad's brought it. Says it's urgent." He beckoned the boy forward. "Here's His Lordship. Give him the note. Take your cap off and bow. Show some respect!"

Tristan gazed at the boy who had coloured at the groom's words. He took the note held out to him and, after a swift perusal, passed it over to Roger then asked, "Who gave you this note?"

"My father. He had it off a fellow that'd stopped by. I was told to tell you it was from Barney and get it to you right quick. Got a lift t'market and ran from there. Dad said you'd be staying here. Good job you were." He wiped his flushed face.

"You did well. Where have you come from?"

"Badger Inn. It's an alehouse up near Beach Wood, sir."

"On the Lansdowne Road, milord," interrupted Roger. "I noted it when I conveyed Lady Charis."

Tristan turned back to the boy. "How long ago did this man give your father this note? Was anyone else with him when he came?"

"Yesterday, late afternoon. I had to wait for a lift into town this morning. The man went off with another chap who was in the bar."

Tristan fished in his pocket for a half sovereign and watched the boy's eyes open wide at the sight. "My thanks, young man. Save this for when you need it most. How are you getting home?"

"I'll get a lift back on the cart I came in on."

"We are heading that way now. One of my men will take you back of him. I want to speak with your father anyway. Stevens, will you oblige?"

"Aye, sir. Right, lad, up with you! We'll have you home soon."

The small cavalcade left the yard and was well on its way out of Bath when Tristan drew near Roger and said in an undertone, "What did you make of the note?"

"No doubt it is a warning. Making a guess as to his identity, does this Barney come from Carwinnion?"

"Yes, Charis said he was an odd-job man-cum-gardener. She thought well of him. One thing in our favour. However, that scoundrel has had a whole night to make plans, so we'd better get a move on. I want quick words with the boy's father about that note. Then, as we ride, we will watch who returns to Bath on this road."

Chapter Twenty-Eight

Charis slept badly that night after seeing Tristan. To her amazed disbelief, she had agreed to wed him. When she had run away from Carwinnion, it had been to get away from a marriage, especially to that hateful man Baron Whaley. Yet here she was, affianced to a virtual stranger, knowing that from now on her life would inevitably change. Although, to be fair, Tristan had promised she could have what she wanted. What did she want? Lonely rides on Cornish beaches? The friends she had made in the village? Or fulfil a life with a husband and children?

Eventually, she rose and, draping a shawl about her shoulders, she sat by her open window to think over her options. She could run away again, but where would she go? There was no one to run to. She could allow her grandmother to override him and insist she went to London, but she suspected Tristan would soon persuade otherwise. Or she could say she had changed her mind and refuse his offer. But she had given her word; she had accepted his proposal. Her upbringing forbade her to break a promise. Nor in the deepest part of her heart did she want to.

She watched the early morning light deepen and glow as the sun rose to greet the start of a beautiful day. The meadows would be rimed with dew, and the river would sparkle as the sun rose higher. Rising quickly, she pulled off her night shift and dressed in her riding gear. In a short time, she was down by the stables where the grooms were only just awakening to a new day and yawning sleepily as they began their duties. Soon, Butterfly was saddled, and she was cantering slowly down past the orchards heading for a good gallop across the open ground.

An hour later found her sitting on a hummock by the river watching the swiftly running current carry the twigs or odd blades of grass she threw into the water. The river was deep here, and she knew it for a place where Uncle Ellis loved to fish. Perhaps he would rise early and join her with his rods. He was a quiet man, and they could enjoy the sound of the running water and peace of the day in mutual companionship. She had grown to like him and was loath to cause him distress, but it seemed there was no option once she left with Tristan.

Spying from his lookout at the edge of the trees, Tenby watched gleefully as Charis sat staring at the river. She had no groom, he was pleased to note, but neither did she roam further afield. No chance of catching her unawares in the distant woodland.

"Barney! Wake up, damn you! We've got her! There's no one near to get in our way. Get a move on, before she returns to the house."

He kicked Barney's thigh to waken him. Reluctantly, Barney got to his feet from the pile of leaves he had gathered to soften his makeshift and uncomfortable bed as Tenby was determined they would remain in hiding until they saw Charis.

He followed Tenby to the edge of the trees and saw the girl by the river. Staring towards the house, he was fearful for her safety. She was all alone, apart from them. What had happened to his note? Was it lost? Why weren't they taking more care of her?

"Get the horses. We'll be down to her before she can reach hers. Look, it's some way off grazing. Move it, damn you! I don't want to miss this chance." With Tenby hopping from one foot to another impatiently, Barney had no option but to obey, and within moments the two riders set off for the river's edge.

The grass muffled the sound of hooves so Charis, lost in thought, was not aware of danger until a hard hand grabbed her arm and yanked her to her feet. "Got you, miss! I'll teach you to run off, whatever Whaley says. You've caused me no end of trouble!"

Tenby raised his cane on high as Charis cowered in stricken terror. Before it could descend, she heard a loud roar as Barney launched himself on Tenby bellowing, "You hurt that girl, you evil mongrel, and, God help me, I'll swing for you!"

Tenby's attention was wholly taken up with teaching his stepdaughter a lesson she'd never forget; to frighten her enough to abduct her as quickly as he could manage. With his back turned to Barney, he never saw the rage that consumed the old man that gave him the strength and weight to lash out at the much stronger man. Barney hit Tenby full-on and, caught off balance, his enemy staggered forward in shock; then, losing his stability, he teetered ungainly on the edge of the bank before finally plunging into the river and going under in the fast flowing water.

"Oh, Barney! You saved me! How brave of you!" Charis flung her arms round his neck then burst into tears.

"Now, now, little 'un. 'Twas nothing really. He's a wicked bully. I gave him a taste of his own medicine, that's all."

Charis turned back to the river. "Where is he?" she exclaimed.

"That bundle yonder looks like him. Caught in the current, I expect. Gives us time to get you back to the house and safe."

"Do you think he will drown?"

"Don't know, don't care...oh, for pity's sake...what now?" he cried out as a troop of men galloped down the meadow towards them.

Seconds later, all four men were off their mounts, and Barney was tethered between two of them.

"No!" screamed Charis as Tristan grabbed her to his chest. "It's Barney! He's my friend. He saved me!"

"Let him go," Tristan ordered. "Where's Tenby?"

"In the river!" Charis and Barney said in unison.

"Drowned or swimming?" The viscount was terse.

"I don't know," Barney said. "We just saw a bundle of clothes moving in the current after I pushed him in, milord. I am right thankful he's out there and not here. Led me a right dance, he has, from Cornwall to here. Bloody maniac he is or *was* – I hope. Men like him need putting down."

"I got your note. We came as quickly as we could though I expected Tenby to take longer to scout the estate."

"He was at it last night. In a great hurry, he was. Whaley was threatening him; holding his debts over him, I expect. He's a killer as well, so I was told. You'd better be warned, milord."

"Yes, I'll take heed." Then Tristan called out, "Everton, Stevens, check the riverbank for a couple of miles. See if the rogue has made it to the bank."

He watched them mount then looked down at Charis. "Back to the house, sweetheart. Breakfast then we'll break the news you are definitely coming with me. We don't need any more scares like this one. Hopefully, Tenby is out of our lives forever. We'll ride back to Bath then leave for

Castle House. I have a fancy to be married in the church there. I trust that will suit you, my dear? I think you've had enough perilous adventures for a while." He pressed his lips to her forehead then lifted her on to Butterfly.

"Come, Barney. No doubt breakfast will suit you as well, as will returning home with us. You can rest easy, man. You will have a job in my service if you want it. Likewise your housekeeper at Carwinnion. I'm grateful for all you have done. You have been a good friend to my future wife, and I shan't forget it. Roger, will you introduce Barney to the cook then join us for breakfast. We have quite a tale to tell the Manvilles."

Charis trotted thankfully ahead of Tristan as they returned to the house, willing the trembling to cease in her body. It was the narrowest of escapes this time, thanks to Barney, and she hoped never to see Tenby again.

At last, she knew she had made the right choice. Held so close to Tristan's body, breathing in the scent of cologne and his manly aroma and knowing she was secure was all she ever wanted now. She knew she would be safely guarded from the clutches of Whaley, a man who had terrified her from the beginning. For the first time, she looked forward to the marriage, particularly seeing his father again. She vowed to make them both happy. Even more joy filled her heart knowing that Daisy and Barney would be cared for too.

Chapter Twenty-Nine

The leave-taking from the Manvilles was not a pleasant affair.

Following breakfast and the story of the frightening events of the morning, Tristan suggested the four of them should retire to the study as there was more to relate. Surprised but acceding to his request, Ellis and his wife had joined Charis and Tristan, and then listened in growing consternation to what he proposed.

Immediately, Ellis protested the changed arrangements even though Tristan had been logical in explaining the reason why he was taking Charis away that very morning.

"Caroline will not like it. She has set her heart on taking Charis to London. She wants to introduce her into society, to the *ton*. We have agreed that is the best way to start her life anew."

"Who is the *we* who have agreed?" Tristan asked.

"My wife has spoken with Caroline and arranged the details with her. I concur with their planning," Ellis said firmly.

"And was Charis a party to these discussions?"

"Well, no." Ellis's face reddened. "Obviously, she is too young to be aware of the problems of moving to the city, and the art involved in being introduced into the social order. We are experienced, milord. We had to do it for our own family who are now well settled in their own establishments. So no, she has not been consulted with those details. Now Tenby has been drowned, the trouble is over. We no longer have to fear an assault from him. We must see to her future prospects."

"On the contrary! My men did not find his dead body or where he might have left the river. If he is still at large, so is the danger. I never take things for granted. I always require proof. As for consulting with Charis, *I* do not consider she is too young to know her own mind; thus

I explained the problems clearly. I then asked her to be my wife, and she has accepted. Caroline was aware that I was going to do that eventually and gave her consent. That, Manville, takes care of her future prospects. While she may have thought that a proposal might be delayed until after the London visit, I deem the danger of delay in protecting my fiancée is not acceptable."

He turned to face Charis who had sat silently while both she and Leticia listened to the tense argument between the two men.

"My dear Charis, please feel free to tell Lord Manville what you want to happen from now on. I know you have said yes to my proposal, but I won't hold you to the promise if you wish to change your mind. Just tell us what you wish to do."

"Oh, this is too much!" Leticia interrupted angrily. "Charis has no idea what a London Season means to a young girl, or what she will miss by not going. A Season is so exciting: dinner parties, balls, picnics in pleasant settings where she will meet the cream of society. In addition, it is her birthday in two days. We have planned a party for her. Surely you are not going to deprive her of that joy as well?"

You should have asked Charis if she thinks it joyful, he thought.

"She needs time to think!" Leticia went on. "You are taking too much on yourself insisting she goes with you now, this very minute. The impropriety of it is not something I condone. What about her maid, her luggage?"

"My coach should arrive shortly, and these things will be taken care of. They will reach Bath by this evening, and rooms are already catered for in the hotel. Charis will ride her horse back with me and my men, so will not go in the coach. As she has travelled before with me and has been safe, you should fear no impropriety. As for her party, I'm sure she will not be deprived of that. Gaining her majority has great significance to us, but unfortunately not to the wiles of her stepfather or any court that he can apply to. Despite the fact we can, and would, apply a considerable defence, I'm not prepared to take a chance on things going awry."

He saw Charis glance at him in surprise, and he guessed she was thinking that he had planned ahead to direct things his way. He had, but at this moment he had no idea how she would answer his question. Would she take advantage of the excuse and change her mind? Would Leticia prevail?

Here it is: a taste of the iron fist in the velvet glove. My future planned for me. No, of course I haven't been consulted. My wishes do not count. Too many people think they have a right to know what is best for me. Would a London Season thrill me? It might be interesting, but I do not crave the experience, though I would enjoy it with a companion like Tristan. Maybe marriage with Tristan would mean freedom after all, and at least I could say I'd had enough and could escape to the peace and quiet of the countryside and be with Daisy and Barney again. At least he is seeking my permission in front of witnesses. I cannot remember having anyone do that before. He is obviously a man of his word, and I cannot ask for more.

Her mind finally made up, Charis took a deep breath and said, "Aunt Leticia, Uncle Ellis, please forgive me for upsetting you but the attack from my stepfather has been most upsetting. Whether he's alive or dead I don't know, but this I do know: I have been guarded and cared for by an honourable man. I've decided to wed Tristan of my own free will, and I know he cares for me."

She stood up and waved her hands to include both the Manvilles. "Thank you for your hospitality and guardianship, and I hope to see you later in London. Tristan's promised me we will go to town so I'll not miss some of the Season, but I will feel safer in his protection."

"Oh well, miss, if that's what you want then it seems we cannot argue with both of you. I can't help but feel you are too young and not knowledgeable enough to know what you are doing." Leticia couldn't help but scowl ferociously and show her deep displeasure until Ellis frowned himself and shook his head at her.

"Letty, for once let the young ones do what they want. I think Lord Fortesque will make a good husband for Charis, and she has also decided this." He turned to Charis. "I will look for you in London, my dear, and wish you the happiness in your marriage that we have enjoyed in ours. God bless and keep you."

At his words, Charis, tears running down her face, moved swiftly towards Ellis and, flinging her arms round him in a hug, said, "Oh, Uncle Ellis, you have been so kind to me. I shall miss you."

Embarrassed, Ellis fetched out a large handkerchief to mop her face saying, "There, there, my dear, dry your eyes and don't get upset. We shan't lose touch with you, I promise. You are as dear to me as your father was. Now, off you go with Tristan and keep safe. We shall see you again before long and will have much to talk over."

Ellis glanced over at Tristan and, eyeing him sternly as though to say 'Look after her', nodded for him to escort her out to the stables.

Charis gave up her hold on Ellis and turned to Leticia with a curtsey. "I trust I will also see you in London, ma'am. I am grateful for your care, and look forward to meeting your family."

Leticia, her motherly instincts coming to the fore, her anger put to one side, grasped Charis's hands and pulled her into her arms to give her a warm and loving hug. "Of course we will see you again. Good luck with your wedding. I wish you every happiness, and I also look forward to hearing all about it. My felicitations also for your birthday. In fact, I may have a surprise for you in your luggage."

At that, Charis raised her eyebrows.

"No, dear child, off with you now. You'll find out soon enough. As I've said before, I will get all the news when I see you in London. Take care and be safe."

The small party left soon after and, before long, reached the hotel in Bath in ample time for an early dinner.

Afterwards, Charis suggested they call on her grandmother and give her the news. She was shocked when Tristan said, "No, my love, you've endured much today and you should retire. We have a long journey and need to leave early. I don't want you so fatigued you fall ill. You'll see her soon and can spend as much time with her as you wish. Sleep well, and I'll see you in the morning." He pressed a kiss on her brow and led her to the stairs wishing he could take her to his bed instead.

Obediently, she went to her room. Once there, her maid was ready to assist and, thankfully, she climbed into bed altogether too tired with trying to sort out the jumbled thoughts that cascaded through her brain of the shocking appearance of Tenby; her timely rescue by Barney of all people; and the appearance of Tristan, who, it seemed, was going to be a major person in her life from now on. Would she mind? Once again, a shiver went through her as she imagined his arms holding her close and his passionate kissing. Hmm, something she could get rather used to enjoying. Certainly better than…no, don't even go there! She wouldn't think of the alternative that she had narrowly escaped from; there was no comparison. And one joy ahead was that she would see the earl again and hopefully make her peace with him.

She fell asleep on that thought of finding someone she could call Father.

Tristan had his own reasons for denying her visit to Caroline. As much as he respected the old woman, she had her own ambitions of a London Season which did not tie with his. More than that, he'd had enough of arguing with people over the do's and don'ts of his actions. Having reached an agreement with Charis, nothing, he vowed, was going to stand in his way.

Chapter Thirty

The welcome at Castle House that Charis received was all she could have wished for, especially from His Lordship Earl Fortesque. Though they had to spend one night at an inn, the journey back was as rapid as weather conditions allowed, and Charis, accompanied by her maid, was able to drowse now and again in blissful comfort in the elegant coach compared with the previous journey she had undergone riding to Bath.

"I collect you've led my son quite a dance, young lady," the earl said when at last she sat before him on the footstool. "Can I hope that you are here to stay, or must I prepare for another loss?" His face was grave though she espied a twinkle in his eyes.

"If you'll have me, My Lord, as it appears I am to marry your son."

"So I've been told. A second marriage, for *my* benefit, I believe?"

Charis blushed rosily red and the earl laughed heartily. "A secret between the three of us, or so I have *also* been told. Yes, I am aware of the whole story. In that case, just between the two of us, may I say I couldn't be more delighted."

"I'm so glad, for I have liked you from the beginning."

"So, therefore, could you spare me more honour? I should like to stand in the role of a father and give you away."

Charis stared at him with such joy in her eyes it brought tears to his own.

Gruffly, he cleared his throat. "Of course, if you'd rather not—"

"I couldn't wish for a nicer person. You'll take the place of the father I never knew. You indeed do *me* the honour."

"Good, that's settled. Ah, here's the man himself!" They turned as Tristan came into the room.

He stared at their smiling faces then frowned. "You both look as though there is mischief in the making." A burst of laughter greeted his words, and inwardly he revelled at the happiness in his father's face.

"Yes, decidedly mischief. So, tell me, what are you both up to?"

"Oh naught but a little forward planning, Tris. Your bride has given permission for me to give her away. But be aware, my son, I give her not only into your hand but also mine own. She is the daughter I never had a chance to possess. And I thank you for bringing this gift to me."

Aware of his family history and the hurtful loss of his mother in childbirth, a flash of emotion overtook Tristan and made him pause before he gave a nod to his father. "Then, without doubt, we are both well pleased," he said gruffly. Turning to Charis he said, "Arrangements are in hand for tomorrow. I trust this is convenient for you?"

For a moment, her heart quaked. He sounded terse and looked so serious, she felt sure he was unhappy with the forthcoming marriage. Perhaps he was having second thoughts. She could not equal him in ancient lineage. She was sure he could do far better in the débutante market.

The silence following was so prolonged that Amery glanced at each of them in surprise. "Is something amiss?"

"Not as far as we are concerned," said Tristan. "Unfortunately, I've just had an uncomfortable meeting with one Baron Whaley. He has managed to track us down and came to protest his prior claim to Charis. He says that he will legally interrupt the wedding if it takes place and will put a stop to it." Tristan shrugged despondently. "I'm at a loss for once in my life. I cannot invoke the law and prevent Whaley from interfering as he can officially turn the tables on us to hold things up even though it is your birthday tomorrow. And more than anything else, I don't wish you, my dear, involved in scandal."

"Are you really sure you want to marry me—"

"How can you doubt it, Charis? However every attempt I've made to solve our future happiness has been fraught with problems—"

"My Lords, please excuse my interruption..."

The three of them turned to see Melrose hovering in the doorway that led to the earl's bedroom.

"What is it now, Melrose? Can't it wait?" the earl said testily.

"If it pleases Your Lordship, I have a suggestion to make—"

"No, it doesn't please. Haven't I told you about listening in to conversations?" The earl banged his hand on the arm of his chair to emphasise his words. "I won't have it, I tell you…"

Tristan stared at the valet's face and unexpectedly held up his hand to silence his father. "You are not usually so forthcoming, Melrose, and I know you hold my father in great respect. Before he sacks you for the umpteenth time, what do you wish to say?"

The valet grinned briefly at Tristan's sally then his face turned serious. "I beg you heed me a moment. You have a licence. We have the minister and a church, but who is to know at what time a marriage service may take place. The estate knows a service is to be held in the morning, but nobody knows exactly what for. Nothing was said about a wedding. Gossip and guesswork are still going the rounds. If the reason for the service is a thanksgiving for a safe return home of you, milord, no one will wonder or object."

Melrose bowed to Tristan. "And if the wedding service is conducted at another time…say, later tonight…?"

"Hallelujah! I knew there was a good reason for keeping you on, Melrose! I doubt you earn a sacking for speaking out. Father, we shall disturb your sleep at midnight tonight. Can you manage to attend my wedding secretly? No one must know the change of time. Perhaps a rumour can leak that tomorrow's service might be cancelled because of unexpected problems. That way we put Whaley off the scent until I can deal with him. I was having Richard Marshall as best man, but Roger will have to stand in his place instead. The doctor will be disappointed, but it cannot be helped. This means only the four of us and our minister will know of the midnight rendezvous. Oh yes, we must have witnesses. Melrose and Kate will do. You can be trusted to keep quiet, can't you, Melrose? Charis, are you happy with this?"

"To evade that horrible man, yes, I'll do anything! But more than that, Tristan, I am content to marry you quietly and without fuss."

The look on Tristan's face was a delight to see, and she knew she had said the right thing.

The night was silent in Castle House as all the occupants were asleep save for six figures that crept quietly across the garden to the tiny chapel that lay at the back of the big house. Amery Fortesque walked slowly but gamely, held up by Roger and Melrose. Charis, robed in a dark cloak, was escorted by Kate, her maid. Tristan brought up the rear, every sense attuned to the surroundings. But all stayed quiet, and they gained the chapel unheard by anyone. Inside, only two candles lit an altar, and a darkly gowned minister stood ready in the gloom to administer the ceremony.

Almost inaudibly, lest the whispers carried beyond the walls of the chapel, the short service took place until finally the ring was on Charis's finger, and at last they were wed. Tristan's kiss sealing their troth was brief and, after a handshake with the cleric, a whispered, "I'll see you tomorrow," and an answering nod, the group left the building and, still silent, filed back into the house and climbed the stairs heading for Amery's suite.

There was a brief hitch as a drowsing footman on duty opened his eyes on the people passing by. Before he could move or speak, Tristan held his hand over his mouth. "As I value loyalty, Jessop, you've seen nothing to disturb you. No one is here. Understand?" he whispered.

The footman nodded and placed his own hand over his mouth.

"Good man. Now go back to sleep. You've earned a rest." Tristan patted the man's arm and followed the rest of the conspirators down the corridor.

In his father's sitting room, he was met by smiles from everyone. Charis had taken off her cloak and, to Tristan's surprise, the dress she wore looked like a wedding gown. Noting his shock, she whispered, "Leticia sent it with my luggage as a birthday present. Her daughter wore it and, fortuitously, it was my size. I thought it suitable even if hidden by a cloak."

Tristan eyed the lacy cream gown designed by first-class *modistes* and grinned. "She turned out nice in the end though she gave us a hard time. You look stunningly beautiful, and I am proud of you. I regret the lack of a congregation to see you and express their approval too." He blew her a kiss, and she smiled and blew one back. They turned to pay attention to Amery.

"By Hades, Tristan, I thought the game up with poor old Jessop. You obviously handled him well. Now, in my book we have some celebrating to do. Melrose, pour the champagne if you please. I need to welcome my daughter-in-law in good style. And needless to say, many congratulations to my son. Your efforts to achieve this marriage will not surprise those who know you for your fine actions, but all the same it is a feat that

I will remember and cherish. So, my friends, with glasses filled and held on high, I give you Tristan and his lovely bride Charis Fortesque. May you enjoy many happy years together."

Edwin had also joined the group and joined in with the toast. He had been aware of the plan and had secretly assembled the champagne and biscuits, sneaking down to the kitchen when all had retired. He had yet to know his master thoroughly, but already had acquired a deep respect for the man and was happy to serve him faithfully.

With the time approaching two of the clock, Tristan signalled to Melrose that it was time the party ended. His father was beginning to wilt and, more importantly, he had a new bride and a decision to make as to whether he could persuade her to come to bed with him.

He knew her maid was now privy to the fact that they hadn't been married before and also that Melrose had warned her to say nothing to the rest of the servants, but she would wonder why he still did not share her bed although legally married. Uneasy to give her more reasons to think of the strangeness of events, he decided that, apart from his intense desires, he had to sleep with Charis, come what may.

Everyone headed for their quarters, and soon no trace of the midnight adventure remained save some glasses, plates and empty bottles. The maids would be somewhat surprised in the morning, wondering who had been guests in their earl's rooms. Only a special few would get to know that a second ceremony had quietly taken place for the benefit of the earl who was unable to attend the first wedding service, though they would not be aware of the time it had occurred. Even cancelling the proposed church service would not be remarked upon. Despite the usual gossip that was inherent in any household, it was not important enough to convey to anyone in the village. No reason had been given other than the viscount had been home some time so he felt it was a waste of effort to celebrate his homecoming at this late date. As it was a chore that upset the usual activities of the household, most were relieved it had been cancelled.

Chapter Thirty-One

Kate assisted Charis to undress and put on her nightgown before brushing her hair and gently smoothing a lavender fragrance over her bare shoulders. "This has been a meaningful day, has it not, My Lady? Brought from Bath to here and then the surprise of a secret wedding. Why, you must be feeling topsy-turvy and no mistake. And to think you are a bride. Wonders never cease how quickly things happen."

Yes, thought Charis, it was the wonder of the century as far as she was concerned. "And time you were off to bed, Kate. Don't wake me too early in the morning. As it's so late, I fancy sleeping in longer tomorrow and recovering from today's excitement."

"Yes, milady." Kate grinned then smoothed her face to neutral as Charis raised an eyebrow. "An extra hour would suit me nicely too if it pleases you. Though that housekeeper is a tyrant and she'll have me out of bed as usual, no matter what I say."

"Then say you have a holiday until noon by command of the viscount. That should suffice until further orders."

The two women jumped in fright as Tristan spoke. "That's all for now, Kate. We will ring when we need you again. Goodnight." He held open the bedroom door for the maid to leave.

"Excellent," he said as he closed it. "Now, where were we, sweetheart? Ah, I know, in the wrong bedroom." Before she could blink, he picked her up and turned to stride through to his own room.

At her strangled yelp of surprise, he laughed. "Bigger bed, my darling. I take up a lot of room."

"What are you doing, Tristan? I think I should stay in my own bed to give you more room. Also we had an agreement…"

He stared down at her in pretended surprise. "Don't you want to sleep with me now, Charis? We have memories to resolve, my dear."

"What memories, Tristan?"

"I recall weeks ago in a bedroom in Liskeard, you said to me, 'Kiss me. If I love you then I should know.' We have kissed quite a few times since then. Have you made up your mind? Do you know if you love me? Or shall we find out?" He let her slide down to her feet.

"Oh yes, I remember my words. But then I was in a daze. If you were deceiving me, and of course you were, that was the only way I might know. Except I didn't find out, not then or even with every kiss you have given me."

"Yes, that was indeed the case. I thought at the time it was the easiest way I could protect you. Somehow, although I knew nothing of you or how you came to be in my coach, I knew I had to keep you safe and get a doctor. Do you think I have tricked you into marriage?"

All at once his blood ran cold. Would she blame him and finally refuse him? Let him spend his wedding night longing for her and feeling at fault that he had gone about things in a dishonest way? His mind churned with remorse. Looking back, there were probably many ways he could have courted her but overall was the danger of Whaley. And, damn it all, he wanted her!

In silence, he waited for her answer.

She blushed with guilt at his words thinking of her own ambivalent reasons for becoming his wife. Then a memory of her mother's principles intruded, and she knew, even if he turned from her in disgust, she had to be honest. "I've married you, and it was by choice. What more do you want me to say? Confess? If that is the case, I own I had not planned to marry anyone, nor wanted to. That is why I ran away from Carwinnion and the unbearable prospect I had facing me. You rescued me from a dreadful fate, and now I feel I have suddenly grown up and must realise the world is no longer an empty beach to walk on barefoot and watch the wild waves roll in from the ocean or mix with the local village people and concern myself with their problems. You have honoured me by making me your wife, but suddenly I have to be a lady and comport myself accordingly. I question my ability to run Castle House. I also admit to feeling extremely nervous now I'm here in your room. I scarcely know you. I don't know what you expect of me. I thought we were only to be friends."

"Yet you married me willingly, knowing I wanted you for my wife and all that means: to live in this house and, eventually, in the future, to have our children. Was it a lie, Charis?"

"My Lord, I don't lie. I hate lies." She spread her arms wide to indicate her surroundings. "It is all this." She frowned. "I should hate to cause you embarrassment. I have come to care for you and appreciate all you have done for me. I also remember the words said when we wed. I promised a great deal, I think, and I have to give you an heir. Though I have no idea how to accomplish that. It's just now I am here with you—"

"Oh!" Was that all? Tristan breathed a sigh of relief. Of course, he should have realised: she had no mother to tell her what marriage meant. He had to take things gently and persuade rather than rush things. He had never made love to a virgin before, and the thought both thrilled and scared him rigid. How he handled matters from now on would make a difference in their relationship for all time to come.

"A great deal has happened since we agreed that way of living. I know you don't love me yet, but I want the chance to prove we can make a good marriage together. Also, you must know that our actions are watched by other people. We don't live solitary lives on the estate. Sooner or later, the household will realise we don't share a bed and gossip will develop. It will affect us and them badly."

He gently stroked her arms. "An heir can wait on nature. First, we must take pleasure in our marriage, and the lateness of the hour means we should be abed." He leaned forward and held up the bedcovers. Eyeing him for a moment, she hesitated then obediently slid beneath them. Dousing most of the candles then casting off his dressing gown, Tristan followed behind her. She lay curled up in a ball on her left side facing away from him, but was conscious of his heat as he swung in beside her, and she recollected he'd said he slept naked.

He lay still for some moments wondering how he could allay her fears and coax her into his arms; then said softly, "Charis? I'd like to kiss you again. Don't make me beg."

She turned swiftly towards him. "I'm sorry; I didn't mean to spurn you—"

Instantly, she was caught in his arms and pulled close, his lips covering hers in the mesmerising way she had felt before. She opened her mouth to his urging tongue and was rewarded with his groan as she responded to his touch with her own tongue.

Soon, the apprehension she felt melted as she became aware of the same pooling of delight in her belly that she had felt before, and she pressed herself even closer to his heat. His hand gently stroked her back, running warm fingers from her neck to her waist then sliding up again to her shoulder and the ties of her nightgown. Before she could protest, he untied the ribbons.

"We'll dispense with this, I think. I won't let you get cold." The nightgown disappeared over the side of the bed leaving her naked and once again trembling as he began smoothing his hands over her body, his lips following every path his fingers traced until she was quivering not with fright but with a new and unexpected passion begging her to surrender to his loving touch. Cupping a breast, he fingered the furled nipple until she gasped at the feeling; then, bending his head, he took it between his lips and began to suckle it within his warm, wet mouth.

Swift sensations of increasing delight sped through her and, responding to his ardency, she curled her hand round his neck then ran her fingers up through his hair sifting through the wiry curls trying to convey in return the pleasure he was giving her. She heard him groan in response then he moved to treat the other breast the same way.

Using his other hand, he gently stroked her from her neck down her spine and over her bottom until she quivered with ecstasy.

"Your skin is like silk, my lovely. I want to touch you all over."

So this is what marriage means? For an instant, she shivered with dread as she thought of her remarkable escape from Tenby; then finally Whaley. To have had the baron hold her like this would have been hell on earth and would have meant her death, for no way could she have borne him touching her. Once again, she shivered at the narrow escape she had and pressed closer to the warmth of the man who had saved her.

Despite his intensifying ardour, Tristan felt the quivers. Sensing surprise at his actions and guessing her innocence of lovemaking and possibly her fear, he thought she was still frightened of him. At once, he knew he must quell his impatience to make her his wife and teach her to enjoy his lovemaking. So, step by step, he ensnared her in a web of feeling that so filled her with ecstasy she relaxed and finally let him touch the very centre of her being, where no one else had ever been.

Unexpectedly revelling in the strange reactions that increased with every movement of his long fingers as they penetrated into her tight moist sheath and a thumb that stroked a spot she had no idea she possessed was like the opening of a door when her body all of a sudden took flight and exploded with pleasure. Never had she known such a feeling. As she cried out in surprise, Tristan waited a moment for her climax to recede then moved swiftly over her, parting and raising her legs to allow him access before easing his erection gently a short way inside her helped by her silky wetness.

Catching a glimpse of his size and realising what was about to happen, her eyes opened wide as she felt him filling her. Swiftly bending forward to take her lips, he said, "Relax, my darling, a moment of discomfort then never again."

As he kissed her, he drove deep against the flimsy barrier of her maidenhood; then paused as she flinched and struggled for breath as the unexpected thrust took her virginity with a stab of pain. Drawing slightly back to let her get used to him before resuming his desire to fill her completely, he said, "I'm sorry, my dearest, this is how two people come together and love one another. The first time is always a surprise. Are you all right?"

She nodded, scarcely feeling the pain, only the strange fullness inside her. As he started to thrust again, she began to feel the tension rise within her and, eager to experience the wondrous feeling she had never imagined was possible, encouraged him as he began a rhythm of intense thrusting until once again she was awash with sensation, feeling it build up in anticipation of another climax.

Fiery tension thrummed though them, the conflagration building slowly, layer on layer of consuming heat, of hungry flames until all at once he groaned, "Open your eyes. I need to see you! I need you to know that you are mine and mine alone." His voice was urgent, his whole body on edge with incredible feeling.

Her eyes flickered open, and the sight of him taut with passion was her undoing. Her sheath pulsed around him as she climaxed yet again. He stilled for a second as he felt the ripple of her ecstasy; then, with two more thrusts, he found his own heaven and at once came with her and, flooding her with his seed, they fell into a heated vortex together. Holding her close against his temporarily sated body following the long awaited and the most joyous union he had ever experienced in his life, he said,

"Now do you believe you are truly mine, my wife, and I adore you?"

"Yes, Tristan, at last I do. I honestly never realised what happens between married people, and it has taken me a little while to understand my own feelings, but I can say there is no one else I'd rather be with. I believe I rather like being married."

Having once heard that it was extremely rare for virgins to enjoy a climax, or amazingly two especially for the first time, Tristan was overjoyed. His patience and expertise had brought out a passion that he recognized, in her response to his kisses, was an inherent part of his wife's nature. He was indeed a lucky man, apart from that word 'like'. How long would it take him to make her say she loved him? As for saying it himself, despite the fact he was in thrall to her beauty, he had once vowed it would never pass his lips.

Yet, in that instant of denial, he realised he had never felt such rapture before with any other woman, not even the one he had once thought to make his wife. Daughter of a rich nabob, he had met her in Calcutta and had fallen for her beauty and charms, even owning that he loved her. On the point of asking her to be his wife, he called unexpectedly to her home one day to propose and, while waiting in an anteroom, overheard her harshly and vociferously berating her maid in another part of the house. Finally, he heard the sound of loud, vicious slaps which produced pitiful wails from the servant. At once, he turned and, briefly saying to the major-domo who was in attendance in the hall that other business awaited him, left. Distastefully, his face a grim visage, he returned to his carriage where Roger waited and, with a terse order, directed him to return to their hotel.

Roger silently obeyed whilst wondering what had happened. He had known of the forthcoming proposal, and speculated whether Tristan had been turned down, feeling strangely relieved if that were the case. He had never liked the woman, always feeling that she put on an act to ensnare his master and beneath the charm lay someone quite different.

Shortly after, he realised that Tristan felt the same way, so he was not surprised when orders came to pack and they moved to Delhi.

Apart from farewells to the other Europeans and of course the nabob himself, there was no mention of another meeting with Salinas nor did Tristan say goodbye. Whatever was said afterwards between her and her father, he wanted no part of.

He had always been aware that kindness played no part in the dealings with servants and slaves in Far Eastern countries, but felt it was the male prerogative rather than the female. His own feelings were based on a tradition and upbringing that was a world apart from those customs, and he decided that he would never seek a wife in that part of the world nor confess to a woman he was in love with her. From that time on, any woman he had relations with was purely for his relief and nothing else. So that way of life had continued all the while they had stayed away from England. In the end, Roger wondered if he would ever marry.

Ever considerate of his master's feelings, despite their close relationship, Roger refrained from discussing that particular episode, but privately mourned the fact Tristan was adamant that he would never marry. Following the death of Henry, Roger knew that Tristan would eventually come round to the thought of an heir. He hoped his choice of a wife would please himself as well, though felt it would ruin the close friendship that had been in place for many years. Finding Charis and subsequently and most unexpectedly being a best man at the marriage that occurred between her and his master filled him with joy. She had never attempted to come between Tristan and himself, and had always treated him with great respect. He made it his job to protect her in exactly the same way he always had with Tristan.

Chapter Thirty-Two

It was almost 11 a.m. the following day before Charis sleepily roused as Kate drew the curtains back from the mullioned windows.

"So sorry to disturb you, milady, but milord, your husband, asked me to wake you. He requests you join him downstairs as he needs you to vouch that you are indeed married. Baron Whaley is with him and also two constables. They would not take my word as a witness. They want to see you in person. Milord says to take your time and be comfortable. I have brought you a light breakfast and your bath is run."

Charis sat up and stretched feeling sensitive in places she'd never felt before, and no wonder for Tristan's lovemaking had gone on until almost dawn always making sure she had her own rapturous release before he satisfied himself.

"I can't get enough of you, my darling," he breathed against her lips as he'd taken her for the third time. "Yet I'm sorry, dearest, you will be sore tomorrow. I expect you to forbid me coming near you, in which case I shall despair for I desire you more than ever, if that is possible."

"No, Tristan, I won't forbid you. I never will. You've shown me a passion I never knew existed, and your care makes all the difference." She couldn't believe she had hesitated to marry him, not once but several times. What a disaster it would have been if she hadn't agreed. She still didn't know what the word love meant exactly, but if the overpowering feeling she had to stay close to him was a guide then she was for all time in love with him.

Charis was dressed to perfection in a gown of turquoise silk when she entered the drawing room by noon to find at least three out of the four men were waiting impatiently to see her. If Tristan was also anxious, he did not show it. He sat at ease until she entered then promptly rose, bowed gracefully and reached for her hand which he kissed with great feeling and devotion.

"I trust you are wholly rested, my dear wife. I regret this irksome request to disturb you. These people have an extraordinary impression that we are not married despite all my assurances, even providing witnesses. I have every confidence you'll confirm the true facts and satisfy their curiosity."

Before she could speak, Whaley rose to his feet and butted in. "You can't be married. You know you were betrothed to me! You've never even reached the church for the ceremony!"

"No? You are absolutely sure? How strange! As is the fact you state I'm supposed to have stood before you and verbally agreed to marry you? Even more untrue." Standing erect, her face and posture showing disdainful disapproval, Charis's voice rang out with deep scorn.

"Well, not actually that. Your stepfather agreed for you."

At this reply, the two constables looked at each other and also stood. It wasn't how Whaley had described the betrothal.

"As I understand it, any woman who agrees to a betrothal has to agree in front of witnesses, be it family, guardian or perhaps a legal body," said one. "Can you produce a witness for this agreement?"

"Well, I can't lay me hands on him at present—"

"To whom are you referring?"

"Her stepfather, of course!" Whaley's voice was growing more irate.

"How interesting," interrupted Charis. "Word has it he is dead. Certainly he is not here to testify, though he would be lying if he spoke of a betrothal. But I digress. There was no contract of a betrothal between you and me, and I will swear to that in court. However, a bride agrees a marriage in front of a priest and I *can* produce the priest. I swear with sufficient witnesses to back me up that I am legally married to Tristan Fortesque and carry the title Viscountess Fortesque, with papers to prove it."

She stared at the two constables who were looking decidedly embarrassed. "You've already met my husband, and now have met me. Will that be all, gentlemen, or have you any other business to relate?"

They both shook their heads and hurried to the door. "So sorry, milord, milady, to have disturbed you. We'll show ourselves out."

They opened it to find the butler waiting with a huge scowl on his face. The door closed behind them, and Charis and Tristan turned to face a furious man.

"Satisfied?" Tristan spoke softly.

"Not by a long chalk, I'm not," was the terse answer. "That blasted fool Tenby has done me out of me due reward. Cost me a lot of money, he has. You two had better watch your backs from now on. If you think you can fool me, think again. I ain't done with you yet—"

"Let me inform you I have two men listening close by who have heard your words, Whaley, so I'd be careful how you act from now on. I don't wish to see or hear of you again. Understand me? This matter is now entirely closed! You will never again protest that you've been associated in any way with my wife. The consequences will be dire indeed for you. Roger, Everton, show yourselves." A door leading to a side room opened, and two men emerged and bowed to Tristan.

Tristan nodded. "Send him on his way forthwith!"

Charis watched with awe and relief as Whaley's arms were gripped tightly by the men, and he was frogmarched outside and thence across the hall and out to the drive where his coach was waiting. There was no doubt her husband handled things with style.

Tristan smiled affectionately and held out a hand to Charis. "Come, my lady wife, I think an early luncheon is ready. That little scene has given me an appetite, and I wish to drink your health for the graceful and most telling way you put the baron to flight. I am proud of you."

"And I, my dear husband, feel the same for you, and also am delighted to tell you I am entranced with the way you deal with your problems." Her eyes rolled with mirth, and she beamed enticingly at him. "Even if I insist you admit I'm the clever one in this family."

"Oh yes?" He raised his brow. "How do you make that out?"

"My amazing ability to climb into a luggage boot!"

Those around in Castle House were intrigued at the peals of laughter that echoed through the rooms of the house as their Lord and Lady went in to luncheon.

That evening, when Charis was dressing for dinner, Tristan knocked and entered her room. Presenting her with a flat jeweller's case he said, "A birthday gift which I should have given you this morning but for the pressure we were under. Father has also planned our dinner tonight so that equally shall be a surprise. I'm sorry we could not have your grandmother join us, but we shall celebrate with her later. Meanwhile, Happy Birthday, my darling. I hope you like it."

Charis opened the case and, with a startled gasp, saw a large pearl held within a circle of diamonds that would hang from a delicate gold chain. Twin earbobs fashioned to match the necklet lay alongside. "Oh, Tris, it's a beautiful gift. I shall treasure it always."

"A beautiful gift for a beautiful lady, I should emphasise! Let me help you put them on, and we will join Father and enjoy his good wishes too. These special two days will be remembered on our calendar for evermore, my love. A story to tell your children and grandchildren in the years to come."

"Hmm, and one that has a happy ending." She smiled joyfully as she took his arm to go down to dinner.

Book Two

Autumn 1833

Chapter Thirty-Three

A cold wind was blowing off the sea, and the emaciated and unkempt man hiding in a coppice on the edge of the estate shivered as he stared at the sight in front of him. He could scarcely believe his eyes at the change that had taken place in Carwinnion since he had last lived there. The fields were now ploughed and sown with crops; the house was painted; and Tenby could see new tiling where the roof had been freshly repaired. Ruefully, he thought of the money that had been spent, money that he felt should have been his – or at least paying his enormous debt to Whaley. Fortunately, that treacherous man or the men he had seen standing in the distance on the riverbank did not know he had survived his plunge into the fast running river which had swept him downstream far enough to connect with the River Chew. Hanging onto a broken limb of a tree which hid his body, he had kept afloat until, spying a battered skiff on the bank, he headed for the shore and thence, by paddling the small boat, proceeded much further down the river until he met the confluence of the River Avon.

He couldn't recall how long it had taken, but eventually he ended up in the Bristol dockyards. By dint of punishing labouring, he earned enough to eat and survive for a bit longer. Finally, he took a job on a tramp steamer and worked his way down the coast to Falmouth where he jumped ship after relieving the crew of some of their hard-earned money. Knowing the area, he was out of town before he could be traced, and was now surveying the ruin of all his hopes.

Nightfall arrived, and a quick and silent scout round the house revealed it was empty of people apart from a watchman dozing by his brazier. It was the work of moments to gain access to the study, pull up the loose floorboard, and lift out the bag of money he had cached there.

With luck, he would have enough to get him to London where he knew he would find the two people he hated most in the world and there do them the utmost harm he could manage.

Chapter Thirty-Four

It took five weeks before Tristan was happy that the town house in Belgrave Square was in first-rate order for him to take his new bride to London to enjoy the revels and partying that were a part of the Season. They'd spent the earlier time at Castle House where Charis endeared herself even closer to Amery, and Tristan was pleased his father was in such good spirits and feeling better. So much so that Amery decided he would join the young pair and enjoy a taste of London, if only for a short time and at least ensure his daughter-in-law was launched into society with all due respect under his sponsorship.

Caroline had reached the city a little earlier along with her cousin Leticia Manville and was staying in their town house. Edwin preferred his country life more than heated ballrooms of the *ton*, and though he was able to make use of the card rooms, inevitably he became bored and longed for the peace of the countryside. Leticia, knowing he would be tetchy if put under too much stress, agreed he could come up later in the Season for a short time. In any case, having such a large family, she and Caroline had escorts in plenty and did not miss Edwin at all.

Caroline was at first annoyed and disappointed by the change of plans, but then was consoled that the girl had done very well for herself by marrying into such a high-born and wealthy family. She admitted, but only to herself, that she could not have done better and probably a good deal worse, as her credentials, while not to be sneered at, were not top-drawer. In any case, she'd not had the rearing of her granddaughter, and indeed the child was a virtual stranger. She just hoped, for all their sakes, that Charis behaved in a style suitable to her rank, though she doubted it would be possible.

Tristan had no doubts whatsoever that his wife would act with elegance. Her display of character in front of Tenby showed, beyond question, her faultless ancestry. Tracing her mother Cecile's family had proved enlightening. Cecile was the granddaughter of the Marquis de Contades and, as a child, was brought up in the splendid Loire Chateau Montgeoffroy. Her French training would have been impeccable.

How Cecile had met David Langdon and married him, he had no idea, although with the subsequent defeat of Napoleon at Waterloo, France would already have been in turmoil, and it was likely that David had saved Cecile from catastrophe. Charis conversed in French like an aristocrat, and her etiquette were no less adept, so Cecile had obviously passed on her traditions to Charis from babyhood. Tristan felt sad he'd never known Cecile. One more reason to despise that evil cur Tenby.

As he escorted his wife down the stairs to the ballroom in the Cholmondeley town house, their commitment for that evening, the butler sang out their names, and instantly all eyes turned to survey the beauty who was descending on her husband's arm.

Tristan felt Charis's anxious quiver and whispered, "Take heart, dearest." Feeling her hand grip his arm in reply, he knew she would respond with courage.

They stopped to talk with the marquess and his wife, Frederick and Diana Cholmondeley. Frederick was a long-time friend, and he and his wife had welcomed Charis with open arms. As they exchanged greetings, Tristan noted the buzz of conversation in the background and guessed the town rakes and libertines, distinguished only by the titles they owned, were lining up to either glimpse or dance with his wife. He was thankful he knew the score and could control the situation. Taking her firmly by the hand, he led her to the Manville family and thankfully became part of their entourage.

Both Caroline and Leticia greeted Charis with loving hugs, saying how charming she looked and how pleased they were to see her before introducing both Charis and Tristan to the family they were with. Caroline noted the specially designed pale aquamarine gown she wore and particularly the diamond necklace and earrings; and, amazingly, the diamond bandeau that gleamed amidst the golden curls of her hairdo. A positive fortune, she thought, in jewellery. She was not to know that Charis had gasped in wonder as Tristan had presented the set to her.

"Part of my mother's jewels. I had them cleaned and thought they would suit your gown."

"Oh, Tristan! Are you sure...?"

"That they will suit?" He grinned. "Or that they are yours?"

"But they are too valuable..." she gasped.

"And absolutely right for my wife who is also valuable, to me at any rate. You look ravishing in that gown, and if it were not your first ball and you are dressed accordingly, I would have it off in a trice and hang attending a scandal-ridden melee that delights in gossip. Don't pay attention to being the prize of the evening, for people will settle down from here on. Enjoy the evening, and be assured I will be on guard."

"I know you will, darling, and, truly, I am not frightened."

She was, but determined not to show it or let him down. Then a distant memory surfaced and she heard a voice in her mind saying: *Face each day with courage, ma petit Chou, and your demons will fly away and leave you free. Never fear anything or anybody. You come from a noble family and will bear life with fortitude.*

The sweet but sad voice from long ago: her dearest mama. Recalling the teaching and happy days of her childhood, she made up her mind that any child she had would likewise be blessed and loved even as she had been – at least, until her stepfather had appeared with his coarse ways and cane. Despite her bravery, he had brought fear to her mother although Cecile faced up to him before her death. Charis vowed she would be as brave as her mother, and would always uphold her husband and make him proud of her.

That evening was successful, and so were many more occasions as society extended invitations until, one evening, Charis stood at the top of the stairs freshly gowned and heaved a tired sigh. Tristan, following behind her, said, "What's the matter, Charis? Don't you feel well?"

"Please don't worry about me. I'm all right; only a little sad."

"Good heavens, sad? What's troubling you, darling?" He turned her about and stared into her eyes.

"I was thinking of walking on a deserted beach, the sound of waves..." All at once, a tear trembled on her lash and ran down her face.

"My dearest, I know what's wrong. You miss Carwinnion, don't you? Don't fret. The repairs are in hand, and I promise I will take you back to see everything as soon as I receive word the place is finished. But it's more than that, isn't it? You are tired of London, are you not?"

"I suppose so. Tired of people; tired of remembering names, of saying the right thing. Just tired, I expect." She yawned, and then said, "We are due at the Northcliffes', and we had better not be late."

"I'll send our apologies if you prefer?" Tristan studied her face.

"No, we'll go. It's too late to make excuses. I'd hate to spoil milady's dinner table arrangements."

He chuckled. "And if you fall asleep over the soup, what then?"

She stared at him in horror. "I won't do that! How awful!"

"I promise we'll leave directly after the meal...or before if you fall into the soup!" Tristan carried on laughing as he took her arm to guide her downstairs. The staff around at the time smiled in delight to see their happy faces, for each of them treasured their Lord and Lady.

In the hall, Charis waited while Tristan draped a silk cloak round her shoulders then donned his coat. Parsons, the butler, opened the door and Tristan, stepping over the threshold, was turning to take his wife's arm to escort her to the coach when a shot rang out. A bullet, narrowly missing him, ploughed into the door.

In a split second, Tristan grabbed Charis round the waist and flung them both back into the hall. His impetus sent him plunging to the floor, but he was able to keep his wife on top of him and so stop her from taking harm. They ended up sliding across the marble floor where his head made contact with an ornate table on the opposite wall. "Shut the door!" he yelled, despite being dazed by the blow. "We have a shooter out there!"

Parsons had already reacted and slammed the door; then was going to help the sprawling pair when a hubbub and violent knocking on it made him glance askance at Tristan.

"Open the door, Parsons, it will be the grooms. I'll see to Her Ladyship." Edging out from under, Tristan helped Charis to stand then smiled in reassurance before whispering, "I should have taken the dress off first!"

"Oh fiddlesticks, Tris, you are quite incorrigible!" Gamely, she tried to respond to his repartee but, noting her blanching face, he held her close to him while he issued orders.

His secretary, hearing the noise, was already in the hall. "Watson, send a note to the Northcliffes to say we regret our last-minute cancellation due to unforeseen circumstances. Ring for Kate then call the doctor."

"Milord," said Parsons, "shall I call for the constabulary?"

"No, I think not for the moment. We shall investigate it without due disturbance from strangers."

"Tristan! I don't need a doctor! I'm not hurt, really I'm not."

"You might not need one, but I do," he pretended, unwilling to argue with her in front of the staff. "I'm not fond of guns!"

"Oh, dear God!" Trembling with fright, she looked at him aghast. "Have you been shot? Quickly, show me where..." Her face whitened more than ever.

"Charis, I haven't been shot, just bruised from the fall...come, my dear, let Kate take you upstairs to recover and change your gown. We are staying home tonight. I will see to things here; then we shall have supper upstairs together later." He handed his wife over to her maid. "See she is made comfortable, Kate. I shall be up soon."

Reluctantly, Charis turned to the stairs. "If you are sure you haven't been hurt..."

"I'm perfectly sure, my love. When do you ever find me at a loss?" He smiled beguilingly. "We are lucky, aren't we? We can take advantage of an early night!"

Chapter Thirty-Five

Tristan was in his study drinking a brandy and pondering the recent event. He'd finished questioning the grooms who had searched the area thoroughly, but they had found no trace of the assassin. At least, he presumed it was an assassin. Taking a sudden shot at someone leaving their home made no sense unless they meant to kill. He thought back to the other attempts on his life, and knew that fate or chance, call it what you will, had saved him. His worry now was not for himself but his beloved wife. If he was in danger then so was she.

A knock at the door presaged Parsons. "Dr Brunton, milord."

"Come in, doctor, take a seat. Sorry to call you out so late but we've had a slight predicament with a shooting. No," he held up his hand, "no one shot, but it was a close call." He went on to describe the incident. "I really called you out on a pretext, though my head seems to have taken the brunt of the exercise when I took a dive into the hall."

"Yes, I can see." Brunton stepped forward and moved Tristan's head gently forward and traced the blood that was staining his collar. "You've had a hard wallop, milord. It will need a stitch or two."

Tristan frowned. "Oh, do you think so? It's not hurting quite so much now and, anyway, that is not the reason I called you."

"We'll deal with this first then you can tell me the rest. If you'll ring for your butler, I'd like some boiling water and towels sent in."

While Brunton was working on the sutures, he said, "So, tell me the prime reason you sent for me, milord."

"My wife unfortunately fell with me, but luckily I kept her on top and, although she was shocked, I do not think she has suffered any damage. However, she was complaining of feeling tired shortly before, and I would feel happier if you checked her over."

"Hmm, you've married recently, I gather."

"Yes, some three months ago. Could it be…?" Tristan stopped as an unexpected thought struck him.

"Yes, it could, but wives do like to be the bearer of that kind of news. I will check, but if I just return and say she is in good health…I would expect you to accept that."

"Yes, I understand." Tristan nodded. "However, if she is *enceinte*, I will want you to keep an eye on her. She tends to be self-reliant so either may not know or won't tell me for fear I may fuss."

"It's a natural process, milord. I do not recommend fussing. In fact, the more a woman keeps to her natural way of living the better chance she will have of an easy birth. Walking, gentle and safe riding, at least in the early stages until increased size makes it uncomfortable. Go on as usual but making sure she has more rest."

"And lovemaking?" Tristan was now feeling anxious.

"Why not? You both need the comfort of each other. But we are pre-empting a diagnosis. I'll see her now and make sure all is in order, and also assure her you are still in the land of the living. Young brides want to know that sort of thing." He grinned at Tristan who suddenly felt better he had called in a doctor with modern ideas.

"Do you know a Richard Marshall in your line of work?"

"Why yes, I interned with him at Guys. Heard he had gone to Devon. Great fellow, we got on well."

"How lucky that is! He happens to be our doctor at home. I'll let him know I've met you, and perhaps you'll pay us a visit some time?" Tristan stood and held out his hand. "I'll see you before you go?"

"Surely will, milord. I hope your expectations come true."

A short while later Brunton returned to the study, and Tristan bade him sit and take a glass of sherry.

"Thank you, but no, milord. I have patients to visit and breathing alcohol fumes over them is hardly conducive for them to trust me. As for your wife, yes, she is tired, but I would say in reasonable good health. I think she has had enough of the London Season, and perhaps some country air would be beneficial."

"And?" Tristan stared expectantly at the doctor.

"And confidentiality is my motto. I'll leave you to draw your own conclusions, milord, but feel that she will be safe in your hands if you follow my previous words. No fussing, just good old-fashioned loving is always the best tonic; but call me if you need me." Dr Brunton rose, bowed to Tristan, and turned to the door. "I hope to see you again, sir, at a more pleasurable time. But, meanwhile, convey my regards to Richard. She will be safe in his hands. He is an excellent doctor."

After the doctor had gone, Tristan sat for a moment contemplating the future. So they were to be parents. His father would be delighted.

A little while later, after arranging for the house to be secured and a watch kept, Tristan ordered supper then went upstairs to be greeted by his anxious wife who gasped at seeing his bloodstained collar. "Oh darling, your poor head. If I had seen that before I would have been sure you had been shot. The doctor told me what was wrong and that he has stitched the cut. Thank you for saving me. That marble floor is very hard, and if I had fallen on it..." She paused.

He stared intently. "And if you had fallen...?" he continued.

"I would not be feeling as comfortable as I am now." She smiled. "Have your bath then we shall eat and enjoy a peaceful evening. How wonderful to be by ourselves and not have to converse politely."

"I see. Should we converse impolitely? I'll look forward to that. By the way, I did not order soup." He grinned at her surprised look.

"You are, without doubt, a most maddening husband. No, I shall never fall in the soup," she giggled, "but make haste, My Lord. I am very hungry and look forward to a tasty supper and to regale you with the most impolite conversation I can manage."

He laughed as he reached out and drew her into his arms to kiss her ardently. "I fear *I* will become more impolite as the evening passes, in the nicest possible way, of course."

Her peals of delighted laughter followed him as he went for his bath, but his thoughts turned serious as he realised she'd had the opportunity to tell him she was pregnant but did not take advantage.

Why not? She must know by now; the doctor would have been sure to explain her condition. Oh well, the evening was young. She would probably wait for the right time to announce the news.

Much later, awake and wondering, he lay by his sleeping wife. The evening had indeed been warm and loving and carried on to be superbly passionate once they went to bed. She was now curled spoon-shaped against his chest, and his possessive hand lay warmly across her bare stomach where he imagined his heir was lying secure. He drifted off to sleep still trying to speculate what was in her mind.

Early the next morning, Tristan gave orders to the staff to pack. He had decided they would be returning to Castle House.

By lunchtime, Charis was settled in the big coach rather taken aback that her request to ride had been vetoed.

"You are tired, my sweet," Tristan said. "I think you should sleep while we journey. You need to be fresh to see Father."

She gave in. Unsurprisingly, she was feeling a little unwell and consequently felt very drowsy.

Chapter Thirty-Six

Fortesque's team of horses pulling the travelling coach were well matched, and Everton's handling of them was superb but, shortly before Glastonbury where Tristan had decided to spend the night, Everton was startled by a knocking on the roof to stop the coach. Instantly, he reacted, and the vehicle came to an abrupt halt causing the outriders to swing around haphazardly as they wondered what was amiss.

"Her Ladyship wishes to walk," explained Kate in a loud voice, and immediately a groom descended from the back of the coach and pulled out the steps as the door opened hastily and Charis emerged in a hurry and made for the woods lining the road followed by her maid.

Everton grinned to himself. *Sudden call of nature*, he guessed. *Obviously can't wait until we reach our inn. Oh well, gives the team a breather, and me also as I've kept them up to speed as ordered.* Then, seeing his master coming back from where he had been scouting the road ahead, he said, "No worries, milord, Her Ladyship is taking a stroll."

"What the devil?" Tristan stared at Everton who just shrugged. "Oh, I see." He dismounted. Handing the reins to a groom, he walked across into the woodland. He hadn't gone far before he heard the sound of retching and, emerging into a glade, saw his wife bent over in distress. Kate stood nearby looking worried.

"Fetch some water from the coach, Kate. I'll see to Her Ladyship." He bent over Charis and held her head with one hand while his other cradled her waist and took her weight.

After a moment or two of dry heaves, she sighed and stood erect. "Thank you, I'm feeling better now," she said wiping her lips with a wisp of a handkerchief. He handed her his large clean one, and she took it with a wan smile, her face still looking ashen.

184

"Darling, you should have told me earlier if you did not feel well. We could have stopped at the last posting house, except I wanted to reach Glastonbury and a hotel where you would be comfortable. Kate is fetching some water. Let us sit over here while you recover." He led her to a fallen tree and urged her to sit down beside him.

She took his hand and, heaving a huge sigh, said, "I don't care for coaches these days. I never used to be seasick but, after a while, they seem like a never-ending rough boat journey. Perhaps that ride in your boot is still with me. I did so want to ride, but you wouldn't let me."

"I'm sorry, Charis, but you seemed tired and after that upset..." He paused, still waiting for her to acknowledge her pregnancy. Surely she realised what had caused her sickness? Had the doctor told her? Or did she hate the idea so much she was refusing to accept it?

"Oh that!" She laughed. "Once you bustled us all to leave London, I knew you were taking care not to be in range of any other bullets, and as we will be safe at Castle House I have not worried. How is your head? Should *you* not be resting in the coach instead of riding?" She smirked, looking more like her usual self.

"It seems to me if you are able to joke then it's time we carried on our journey. It's only about five miles more and I will join you in the coach and see how seaworthy it is. I have to confess it has never made me seasick, but then I ride outside more often than not. Perhaps, if you are good," he grinned at her, "I will allow you to ride the rest of the way home tomorrow."

"If I am good...!" She squealed as he swung her up in his arms and began walking back to join his men. "Sir! I did not promise to obey you when I made my vows. If you remember, I coughed when it came to that part and did not voice the word when I was asked by the priest, so from now on consult me and I will let you know if I agree."

"Baggage!" He pinched her bottom and she squealed again. "We shall see about that, my errant wife. Later tonight, when I have you at my mercy, you'll agree to all I desire." He smirked back and was rewarded by her giggle.

"And if I don't?" The riposte came out before she could stop it or add anything else as a wave of nausea beset her again.

He looked down at her face which had swiftly turned white again and felt an icy shiver run through his veins. Had she married him under sufferance? Would this pregnancy set her against him? If it did, his marriage could turn out to be a dreadful mistake that would blight both of their lives? And not only theirs but his father's too.

"Madam, your wish, as always, is yours to command."

She stared up at his grey eyes which had turned to flint. He had taken her words awry. "Put me down please. I'm going to be sick again."

Chapter Thirty-Seven

Tenby loitered in an alleyway leading to the mews that served to stable horses and carriages for the rich owners of properties in Belgrave Square and scratched his lice-ridden head angrily, thinking of the rough lodgings he had to put up with these days. Dusk had deepened the shadows, and he felt safe enough to once more survey the town house of the Fortesques. Last night, he had seen the viscount fall back into the hall following his shot, so hopefully that had put paid to him. Though, strangely, there was no word on the street about his death. Still, the nobility could command secrecy if they desired, and he could well be mortally wounded and close to death. Now, all he had to do was to get his hands on Charis, and he would take the next part of his revenge. He licked his lips in anticipation and edged closer along the street until he was standing opposite the mansion hidden in the shrubbery fronting another town house.

He stared at the windows. How queer; they were shuttered and blank showing no lights. His eyes went to the door and realised the large commanding door knocker had been removed, indicating to callers that the family was not in residence. Not merely in mourning, but gone.

Gone! How was it possible? It wasn't even twenty-four hours since he had stood in this same position and lined up his shot. Admittedly only barely within range, but then he had always prided himself on his knack of marksmanship. The place seemed empty but, to verify the fact, he scuttled hastily across the road and headed for the rear of the property where he found only a single light of a caretaker in the servants' quarters. Christ and damnation! They *were* gone! But where?

As he stood debating his next move, he felt a hard hand grasp his shoulder and a knife edge slide below his chin. "What the hell...!" he gasped. "Who are you? What d'ye want?" He tried to turn to see his assailant but the knife pressed even closer to his flesh.

"Stand still, you misbegotten pig shit! I've been watching you for the past week wondering what you were up to but, damn it, never thought you'd try anything as bloody stupid as to fire at a front door."

"I wasn't firing at the door but at His Lordship. Hit him 'n all!" Tenby claimed, instinctively feeling that it wasn't the law he had to deal with, keeping his right hand that held his cane firmly down by his side. Given the opportunity, he'd make short work of whoever this was.

"Daft bugger! Of course you didn't hit him, and now him and his wife and servants have left London for a place much more secure than this. You've spoilt my plans big time with your damned interference."

The bitter voice sounded educated, so Tenby took a chance. "I'm sorry, Your Lordship, you should have spoken up earlier. Could it be we are of the same mind? Do we want the same thing? Namely, the demise of Viscount Fortesque? I'd appreciate you leaving my throat intact so we can talk about it."

"Drop your cane and I'll think about it. One stupid move and I won't hesitate to forget you ever existed," retorted the pitiless voice.

Tenby promptly dropped the cane. "I wasn't going to use it, sir," he whined, "but I've got this gammy leg—"

"Yes, I saw you twisting your ankle as you ran yesterday. Nearly got caught too, didn't you? Lucky for you the grooms didn't see where you slipped to or you'd be worrying more about a rope round your neck than my knife if they'd caught up with you. Right, come with me. I'll give you five minutes of my time to listen to your tale. Don't do anything stupid, mind. I'm good at throwing knives as well."

The knife retreated, and the hand came off his shoulder as the speaker stooped and picked up the cane. Tenby turned round and eyed him carefully, somewhat surprised to see a stocky, well-muscled man of middling years wearing good quality town clothes rather than someone who looked like an obvious criminal. With a toss of his head, he indicated to Tenby the direction they were to take and, before long, Tenby found himself in a walk-up flat somewhere in a cluster of buildings not far from Belgrave Square. The flat was clean and reasonably well-appointed with plain but serviceable furniture.

"Take a seat and start talking," the man said harshly. "Who are you, and what's your business with the Fortesques?"

Despite being loath to divulge much to a stranger, Tenby felt he might find out more of this individual if he offered something himself. In any case, menaced by the knife that was still on show, he did not want to aggravate the situation. "I'm Her Ladyship's stepfather. I almost died by her hand, and I wanted to get even with her and kill him as well."

"Why kill him?"

"Well, he married the chit, didn't he? Lost me a lot of money in the doing of it. Ruined me, in fact." Tenby's reply was surly.

"Ah yes, I recall your misdeed of trying to sell your stepdaughter for a goodly sum. Hardly the most charitable act towards a relative." The raised eyebrows were disdainful. "However, your debts were becoming perilous, I believe."

"Yes, well, I wasn't aiming to go to a debtors' prison, was I? Now, I'm just as bad off; skint, and likely to stay that way. All I have is revenge, and even that's been set at naught," Tenby said truculently.

"Maybe not, if you are prepared to work for me and take orders."

At that remark, Tenby visibly brightened. "Yes, sir, I'll take orders, but who will I be working for, if you don't mind me asking?"

Gazing thoughtfully back at Tenby for a moment, the man said, "You can call me Mr Reg. You don't need to know more than that, but what you do need to know is if you cross me or fail to do as you are told then I make a bad enemy. On the other hand, you'll earn, and I'll pay your keep. I have a spare room here, and I'll kit you out in fresh clothes. Is it a bargain, Tenby?"

With a sigh of relief, Tenby nodded and held out his hand. "It's a bargain, sir. I'm grateful for the chance. I'll do anything you say."

"Right, we have a bargain. See that you do." Mr Reg glanced down at Tenby's grubby hand and, declining to shake it, said, "I think a bath is in order before we proceed further. My man will show you the ropes. Obey him precisely. He runs this place exactly how I prefer." He went to the wall and rang a bell. When the manservant answered it, he said. "This is Tom Tenby. See he is clean before he touches anything. I'll be back in half an hour with fresh garments. When he is dressed, he will eat with you in the kitchen. That is all, Wallace. I rely on you to keep him in order."

Wallace bowed silently and gestured to Tenby to follow him.

Bloody hell, thought Tenby. *Back to the flaming schoolroom with a vengeance. Still, it's fine for now. I'll bide me time and see how I get on. I can always scarper when I need to.*

Chapter Thirty-Eight

Tristan dispatched one of his men to ensure their accommodation was secure in the Glastonbury hotel and, once she'd recovered from the second spell of sickness, made his wife comfortable in the coach which began travelling at a slower speed to make her feel easier. A little later, safely arriving at the George and Pilgrim, Charis was urged to rest in bed until she felt better. Grateful to lie down in a bed that did not rock, she soon fell asleep. Kate knocked on the door opening to the adjoining parlour to let His Lordship know that his wife was feeling recovered and was resting quietly.

Tristan beckoned her in and bade her sit. "Kate, what caused Her Ladyship to be so sick?"

"Mushrooms, I reckon, milord," she replied, uneasy to be sitting in his presence.

"Mushrooms?" He was taken aback. "What makes you say that?"

"She doesn't like 'em, or they don't like her. There was some in a particular dish which she ate when she was at the Manvilles', and I recall she was very sick that night. She said she usually avoids them."

"When did she have them recently?"

"You ordered them when you had supper sent up in your room." Kate blushed uncomfortably. "Maybe I shouldn't say, milord, but you persuaded Her Ladyship to try them as you felt they were so good, and as she has such a kind heart she did not want to disappoint you."

Tristan felt a wave of deep regret wash over him as he recognized it was his fault, and she wasn't having his child after all.

"What did the doctor say to my wife when he saw her? I presume you were in attendance?"

"Asked her some personal questions..." Kate blushed again.

"Took her pulse...to be truthful, I was standing over the other side of the room and did not hear all he had to say. But she seemed relieved when he told her that you were not badly injured and explained about the cut. That's about all, milord."

"Thank you, Kate. Tell Her Ladyship when she wakes we will dine in here when she is ready. Let me know if this suits. In the meantime, I will be absent until later."

On his way to meet Roger in the stable mews, Tristan pondered on the conversation he'd had with the doctor as he left after visiting with Charis. What had the doctor really said to him? Tristan tried to recall his words and concluded he'd said nothing about a pregnancy; only that she was tired of London. It seemed he had got it wrong. His only advice was no fussing and that good old-fashioned loving was the best thing. Well, that went without saying. Loving, he could certainly give her, and plenty of it. Up until now, he had not given a thought to them having children. He was enjoying his wife too much to worry about consequences, but now the idea was in the forefront of his mind, he suddenly yearned for that event to become real. Though together with that thought was an uncomfortable feeling that maybe he ought to ask his wife if she wanted a child now, or should they postpone it until a later date. It would mean he would have to take care, or indeed refrain from touching her altogether. Oh God, married life was hell.

Roger was sitting at ease in the public bar at the back of the hotel, a place available for the coachmen and grooms while waiting on their betters. He took one look at his master, gestured to his tankard, and said, "Will you join me, milord? It's quiet here at the moment, the beer is tolerable, and I doubt you'll get better inside."

Tristan nodded and chose a seat beside his groom. When his ale arrived, he took a large swallow; then wiped his mouth and sighed. "Yes, you are right. The beer is good. One can't beat Somerset ale."

"How is Her Ladyship?" Roger asked.

"Resting now, but I think recovering from the stomach upset. It was mushrooms so Kate tells me; seems they affect her badly. I never knew. In fact, there is probably a lot I don't know about my new wife." He sighed again.

"Time will cure that problem, sir," said Roger quietly.

"Yes, undoubtedly. Now, about tomorrow. I'll let Charis ride with us.

The next stretch is not that far to Taunton where we'll rest up and wait for the coach. Then, if she is still able to carry on, we can go on to Castle House the day after. I feel she will be happier riding than in the coach. I have to admit it does have a deal of sway, and I suspect it did not help her nausea. Are your quarters comfortable?"

"Yes, milord, we are placed nicely, thank you. I'll set the guards as necessary and make sure all is secure."

"Good. Perhaps we left too soon for anyone to follow us."

"That sudden departure would surprise anyone," Roger said. "It definitely took us by surprise, though I ought to know you well enough by now to know you never take the obvious path." He grinned. "Keeps us on our toes, and that's no bad thing at this moment. I'll make certain everyone keeps alert."

Tristan took another swallow of ale and envisaged the shooting as he had stood at his front door. It might have been fatal this time, as indeed the other attempts at killing him could have been. Who the devil wanted him dead? And why? A thought struck him, and he said, "Roger, even though Castle House is relatively secure, I particularly don't want to take chances with my wife's safety. Until we find out who is after – well, I presume me, it could possibly turn really nasty and involve Charis as well, so we must investigate anyone who might be the culprit. I won't rest until he is caught. I won't tell her directly, but she must be guarded at all times. Don't make it obvious, but so manage it that she is never out on her own. It puts a burden on you, but nothing you can't manage with your usual deviousness." He smirked at Roger then went on, "We made a few enemies out East but no one, I believe, would carry on a vendetta and follow us back here, so it has to be someone from this part of the world."

"It could be that Tenby fellow. We never found a trace of him. Yet he had to get from Bath to London, and I'll bet he hadn't a penny piece on him if he ever got out of that river. If it is him, he'll have to get from London down here, and I can't see that happening in a hurry unless he does a quick job of thieving which I wouldn't put past him." Roger shook his head in puzzlement. "Well, whoever it is, we'll put up a barrier that a rat can't slide through, and maybe we'll catch the blighter. I'll keep the lads primed and ready, so rest easy, milord."

"I know you will, Roger. I'll be off and change for dinner. Make sure you all get your vittles, and the men are well housed. See you early tomorrow. I've had enough of this journey and want to be home." Tristan rose and made his way back to his rooms, hoping that he would find Charis feeling a great deal better than earlier that day.

She was waiting for him in the parlour after he'd had a bath and changed, and he was pleased to see her looking more her usual self. She was wrapped in a full-length silk gown tightly buttoned all the way down the front from her throat to the hem. With her hair tied in loose curls, she looked beautiful. He hardened instantly and, drawing her close in his arms, said, "Darling Charis, the change is magical."

"Watching me cast up my accounts this morning was not the most edifying of sights, My Lord," she said pertly as she hugged him.

He threw back his head and gave a great shout of laughter. "Charis, where did you hear that expression? Not generally a term used by the ladies who attend Almack's, I collect."

"It was used by mostly everyone in Cornwall, or at least the part I came from. So much nicer than saying one was heaving one's guts up! However, I perceive I've still said the wrong thing." She scowled and drew back from him. "How would you describe that appalling situation which embarrassed me dreadfully?"

"I'm teasing you, sweetheart. I would have said the same as you, or possibly used the second description depending on whom I addressed. This reminds me, I have an apology to make. I'm sorry I made you taste those mushrooms. I had no idea they would affect you so badly. You must always tell me if there is something you don't like. I have a hatred for turnips as I once had to exist on them for over a week when we got lost taking a field trip to an outlying village in India. It took twice that time for my stomach to settle afterwards."

"You must have enjoyed many adventures when you were out East," she said wistfully.

"Some, yes. But not as much as enjoying life with you, sweet. Don't fret. I'll take you travelling once we get over..." He stopped.

"...someone trying to kill you, I believe you were going to say. I overheard you declaring to Roger this was one attempt too many and you've had enough, which made me chase everyone into action when you said we had to leave even though my stomach was upset."

"Most efficiently done too, My Lady. I was impressed. However," his eyes narrowed and he frowned, "the last time you eavesdropped, you ran away. I hope I shan't have to chase you again."

"No, My Lord," she said haughtily, "things are different now. I am your wife and, as I am supposed to trust you, I also expect you to trust me. Don't change the subject. How many attempts, sir?"

He stared back at her wondering how he should answer; then decided the truth should be the only way to deal. "I think three so far with a question mark over a fourth."

"And you have no idea who it is?"

"Unfortunately, no. Whilst I have had some difficult assignments abroad, I can't recall making an enemy who would follow me here."

All of a sudden, he thought of his brother and his face blanched. She stared at his grim face thinking the worst. "Tristan! Is it someone you know? That we both know? Is it my stepfather? Or, heaven forbid, Baron Whaley? He did threaten us."

"As far as Whaley is concerned, he has returned to Cornwall. Also, he knows I would send Roger after him."

He shook his head, tried to govern his face to show he was still calm. "Unfortunately, Tenby's whereabouts is unknown at present, that is, if he survived the river without drowning. Apart from the last attempt at our house, the others were made before I knew either of those men. So, I don't think it concerns you directly, but there is more, Charis. I am loath to tell you, but it will serve as a warning to take great care. I believe my brother was murdered."

She gasped and put her hand out to take his. "Oh, Tris, how awful for you. Whom do you suspect? Can you prove anything?"

He put his arm round her and sat them down on a couch. "Sadly, I can't prove anything beyond a suspicion someone may want to become an earl. A distant member of my family might inherit if either my father or I were dead. I am more concerned about you if you should bear a child. Your life could be in danger too. Not that we need worry about that at present." He felt her jerk in shock.

"Oh dear, perhaps we do." Tears welled in her eyes and ran down her cheeks. "I was going to wait until I was absolutely sure, and made the doctor promise not to say anything, but I fear I am increasing and will indeed become a worry to you."

He stared at her in astonishment before pulling out his handkerchief to mop her eyes. "Oh, darling, what wonderful news. I couldn't be happier. I hope you are too. I did wonder when you were sick; then you said it was the mushrooms so I put the thought out of my mind, but now..." He held her close in his arms and kissed her wet cheeks before finding her mouth and kissing her till she was glowing. After taking a breath, he said, "When will you definitely know?"

"Quite soon now, so the doctor said. Although I was sick with the mushrooms, I feel fine, though I do get sleepy and hungry at odd times. Speaking of which, do you think we can eat now?"

He laughed again with delight. "Certainly." He rose and led her to the table. "I have a notion to feed you on nectar, I am so pleased."

She stared at the laden table and, smiling, said, "I think this food is more to my taste at present, but after supper maybe there will be different tastes to enjoy." Her eyes twinkled with promise.

"Hmm," he smoothed his hands over her silk clad shoulders before pulling out a chair for her to sit, "I'll have quite a task undoing all those buttons on your gown. You have dressed to tease, but no doubt I'll manage," he vowed with assurance as he bent to kiss the soft skin on her neck and fondle her curls. "Nevertheless, you must get plenty of sleep tonight as we shall be away early tomorrow morning. Don't forget your habit as you have my permission to ride tomorrow."

"Your permission?" Taken aback, she stared at him in disbelief.

"Naturally, Charis. Permission always has to be given to the grooms to ready a horse for riding." His lips curled with humour.

She decided not to embark on an argument as he was in such a good mood. Besides, she wanted her night to be filled with joy, not bad feeling, but she vowed to change his high-handed ways before too long. She had enough of being oppressed by a man.

After a comfortable sleep, she ate an early light breakfast, and was dressed and down at the stable with him to watch Butterfly being led out. At once, she looked intently at her saddle. "That's not right. She's got a side saddle on. I am going to ride astride. See, I have my divided skirt."

"I think not, Charis. Don't forget your condition," Tristan replied.

"My condition! What condition?" she retorted.

"Do you wish me to shout it to the world?" he said quietly.

She blushed with vexation. "Oh, that condition. Well no, I don't want to mention it to anyone at present! I've only just started a baby. I am not an invalid, and I see nothing wrong with riding astride."

"Except these are early days, and I wish my heir to be comfortable and not leave us too soon. I promise not to fuss you too much, but in this instance you either ride side-saddle or go in the coach." His face was set and his tone adamant.

"Oh, very well, I'll ride as you wish," she agreed with a pout.

He grinned as he lifted her up into the saddle and arranged her skirts correctly as she took up the reins. "There's a good girl. I knew you would see reason. Just let me know if you feel tired and we shall stop for a rest." With a pat to her leg, he swung away and mounted his own horse; then gave the word to the escort and carriages to start away.

Charis muttered a curse under her breath, but she was so pleased to be once again on the back of her favourite horse that her bad humour lifted and she was soon in good spirits again.

Chapter Thirty-Nine

Charis was asleep in the coach when the party arrived at Castle House. After listening to Tristan's remonstrations, she admitted she was tired after riding many miles on horseback and, although most unwilling, consented to ride in the coach. Once laid out on the seat, Tristan tucked her up in a blanket, and she was asleep in seconds. He shook his head and smiled tenderly at her wilfulness. Marriage to her, he felt, would be an extraordinary journey of trial and error until they got to know each other's ways. For now though, she was safe, and he exhorted his servants to make all possible speed home.

She woke up as he lifted her out of the coach. "Home already," she whispered. "Tris, I can walk, you needn't carry me," she protested.

"Seems to be a habit with me. Lay still, wife, you are exhausted. I'll have you upstairs quicker than you can climb. Bed from now on until you regain your energy, which may take some time as I join you from time to time and deplete it." He smiled at her with a wealth of teasing meaning in his eyes, and before long had her sitting on her bed.

"I'm going to see Father now. I have matters to talk over. Be restful, sweetheart, until we meet for dinner. Although I enjoyed London, I am happier to be here at home and looking forward to a great future with you while we make our family. See you soon." He leaned forward and pressed a kiss to her lips, and then was gone.

She sighed as the door closed. He was so exasperating one minute and yet so loving the next, it was going to take a lifetime to get to know him. She rang the bell and Kate appeared. "I no longer feel tired so I'll change into a light dress and walk in the garden," Charis said.

"Oh milady..." Kate paused, then, "Do you think you ought? That is...Roger is busy in the stables. I don't know if he can come just now."

"What has he got to do with whether I walk in the grounds?"

"Well, I've been given orders that, when you are outside, you must be accompanied by Roger. I'm sorry, milady, but I daren't disobey."

It took no great genius to know who'd given orders or to realise that this damned threat hanging over them was making her a prisoner.

"Oh, for goodness' sake, this is ridiculous. Is it *our* land or isn't it, Kate?" Charis said crossly. "I only want to walk in the garden. Well, I'm going anyway. You'd better fetch a shawl and come with me. I assume if there are two of us to scream that may suit His Lordship!"

Kate pursed her lips, but decided not to argue. Instead, she flew to fetch her shawl; then, with a hurried message to one of the maids to let the butler know what was happening, she was ready to attend Her Ladyship and escort her into the garden.

A knock was heard at the earl's door. Engaged in the forceful discussion of Henry's death and the consequences that lay ahead, both the earl and Tristan ignored it. "'Tis my fault, Tristan," said Amery, gloomily shaking his head. "I was told of this person, but the possibility seemed so remote I ignored the whole thing and never even discussed it with Henry, nor even considered informing you. I'm getting old and thoughtless, Tristan. Thank the Lord you are here to carry the burden. I confess the thought of an unknown relative who can inherit this earldom should we both die, especially without issue, is disastrous to say the least."

"None of us can see so far into the future to predict or prevent the tragedies that are sent our way, Father, but we do have to take notice of warnings." Tristan sighed. "Henry's death tells us loud and clear that we have an enemy—" A second knock at the door cut short his next words. "Yes, Maxwell, what is it?" he asked the butler sharply when he entered and bowed.

"Her Ladyship has gone outdoors, milord." Maxwell paused, and then said, "Unescorted, at least not by Roger Maberly. Though she has Kate with her, or so I have been told. But I felt you would wish to know, milord. Do you wish me to send for Roger?"

"Thank you, Maxwell, I shall deal with it."

"Very good, milord." The butler bowed and left the room.

When the door had closed, Tristan shook his head and grinned at his father. "She's a minx! Gets the bit in her teeth and tries to defy me.

I thought to have Roger run a little surveillance on her as a precaution when she wished to walk in the gardens if I was not with her, and now she'll likely run me ragged until I explain."

Amery stared at him in shocked surprise. "You'll tell her? I mean about this Reginald Mountford? Is that wise? Womenfolk in my day were kept in ignorance of everything except their familial duties. It saves a lot of interference and unnecessary arguments. Besides, she will have other things to concern her, unless I miss my guess."

Tristan cocked his head at his father. "Oh, what makes you think that? We've scarce been married that long."

"The Fortesques might lack some things, but never in breeding the next heir for their dynasty. Why, your mother and I…" He halted, a sudden and most unusual blush reddening his cheeks. "Well, never mind, just nostalgic memories. Get along with you now and see to that minx, as you call her. We can speak after dinner."

Tristan absorbed the wistful regret in his father's voice, seeing more clearly than ever that their marriage had been a love match, one that he hoped to emulate himself. "Yes, I must explain a little, though Charis is far too intelligent to be fobbed off with excuses, and certainly not lies. It is not how I wish to conduct my marriage. She knows, especially after that shooting and our hurried departure from town, that something's amiss. She also knows we have an assailant to be concerned about. I have to say something but perhaps not everything, so if you will excuse me, Father, I'll meet her in the garden."

Tristan rose, bowed to his father, then hurried to a side door and went outside. He saw the two women strolling slowly through the herbaceous area below the terrace, Charis bending now and again to look closely at the foliage, her hands gesturing gracefully as she drew the maid's attention to a plant.

He advanced slowly and quietly as he gazed at the lissom figure he had held so close to his straining body in London and recalled her rapturous cries as he brought her to fulfilment. Long versed in sexual expertise, he was continually being surprised with her joyful response given freely with no guile masking the truth that she enjoyed his lovemaking every bit as much as he did. He felt blessed that fate had kept him waiting until he met this woman that was so unlike any other, and one he adored to the depths of his soul.

"Just look at this lavender, Kate," Charis said as she bent over a profuse bed of the flowers. "That's our next project. I will have all the maids stitch bags for the harvest and fill the still room with what's left over to scent our baths. It smells heavenly, don't you think?"

"Thank you, Kate. I shall escort my wife from here. You may attend her later when she returns to the house."

Charis spun round to find Tristan standing behind her. "Gracious, Tristan, you startled me. I thought you'd be still with your father. You don't have to excuse Kate and leave him on his own. We are perfectly all right enjoying our walk while the day is mild," Charis said rather tartly, as Kate curtsied and walked away, knowing he had come deliberately to question why she was outside instead of resting.

"As you say, my dear, the day is mild. I'll be happy to walk with you instead and enjoy the fresh air."

"And, I trust, be so good as to tell me why you are fussing me to death!" Her temper was beginning to rise with what she took to be an excuse to keep her under control. "Are you trying to wrap me in a cocoon until I have your baby? Tristan, I won't stand for it!"

Tristan stared at her angry face sensing he had to placate her without losing his authority of being master in his house, well knowing she had the temperament and ability to run from constraint. "Charis, I've given you the reason why we had to leave London."

She nodded, staring back at him with a mutinous pout to her lips.

"You also know my father and I think that Henry was murdered. Another death, be it father, myself or, God forbid, you and a possible heir would be disastrous. No one, least of all me, is keeping you penned up and denying you your freedom. I have set things in motion to try and discover who seeks us harm, but meanwhile we have to take care and not relax our vigilance. Despite this place being safe most of the time, by its very nature of being surrounded by open land, it is still open to trespassers who can gain access to the gardens close to the house. I have organised extra guards to patrol the place especially at night, but even they are not infallible, and I don't intend to rely on their expertise. I beg you, Charis, have patience with me until this crisis is sorted and we can go to Carwinnion and enjoy the sea."

All was silent as she lowered her head and stared down at her hands twisting her fingers until eventually she raised her head and he saw her eyes awash with tears. He took a step forward to comfort her.

"No!" she sobbed, swiftly retreating backwards. "Don't show me sympathy. I deserve to be scolded. I'm so sorry, Tristan, I'm acting childishly, but I truly didn't think… I thought it was safe here," she cried wildly. "All this…" She waved her hands at the huge house behind them. "All this estate is too much. My grandmother and Lady Manville are perfectly correct. They said I'd never be able to deal with…" Her eyes closed as copious tears spilled over, and she hugged herself as she sobbed in despair.

"What damned rubbish!" Tristan declared, folding his arms about her and pressing her close to his chest as he reached for a handkerchief. "They have no idea of your ability. Of course, you manage, and *I* say you are coping beautifully, sweetheart. The servants adore you. My father adores you, and undoubtedly I adore you to distraction. It is my fault for not talking this through before we left London. It's the thought of you carrying my child that has overwhelmed me and made me want to wrap you in swansdown." He handed her his handkerchief to mop her eyes, and as she did so she giggled suddenly.

"Swansdown! How absolutely awful! Don't you know feathers make me sneeze?"

"Is that so? Dear me, you'll have to make do with only me covering you and keeping you safe from harm, and also telling me all of your likes and dislikes." He took her in his arms and bent to stroke her quivering lips with his while she opened up for him to kiss her properly until she was breathless.

Raising his head, he smiled down at her. "Are we friends again?"

"Much more than friends, I've discovered. I doubt that friends act as we do, even though…" She paused and shook her head.

"Even though…?" he persisted, wondering what she meant.

No, even she did not have the courage to ask him if he loved her. Love, it seemed, was not spoken of in the *ton*, especially between married people. Whatever went on behind closed doors was kept hidden, and to declare one's feelings was strictly unthinkable.

She amended her words. "Well, you do tend to be very masterful."

"And you tend to be very skittish. Like you, my darling, even when I have you close. I shan't change, Charis. It is up to you if our lives will be compatible and affectionate, or whether you will defy me every time it suits you."

She blushed at his words knowing he was asking if she would accept him as her lord and master and remain faithful to her marriage vows. As she gazed up into his serious grey eyes, she knew he would always treat her with kindness. He was nothing like her stepfather. "Tristan, I ask only one thing. Will you always explain things?"

"Yes, whenever possible."

She noted the caveat but decided she'd gained enough ground not to argue. "In that case, whenever possible, I truly promise to obey you."

Minx! Double-dyed-in-the-wool minx! Still, they had reached an understanding, and he would never attempt to break her spirit. "On that note, I suggest we dine early and retire early."

Chapter Forty

The lodgings seem adequate, thank the Lord, thought Tenby as he tested the bed allotted to him following the two-day wearisome ride from London, during which he and Wallace had suffered far worse quarters in shabby out-of-the-way inns that Mr Reg had deemed suitable for the journey. Where Mr Reg stayed each night, he didn't know, nor had Wallace, a taciturn individual at the best of times, enlightened him beyond saying, "If he needs you to know, he'll tell you." As the only conversations between the master and his manservant occurred out of his hearing, he could only obey the abrupt order "Saddle up, and get a move on" that was voiced early each morning when Mr Reg appeared.

Silently, he had done as he was told, never meeting the man's eyes and exposing the vicious anger that glinted from his downcast gaze. Now was not the time to show his aversion to commands, for at last he was on the road to gaining what he most wanted: revenge.

On the last day, Wallace had unexpectedly ridden off, leaving Tenby to continue towards the Fortesque Estate with Mountford. "Where's he off to?" he asked as Wallace disappeared in the distance.

"Oh, just doing a job for me. You'll see him later, no doubt."

Tenby had expected a swift "Mind your own business!" He was quite surprised at the soft rejoinder, and felt that at last Mountford was beginning to trust him. *All to the good*, he thought complacently. *When I makes up me mind to do what I want then I won't be stopped.*

Little did he know that, as far as Reginald Mountford was concerned, whilst the initial failure of the shot to kill Fortesque had pre-empted the removal of the family to Devon and filled him with fury, he had revised his plans and now thought he had a far better chance of ridding himself of any heirs to the earldom whilst being beyond suspicion. Fortesque senior would not last long, especially if he was grief-stricken over the loss of his remaining son. And if his daughter-in-law was pregnant, her loss would be a double blow. With Tenby under his control, this could easily be achieved, and he would see to it that Tenby was the only culprit on the scene.

An alibi had already been set in motion, and it would be verified that he was miles away from Castle House when the murders happened. Wallace would be on hand to see that the plans were carried out.

In his mind's eye, Mountford was practising the shock he would display when he was informed of the fatalities. Yes, things were working out much better than the previous attempts on Tristan's life, although the killing of Henry had been most successful. Approaching Henry that morning as he was returning from an early ride, his horse lathered from the gallop over the downs, Mountford had ridden close as though to greet and get into conversation with him. Then, with no one else in sight, he quickly wrestled the man off his horse and broke his neck.

Henry, though taken completely by surprise, tried to fight back against the aggressor, but Mountford proved the stronger and, after killing Henry, had viciously beaten his horse with a whip then watched it heading back to the stables with the reins trailing. Setting the scene with the dead body took only a moment or two. Then Mountford quickly made his way off the Fortesque Estate and was soon many miles away with not one finger of suspicion directed his way.

Excellent! One dead, two left to get rid of later. However, the discovery of Tristan's marriage had complicated the situation with the threat of a future heir. At least, until Tenby appeared on the scene. It hadn't taken long to get the full story out of the man nor gauge his ire at losing all he'd owned and his pursuit of vengeance. Mountford's initial reaction of sliding a stiletto into the stupid oaf's heart for being such a fool and only shooting a door abated as a glimmer of an idea entered his mind and, deciding to let him live and take him back to the flat, he began to review his plans. Now he was pleased he had refrained from killing Tenby. His use as a scapegoat was vital for his own protection in case the alibi he'd set up did not hold water.

Mountford had been fortunate in finding a criminal who bore a faint resemblance to him. It was arranged for the man to liaise with Wallace and book late in the day, after most people had retired, into an inn with his manservant. Regrettably, it seemed, he was forced to take to his bed with a chill. Wallace, as the supposed manservant, with the thankful agreement of the innkeeper, had agreed to take charge of the nursing of the poor fellow, and thus no one at the inn had taken note of his features. Thus it would be simple for Mountford to take his place after the demise of the viscount and his lady, and the capture of the supposed killer, namely, Tenby, and confirm that he was the unfortunate person with a chill. Yes, all his plans were going well.

Thomas Tenby was a mediocre horseman; in the past never enjoying exercise for its own sake, much preferring to ride in a coach. The dilemmas he faced after falling into the river had toughened him a little, except his body had never owned a trace of flexibility in its structure or the ability to relate to the movements of a horse. He had not even mastered the art of conveying commands to the animal by the use of knees, voice, or gentle hands on the reins. Consequently, if speed was required, he merely resorted to using his cane, which he was never without rather than the customary whip. Mountford, noting the man's defects, rode alongside as he raised the stick over the unfortunate horse's rump and remarked, "Fond of using that weapon, are you?"

Tenby paused and lowered his arm as he stared at his companion. "Oh, it has its uses, Mr Reg. Got me out of trouble many a time in the past. Using a sword can get you hung, while with something like this, one can argue it's for safety against falling and for defending oneself if necessary. Course, used the right way it's enough to kill."

"So you were near to getting hung at one time, were you?" Mountford flashed back, taking Tenby by surprise.

"Well, er, sort of, though it weren't my fault," he added hastily, taken aback by the perceptive reply.

"No, never is with felons. The gaols are full of innocents."

"Well, in my case, it was either him or me, and the judge was a bit dozy that day and took me at me word that it was the other fellow's fault. Which it was in a way, as he took exception to me helping myself to his gold. I left London soon as I could and found me a nice little billet in the West Country with the proceeds, and acquired a stepdaughter, as I told you. I thought she'd make a nice little earner but things didn't work out. She didn't do me any good in the end. Nearly got me killed she did, but I always land on my feet and meeting you is a godsend.

'Spect you got your reasons for wanting them two dead, and I surely have, so I'm your man for this." Tenby grinned wolfishly.

Mountford nodded as though in perfect agreement, but almost laughed out loud at the thought of Tenby changing his mind when he ended up with a noose round his neck. "I've hired lodgings in North Molton close to the outskirts of the Castle House Estate. Near enough to reconnoitre, but easy to escape from when the deed is done. We'll settle in and wait our opportunity."

Tenby nodded happily and raised his cane once more.

The lodgings consisted of two rooms above a cobbler's shop in a side street off the village. A barn at the rear, mostly filled with old saddles and a variety of leathers, had been partitioned off to allow the stabling of a horse or two. Mountford had arranged for feed to be supplied, and Tenby was ordered to see their mounts fed and watered before he joined Mountford and they found one of the inns close by where they could obtain food. With relief, Tenby sat down on a stool that did not rock him from side to side and, after taking a large swallow of ale while waiting for their meal to arrive, said quietly, "What comes next, Mr Reg?"

"Impatient, Tenby?"

Tenby tamped down his irritation at the inane question, for of course he was impatient; damned right he was bloody impatient to know what was coming next. Mountford was slyly holding things too close to his chest. Feeding him instructions bit by bit was not to his liking.

"I like to be prepared, sir." Tenby kept his tone even. "I don't like to act without giving a matter full thought. You'll have plans already in hand, I can see. No doubt of your planning. I don't intend to disagree, but now and then someone else can offer an alternative which might suit better. However, just to know what's to happen a little way ahead might be reasonable and enable me to act as you want."

Mountford nodded. *Yes, the man made sense.* Then he quickly pulled back from the table as plates were dumped in front of them. Hunger kept them silent for the best part of twenty minutes. Then, replete from the meal and with another tankard of ale in front of them, he narrowly surveyed Tenby as he reviewed the man's former statement.

"When we leave here, we'll head for our lodgings. Then we will wait awhile till the town settles; then find our way to the back of the estate and reconnoitre the area. I've seen it before, but of course you are right. Knowing the terrain is sensible. Come, drink up, it's time to go. We don't need to show our faces more than we have to."

Chapter Forty-One

Several weeks passed during which time Charis settled into the routine of the house and finding her way around not only with the staff but in the surrounding countryside and nearby villages. Knowing this would be her home for all time, she was eager to discover all about the area and the people she would eventually get to know. Her husband was busy with estate affairs, so they only met each other at intervals. However, the nights were theirs to enjoy, and Tristan, in particular, looked forward to the moment when he could hold his wife close and make her writhe in ecstasy. At first, she would rise early with him to enjoy a pre-breakfast ride on Butterfly, but soon, with pregnancy tiredness taking over and a suspicion of morning sickness, she had to cry off that pleasure and stay in her room until her stomach settled. However, by mid morning she was up and about taking on duties formerly managed by the senior staff, much to their delight. They had long wished for a countess to head the household, and one and all decided that Charis fitted the role perfectly. The fact that the earl and his son tacitly agreed with this finding made for a very happy household indeed.

One day, at the behest of his father, it was decided that Tristan and Charis should host a small dinner party for a few local dignitaries and their wives, who were both eager to meet the viscount's new wife and to dine sumptuously at an earl's table. There had been no chance of an invitation before as the earl declined to entertain after Henry's death and Tristan was too head over heels in love to want to share Charis with others. His father added that it would be wise to introduce Charis to the neighbourhood and allow her to make friends with other women. Before the event, Tristan was called to his room to discuss it.

"She's a stranger to the area, son, and it's up to us to make her feel comfortable in her new home. I know you have kept her occupied so far, but when you are busy with estate affairs she needs her attention happily engaged with the things she likes doing, or indeed with the friends she will undoubtedly make. She is intelligent and outgoing and already has taken to visiting village people who are ailing and need our help, and she's making a success of it. Naturally, either Roger or a groom has accompanied her and her maid on their local visits. She is also taking on the reins of managing this household and very capably too, so Harwood tells me. It is up to us to back her to the hilt."

Tristan blinked with surprise at the firmness in his father's voice. Then, recovering, he knew his father was right and he was at fault for not realising he had neglected to think of more than his own needs, that of making love to the most alluring woman he had ever met, who was now carrying his child. Was he more concerned with showing her he was her master rather than showing her how she could be happy in the new life he had forced her into?

He flinched at that last thought. *Forced? Yes, face it. You did everything you could to make her marry you, even using underhand tactics against her closest kin. Except I've made her happy, haven't I? She says she loves me. Ah, but does she really mean it or is it because she feels trapped into a marriage that she didn't want and is trying to make the best of things? Yet, her passionate response tells me she enjoys making love. She follows my lead in everything and even comes up with thrilling notions of her own to increase our pleasure which has been quite a surprise. She had no experience before, for undoubtedly she was a virgin when I first made love to her, but is her love genuine or simply make-believe? A method of getting her own way? Trying to wrap me round her little finger? She won't succeed, but she might attempt it.*

All at once, he was appalled at the route his thoughts were taking. Then his mind went back to the woman in Calcutta. Salinas! She had turned him against women for a long time until he met Charis. But what the hell, Charis was nothing like Salinas; quite the opposite. Whatever was he thinking of to distrust her so?

He suspected that the instinct to manage people ran in her blood, an inheritance from her forebears who had descended from the ruling class of France; in fact, like the similar instincts that ran in his blood. Primarily born to rule, he was also a hunter/killer from his army days, though in his wife's case he was all protector and guardian of her welfare and safety, particularly now there was the child to consider. However, the issue at hand, according to his father, was to give her more freedom. A hard thing to decide, especially with enemies who, he was sure, lay in wait to do them harm. He accepted his father's point of view, but Amery had not been in London when that bullet hit their front door. That, more than anything else, brought his hunter/killer instincts to the fore. Inwardly, he groaned with frustration. How to take into consideration his father's advice and keep his wife sweet, yet guard them all against an unseen enemy?

"I hear what you say, sire, but until we have evidence of whoever means us harm and can catch the brute, I deem it necessary to take the utmost precaution. Despite the fact we've had no sighting of Tenby and it's been some time since his apparent demise in the river, I am aware he could still be alive. Without proof of his death, I must still take that stance. As for Mountford, he is an unknown adversary, if one can call him that. Certainly, he stands to gain immeasurably with our deaths and, in each instance of my previous, shall we say, accidents, he could have contrived them. That shot hitting the door has me puzzled. Whoever ambushed me came so close to killing me that day I was riding back from Caroline's cousin that the shot actually singed my collar. I am amazed he didn't succeed the second time. I was standing in clear sight for some moments before I turned to take Charis's arm, so I was an easy target. It may be that there are two gunmen possibly working together. In which case, we have a great deal to worry about."

"You make a good case, Tristan. I confess I've not taken all the London facts into consideration. My deep concern is because I have learned to love Charis dearly. She's brought back thoughts of your dear mother to mind, and my deep regret and sorrow that she's not with us today. Expecting a grandchild would, I know, have been one of her dearest wishes as mine is now. Pray God that we come through this bad patch safely and are blessed with that wonderful event." Amery swept a hand across his brow as though to brush away a tear or two.

Watching him closely, Tristan could see the lines of age in his father's face had deepened considerably while he was absent from home for so long. Since his return home, he had felt a pang of sorrow for all the lost years and that he had almost left it too late to take pleasure in being with his father once more. All he wished for now was to enjoy his wife and the coming child, and join with his father to make a loving family once more without the dreadful threats hanging over them. His secret grief at losing his brother might be gradually appeased if he could ensure the others were kept safe. He felt at times he was fighting an invisible foe, not knowing who they were or when they would strike next.

Chapter Forty-Two

It was close on ten o'clock and darkness well set in when Mountford and Tenby saddled their horses; then, in the faint intermittent starlight that gave off just enough light to see their way ahead, found the road that led towards East Buckland. Short of the village, they turned south towards Castle House and, at the woodland backing onto the estate, found the small lane that eventually led through to the huge garden behind the house. Mountford had reconnoitred many times so that he could almost navigate the path blindfold. Wide enough for farm carts, it was used to ferry in garden supplies and unwanted waste out.

Leaving the horses in a small glade off the track, they silently and carefully, conscious of any night watchmen that could be prowling around, approached the terrace at the back of the house. Lights were blazing in all the downstairs areas, and they could see a gathering of people in a large dining room attended by several servants.

"Dining in style tonight, I detect. How fortunate they have the wherewithal to indulge," growled Mountford in Tenby's ear. It filled him with bitterness that it was not he who was seated inside playing the host. One day, he vowed, it would be. He had gone over all his plans so many times he knew it would come to pass, and he would gain the earldom, the estate and money for himself. Only a few more days and he would achieve it all.

"Memorise the area, Tom. We shall return tomorrow. Sadly, it is useless tonight, too much going on, but with the benefit of those lights, see if you can spot where we can get closer to the house and hide. Might have to wait it out several nights, but we'll get them in the end."

Tenby gave a grunt in reply then whispered, "That stand of shrubbery could do us all right. From here, it looks deep enough for both of us to hide in; unless the keepers have dogs with them. They'd sniff us out in no time. Have you seen any?"

"The old earl used to keep a pack going for the local hunt, but since his eldest son died and he doesn't ride any more he got rid of them. There might be the odd animal around but, no, I don't think they use them regularly. Leastways, not the last time I was here," Mountford whispered back. "Seen enough? Come on then, we'll get back to the village and scout the roads round there. We need to move fast out of the area once the deed is done."

Not that he would let Tenby move anywhere to escape. With the element of surprise that he had carefully planned, he would disable him and leave him to be found, complete with the guns that would hang him.

As the last of the guests said farewell and withdrew to their waiting carriages, Tristan turned to his father who had lingered to bid goodnight to Charis and himself and groaned, "Thank goodness that's over. I'm sure you are tired. I know I am."

The earl smiled and nodded. "Yes, a little weary now, but very content. Excellent evening, I'd say, wouldn't you? Considering you knew hardly anyone except maybe a few from your youth, and Charis no one at all, you were most proficient. As an opening endeavour for our neighbours, you've both made a good beginning. Charis, I commend your choice of menu; most suitable for the company."

She blushed at his words and said, "I did consult with—"

"But you had the final say, I perceive, did you not?"

"I suppose so, but—"

"Take the credit when it's due, my dear girl. I knew you had the makings of a good hostess and am pleased to be proved right. Without doubt, you charmed us all. Take her up to bed, Tris, and see she has a good rest. She's earned it. Goodnight, my dear, sleep well." Signalling to the waiting footmen that he was ready to retire, Amery allowed them to carry him upstairs to his rooms.

Tristan waited until he disappeared then turned to Charis, took her hand, and led her to the stairs. "Our turn now, darling. I've been waiting all evening to get you to myself." He frowned wryly. "I trust our dear papa does not enter into an orgy of entertaining now that he has found

214

an able hostess. I must remind him that you have to keep your energy for other things."

She raised her brows as she began to climb the stairs with him, and then halted as the significance of his words teased her mind. "Oh yes? What other things have you in mind?"

"Me, for instance. I'll explain as we go along." His eyes blazed hotly as he looked down at her. "Or maybe I shall just demonstrate."

She shivered as a thrill of anticipation ran through her. She was pleasantly tired from her evening's efforts, but not too tired to respond to what lay ahead. His talent for lovemaking was a prize indeed. Since their marriage, she had followed his lead without reservation. To touch, caress, and wonder. To take joy in each other's delight and pleasure in every sensual exploration.

Upstairs, he relinquished her hand momentarily as she opened the door to her bedroom where Kate was waiting to ready her for bed.

"See you soon," he said as he blew a kiss at her and went to his own dressing room to undress.

A short time later, he padded in with bare feet to the master bedroom and found her by a window gazing down at the garden below which now and then was revealed as a fitful moon emerged from the passing clouds. "What are you looking at?" He came behind her, and placing his hands on her bare shoulders gently smoothed them over her skin.

"I was wondering whether we could organize a summer fête for the staff, and how much room would we need for it."

He laughed. "From what I remember from my boyhood, it's easily done, but then I did not do the arranging. However, if that is your aim then I guess you will have ample support from father, not to mention our people. Judging how Maxwell and the rest of them all looked for your discreet signals and how well the evening flowed then I expect they will be eager to participate."

His hands slid under the ties of her nightgown and curved over her breasts, palms caressing the furled nipples until they swelled at the touch; then he retreated to undo the ties and allow the heavy silk of the gown to fall of its own volition to the floor. Turning her around to face him, he bent his head and took her mouth in a passionate kiss that caused a wave of heat to stream through her. In turn, she undid his dressing gown and slid her hands beneath to stroke his chest muscles and tease his nipples; to lay claim to possessing his body as he owned hers. The exquisite melding of their mouths grew hotter, hungrier, their demands rising by steady degrees until he bent, lifted her and walked to the bed. The silk sheets cooled her skin momentarily as he laid her down; then the heat rose again as he folded her close to his warm body, and she felt his hands stoke the surging, swelling desire of her need. He took all she had to give and returned it in full measure until she crested and joined with him on the rising, spiralling path to completion.

Chapter Forty-Three

The night was dry and still as Roger watched the last of the guests depart and the grooms scamper off to bed. He didn't feel tired enough for sleep and, glancing down at his feet where a black Labrador sat patiently waiting for him to move, he decided to have a last stroll before retiring. He clicked his tongue and Bess rose, somehow sensing that a walk was in order. After he had been at Castle House for a few days and was beginning to settle in, she apparently decided to adopt him and, changing her usual territory of the stables where she kept a maternal eye on all and sundry, he was aware that she became a constant shadow. So much so that her bed now occupied a corner of his bedroom.

Deciding to circumnavigate the house to make sure the extra night team were in place to patrol the surrounding area, Roger headed for the back terrace, Bess happily roaming a few yards away. Reaching the wide stone terrace, he stood for a moment or two, his eyes looking over the huge expanse of parkland; then he turned to resume his walk.

A sudden growl caused him to stop and watch Bess as she sped down the steps and headed off towards the woodland. *Damn*, he thought, *she's scented rabbits*. Tired now and ready for bed, he whistled for her, but she ignored his call and stood quite still, nose pointing to the shrubbery like the well-trained gun dog of her youth. Puzzled and a little bit on edge, he walked warily towards her, eyeing the area all around. The dog had smelt something, and maybe that something was an alien smell that shouldn't be there.

He stood silently before the border allowing his senses loose to determine if anyone was hiding there. Only a light rustling breeze was heard, and watching Bess he saw her relax. "Come on, lass, time we were in bed. We'll come here tomorrow early when it's light and see what's up."

Appearing to understand every word, she obediently followed him as he carried on perambulating the house, stopping briefly to have a word with the man on duty before heading for bed, but he didn't doubt that someone had been trespassing illicitly.

The next morning, Roger stood on the path before the shrubbery to survey the area before he ventured into the bushes. A morning mist disguised the pastures, and moisture coated the leaves and laid damp patches here and there on the stone paths that led back to the house.

It would clear when the sun rose but, for now, the silence was ghostly, almost eerie with otherworldliness. Bess raised an inquiring nose to him, and he motioned with a hand to the tangled undergrowth before them and said, "Go seek".

Soon a short yip was heard, and he thrust his way to the sound. Calling her to his side, his expertise at tracking which had stood him and Tristan in good stead when they were in India recognised the signs that two people had recently hidden there.

With the help of Bess, he backtracked through the wood until he reached the glade where horses had been tethered. For quite a while, he surmised, as under the trees there was little grass and the earth still held the mark of their shoes. The pattern of one shoe held his interest. He recognised the unusual style of nailing. Where had he seen the like before? Not round here, he would swear. The local blacksmith who handled all the Castle mounts had a different technique. Then where?

Walking swiftly back to the house, he deliberated whether he should warn His Lordship or just keep watch himself. Except it did not just concern a man he had guarded for so many years but his wife as well; someone he had vowed to protect with his life. And, if his intuition served him right, was carrying his master's heir. Some things he could and did hold back if he felt it was right for the occasion, but this was too dangerous to keep to himself. Brushing down his clothes after charging through the trees, he headed for the stables. Tristan was probably due there about now for his morning ride. Except this time he wasn't. Roger hung about for a long time until he discovered the ride had been cancelled. Lord Fortesque was remaining with his wife.

Chapter Forty-Four

Feeling decidedly nauseous when she woke, Charis tried to slip out of bed without disturbing Tristan, but the heavy possessive arm that lay around her waist was hard to dislodge. She tried to push herself free, but the arm closed tighter in spite of her struggles. The fierce tone of "Leave me be!" roused him and, half awake and totally surprised, he released her. A moment or two later, the sound of retching came from within a small marbled bathing chamber set between the two bedrooms.

Recently converted, with the newest fittings that pleased him enormously, Tristan's delight in tranquil bathing, resulting from his long time abroad and knowledge of the Eastern way of directing water, had produced a huge and comfortable bath set in a chamber designed for easy use. His ability to create and devise the necessary equipment had impressed his father, who was presently having a similar room converted in his own suite.

Tristan, hearing the sound of one being dreadfully sick, knew his wife was in trouble. Instantly, he thought of mushrooms but recalled no dish the previous evening had contained them. Then it hit him! Poor dear, the babe was responsible for the malaise. He flung back the sheets and, padding over to the room, found Charis on her knees bent over a basin.

"Oh, sweetheart, how can I help?"

"Go away! For pity's sake, leave me! It's none of your affair!"

He ran a hand through his tangled locks and groaned, "For God's sake, Charis, it is my affair! I've damn well caused your pregnancy. I did not know it would be as bad as this. What can I do to make up for my heartless behaviour? What can I get you?"

She raised her head from the bowl and muttered, "A cup of water would be helpful."

The tap that ran water from below stairs was to hand and he filled a glass. Taking it from him, she rinsed her mouth and spat. Then, after waiting a moment or two, she said, "I think that's over for the present, thank goodness." Rising to her feet, she looked at him and smiled. "I'll take odds your face is whiter than mine. What do we call it this time? Casting accounts or heaving guts? Whatever! I'm feeling better and will have the required tea and a little toast as recommended."

Putting an arm round her, Tristan led her back to bed and helped her to slide in under the covers. Relaxing against the pillows, she closed her eyes and sighed. "Ring for Kate, please. I'll stay here for a while and rest. Are you going riding now you are awake?"

"No, I'll join you. A cup of tea and a smidgeon or two of toast might help settle *me* for a while, and allow me come to terms with our lives and the forthcoming event which I can see is going to make considerable changes."

At once, her eyes opened wide and she stared at him in dismay. "Oh dear, I knew I shouldn't have let you see me like this. I expect you will regret us starting a family. Perhaps I should sleep in my bedroom until this sickness passes—"

"Just try it, and you'll find that I'll haul you out of bed and in here every night until you desist!"

He scowled ferociously, though his eyes belied the display of anger, and she spied the warmth and humour within. Abruptly, with a right about face he grinned. "I'm going to rename you a Cornish pixie. I believe they are full of fits and starts just like you. Truly, I never know where you are going to jump next. If anyone needs comforting, 'tis I, a poor long-suffering husband."

She giggled at his play-acting and, no longer feeling queasy, enjoyed another hour with her loving husband.

The early dinner that evening was low key with only Tristan and Charis dining in the smaller room they kept for themselves and immediate family. The earl had sent his apologies for not joining them. He was resting, he said, following the previous night's dinner party.

"He enjoyed it, I know," said Charis, "but is probably paying for it with painful joints. I must try hard once again and persuade him to take a tisane of willow bark. Daisy, my former housekeeper, used to make up potions for the village with great success at easing their pain."

"Ah yes, that reminds me, I've had news that Carwinnion is finished and ready for us to visit. I sent Barney back a while ago to keep a watch on the house, and he and Daisy are organizing the extra staff we need. The furniture you've chosen from here has been delivered – God knows we've ample to spare – and you've created space that looks far more pleasing. A positive museum this place is, crammed with centuries of avaricious collections." He chuckled. "But, you know, you didn't need to be so thrifty. I was more than prepared to order new furniture."

"So I gathered, but I felt more at home choosing pieces from here that will be familiar to you and give you a feeling that it is your home too. After your man of business informed me that I still retain rights to the ownership of Carwinnion and that I can keep my trust as well, I'm overwhelmed, Tristan. You know you have every right to own it and me." She had been waiting for an opportunity to thank him for his gift, and unaccountably her eyes brimmed with tears.

"Charis, my dear, I don't need it. I have funds enough to spare, and I know how much the property and your people mean to you. If you will allow me to guide you with the financial aspects of the trust then consider it entirely yours to do as you wish."

With the table cleared apart from tea for Charis and a brandy for her husband, there was no one around to see her leap into his lap, throw her arms around him and take his lips in a deep and loving kiss. "Darling man, whatever have I done to deserve you?" she cried.

"You've given me the honour of marrying my sweetheart. I'll always care for you." He flinched. What a bloody fatuous thing to say. Care for her? Of course he cared for her. Why hadn't he said he was head over heels in love with her? That damned vow he had made? The pledge loomed large, and he knew it was no longer valid.

He took a deep breath and was about to confess when she slid off his lap and said, "It's far too early for bed. Let's walk on the terrace for a while. I do love looking out on the park at night."

He rose to his feet thinking that, before the night ended, he would tell her he loved her and fulfil his dearest hope that she would respond and tell him that she loved him too. Sliding a wrap round her shoulders, he led her to the French windows and opened them.

Standing on the terrace looking westwards into the far distance where the very last of daylight cast a slim band of pale pink across the horizon below the darkening blue, he said, "Out East one never gets twilight. One moment there is a blazing sunset, looking as if the sky is on fire; the next it is night. Black as soot if there is no moon."

"Do you miss it?" she asked wistfully, eager for him to go on reminiscing as she held his hand and they strolled to the parapet.

"No, not a bit. I have all I want here to satisfy me. You, my sweet love, my father, this house, which I accept is the cornerstone of my being, and the joyful prospect of a family and the contentment of everything I hold dear. I love you, my Cornish pixie, and will forever and ever."

Holding up her face for his demanding kiss and trying to take in the unexpectedness of his words – words that she never thought to hear from a man so reticent and self-contained – caused a shiver of ecstasy to race through her. "I love you too, my dearest Tristan, and yes, always and forever."

Mistaking the shiver for the chill of evening, Tristan braced an arm about her shoulders and, turning her round, said, "Come, we will seek a warmer place to rejoice in this love of ours. Tomorrow, we go to Carwinnion, and you will show me the places where you have been happy, and I will make you happier still. I've already given orders for the packing, so you may rest content that all is in hand."

Once again, she felt swept away with the arrogant planning he had ordered without consulting her, but consoling herself with the fact that at least he had admitted he loved her, she decided not to cavil at his high-handedness. There was plenty of time to get her own way, and at least she was returning to Carwinnion.

The trespassers arrived quietly at the same spot overlooking the terrace to see the people they had come to murder disappear back into the house. Watching for a further two hours brought them no comfort bar freezing feet and an escalating anger from Reginald Mountford.

"Bloody hellfire!" he swore. "It'll have to be tomorrow. We'll come early and settle in the nearest shrubbery. They obviously have a moment or two of an evening outside which will be time enough for us. Come on, let's get back. It's cold enough here to freeze brass monkeys." In high dudgeon, he trod back to the horses followed by his partner in crime who was no less cold and disappointed.

The next evening on their return, they stared at the darkened back of the house. Curtains were drawn over the lightless windows, both down and upstairs in the main bedrooms. Only a few lights shone at the end of the building where the kitchens and staff dining room lay.

It was obvious that the Fortesques were no longer in residence. They had gone elsewhere. Dumbfounded, Mountford could scarcely believe his bad luck. Exactly as had happened in London. Where the hell had they gone? It was three days before they discovered milord and lady had gone back to Carwinnion. Mountford was furious at the delay for it would take days for them to get to track the Fortesques back to Cornwall, and who knew where they might jump to next. Without revealing his thoughts, Tenby cheered up at the news. On his own territory, he was king. All he had planned would be simple to organize. He was in alt.

Chapter Forty-Five

Roger was especially relieved that Tristan had decided to take his wife back to Cornwall. It still bothered him that he'd had no chance to describe what he had found, but the fact that they were separating from the immediate danger was reassuring. He undertook to keep a special guard over the two of them, but for now to say nothing until he could produce evidence that they were in danger. When he heard from the housekeeper they were to travel back to the former home of Lady Charis, he had pursed his lips and frowned but merely nodded. "Thanks, I'll pack, Mrs Tawton. Early start, I expect, if I know His Lordship."

"Oh, are you going too, Mr Maberly?"

"Of course. Neither milord nor Her Ladyship will travel anywhere without me. You know I am his body servant and have been for many years. He goes nowhere without me to protect him. Likewise Her Ladyship."

"*Humph*!" Mrs Tawton scowled fiercely. "Comes to something when a servant tells *me* what he will do."

"Except, Mrs Tawton, I am not a servant of *this* house. I belong to His Lordship and take his orders. Ask him if you don't believe me." He grinned to himself. That should shut her up, he thought, well aware of the hierarchy in a large establishment and the jealousies that emanated between the staff. Leaving her fuming, he retired to his room, another bone of contention with Tawton that he was allowed a room below the attics where other members of the household slept.

Working quickly, he filled a small bag with his necessaries whilst pondering on the current situation. Was Thomas Tenby actually dead? What about that gunshot in London that had prompted their rapid exit here? Plus the other attempts at his master. He felt fortunate that Tristan never kept things from him but would cogitate aloud and let Roger make what he willed of the intelligence. Always slow to give advice which Tristan appreciated, once given, he knew his master would take notice.

Thankful that he hadn't let loose a false hare with the incident of Bess unearthing the scent of villains, he decided to continue to hold his tongue yet keep a strict watch.

Instead of returning south through Launceston this time, Tristan decided that Tavistock would be a suitable town to break the journey for the first night, staying at the Bedford Hotel which had once been a Benedictine monastery. Charis was too tired to take in more than the transformed elegant rooms, even though surrounded by granite walls, the welcoming fire, and large four-poster bed already turned down for her comfort. Dining simply in the adjoining parlour also suited, and when Tristan came to bed after ensuring his servants were adequately settled, she was sound asleep.

He slid quietly into bed unwilling to disturb her and lay for some minutes thinking over the few words he had with Roger before retiring. For once, his groom was looking unsettled, not a characteristic he generally displayed. Most times he was a positive fellow, seldom allowing the day to day problems bother him. Taciturn by nature to his fellow men, he would only unbend to Tristan and only then if he felt it was necessary. The two men had been together for so long that an intuition had developed between them which Tristan valued.

He was bidding goodnight to Roger when he paused. "What's vexing you, Roger? Problem with the cattle? Everton said they were running well. At least coming this way, although it's longer, the roads are better. Though from Plymouth onwards we might get held up. Still, the weather is with us for a change, thank goodness."

"I'm still thinking about Tenby and whether he is actually dead. Seems to me we are going to his former hunting ground, that's if he has made it back there, and we need to take care."

"I believe Barney or Mrs Fenton will have an eye out for him too even though Barney was sure he drowned. From what I gather from Her Ladyship, the village area is too small to hide someone like him. He'd be recognised in a flash." He raised a questioning brow. "Unless you know more than you are telling me?"

"Only a feeling, an itch, one might say, at the back of the neck."

"Hmm. Keep watch and don't scratch too much. Goodnight."

Roger's uneasy feeling was echoed in him too, Tristan thought as he composed himself for sleep. Proof of Tenby's death was what was needed and he had never had as he'd said to Manville. That they were being dogged by one or more killers he had no doubt. Yet, he reasoned, if one went through life fearing trouble at every corner, one would never get out of bed.

Turning over onto his side, he put his arm round his wife's waist and, cuddling her closer, fell asleep.

A further night's halt at St Austell saw them on the last leg of their journey into Falmouth where Tristan stopped to have a word with his shipping agent. He had kept up a steady correspondence with the man, and was pleased with the reports he was sent. He planted the thought that he could be interested in buying another ship; then, bidding the man goodbye but promising he would call in on his way back to Castle House, he went back to the inn where he had left Charis and the meal they had readied for him.

"We've still a way to go before we reach your home. Do you wish to stay here and rest overnight or go on? You are looking tired, my love."

"Oh, Tris, I can't bear to be so near and stay here. Truly, it is not so far. I've had enough of the coach, so please can I ride the rest of the way with you? I can tell you of all the places I know."

He smiled at her excitement, the way her face lit up at the prospect of seeing her home again, and couldn't deny her. "Very well, I'm sure Butterfly will be pleased to be ridden instead of being hauled on a leading rein. If you are sure you can manage, we will leave shortly. I'll send someone on ahead to warn the house we are on our way."

She hugged him close then, calling her maid, went off to change into her riding habit, thinking with a thrill of delight she might have left Carwinnion as a stable boy in rough clothing but she was returning as a beautifully attired lady. *Goodness*, she contemplated, *I must remember to act like one too instead of being considered a hoyden. But, oh, it will be marvellous to be home again and see Daisy.*

The last stretch of countryside to reach home was as wonderful as anything she had ever done in her life before. Talking continually, Charis described the places they passed, and the people and who lived where, which kept Tristan more entertained than he expected. The change from someone who was not a chatty person, who only spoke when she had something pertinent to say, was a revelation. Within a short time, he knew more history of the county he was riding through than he could have learned reading a book. That she had loved her home and still did was made apparent. He delighted in her excitement and was not only pleased they had travelled back to her place of birth but was looking forward to sharing the surprise he knew was in store. He had deftly kept her from knowing about his directions to the builders he had employed.

Finally, they reached the gates of Carwinnion, and all of a sudden Charis stopped dead, amazed and totally silent as she stared at the brand new iron gates, now standing wide open, the newly stoned drive without the former potholes, and, most significant of all, the gracefully pruned trees guarding the grassy verges.

She swung back in her saddle and gazed at her husband with tears in her eyes. "Oh, Tristan, what a lovely, lovely surprise. It's beautiful! Thank you so much for putting the estate in order."

"You haven't seen it all yet. How do you know everything is done? It could just be a mirage, a dream and all is as it was before."

She smiled mistily at him. "And pigs might fly, my love. You've never done things by halves in your life. Come on, we're wasting time. I need to see the rest of my surprise." She dug her heels into her horse and headed up the drive. Tristan followed suit, but he was left behind as she raced Butterfly up the approach to the house.

When he caught her up, he found her standing rapt on the swept and weeded forecourt gazing at the weathered oak door, the iron rivets now braised from their rust and gleaming black; the repaired roof and gleaming windows; the pruned ivies fastened against the warm brickwork, as copious tears filled her eyes and wet her cheeks. As he approached, the door swung open and Daisy raced out, apron and dress flying wildly, her arms spread wide to embrace her adored mistress.

"Oh Charis, my lovey, uh, I mean Your Ladyship, you've come home! I'm right glad to see you, and this handsome husband of yours!"

As they hugged, Tristan could see the joy on both of their faces and was glad he had brought her back. He thought briefly of the turmoil she had gone through, and vowed to keep her safe and happy.

"Come along inside, milady, milord. I have everything ready for you.

Dinner when you want it – or anything – just let me know!" Daisy's excitement had almost got the better of her, and Charis took a moment to calm her down and then, turning to Tristan and curtseying, said, "Come, My Lord, I shall show you around your new estate."

He quirked an eyebrow at her. "My Lord? My estate? I believe you misrepresent things, my dear. No need to be so formal. I collect, if I am not mistaken, it belongs to you."

She chuckled. "Ah, Tristan, dearest husband, it is ours to enjoy. The transformation from its former neglect is just as I would have wished. It is quite wonderful. I once despaired of ever rescuing the place and making it a real and lovely home again."

She took his arm and led him from room to room until, finally, they reached the master suite where she stood and gasped at the new furnishings which he had especially commissioned and which she had known nothing about. Palest eau de nil, with subtle tones of blue and here and there a warming peach, was displayed in the brocade curtains and chair covers. All set against dainty white furniture carved with delicate gold tracery. Gone was the ancient dark oak furniture. Instead, the room gleamed bright with beauty and light. She was stunned with the transformation.

"This is for us, my love. Nothing to remind you of bad times; only, I suspect, a memory of your mother."

"How did you know she loved those colours?"

He tapped the side of his nose. "I know many things."

She stamped her foot in frustration. "Tristan Fortesque! You are absolutely exasperating at times. Tell me!"

He grinned at her. "Well, I teased your grandmother into telling me that she would never recollect how the house had once looked when your parents were in residence. To my surprise, she did well, and also remembered that Cecile, your mother, was nostalgic for the home of her youth. I gathered they never changed the oak furniture that your grandfather had used, possibly because they couldn't afford to. But her dream of ideal decor was of the French persuasion, fragile furniture, delicate and flowery; what she had been used to in her childhood. She once confessed it to your grandmama who became aware eventually of your mother's descent from one of the oldest of French aristocratic families. Caroline idolised her son, your father, so of course was elated that, instead of marrying a refugee, as she thought, he had married a noble lady of the realm, as by descent you are too."

She stared round-eyed at him. "Me? How is that possible? No one said. Certainly my mother never told me."

"By the time you were old enough to understand her French background, she was probably aware of your stepfather's grasping motives. Almost certainly she tried to protect you from his avaricious intentions. If she had told you and you inadvertently let it out once you reached an age of understanding then, if I read the situation right, your safety would have been compromised. I believe that somehow she intended letting her relations know of you, but unfortunately her death intervened. Doubtless it was impossible to get a message to France."

He held her close and wiped the tears from her eyes as she wept over the long-lost memories of her mother and the conclusions Tristan had revealed. "Oh, I wish you could have known her, Tris. She was a sweet and gentle person and did not deserve her bad ending."

"Yes, I have gathered that too. But her legacy lives on in you, and I am profoundly grateful that it does. We shall dispense with history and look forward to the future, my love. Leave the sad events in the past. Come, I'm sure dinner is ready, and you must eat and then rest. Our hope is bound up in that adorable belly of yours and must be taken care of. We shall return here after we dine and enjoy our first night in Carwinnion, and I'll tell you how much I love you."

He swept his arm round her and led her back to the stairs and thence to an elegant dining room. "No need to change, Charis. You are charming as you are. To wear a gown for an hour or so before I take it off is, I am persuaded, a futile exercise. In any case, I believe the coaches have just arrived. The maids will be busy unpacking so it behoves us to enjoy Daisy's cooking and leave everyone to settle." He turned to Daisy who had suddenly appeared in the hall. "Dinner ready?"

She swept a deep curtsey. "At once, milord. Please take your places in the dining room. I have made all My Lady's favourites which I hope you will enjoy as well." She whisked off to the kitchen and, with an amused smile on his face, Tristan guided his wife to the table and, with a flourish, seated her.

"So I have to enjoy your favourite food, have I? I trust I will survive the experience, my love. As long as Daisy does not produce turnips, I will endeavour to take pleasure in her cooking."

Charis giggled at his words. "She might take it into her head to give you stargazy pie, just to see you flinch!"

"What in heaven's name is that?"

"Baked pilchards set in pastry with their heads poking out!"

He shuddered. "Sounds awful! Charis, I trust you are not trying to put me off dining?"

She chuckled once again. "Would I be so perverse?"

"Knowing you so well now, my sweet minx, yes, you would."

However, the meal set before them was excellent, and, much relieved, Tristan enjoyed every morsel. Escorting his wife to their room later, he looked forward to showing and sharing his contentment with the woman he adored.

Chapter Forty-Six

It took a week before Mountford and Tenby came within sight of Falmouth, and another four days longer before they skirted the town and found a tavern just outside of Helston at Turnpike Cross that would put them up for a day or two. Tenby had already warned Mountford that it was not wise for him to be spotted close to his former home in case he was noticed.

Mountford determined it was too early to put Tenby in the firing line as a culprit before the Fortesques were killed, so he chose to reconnoitre the country lanes to Carwinnion in daylight himself; and, with any luck, assess the land around the house and pick out the best spot for the shooting. It wasn't long before he found, after making discreet inquiries, that the former dilapidated estate that Tenby had spoken of was thriving prosperously. Several men from local villages had been employed to farm the land, which made it impossible to get close to the house in daylight, and Lady Charis had become a well-known and much loved benefactor in the district. *All to the good*, he thought, *I shall inherit even more wealth than I formerly knew would be handed over. At last, I will succeed to what is owed me.*

Riding back along a narrow track that he hoped would take him to the highway that led towards Helston, he was unaware that a rider ambling along and well hidden behind the Cornish hedge had spotted him as a stranger and was curious to know what he was doing in the district. While his master was busy with estate matters, Roger Maberly was content to patrol the locale and generally keep a watchful eye on all and sundry. He enjoyed being out in the fresh air, and combining this with finding his way around unknown territory was his way of relaxing. The man he presently had his eye on seemed, if not wearing all the attributes of a gentleman, at least decently dressed, and had a prime horse under him but no sign of saddlebag or luggage that might denote he was just passing through. He could be visiting friends or relations, or had put up at one of the acceptable hotels in the neighbourhood. Interesting. Maybe more than interesting.

Deciding there was still ample daylight left, Roger continued to trail the man, keeping well back as they reached a wider road and then taking to the fields so that he would remain hidden. At no time did Roger feel that he had been spotted. He was determined to keep it that way especially as he noticed that, every so often, the stranger would cast a look behind him in case he was being followed.

When he turned off the road that led to Helston and took the lane to Turnpike Cross, Roger felt the familiar prickling sensation at the back of his neck. Ah, my beauty, you are up to something, I'll be bound. Whether it concerns us, I'll try and find out, but find it I will. He watched for some time after the man went into the small alehouse that served as the only inn midst the few cottages that composed the village, but when he did not appear again as it grew dark, Roger assumed that he was staying there. The man's clothing and inferior accommodation did not add up. By all accounts, he ought to have chosen better lodgings. Had he gone there to meet someone, or was he hiding from something? Time to find out.

Once it had grown completely dark, Roger tethered his horse and, taking advantage of every shadow and the absence of anyone in the yard, ended up crouching below a gaping window that let out the fumes and smoke from the only saloon bar the place possessed. Snatching a quick peek through the opening, Roger saw his quarry sitting at one of the tables with another man. Dropping his head, he drew in a quick breath then raised it for another look. Bloody hell!

No doubt about it: Thomas Tenby, alive and as healthy as ever. He even had the surly frown on his face that Roger remembered well from following him about Bath. So he had survived his dip in the river and was back in his old haunts and presumably up to no good? So what was he doing with this stranger? Who was he, and what connection might he have with the Fortesques other than Tenby's relationship with his stepdaughter? Was he around to help Tenby? How to find out and how to warn His Lordship there was danger around? In the end, there was only one way. Sliding back through the shadows to his horse, Roger made urgent haste to get back to the estate and forewarn the viscount that trouble lay ahead. This appearance of an undoubted enemy and an unknown man could have connections with the shooting in London, or indeed any of the attempts made on His Lordship's life.

Though Tristan had spoken little of the recent affairs affecting his life, Roger, by dint of overhearing talk, listening to conversations not for his ears, had gathered what was amiss. Tristan had made a comment about an unknown relative who might cause trouble, which was why the security had been so tight. This raised the likelihood it could be this relation which no one had heard about until now.

The house was mostly dark and silent by the time he got back to Carwinnion, and Maxwell, the butler, who had travelled down with the staff, was doing the final rounds of the house, locking up and chivvying the last of the servants off to bed.

"His Lordship? Oh, long since retired, Maberly. No, I durst say he would not be amused to be disturbed at this late hour. Is it urgent?" He gazed at Roger's face with raised brows.

"No, I suppose not," Roger admitted, though he was torn with indecision and the gravity of his news. "It can wait till morning. I'll see His Lordship then before his morning ride. Thank you, Mr Maxwell, I'm much obliged." Giving a respectful nod to Maxwell, he said, "I'll bid you goodnight, sir." The butler nodded, and soon the house was silent. Roger made his way to his room using the servants' stairs. Once there, he stood in thought for some moments. Should he remain and rest himself, or go back to Turnpike Cross and keep watching? In the end, he decided to stay and let Tristan choose what course of action he preferred.

He was waiting in the hall when Tristan appeared the next morning. Glancing at Roger's face before heading to the stables, he frowned and said, "What?"

"A word, if I may, sir," Roger said briefly.

Tristan nodded to his study, and Roger followed him in then turned and shut the door behind him. Surprised at this unusual action, Tristan leaned against his desk and stared at his henchman. "Well?" he said.

"I've found Tenby not far from here. Also, another man is with him. Spotted the stranger yesterday and followed him to Turnpike Cross. Found the pair of them conversing close in a rough old excuse for a tavern. Not a place I'd care to visit dressed as Tenby's companion was, though none around took heed. He wasn't extravagant, more middle-of-the-road gent, but if he's staying there he'll need lye washing for fleas!" Roger grinned pithily.

Ignoring Roger's last sally, Tristan scowled and rubbed his hand over his chin. "Tenby, what was he like?"

"Healthy as you please, sir. A bit thinner mayhap, his face more gaunt. Hair fully greyed now; looked as though he hadn't fared too well since I saw him last. The pair of them had their heads together obviously plotting something. Should we get the law involved now?"

"And prove what?"

"Her Ladyship can prove Tenby was going to kidnap her."

"This would precisely give rise to a scandal once the facts were known. Considering all that has gone before and the efforts that have been made, you know that is something I will not tolerate. And in any case, I do not know the local constabulary. Bearing in mind Tenby was a previous resident, who knows which man he could subvert to his cause, even though both Barney and Daisy say he was not liked in the area. No, Roger, we have no option but to handle this ourselves. I'll forego my ride this morning and have an early breakfast. See to your own and be back here in an hour. We'll review the situation and discuss our options. I don't intend to jump into action before thinking carefully. There is too much at stake with the safety of Her Ladyship to consider, let alone the people here that may be in danger."

"I take it you include yourself among those that need to be safeguarded, milord? Something tells me that Tenby's mate could well be the blackguard who's tried to do you in before this."

"Possibly. Still, we are not jumping to conclusions yet. Facts, Roger, that's what we need to scotch any foul play. Off with you! I'll see you later. Tell Maxwell I shall have breakfast now. I shan't be riding."

Roger bowed and went to find the butler, his mind working furiously over the next steps that they could take. Overall was his apprehension that his master was going to put himself in the line of fire. Knowing him of old and the outrageous adventures they had in the past, he knew His Lordship would not hesitate to call the bluff of these villains and, if luck went against him, fall foul of their machinations. Except for himself, renewing his mental vow for the umpteenth time, he knew there was no way he would allow harm to come to the man he revered. He'd go along with whatever was suggested but at the same time his foremost aim was his guardianship.

Sensing his master was deep in thought, especially after calling off his morning ride, Maxwell, contrary to his usual light conversation, served the breakfast silently, fetched the news-sheets then left His Lordship to eat and read alone. Whatever was amiss, and thinking of Maberly's concerned wish to have words with His Lordship the previous evening, he knew something was definitely not right. His own constant ambition was to emulate his predecessor's ability to know what was going on in the Fortesque family at any time so that he could offer his advice or help with whatever was needed.

Harwood, who had risen to the fount of all knowledge at Castle House and was seldom caught napping, was the epitome of resourcefulness. Old as he was, his duties solely for the benefit of the earl, Maxwell had never seen him at a loss regarding his knowledge of the rest of the house. If he, himself, was able to reach that pinnacle of experience concerning the estate and all who lived therein, it would be a dream come true. Allowing that hope to percolate through his brain, it still would have been good to pass the time of day with Harwood and venture a question or two that might throw some light on his suspicions. However, he was in Cornwall and Harwood in Devon, and he would have to make the best of it and rely on his own intuition and judgement.

Could it be that this recent trouble stemmed from that shooting in London? The abrupt removal to Castle House and thence down to this furthermost estate, away from the customary amenities he was used to, hadn't been to his liking. There was hardly any room for servants. He had the pokiest space to sleep in despite the new extension, although at least he had a room, if one could call it that, and not a cupboard to himself. But he could sense trouble approaching and was at a loss to know how he should act. Maybe he would have words with Maberly and prise some information out of him. When he eventually ran Roger to earth later that day, he was in the stables.

Roger's usual impassive face met Maxwell's with puzzlement. "Trouble? Not that I know of. Ask His Lordship. Still, it's always wise to keep a lookout and the staff up to scratch. We are in foreign territory here; for all that it is our country. Best beware."

Beware? But what of? Another shooting? Had the scoundrel followed them to Cornwall? He felt out of his depth but, with that subtle warning, Maxwell had to be content. However, his antenna was on alert, and he would make sure he and the servants would cope with whatever.

Tristan accompanied Roger to the edge of the village and, keeping out of sight, he got a glimpse of the tavern. The place was deserted; even the cottages looked desolate. He wondered who the local landlord was and why he did not care about their upkeep. Maybe, come dusk, the inn had customers, but it did not seem an inviting place to drink.

"No smoke from the chimney. I'd venture the place is empty. Well, we've wasted enough time here and I must return home where I've more to keep me occupied than chasing after ne'er-do-wells." Turning his horse, Tristan set off for Carwinnion.

Riding alongside, Roger said, "What do you wish me to do now, sir?"

"Keep a general lookout as before. Let the scoundrels come to us if they've a mind to. I'm not chasing them over the countryside unless I'm well and truly provoked."

With that, Roger had to be content if not happy with the outcome.

Chapter Forty-Seven

The previous day's rain had cleared overnight, and the day started bright and sunny. Feeling better that morning, with little sign of the usual nausea, Charis decided to enjoy some fresh sea air and take a ride to the beach to see her favourite places again. She guessed Tristan would also be out riding, and maybe they would meet up, but she wanted to be by herself for the present and think over all he had told her about her mother's family background. So much had happened since she was last in Cornwall, she could scarcely believe how her life had changed, how she had changed and become a wife and soon would be a mother. No longer the lonely girl who preferred wandering barefoot along the seashore, but a titled lady to boot, owning the estate she had always loved. Might there also be a possibility she could connect with her relations and hear more of her mother's youth? That would be truly wonderful, and she hoped Tristan could arrange matters so. Dressing quickly in her habit without calling her maid and walking through deserted corridors, she arrived at the stables to find only a young lad doing the stable chores.

"The grooms are in the paddocks, exercising the horses, milady. Shall I run and fetch someone?"

"No, don't bother, just saddle my horse. I am going for a short ride and will meet up with His Lordship."

It was beyond his power to question her, or even think of doing anything other than obey, so he quickly saddled Butterfly and, when she mounted, doffed his cap, bowed and thought no more about it.

Taking the back lanes she had known since childhood that took her off the estate and led to the sea, she was deep in thought and unaware that she had been spotted by the very people who wished her harm.

Mountford and Tenby had ridden clear round the village and the land abutting Carwinnion, reconnoitring the district for Mountford's benefit. Tenby had been agreeable. He knew the place so well he could travel it blindfold, and it gave him time for his fertile brain to work on his plan to scupper this madman who was so intent on killing the Fortesque family as soon as he could. He, personally, could not care less about His Lordship, but he wanted Charis for his own ends. He not only had a grim score to settle with his stepdaughter but he also had to get himself out from under Whaley's murderous intent and clear his debts. To do that, he planned to hand Charis over to the baron. What happened after that would be none of his affair.

"Bloody hellfire! Do you see what I see?" Tenby gasped in surprise as he recognised the slight figure cantering slowly seawards. "It's her! And, by the Devil's own luck, she is by herself!"

Without a word of warning, he dug his heels into the sides of his nag and raced over the soft turf leaving Mountford gaping in shock at his rear. About to bellow after Tenby that this approach wasn't part of the plan, but realising the man was too far ahead to take notice, he set off after Tenby, his mind working furiously at finding a way to prevent the stupid oaf from spoiling his plans.

Lost in thoughts of the future, her eyes on the path ahead that led through the dunes to the shore, Charis was oblivious of the approaching danger until a clutching hand pulled her from her horse and hauled her to her feet to stand facing him but unable to free herself. Horrified, she gazed up at her stepfather in appalled incredulity at his unbelievable reappearance. "You!" she cried out in terror. "We thought you were dead!"

"No thanks to that Barney, I ain't. I still got a score to settle with him. Meanwhile I gotcha good and proper this time, and I'll deal with you first." Standing taut and holding her firmly in his grasp, he shook her brutally causing her to lose her balance. Hampered with the skirt of her habit, she thrust out a leg to steady herself and, in so doing, her knee hit his groin fair and square. As the resulting agony shot through his body, his face turned purple with rage. Raising his cane, he was about to bring it down on Charis when it was wrenched out of his hand by Mountford who had at last caught up with them and swiftly thrown himself off his horse to confront Tenby.

"Oh no, you don't!" he roared, raising the cane himself meaning to whack Tenby over the shoulders with it. But Tenby, a careless fist hitting Charis's cheek and throwing her to one side, wheeled to have at Mountford. The cane in turn swiftly slashed across Tenby's cheek, leaving a deep gash that rapidly filled with blood. In a flash, Tenby pulled out his firing piece from his pocket and aimed it square on Mountford, his other hand gingerly touching his face.

"You mangy spawn of the Devil. Hit me, would you? You are due for your comeuppance anyway and now is as good a time as ever," he sneered. "Think I don't know what your little game is, thanks to your man Wallace. Partial to a good drop of ale he is, and as loose tongued as an idiot when he's had it. Likes to boast as well, so I know you are a long-lost relative of the family who thinks if they all die off you are going to inherit the leavings. Well, well, dammit if it ain't a good scheme, mate, especially if you kill off your accomplices so they don't peach on you. Boot's on the other foot now, and I'm following me own plan which doesn't concern you—"

The sound of a shot rang out without warning, shocking Charis still further as she lay prone on the ground praying that her fall had not injured the baby. She stared up at the two men, fearful of the outcome of that shot, and saw Tenby gaze down at his chest where a crimson spurting hole had appeared.

His glazing eyes lifted to Mountford and he muttered, "Bloody swine, you'll hang..." The next moment, he dropped where he stood and, breathing a last gasp, mumbled, "See you in hell..."

Mountford looked down at his coat pocket and grimaced at the singed hole. His hand had been on the trigger since he had come face to face with Tenby and perceived the man was about to kill him. Well, he had beaten him to it, and now was not the time for recrimination. He still had to keep to his strategy and gain the wealth of the title.

Mountford stared down at Charis; then held out his hand to lift her up. Bowing ironically, he said, "A slight alteration in my plan is called upon, I fear. However, I always come about so you will oblige me by not giving me any trouble, my dear, and I will let you live for now. Come, get up!"

He gripped the hand Charis held up and hauled her to her feet. At once, she began to arrange her clothes and sweep back the loose tendrils of hair, and she picked up her hat. Neither noticed the broken feather that had formerly graced the milliner's creation that still lay on the ground. Trying to bring her shattered senses under control after being privy to the outright murder enacted before her took a great deal of effort but Charis was determined not to resort to hysterics and, if possible, to escape from this situation..

Had Tristan known of Tenby's escape from drowning? Had he known who had committed the attempts on his life? Possibly not, but she knew his sharp brain would have reasoned things out by now. Had Tristan ever shared his thoughts or discussed the danger with her? Well, in a way, but only by issuing orders and telling her he would protect her with guards. But details? Only dribs and drabs, hardly anything at all. Not enough to let her know who else she had to beware of other than Tenby – who it seemed had not drowned after all.

Tristan was a past master at not answering questions or redirecting them, so one lost the crux of the matter. Maybe he thought he was protecting her now she was pregnant? Well, bully for him! It was out in the open and now she was facing this relative, whoever he was! Enough of Tristan's arrogant high-handedness. When she got out of this mess – she paused in her thinking – *if* she got out of this mess, and God willing she had to, there would be a reckoning with His Lordship!

Turning to the stranger, Charis saw him facing her and holding his cravat in his hands. Ignoring his stance, she asked, "I don't know you. Tenby said you were a relative. What do I call you? Surely you can give me a name."

Mountford took in her intelligent features with an unexpected wryness. She was beautiful in every aspect of womanhood, and again he envied her husband's possession of her. Much as he coveted that role, he knew he could never aspire to ownership. The estate would suffice, and the benefits accruing from that. She would have to go but not, he thought, immediately. She might afford him some pleasure before he got rid of her.

"I suppose any name might do, but it doesn't matter you knowing. My true name is Reginald Mountford, and I am distantly related to you, perhaps only for a short time, of course. Hold out your hands!"

His abrupt order made her flinch along with the ice curdling in her veins at his words. She held out her hands and, with his cravat, he swiftly tied them tightly together with close knots. "Pity your horse made off when that fool pulled you down. You'll have to ride his, and do without a side saddle."

"I have a divided skirt, Mountford. I will manage quite well. But you would be wise to leave me here. My husband is not known for leniency in dishing out retribution. Your intention to kidnap me is not in your best interest. I suggest you escape while you can. Someone will be searching for me as we speak, and I give little for your chances when they find you."

"Well, you're the cocky one and no mistake. Find me? They'll have a cat in hell's chance of that." Taking a large handkerchief from his pocket, he twisted it cornerwise then, passing it across her open mouth, tied it tightly behind her head. "Scream if you like. With that on your mouth, the noise won't get far. Now, get a move on," he growled, thinking she needed precise instructions on how to mount a horse without a side saddle. "Put your foot in the stirrup and swing your other leg over the horse. Don't do anything stupid. I have another loaded gun ready, and it won't cost me dear to kill you here and now."

Inwardly terrified at his threats but equally determined not to show her fright, Charis did as she was told and finally sat in the saddle while he adjusted the stirrups. Then he tied her wrists to the saddle horn and took hold of the reins. He was not to know that riding astride was second nature to her as she had ridden that way all of her life. She thought of Tristan's ruling that she protect her baby and hated that she was not in control of her mount. It was a disadvantage but, come what may, all she need do was not fall.

Within moments, they were travelling east, and her captor rode them hard down deserted tracks, pulling off the road if he saw anyone en route. Eventually, they bypassed Penryn and took shelter in a vacant barn. By this time Charis was cold, hungry and exhausted. She collapsed wearily on a pile of straw, too spent to more than moan as he tied her wrists to a spike on the wall.

"I won't be long. I'll fetch food." He was gone before she could nod, and her eyes were closed in sleep when he returned. She roused when he spread a horse blanket over her and, releasing her wrists from their bindings, held out a rough piece of bread with a hunk of cheese on the top. She was too famished to deny the offering, and even the mug of water he gave her tasted like champagne. After eating, she curled up and went to sleep.

Chapter Forty-Eight

Tristan strode in through the side door heading for the breakfast parlour, only stopping briefly to wash his hands in a retiring room.

Maxwell met him at the door looking concerned. "Milord, I beg your pardon, but is Her Ladyship with you?"

"No, she is still abed, I would imagine. Why do you ask?"

"Oh dear." Maxwell wrung his hands. "Her maid did not realise she might have gone out. In fact, no one did, at least no one from the house has seen her. Her horse was missing, and the young stable boy said he had saddled it for her…" He paused to take a breath.

"Get on with it, man!" Tristan was beyond terse.

"We thought she was with you, but her horse has come back and she is not with it."

"Christ! Where the hell were all of you? Didn't I give orders she was to be protected and cared for?" His face beginning to frown before was now graven in stone. "Where's Maberly? Fetch him!"

"We have no idea. Apparently, he went out early. We thought he was with you."

Tristan stood silent for a moment while fury and anger raced through his system. She'd come off her horse, that was evident. She could be lying injured God knows where. Or dead! No, he would not, could not go down that path. She was far too precious to contemplate something so awful. Oh God, if he lost her? Gritting his teeth, he pulled himself together. "Warn all the men available to get saddled. I want the estate searched immediately. You and the indoor servants are to search the house. Every room, top to bottom, attics to cellars." Though what she would want in the cellars escaped him.

"Yes, milord, at once. Where do we find you if there is news?"

He paused. "I'm off to Turnpike Cross."

His butler's face changed from his usual blandness to surprise.

"Roger Maberly is there. I need to find him."

"Very good, milord. Should we find Her Ladyship, we shall send immediate news."

Roger had indeed left early that morning for Turnpike Cross again, hoping to find and track the two men he now thought of as villains. As ever, fate liked to throw in a party piece. Halfway there, his horse cast a shoe and began to hobble. He cursed his nemesis up hill and down dale but, with no choice but to lead the animal, he decided to carry on to the village. He couldn't recall if he had seen a smithy, but surely he would be able to hire a nag of some description and send later for his own.

The alehouse was shut when he arrived, and an inquiry at a nearby cottage said the owner was in Helston at a local fair. No, the place was empty; any guests had gone. Not that they had many of those. It was, after all, just an alehouse. Yes, there had been two callers who'd stayed but they had vanished overnight. Cursing his bad luck as he could not find anyone in the village to loan him a horse, Roger, hauling his horse behind him, directed his feet towards Carwinnion knowing he had a long, tiring walk ahead.

Two miles later, the group that rode towards him filled him with joy until he saw his master's face frowning down at him.

"Well?"

"They've left, milord."

"And?"

He shrugged. "I've no idea where. I think—"

"I don't pay you to think. I pay you to follow orders. You did not tell me you were coming back here. I thought it was decided to leave well alone for the moment. However, we have more to consider. My wife is missing. The horse she was riding, presumably without an escort, has returned to the stable. We have no trace of her whereabouts. I rode this way to see if you have news. Obviously not. Get back to the house quick as you can, get another mount, and join the others in the search. I will speak to you later." Tristan turned and galloped back the way he had come leaving Roger ashen-faced with distress.

Clambering on the back of a groom's horse and still holding the reins of his horse, he spent the next half-hour feeling disheartened and thoroughly miserable as he thought about his careless action of pleasing himself and not attending to the orders of his master. Had his neglect contributed to the disappearance of Lady Charis? His vow to protect her wasn't worth twopence. His Lordship would rightly think that neglect would apply to him as well.

His despairing sigh reached the ears of the rider in front. "Let it go, mate. He'll forgive you in time."

"I doubt it," Roger replied. "His Lordship is not a forgiving man."

With his body clenched in anxiety, Tristan returned to the house to plan his next move knowing he must keep his wits together to face what peril or danger was before him. He was in the breakfast parlour quickly having a bite to eat before going out again when Maxwell came in, his face as white as chalk.

"A messenger has arrived, milord. They have found a body..."

Half-rising, the blood draining from his face, Tristan stared back at his butler, his eyes like shards of ice. Oh God, was it...

"No, no! Milord, it's not Her Ladyship." Equally distressed, Maxwell hastened to say, "It's a man. A local man from the village who was helping with the search recognises him as a previous resident of this house. They are leaving him until you see what's happened."

"Do you know where Maberly is?" Tristan, with an iron effort, brought his nerves under control, realising now more than ever that he had to retain a sensible attitude of command in his household.

"He is with the...er-er...body, milord," Maxwell stuttered.

"Thank you, Maxwell. Send to the stables to saddle my horse, If Everett is there, he is to come with me. Courage, Maxwell. We must, God willing, come through this and find Her Ladyship. Oh, find my jacket, please." Striding out of the room, his brain a welter of conjecture, he was already garbed for riding, so it took no more than minutes before he was on his way accompanied by Everett. If the man had been recognised, it could only be Tenby. Had there been a falling out between the two men? If so, that still left the question of his wife.

Maberly was crouching a few yards away from the body when Tristan arrived. He stood, walked over to stand by His Lordship's horse and bowed low, his face a mixture of anxiety and despair. "Milord."

Tristan gazed down at the man he had berated with such angry scorn and knew he was at least partly to blame. His unthinking words had bitten deep into a man he not only respected but had been his staunch companion for so many years he could scarcely remember how long. Even excusing the emotion tied up with all that had transpired, he had to make amends. He dismounted and walked towards the body with Maberly following close behind.

"Roger, what do you make of this?" he said, gazing down at a man he had heard of but had barely seen that day in Bath at Caroline's.

Hearing the familiar name, Roger almost wept. Glory be! He was forgiven. "Gunshot to the chest killed him. He was also hit with that cane lying there. A savage blow, by all accounts."

"I heard he was uncommonly free with that missile. I collect he may have had his comeuppance, and deservedly so. Anyway, you confirm he is Thomas Tenby?"

"I do indeed, sir. But there's more. I discovered a broken feather that I think belongs to Her Ladyship's riding hat. A peacock's feather." He held it out to show his master. "I found it on the ground close by the body. Then, just now, I saw the imprint of a horseshoe over there in the mud." He waved his hand at the edge of the field. "I've seen the particular nailing the shoe makes on soft ground before at Castle House. Rear side of the estate and in a small glade in the woods. The gate was tampered but so cleverly one would have to know what one was looking for."

"You never said." Tristan looked quizzically at his groom.

"I never got a chance. We all left immediately for Cornwall, and I felt we left that particular trouble behind. I was going to keep a watch on our return, but from this imprint I'd say trouble followed us here."

"So, that was the itch you spoke of. Hmm, a powerful prophesy, methinks. I recollect you talking of it before, and always we got out of trouble by a small margin. I think we can assume now that the two men did indeed have a falling-out, and Tenby lost. The other man has my wife. If it is that relative of mine, has he taken her to blackmail me or to kill her? Either way, I intend to tear him apart."

The clear but softly spoken words lost none of their lethal intensity because they were quiet. Roger felt a shiver go down his back as he listened. His master was a man who unfailingly followed the path of justice. Someone had crossed the Rubicon, and Roger knew his master would never let go until he found the culprit. So be it; he was with him all the way.

"What now, sir? What do you wish me to do?"

"Back to the house and a meeting. I want to go over every clue we have as soon as possible. The body can be taken back as well, and the constables told. I must have words with the authority here and give them the facts. Also, I must say I was wrong, and your intuition or itch, call it what you may, was right, Roger. I have no excuse."

"Oh, you have, sir, and have had for a long time. This last thing with your wife is unbearable; at least it is to me. Since we first met her, I have respected her enormously, and I am so glad you married. My role at your wedding will be remembered for the rest of my days, and if I am lucky enough to meet someone…well, enough said."

"When you meet someone, I shall be pleased to return the compliment and act as your best man. So don't put off in your search. Time is passing quickly for us both." Tristan clapped Roger on the back; then headed to his horse and mounted. Turning back to Roger, he called, "Hurry, we have much to talk over and decide."

Chapter Forty-Nine

It was almost three days before Charis and Mountford reached North Molton; days of hard riding and poor accommodation. Charis was so exhausted it barely impacted on her mind that she was once again in the vicinity of Castle House. Concerned that his lodgings might have been let to someone else while he was absent, Mountford's attention was concerned with getting Charis hidden away as soon as possible. Pulling her off her horse and, because she could hardly stand, hoisting her up and finding that all was quiet and the place still empty, he opened the door and carried her up to a bedroom.

Dumping her on a bed and throwing a blanket over her, he muttered, "I'll bring food." Not even bothering to lock the door, knowing she was in no fit state to escape, he went back downstairs and walked the horses round to the stable. Fortunately, there was still fodder so, unsaddling them, he put each into their stall, filled the troughs with hay and corn pellets and, deciding he was too tired to groom, left them to get on with it.

Next stop was a bakery. The owner had only just come down to begin his nightly baking and was in a back shed shifting bags of flour. Mountford was in and out of the shop in a flash, grabbing two stale loaves of that day's baking from a bin and a hunk of farm cheese that was kept for local people. It never occurred to the baker he had been robbed until his wife taxed him with giving the food free of charge to the gypsies. Denying he was at fault, he remained totally mystified.

Back at the lodgings, Mountford left a plate of bread and cheese and a cup of water beside the recumbent figure, which still did not stir or even moan. Too exhausted to find a rope to bind her, nor even locking the door, he filled himself with food and sought his own bed. Within moments, he was fast asleep.

A short while later, the figure in the next room uncurled and, realising she was no longer tethered, stretched. Charis had been asleep until disturbed by Mountford coming into her room and, deciding not to move or blink an eye, kept still until she heard loud snoring from the room next door. Sitting up and eyeing the unappetising fare beside her, she nevertheless broke off a crust and started munching. What now? Could she escape this fiend who was intent on killing her? Now, more than any time in that dreadful journey, she thought there might be a chance. Any chance was better than none.

Catching sight of familiar names on the odd signposts pointing down indistinguishable lanes in their wild race through the countryside as she neared home, her memory was jogged from her previous trips round the district in Tristan's curricle and her foray's riding to the local villages accompanied by a groom. She realised she was close enough to safety to escape from her persecutor, if only she had the courage. Stretching and bending her legs restored the circulation and, at last, she stood up to determine her ability to move. Making an allowance for the fact her thighs ached abominably, she still felt able to make the attempt to flee.

After taking a last bite of the bread and cheese, she moved to the door and listened. The snoring sounded even louder, so she tried the door and found to her relief it wasn't locked. He must have been too tired to remember. Edging to the stairs and holding onto a side rail, she moved down one step at a time on her bottom thus spreading the weight on any loose board that might squeak with the weight of a single foot. Reaching the ground floor, she discovered the main door was securely locked and bolted high up where she could not reach but, tiptoeing to a rear kitchen, she saw a flimsy door that led to another room. Elated, she saw rough wooden stalls and the two horses.

She realised she hadn't the strength to saddle the huge grey that Mountford had ridden that had suffered less than the nag that had been her mount, but it was the one she intended to use, so she just tossed a horse blanket over his back and decided she could manage. Speed was her only ally, and the grey certainly had stamina, and bareback riding was a skill she had learned from her childhood.

Opening the back door, she peered out and saw it led to an alleyway and thence to the village street. Pulling a chair carefully and silently to the side of the horse, she climbed on it and then managed to clamber directly onto the horse's back. Loosing the tethered reins, she backed the animal out of the stall then guided it to the open door. Walking it to the main street, her heart in her mouth as she heard the echoing sound of its hooves, she kept the horse moving steadily along the lane, holding her breath in sheer fright lest Mountford heard her leaving.

Once into the main thoroughfare, Charis dug her heels into the horse and took off, but it was an age before she inhaled and lost her dizziness. Reaching the last house of the village and following signposts, bending low over the steed's neck and gripping onto the reins and the coarse hair that formed a rough mane, she managed to keep her seat and maintain the horse to a constant hard gallop. Fortunately, the sky was clear, the night not so dark that she couldn't see hedges on either side. Even the road surfaces seemed amazingly clear of ruts. All the same, as she clung to her racing and barely controlled animal, she kept praying that it wouldn't come to grief or that she would fall off.

In her mind's eye, she imagined the appalled, frankly horrified anger that Tristan would explode with if he could see her now. She daren't think of how she was treating her baby. She only knew that this time, above all the other times, she was running away to freedom and to her love.

Mountford stirred briefly in his sleep as some sound marred the silence of night. Then he swiftly sank again into a far deeper slumber. He was dead to the world until late in the morning when a rumbling cart brought him to wakefulness and then to utter rage. Finding Her Ladyship gone was bad enough, but when he discovered his horse had vanished too his wrath was beyond volcanic. Without exception in this long-running strategy he had put together, totally convinced that it would bring him success, nothing but nothing had gone right. Disaster had met him at every turn.

Well, he had enough! Even if he went down for it himself, he would kill these two opponents who stood in the way of him inheriting an earldom. That streak of envy and madness that had been with him since childhood began to escalate into a lunacy that lost all reason. He was on a collision course to murder, come what may.

Chapter Fifty

By the time Charis reached the gates of Castle House and turned up the drive, her sharp brain was turning over the action she needed to adopt when she arrived home. Most important of all, she needed to evade Mountford as she knew he would attempt to kidnap her again, so she had to stay hidden. Then, too, she knew how hard Tristan had worked to make sure any scandal of their speedy and unusual timing of a marriage did not reach the *ton*, the social structure ever on the hunt for salacious tittle-tattle. It was bad enough that news might come out about the murder of her stepfather, though that could be glossed over, but a kidnapping of a viscountess would provide endless gossip that the family would hate.

She turned off the stony drive onto the grass to silence her approach to the house; then slowly and quietly made her way to the stables. Dawn was just laying a finger of light across the sky when she slid down from her mount and stood, still holding onto the reins and the horse blanket, to catch a breath of relief for her amazing escape and the fact she was home. Despite her care to be quiet, a window opened above the stables and a voice cried out, "Who's there?"

"Shush, Hewitt, it's me! Lady Fortesque! Come down, but quietly, I beg. I need your help."

Stopping only to pull on trousers and a jacket, Ted Hewitt, the head groom, came into the yard at a rush, astounded to see Her Ladyship holding onto the horse as if she might fall any minute. Ignoring protocol, he leapt forward and took her weight, helping her into the stables and settling her on a stool. "My God! Whatever has happened? Why are you here on your own like this? You're exhausted—"

Weakly, she raised a hand to stop his exclamations; then slowly told him what had happened to her. "You have to keep silent on this, Ted.

His Lordship will require this above all things. Now, I want you to bring Melrose to me and also a young maid you can trust to keep silent. My own maid is still in Cornwall..."

"Your Ladyship, worry not. I will fetch your trusted servants."

Melrose proved able to manage everything for the comfort of Charis. She was installed in a bedroom in the west wing as she knew if she went back to her own bedroom the whole of the house would know. Once bathed, and her hair washed and brushed by the maid, she had eaten a light meal. Then, thankfully, she was tucked into a warm bed to close her eyes and sleep. Amazingly, the morning was hardly begun, the house rising to its daily tasks, and the earl not yet awakened for his morning tea.

"I have to alert His Lordship, ma'am. It would distress him to know you are here and have not spoken with him," Melrose had said before she retired to bed.

"By all means, Melrose. He is the last man who would disclose my hiding place. Tell him I will attend him as soon as I have rested. I am worn out; I need to sleep but not too long. Wake me in two hours. I will see him then."

It was shortly before luncheon before Melrose felt able, with the permission of his master, to rouse the exhausted woman, and even then bade the housemaid to treat her gently and take her time. Eventually, she entered the earl's sitting room and, with a sigh, knelt down before him and laid her head on his lap. "Father, you have no idea how thankful I am to be here..."

"Hush, my dearest girl, no more thankful than I to have you safe. Melrose has told me some of the story, but I'm sure you have more to tell. We shall dine here, if it pleases you, and you can relax and tell all. I have not sent word to my son yet. Not knowing the circumstances, I needed to wait until you gave permission."

"It will be hard on him, but I think we should wait until you have heard all and then decide how we may proceed." They proceeded to eat their luncheon as Charis told Amery the full story from being accosted in the meadow by the beach, the murder of Tenby, what had transpired since then, and the details of her escape.

"I must say you are a brave woman. It is an incredible story," Amery said in admiration. "I don't know another lady who would have been able to accomplish such daring, but then I forget you are already a fearless traveller if not a prime escapee."

"Not so, Father. I am terrified of that scoundrel finding me again. If I seem brave, it is only because I grit my teeth and try to do what is best. Inside, I am truly scared. I really must stay hidden until Tristan eventually returns and decides what to do."

"Yes, I agree. Hewitt has hidden the horse you arrived on, and sworn his stable lads to silence. Harwood has control of the household, so I swear you can rest easy that Mountford will never find out you have arrived here. Likely, he will be searching around North Molton to see if you have fallen by the way and are seeking local help. Now, my dear, you will please an old man and agree to Marshall having a good look at you. I dislike your strained face, even knowing the reason for it. You are carrying my son's heir and have faced a terrible time. You need care and attention, dear girl, so I insist Marshall attends you."

Charis smiled. "To put your mind at rest, I will see Dr Marshall. I presume, knowing you, he is waiting to be announced." She grinned at him, her eyes dancing with mirth. "And you have already instructed Melrose to tie me down should I not agree?"

Amery grinned and shook his head. "Tristan calls you a minx, and I daresay I agree. Run along, Charis, and see Richard. I shall expect a full report later. Then we must decide how we shall manage until we see Tristan again. Meanwhile, I shall rest. See you later."

Charis gave him a deep curtsey then went off to see the doctor.

Richard Marshall's examination was thorough, and finally he sat down on a nearby chair and smiled at her. He was privy to all that had transpired and was amazed she been saved a miscarriage. "Considering the trials you have put this infant through, he or she must be amazingly tenacious. The only thing amiss is a loss of weight, accountable by your poor diet over the last few days, which will be remedied from now on. As will your exhaustion lessen with rest. Other than that, the babe is still safely held and looks to remain. However, I shall ring a peal over you if you do not mind my instructions."

Smiling back with relief, she said, "Tristan will be pleased at your verdict and yes, until he arrives, I promise to rest. In any case, I must not show my face outside these rooms, so I will amuse myself and my father-in-law playing chess. He is a staunch competitor and I have yet to beat him, though I'm determined I will in the end."

Richard chuckled at her words. "I swear his health improves

enormously when you are around. You are the best tonic he could have, and he loves you dearly. In fact, we all benefit as he guards his temper when you are with him. The pain has also improved with the willow tisane you recommended. I also tried it on others in the village."

"Maybe it is an old wives' remedy, but Daisy my housekeeper used to brew up bottles of the stuff for ailing people in the village, and they all swore it helped a lot."

"I have begun work with a medical friend of mine to investigate the efficacies of old remedies and herbs, and he has surprising results to show for his efforts. I hope to send a paper to the Medical Council to alert them to our findings and maybe join with others in the same search. I count this due to you, My Lady. You have a habit of making a body think and confound our preconceptions of medicine."

She laughed and held up her hands in denial. "Not so, Richard. I'm sure you will find many women who have had medicinal lore passed down through generations of families."

"Be that as it may, you have started me on a crusade which I hope will benefit many." He stood and held out his hand to shake hers. "Now, I must be off, My Lady. I shall report as ordered to the earl," he grinned, "and, with reservations of course, let him know how I find you. No doubt, I shall also see your husband when he returns. Anxiety will have taken a toll of him too, so I counsel you to look after him as well."

Dr Marshall bowed to Charis and opened the door; then turned back to her. "Oh, by the way, Dr Brunton, the man who saw you and your husband in London, has been in touch with me and hopes to visit. He is a great friend of mine. We interned together. He sent his regards." Bowing once more, he left before she could comment further. It would be pleasant to see the man again, she thought, this time socially, though possibly he would be equally pleased her pregnancy was confirmed. She yawned deeply and, throwing back the covers, slid into bed. A nap was due. She would need all the rest she could get before Tristan arrived.

Chapter Fifty-One

It was late in the afternoon when the bedroom door was thrown wide open, rousing Charis from a deep sleep. Alarmed at the noise and bewildered at the sight she saw in the doorway, she hurriedly sat up, her mouth opening in surprise. "You!" she gasped.

"Yes, me," he growled. "Who did you expect? And what are you doing in this room? I collect your quarters lie elsewhere."

"I-I..." Lost for words, taken aback at the blazing fury she beheld, she stuttered, "D-didn't y-your father tell you?"

"Haven't seen him; only Harwood. He told me where you were. Now I'm going to kill you, slowly and painfully, taking a long time..."

"Tristan, you wouldn't!" She giggled; then stopped as she gazed at his hard, angry eyes glaring back at her.

He strode over to the bed and loomed over her. "Right now, I'd do it without a shred of compunction! Do you know what I have been through? Every mile here filled with terror I might find you dead!"

Oh ho! So because he had been frightened, he wanted a fight to assuage his feelings. Well, she had plenty of issues and feelings too with this damned high-handed arrogant brute she had married. Charis gathered her courage and stared back at him. Time for a reckoning! Let battle commence!

"Yes, I might well have been – no thanks to you. Did you tell me you knew Tenby was still alive? No! But you knew, didn't you? As you knew who it was who was trying to kill you. Did it ever occur to you that, apart from issuing arrogant orders, I would need to know too if only to take better precautions? I believed I was safe at Carwinnion. No one said otherwise. And in the end, I rescued myself. Not you! Nor the whole caboodle of servants you have dancing to your tune. Me! And you have the gall to come here and bleat about your fear! If you had stopped to confer with your father, he would have told you that, with his agreement, it was better for me to hide in this room so that Mountford would not know I had managed to return home and have him kidnap me again."

In sheer surprise at the outburst, Tristan took a step back and held up his hands as though to either placate or stem the torrent. With her eyes blazing and her breasts heaving with passionate anger, Tristan had never seen her like this. She looked glorious! And those breasts, almost exposed in the flimsy nightgown. Filled with lust and an eagerness to claim her, he stepped forward again.

"Don't you dare touch me!" Her acid tone brought him to a halt.

"But, Charis, sweetheart, I'm sorry if I had the wrong impression. Truly, until I arrived here, I did not know you had escaped. I thought – no, I did not know what to think. Only that you were missing while I was—"

"Go away, speak to your father. I have nothing more to say and I wish to bathe before dinner." How she managed the curtness in her voice was a miracle, except she knew she must not give way.

His face turned to stone. He bowed and pulled open the door. "I too must bathe. I shall see you at dinner then. *Au revoir.*" He left.

Tears she had held back with such an effort cascaded down her cheeks, and she turned and sobbed into her pillow as though her heart would break. Oh, this was one almighty quarrel that they might never get over. His pride was such that her outright accusations had hit home in a way he would never forgive. Had she gone too far?

Dinner was a disaster. The atmosphere even affected the servants who crept round the table scared to disturb the silence, serving food that stayed untouched on plates. Sitting at the head of the table, the earl gazed in consternation at his son and daughter-in-law. What had gone wrong with his family? His earlier talk with his son was unexpectedly strained, although he knew how upset Tristan was with the dreadful affair and thought how relieved he should have been to see his wife safe. Significantly, he thought something had happened when Tristan had seen her earlier. That they had quarrelled was obvious, but what the hell was it about? Charis's puffy eyes still showed on her downcast face, so whatever had caused it was serious.

All too soon, once covers had been removed, Charis stood, curtsied to the earl and, without a glance at Tristan, walked out of the room. Amery waved a negative hand at the butler offering the port. "Not for me, thank you. Tristan?" His son shook his head.

"I'll ring when I want you," said the earl to the butler, and both he and the footmen left the room. When they had gone, he gazed at his son. "An explanation is called for, I believe."

His son shrugged. "I seem to have hurt her feelings."

"Oh?" The terseness of the single syllable held displeasure.

Tristan flung his napkin down and stood. "I will speak to you in your room when the footmen have taken you upstairs." He rang a bell for the footmen adding, "See you shortly," and stalked off to the study.

Amery watched him go, recalling him as a lad. When he didn't get his own way, he was as stiff-necked as a rooster. He chuckled to himself. Charis, it seemed, was on a warpath. Not before time, he felt. Tristan had taken no notice of his advice to treat her gently and let her have some say in matters. He'd bet a pound to a penny that she had rebelled. Well, good for her! Taken upstairs to his sitting room the earl sat in his comfortable wing chair, a glass of prime malt whisky in his hand, quietly ruminating on the quirks of newly-weds, and came to the conclusion Tristan would have to learn the hard way.

Leaning against his desk in his study, Tristan also had a drink in his hand. He surveyed the half-empty glass of brandy ruefully. Dutch courage no less, in order to face his father. Better than a book in his pants, he supposed, but he was not looking forward to facing his sire any more than he had as a young boy. He tossed the remainder of the liquid back then set out for the west wing. He knocked and entered his father's sitting room to find him seated in his usual chair watching the door, his expression somewhat dispassionate.

Tristan moved into the room, scarcely knowing what he was going to say. Then he shrugged. "I'm here. You wanted to talk?"

"No, I believe you must." The voice was cutting, and then abrasion came into play. "What the bloody hell did you say to her?"

"That I was going to kill her!"

"*Humph*! Times have certainly changed. Replacing loving words to one's dearly beloved with vehement expressions of brutality doesn't seem to resemble the way I was brought up."

"Look, Father," Tristan scraped frantic fingers through his hair until it almost stood on end then opened his arms out wide, "she went missing from Carwinnion. Her horse came back to the stables with the reins hanging. We searched everywhere. Then news came in that a body had been found. Believe me – you must believe me – I nearly died too. When I discovered it was Tenby, and Roger found traces of Charis and who we now know is Mountford, we still hadn't a clue where he had taken her, though somehow I knew he would bring her back here. I've had my mounts nearly die under me in an effort to reach you—"

"Is that so? Well, shall we compare? Charis arrived before dawn riding a huge almost uncontrollable gelding, bareback if you please. He was too big for her to saddle. Hewitt carried her into the stables and fetched Melrose. She was so done up and couldn't walk he had to get Jordan, my footman, to carry her up here. It took two maids to bathe and tend her and put her to bed. Hours later, she came to see me, still exhausted, only concerned that Mountford wouldn't find her or that we would not have to face the scandal of her kidnapping. You look hale and hearty, my boy. She has slept in barns, had little or no food. Has lost weight and, moreover, is carrying my grandchild! According to Dr Marshall, we, you and I, are very fortunate she hasn't lost the baby. And your arrogance and threats, no doubt gained in foreign places, has brought intimidation to a fine art. If she never speaks to you again, it will only be what you deserve." Amery stopped to cough, his throat dry with effort, as he pressed a shaking hand holding a handkerchief to his lips. He took a sip of his whisky and went to speak again, but Tristan forestalled him.

"I've really bungled matters, haven't I?"

"Bungled? I'd say that is the least you have done."

Then all of a sudden the door opened, and Charis came in. She was dressed for bed, her feet bare, a dressing gown buttoned tightly to her neck.

"I heard you shouting. Please don't quarrel on my account. I can't bear it..." She flew across the room to Amery and buried her face in his lap. Raising it a moment later, her tears already soaking her cheeks, she said, "I won't come between you both. I'll go away..." She sobbed then curled closer to Amery who, holding her tight, looked over her bent figure at his son.

Tristan was still on his feet staring down at his wife, his face ashen with misery. He rubbed a hand over his eyes then said brokenly, "I'd better leave you. It seems I'm not wanted..." Moving swiftly, he was gone before Amery could speak.

Gently, easing the overwrought figure in his arms, Amery made Charis sit up and, when she raised her head, mopped her face and smiled. "You promised me you were done with running, my child, so why torment me now?"

"I don't want you to quarrel and-and –" she hiccupped, "he doesn't want me anymore..."

"What rubbish! Of course he wants you. He is head over heels in love with you."

She stared round-eyed at him. "He loves me still? He said so, but I'm sure he has changed his mind. He was in such a furious temper—"

"May I make a suggestion?" Amery kept a straight face though it was difficult to contain his chuckles. Oh, this lovesick pair really needed a push to find their way back to happiness.

Charis nodded.

"Go find Tristan. He'll probably be in the master suite. Go in but don't say a word. Mind me, not one word. Just stand and look at him. Then you will find out if he truly loves you." He bent and kissed her cheek. "Now, off with you. I'll see you tomorrow. Go on, hurry!"

After the door had closed behind her, Melrose appeared from the dressing room. "Ho, milord, shall I ready you for bed? You must be tired after playing matchmaker."

"Melrose, confound you! What have I said about listening in?" Amery smiled and added, "Do you think it will work?"

"With your craftsmanship, it could hardly fail."

The two men, master and servant but close friends for all that, grinned at each other. Amery, feeling satisfied, nodded. "We'll see the result tomorrow."

Chapter Fifty-Two

Still barefoot and in her nightwear, Charis, after peeping into the study to find it empty, did as she was bid and went upstairs to the door of their bedroom. She stood there for a minute, wondering if her father-in-law had advised her correctly. If she was spurned? No, she must not be so negative for here and now her marriage was at stake.

Opening the door quietly, she saw Tristan standing looking out of a window, his hands in his pockets, his shoulders bent as though all the cares of the world were on them. She entered and turned to close the door. The click of the lock alerted him, and he spun round. She stood silent looking back at him. He took a step towards her.

After a long moment, he said brokenly, "Charis, I am so sorry. My dearest love, will you forgive me?"

She smiled joyfully. "You know I will."

At that, he leapt towards her and enfolded her in his arms burying his face in her curls.

"Oh, my darling, I love you so much, it hurts. I thought you wanted to leave me..."

"I won't leave you if you really and truly love me, but you were so cross..." She nestled close to his body overjoyed that at last she could share her own love for him.

"I'm an utter cad to treat you so badly, but I do love you. Forever and ever. My oath on it."

"As I love you, too, my darling. Forever sounds just right."

He stared down into her eyes and saw the truth of her words, closed his arms tighter, and bent his head and set his lips to hers. Then together they reached for and found the supreme pleasure of finding each other again, of forging a relationship based on true love, a partnership that had carried them safely home and into each other's arms. They came together as though newly forged in fire, the flames of their uniting carrying them through passion and desire into ecstasy.

As he held her in his arms, then joined their bodies time and time again throughout the night, he thought just once of the imminent days to come and his intention to kill Mountford. Imprisonment would not be enough. He wanted him off the face of the earth, no longer a danger to his kin now or his family in the future.

Charis stirred drowsily, conscious she was by herself in bed, and then she heard water splashing in their bathing chamber. She sat up as Tristan appeared in the doorway towelling his head, looking freshly shaven. He smirked as his wife yawned sleepily and said, "Someone keeping you from your nightly slumbers, my love?"

"Too true. Is that someone going riding?"

"Not this morning, I'm pleased to say. We'll enjoy breakfast here, sweetheart. Maybe lunch later. Dinner? I suppose yes, we shall go down to dinner. Perhaps I shall have caught up by then on all I have missed these last few days and let you rest."

"Tristan! For goodness' sake, we can't stay here all day! What will your father think? Or the servants?"

"They can think what they like. I've got my wife back with me and that is all I'm concerned with. Still, if you are bored with me..."

She giggled. "Not yet, My Lord, not while you are so inventive."

He beamed again and bowed extravagantly.

A knock on the door heralded breakfast and stilled their repartee. Then, true to his word, he stayed by her side until late afternoon.

Fetching the earl's luncheon gave Melrose a chance to inquire, "Er, about the young couple, have you heard anything?"

"No, the silence is golden, I'm pleased to say." Amery smirked contentedly. "As is their absence from the many daily duties we humans inflict on ourselves. A rest from those chores can be most appealing. Melrose, my trusty servant, I believe the contretemps so far suffered is healed. My children have reconciled."

"Congratulations, milord, your discernment leaves me dumb."

"Dumb? Good lord, a huge benefit for my ears, I declare. I have

261

never known you short of words before."

"No doubt, I shall recover, milord."

"Hmm, pity."

Much later, at dinner, the atmosphere was congenial and the earl basked in the knowledge that his cherished children were once again as loving as before. That was until Tristan said quietly, "Before you retire, sir, I'd like you to join Charis and me in the study. There are still matters of import to resolve, and your advice will be welcome."

"Yes, Tristan, that subject has concerned me also. I believe we have a task ahead of us that must not fail. I am happy to assist."

It was late when at last the three of them retired to bed. Every detail of attacks by Mountford, including the failed attempts over a long period on Tristan, was discussed.

Charis sat quietly listening, absorbing the significance of the underhand way in which Mountford operated, until it was her turn to speak of her ordeal. She interrupted only once apart from that. "It seems to me that he hides, advances a little with an attempt, tries to use someone else to front him; then, when he fails, he melts back into the shadows and patiently waits for another opportunity. Is he a coward at heart or just very wary?"

"He had to present an innocent front to the world if he hoped to inherit the earldom. An innocent with a good alibi was what he craved until he made the mistake of shooting Tenby and kidnapping you," Amery explained. "I wonder if he realises after all that has taken place he will never succeed to that office. Your escape, my dear, put paid to his aspirations with a vengeance." He looked at his son. "I believe, Tristan, your men are still searching for him as we speak?"

"Correct. They've covered his old home, haunts he has used, any sightings by friends or neighbours, not that he has any of the former, by all accounts – everywhere they can think. I had a message through before dinner that no trace has been found. Where he is at this moment is baffling. He may even have gone abroad. In opposition, I have enlisted almost an army of men to defend this place. A mouse might slip through, but no one intent on vengeance. And, with his pompous ambition thwarted, that is all he has left in this sorry débâcle."

Charis shivered as he spoke. His tone left no room for pity or forgiveness. Once he had seen her bruised cheek and the bruises on her upper arms and wrists then Mountford was a doomed man.

"Thanks to your efforts, son, I judge we can sleep soundly in our beds tonight. I'm off to enjoy my rest. I suggest you both follow suit. Charis, you must take great care from now on of yourself and my grandchild. Try to be patient with us old fusspots that want to wrap you up safe. I'm sure we both will try not to crowd you too much."

"Thank you for that accolade, Father! I am neither an old fusspot nor one who pampers too much. In fact…oh, never mind!" Tristan rose to ring the bell for the footmen to take his father to bed.

Charis smothered a grin at his testiness. Although things were happily resolved between them, any allusion to control put him on edge. Still, in the night ahead, she would take the scowl off his face and kiss him better.

A fortnight later, tension escalating as each day passed, Tristan strode over to a window in his study and glared out of it for some moments until he finally threw up his hands in frustration. "I can't accept he has given up! Hellfire! What is he waiting for? Does he think *I* will give up and send the men home?"

"No one who knows you, milord, will ever draw that conclusion," his secretary said quietly, searching his brain to find words to placate the temper that seethed beneath the surface of his employer. Yet, with all that was going on, he personally was well satisfied with the estate affairs. Taken on soon after Tristan had come home, John Watson had relished the job both at Castle House and a short stint in London. His references were immaculate, and Tristan and he had got on well. Tracing the records of the estate back in history, he had never found a time when everything was so beautifully in order. True, both he and the viscount had worked hard to create that stability, but nevertheless it was a pleasure to know he had played a large part in making it so.

"I'm tired so we'll stop now, and I'll join my wife and take tea with her. Thank goodness we are up to date. It was a chore I was loath to start but a good finish."

"Oh, just one thing, milord." Watson flinched as he heard the groan. "Won't take a moment, I assure you. The post was late today but nothing came of great import except a letter from Parliament for you. Sorry I did not mention it before but it slipped my mind."

Tristan cocked an eyebrow at his secretary. "Not your style, Watson, to let anything slip, but we'll let you off this time. Give it here." He took the crisp parchment and opened it up, rapidly perusing the details. "Glory hallelujah! At last, the Poor Law Amendment Act has come to the table. I have been praying for this to happen to give succour to those most in need. The old law was a travesty of neglect, and so many people suffered because it was useless in the end. I am called for the concluding debate before it is finally ratified, but at least there is a good chance it will be. That means we must return to London. Perhaps a change of scene will do us all good. I will inform Lady Charis she is to pack."

"You will be taking your wife with you, sir?"

"Naturally, she goes where I go. I daresay she will enjoy seeing how officialdom works in the House, or doesn't." He pulled a face.

"What about the security?" Watson couldn't help but caution.

"As to that, we have enough men to guard, and maybe it will encourage this villain to show his face. If it provokes a reaction, no one will be more pleased than I. Waiting has never been my strong suit."

Chapter Fifty-Three

Supping a glass of brandy, Mountford was sitting by the window in his London lodgings gazing at the rain falling steadily outside. The scowl on his face bore testament to his inner feelings. Nothing had gone right; indeed, everything had gone completely wrong. Not only had he lost Lady Charis as a hostage but, briefly scouting Castle House, he knew that any entry there was impossible. The place was guarded like a nation's gold reserve. Forced to buy another horse as the nag left behind was only good for the knackers' yard, he eventually headed for the inn where Wallace and his stand-in were waiting. Reflecting on the taunts that Tenby had uttered that Wallace was a loose mouth, he seethed with venom. He needed neither him nor the man who was giving him an alibi. Things had gone too far for that. Yet, bodies around who would shoot their mouths off at the drop of a hat had to be silenced.

It was late when Mountford scratched a signal on a window, and Wallace let him into the tiny suite where he and his companion waited. Once in the darkened room, Mountford hushed his valet. Then it was the work of seconds to slide a stiletto into the man's heart. Catching him before he fell and careful not to get blood on his clothes, Mountford hauled him into the adjoining room and laid him on the floor.

The stand-in woke and, confused, muttered, "What's up? Oh, it's you! Wallace—"

"…is ill. I've only just got here. Have a look, will you?"

As the man bent over Wallace, again it was the work of seconds to drive the stiletto deep and finish by pushing the unsuspecting victim back on the bed. Placing the stiletto in the man's hand and the knife that he knew Wallace kept in his boot in Wallace's fist, it looked as though the two of them had fought and both lost. Satisfied that he had done for the pair of them and would not have to pay out unnecessary money, he searched the rooms for any cash then slid out of the window as quietly as he had come. Retrieving his horse from nearby and turning his face towards the capital was not a problem. Two days of hard riding saw him once again in his rooms filled with greater spleen than he had ever known.

Charis was pleased to be back in their London residence again, and lost no time visiting her favourite fashion house to order comfortable gowns to suit her pregnancy. Still slender, the tiny bump barely noticeable, she knew that condition would not last long, and she would need dresses to take her through to her confinement. Also, to her joy, Tristan had sent his carriage to Bath, and her grandmother had come to spend time with her. The surveillance was rigid but, by the time Caroline knew all the facts and had agreed the necessity of them, they settled happily to shop and exchange news.

Their visit to Parliament was an added delight to Caroline who revelled in the treat. So too was the dinner party the Fortesques gave to various friends, particularly the Manvilles who were in town awaiting the birth of one of their grandchildren. Tristan, sitting at the head of the table, watched, rather amused it had to be said, at the barely hidden stunned look on Caroline's face as his wife elegantly controlled the proceedings and delighted her guests with her repartee. His pride knew no bounds when, later, Caroline whispered to him, "Has she been taking lessons?"

"Lessons on what? Enlighten me, dear lady."

Flustered, she waved her hand. "You know – the social graces."

"Oh, those. But surely you know she was born and reared to cope with entertaining in every sense of the word. It is bred in her blood. I have a wife of par excellence, I assure you, who can deal with any engagements we create. Furthermore, we will forget this conversation ever took place. I'm sure you understand me."

Caroline took the hint and bit her lip for evermore on even the slightest criticism that might pass her lips. She sensed that the viscount would not tolerate even the least disparagement of his lovely wife and was definitely displeased she had dared to voice it.

Soon the Fortesques' arrival in town was heralded in the news-sheets, avidly read by those in town for the London Season, so requests to dine from people who were in the city to attend Parliament began to appear.

Reading the papers one morning and realising the significance, Mountford's spirits took an upward leap. At last, his day had arrived. Security was beyond a joke in Devon, the estate out of bounds to trespassers, but here in London it was a different story, especially as it seemed that milord and milady were going about their affairs, accepting invitations without a care in the world. Even so, his innate wariness made him plan carefully and take care. He would not fail this time.

Chapter Fifty-Four

Tristan, for the sake of peace and quiet, gave way to the pleas of Caroline who kept entreating Charis that a trip to the opera must simply not be missed. "Bellini's Norma is on at the King's Theatre. We definitely mustn't miss it. Everyone speaks so highly of it."

"When will she return to Bath?" he said that evening as they were getting ready for bed. "A little goes a long way with your grandmama. I've scarcely seen you these last few days except when we retire. I had the notion today to introduce you to our man of business to go through some of our holdings and ask your opinion about your trust. I didn't intend to broach it while she was present, but I'd like you to come soon so you can guide me with your wishes."

"The fortnight is almost up that we promised, so I can tactfully say that, barring some plans you have arranged for me, we are due to return home, so we must bid her farewell. The visit to the opera will be a last treat, and I'm sure she will be content with that, darling."

"*Humph*, let us hope. Very well, we shall go and, I think, include Lord and Lady Manville. The party will round things off nicely."

Two evenings later saw them all ensconced in a box enjoying the arias that were beautifully sung by the eminent performers of the day. At the interval, the Manvilles and Caroline rose to promenade the theatre to converse with their acquaintances.

Tristan laid a hand on Charis as she was about to rise. "Do you really want to face the crowds outside? I'd rather stay here with you and talk."

Intuitively concluding that he preferred them to stay out of the limelight, even though their guards were in place, Charis said, "I am rather tired, and as you know I don't like crowded places. We'll stay here."

They waved the others off and settled to relax. Tristan heaved a sigh as he slumped comfortably in his seat. "I've been meaning to ask if you would like a belated honeymoon before our infant is born, and probably go in the next few weeks. It will help to restore your health, I think, from the morning sickness and some of the physical trials you've endured this past year."

"I really am feeling better, but a honeymoon sounds lovely. Where will we go?"

"I could keep it as a surprise, but you need to know to order your wardrobe. I rather thought to return to Italy and show you some of the delightful places I know." His mouth curled in a smile as her face lit up with excitement. "The weather at the moment is not too hot, and I'll ensure your every comfort. Carrying a child is no small matter, and I want you fit and well to cope with the birth."

"How wonderful, Tris. Yes, oh yes, I'd love that above all. I've read so much about those countries and never dreamt I could visit."

"We would take in France first of all and visit your relatives; then go on to Italy where I have good friends I do business with; then a sea voyage to return home. A Grand Tour all of our own."

"Heavens, Tris, I should learn Italian and there's no time."

"Worry not, sweetheart, my friends speak English, and I believe I can manage to cope." His grin was infectious.

Rolling her eyes, she giggled. "Oh, thou paragon of virtue! Is there anything you can't do?"

"Contain my patience for much longer while this fiend roams free," he retorted, and then, irritated for spoiling the ambience of their closeness with thoughts of danger, he leaned forward to kiss her cheek. Before he could make contact, a brief knock at the door which swiftly opened had him pulling back thinking the rest of his party were returning. The man who stood in the doorway took him aback. He was neither dressed for the evening nor wore a servant's uniform. What the devil was he about?

Tristan shot to his feet, abruptly realising that, with his men near, no one should have entered their box. He glared at the intruder. Mountford! He'd swear it was him! "You've no business here. Get out!"

"I think not, milord. My particular business will not wait. You and your wife have an appointment with fate, I fear, before your companions return." He waved the gun he held in his left hand.

"Hah! One shot and you'll have half the theatre at your heels."

"Again, I think not." He lifted his other hand which held a slim throwing knife. "Silent and most effective. But I must not waste time talking. I've dealt with two of your men, but merely evaded the third."

Tristan watched him raise his arm to throw, knowing there was no room in the area to dodge. He could only stand guard in front of his wife to protect her and pray that help would arrive soon. Glancing swiftly at the next box, he realised it was empty so no help there. At the same time, he saw the door handle jiggle as though someone was testing it gently, but could not spare another look in case he missed the throw of the knife. Then the door swung open with a crash knocking the killer off balance. Roger burst in as the gun fired and the knife fell from Mountford's hand to the floor. Instantly, Mountford crouched to scrabble for it but Tristan was faster. He flung himself forward at the man's back and pinned him to the floor before he could reach it. Helpless, Mountford still tried to heave Tristan away, but by this time Roger had launched a kick at his head and, dazed with the heavy blow, he slumped down.

Tristan stared at Roger who was panting as he rubbed the shoulder where he'd hit the door. "What kept you?"

"I was warning the men to keep a closer watch in view of the crowded corridor; then came across Stevens in an alcove. He's been knifed and, yes, sadly he's a goner. I had to push through the mob to get here. Some are not too pleased with me." He shrugged as a hubbub was making itself heard through the open door.

"Was that a shot I heard?" Just then, a man appeared in the opening, his elaborate bright green coat overlaying a yellow embroidered waistcoat all topping silk pantaloons portrayed him a dandy in the first degree. He was waving a handkerchief in one hand and a quizzing glass in the other.

"I say, sirrah! Hooligans are not to be tolerated in these august halls. You, sir..." he waved at Tristan, "what the devil are you doing on the floor? Brawling is not allowed in these boxes, I'll have you know. Disgraceful conduct in front of the ladies..."

Tristan heaved a sigh and stood up. "Get out!" he said succinctly.

"What! How dare you address me in that fashion—"

"You either get out or end up like this man here who is due to be arrested for murder. Make up your mind!"

Expostulating about the low order of ruffians and how he had a good mind to call that uncouth fellow out for his damned rudeness, he allowed Roger to hustle him out. At the same time, Tristan gave a glance behind him to see how Charis was coping. Her ashen face and slumped head against the velvet chair back revealed she had fainted. At once Tristan's face blanched as he saw the stain spreading down her chest. Completely forgetting the man on the floor, he raced to her side. The gun! He knew it had gone off but, as he had to immediately react to stop Mountford getting to the knife, he had ignored the noise.

Furthermore, the general clatter in the theatre from the stalls to the gods and the movement of people in the corridors had served to deaden the sound. It had not travelled far enough to cause alarm. As he reached Charis and fell on his knees beside her, he saw the hole in her shoulder which still bled sluggishly. With fingers that shook, he searched for the pulse at her throat. The beat was there, weak but steady. He drew in a ragged breath and briefly closed his eyes in grateful thanks that she was still alive; but for how long? Dragging off his cravat, he folded it into a pad and slid it under the edge of her dress and pressed firmly against it. She stirred and moaned at the movement.

In a flash, his speed exceptional considering the blow to the head, Mountford rose to his feet, then ignoring both Tristan and Roger, who was still in the doorway and using a chair seat, he leapt onto the dividing balustrade between the boxes. From there, he jumped into the next empty box and vanished through the door before the two men could react.

Knowing pursuit was useless, Tristan bent to pick up his wife. "Forget him. Charis has been shot! Get the carriage, Roger, quick as you can!"

As he angled himself out of the doorway to avoid bumping his wife against the entrance, Caroline and the Manvilles approached.

"Good heavens, where are you going, My Lord? Is Charis ill?" Caroline burst out.

"Yes, I am taking her home." Tristan kept walking.

"Then I'll come too. She may need me," she started to insist.

"I'd rather you didn't. Stay and enjoy the opera. I will see you later," Tristan shouted back over his shoulder.

"Well, if you can manage..." Aware that she was speaking to empty air, she turned back to her companions. "We are not wanted, it seems. He is very independent and likes his own way."

Caroline was not a contentious person, though she had quarrelled with her long dead father-in-law for being the cause of her husband's death. But the relief in moving back to Bath had since tempered that ancient memory. Recently, her quarrel with Tenby had upset her normal tranquil peace. Accustomed to running her own life, she had attempted to take on Charis too, but twice if not three times she had lost out to Tristan's will. Sensing he was not pleased at her insistence they attend the opera, especially with Charis becoming ill, she was not tempted to gainsay him and risk further contretemps especially in front of her cousins. So she decided to forget Tristan's abruptness and followed them into the box.

"Come along then, we might as well enjoy the rest of the performance." They moved inside to their chairs as the curtain went up, completely unaware of the drama that had been enacted before.

Moving swiftly through the now empty corridors, Tristan reached the coach and, passing Charis to Roger, climbed in. Then he took his wife carefully again and laid her down on the seat hauling out a blanket from a locker to wrap her up before checking on the wound.

"Back to the house, quick as you can. Then warn Dr Brunton he is needed urgently. I don't care what you have to do but get him!"

Grim-faced, Roger climbed up beside the coachman. "Move as fast as you can, but try not to rock the coach too much. Her Ladyship has been shot, and speed is essential but we must take care as well. Also, no gossip about this, Henry. His Lordship requires guarded tongues. Understood?"

Keeping the speed constant and steady through fairly clear streets, Henry replied, "Yes, I knows the drill. Don't fret, won't breathe a word anyway. I got a lot of respect for them. They're the best, in my opinion."

Inside the coach, Tristan held onto his wife to prevent her moving, his face a stony mask. He had tended wounded soldiers often enough. The wound was serious but not necessarily fatal. On the other hand, the ball had lodged deep in her flesh, and the agony would come when it was removed. The short ride home was the longest Tristan had ever travelled. Charis remained unconscious, which was a blessing. To have her severely wounded was one thing, but to watch her suffer was far worse. His guilt at allowing the visit to the opera filled him with black despair. He had mentally hoped the villain would appear and they could be done with him for all time, but now with things going so badly wrong they had not only lost him but his wife might lose her life too.

Chapter Fifty-Five

Finally back at the house, Tristan carried Charis upstairs and laid her on her bed; then began to remove her clothes. The maid, standing at his shoulder, at once protested. "I think I should undress Her Ladyship. After all, I do everything for her—"

"And I think not! I know my way around her clothes, and I know how to handle her so that she is not further hurt. Fetch hot water and plenty of bandages, and then watch for the doctor." He turned back to the task of carefully disrobing his wife. When she was down to her chemise, he changed the pad over the wound and covered her with a blanket.

Just as he finished, he heard the doctor's voice talking to the maid. "A trestle table must be fetched as soon as I've seen the patient. If it's a case of shooting, no better way of dealing with it. Hurry along."

Briskly, Brunton entered the bedroom, his gaze going first to the bed where Charis lay; then to the viscount. He bowed to Tristan then, frowning, remarked, "Hmm, it seems dangerous to deny your servant. The one called Roger, so I was given to understand. He is exceptionally persuasive."

"My apologies, doctor. My fault entirely. I told him not to take no for an answer and to hurry. My wife has suffered a bullet in the shoulder and is still unconscious."

"For that, we must be thankful. Tell me, sir, you seem to be prone to these shooting accidents. I trust you have caught the perpetrator?"

"Not as yet. Charis had to be seen to urgently."

"Then we will proceed in the same manner. I take it you will assist? She will need to be held down. I'd prefer to not administer a sedative yet, and the fact she is comatose is fortunate. I have called for a table. Trying to operate on a bed is not only foolish, it is dangerous."

A knock on the door brought two footmen with the table and the housekeeper with blanket and sheets to pad it. Tristan was both amazed and relieved as, directed by the efficient doctor, who was rinsing his hands in a basin, he carefully placed Charis on it, and the doctor covered her with a sheet.

"I lose fewer patients this way, milord. Trial and error has shown us that an operation can be successful, but the aftermath fever is often fatal. Stand on the other side and hold her still. She will rouse when I begin to probe, and you must hold her still."

The doctor's forceps dug deep into her shoulder. Charis, rousing from her oblivion, gasped and struggled in vain as Tristan firmly held her down, even though his nerves shredded with her whimpers and choking sobs until sweat beaded his brow with anguish for her pain.

Finally, Brunton straightened with a triumphant grin. "Got it!" Dropping the ball and his forceps into a basin, he set about staunching the blood that was flowing copiously once again. Packing the wound with Tristan's help, and setting bandages to keep the wadded pad in place took no time at all, and at last Tristan put her back to bed where the doctor dosed her with laudanum. At length, Tristan heaved a final sigh of relief.

About to leave, Brunton shook Tristan's hand. "I understand, according to Roger, my visit here is to see someone…?" He paused and waited for an answer.

"Yes, that is so. An elderly housemaid who is feverish."

"In that case, I will be along in the morning to attend her again. It does you credit, milord, to look after your servants so well. I wish some of my richer patients were so compassionate." His lips curled in amusement. "Goodnight, milord. Try not to worry." With a last bow, he left the room.

Tristan turned to look at Charis who was deep in sleep. Then, calling for the table and debris to be removed, he gave orders for a maid to sit with his wife, and Roger to attend him in the nearby sitting room. Arriving there, he went at once to the decanter, poured a large glass of brandy and took a hefty swallow.

As he sat waiting for Roger, he contemplated his reactions to her injury. If he was so chicken-hearted now, how the hell would he get on when she was in labour? God, he loved her so much he felt terrified she would suffer again and this time for him so he could get his heir. Emptying the glass, he was about to fill it up again when a knock at the door made him pause.

"Come in!" he growled. "Oh, it's you! Roger, we have to talk."

"I was on my way to see you. I've found Mountford's lodgings."

Tristan gaped in shock. "How the hell did you manage that?"

"I remembered a smithy close to this house and called on him after I brought the doctor. He knew Mountford and where he lived. I've got the directions. A case of overdue debt for the nag the smith supplied. He's likely skint!"

"Chasing up and down the countryside after us has not been too profitable, I collect, and I deduce he was not flush with money before that. In fact, I reckon his persistence is more money orientated than otherwise. I could be wrong. An earldom was a target he originally aspired to. His ambition is now severely curtailed. What say you, Roger? Shall we pay him off and let him go?"

"And pigs might bloody fly, begging your pardon, milord."

"As ever, we are of twin minds." The icy smile was malevolent. "Charis will sleep for a while. I think we will pay a visit to our friend tonight and make him aware we are not pleased with his actions."

Taking advantage of the shadows, the two men soon arrived in Belgrave Square. Dressed overall in black and armed with a pistol each and a knife each for their boots, they warily approached the area. Roger, who had spoken at length to the smithy and been given precise guidance, took his master through narrow alleys until he stopped outside a three-storey tenement house hemmed in between others of like nature.

"Back entrance?" Tristan whispered.

"Yes, but only way out is to this lane. He's on the third floor."

"What about the roof?"

"Bloody death trap, if you ask me. Look up there: those slates look rotten."

"Right, let's go." Tristan felt the thrill of anticipation wash through him, resurrecting his army days. He hadn't lost his touch.

Quietly forcing the main door, they eased their way up two flights of stairs and stopped to listen. Late as it was, all they heard was the occasional snore, loud enough to penetrate the thin doors that led to the individual flats.

Roger stopped outside one of the three doors on the third landing and listened. Not this one, he sensed. He nudged Tristan and pointed to the base of the third door where a glimmer of light showed under the threshold. "Could be?" he breathed a whisper.

Tristan made a pushing gesture. Roger nodded and held up three fingers. Right! One, two, three and go! He held himself ready. The door crashed open, and a startled Mountford who was standing in the doorway of a kitchen stopped dead for only seconds then spun into the room and slammed the door closed. At once, they heard the dragging of a heavy piece of furniture and a crash as it slammed against the door.

"That boyo has the speed of a bloody tiger, damn his soul!" swore Roger as he heaved against the door. Tristan joined him and together they managed to shift the dresser.

In the kitchen, the window was open, and they could hear a scrabbling sound as Mountford clawed his way up an iron ladder fixed to the wall.

"My God, the man's well prepared!" Tristan stretched out to grasp the ironwork.

"No, sir, let me go," begged Roger.

"Not this time. My wife, my quarrel, and I believe it's my turn. You've done enough. Get to the road and catch him if I lose him."

By the time Tristan was at the gutter edge of the roof, Mountford, half bent over, taking care with the sloping roof, was making his way across the slates to the chimney pots that divided the terraced houses. He disappeared behind them. Quickly, but balancing carefully, Tristan reached the pots and saw a short section of roof beyond that seemed lower than the height they were on. Probably the neighbouring roofs descended in like manner thus offering an escape route. Disregarding the sound of cracking slates beneath him, he moved as rapidly as he could to the peak of the roof to see over to the next house and spot the direction Mountford would take. A foot on each side of the crest to steady him, he saw the crouching figure ahead scuttling rapidly to the far side of the next house.

Mountford had almost reached the next set of chimneys when, all of a sudden, he gave a startled scream. Tristan saw his arms wave violently as he tried to regain his balance when a large hole opened up in the tiles alongside. He attempted to avoid falling into the hole but staggered ungainly, his body out of control. The next moment saw him tumble awkwardly down across the lower slates and, in an instant, slither off the eaves. A resounding crash echoed loudly as the body hit an obstacle. At once, Tristan hastily started back to the kitchen then slid down the stairs as fast as he could before he attracted attention. Once out in the street, he spotted Roger standing further down the road gazing at a body lying twisted on the roof of a derelict shed.

"Dead?" was all he could voice with the effort to inhale more air.

Roger nodded. "Yes, I'd say he's a goner."

"Home, I think. We've done enough."

Silently, they walked home, both wrung out with the unexpected finality of the night. Even after all the shocking attempts on his life, Tristan had previously felt detached from revenge. It had been the shooting of Charis that had brought his blood to the boil. Knowing he no longer needed to seek vengeance, he still could not believe it was all over and they could live their lives free from danger. He quickened his steps in a hurry to get back to his dearest love. God grant she would recover from the attack and they would enjoy the belated honeymoon.

As far as Roger was concerned, it was a job well done, and he had upheld his oath to protect his Lord and Lady. God grant he would be at their sides to protect as long as he was spared to do so.

Tristan dismissed the maid saying, "Go to bed, I am here now." As he undressed and slid into bed alongside Charis, she stirred and wriggled uncomfortably. "Do you wish to pass water, my love?"

"Hmm. Oh yes, I do! How did you know?" Then, as he helped her out of bed, "Tristan? You are here?"

"Of course, where I shall always be." He promptly fetched a chamber pot and helped her to sit. She sighed in relief as she relieved herself. Then he picked her up and put her back to bed. "Oh dear, perhaps I should have had the maid assist me. I am beginning to feel somewhat—"

"Embarrassed?" he interjected with a grin. "You can't be after all the time we have been married. Besides, how do the words go? In sickness and health – do you want me to recite it? I can only add: forever and ever, my love."

"But what of Mountford? We still have to face him."

"No, Charis, he is gone, never to return."

"Did you kill him?" In the light of the candle, her eyes widened.

"No. He managed that perfectly, all by himself. Now, go to sleep, my darling. I need you to get well before we take our trip."

She yawned contentedly and cuddled closer to him wondering why she felt so wrapped and up and stiff, but the laudanum was still strong in her body, and she fell asleep to dream of halcyon days in Italy.

Roger snaffled the news-sheets in the morning before a footman ironed them for His Lordship. There was only a short paragraph recording the mysterious fatality of a man falling off a high tenement roof which had proved to be rotten. To date, no relatives had claimed him. As far as the constabulary were concerned, he had no business climbing there and was only one of an anonymous breed to be found in the city. He would go to a pauper's grave. Roger chuckled; a fitting end for the villain. At least his evil exploits would not impinge on the family. They would escape the notoriety and gossip from the *ton*. Society would never get to hear of the events that had almost brought the Fortesques to ruin. His Lordships would appreciate the reality of that.

Epilogue

Castle House was unusually quiet; orders given in the lowest of whispers as the staff carried out their duties. The silence had carried on for several hours until listening ears caught the sound of a baby's cry. Immediately, joyful faces were seen. "She's had it!" Voices passed the wonderful news around the house and then to the outside servants and grooms who were equally on edge for news.

A few minutes later, another cry was heard and someone said, "Gawd! Hope he's not going to be a squealer. They're the worst."

Amery was in the study trying to keep Tristan calm. He beamed as his son jumped to his feet as the first cry came through the open door then paused as he heard the baby cry again. "Ah, praise the Lord, just as I thought."

Tristan halted for an instant, perplexed at his father's words.

"Thought what?"

"I'll wager you'll find you have twins, my boy. Your mother was one of a twin, and, to be truthful, Charis was uncommonly huge for her tiny figure to cope."

"Robert never mentioned it."

"He did not wish to alarm you more than you were. Even with a natural birth, accidents happen and one baby is lost. Go quickly. Tell Charis she has my blessing. I will see her later."

Tristan took the stairs two at a time; his first thought was Charis. Sitting on the bed beside her, he bent and kissed her lips. "My precious darling, how do you feel?"

"Tired, sore, but very pleased. Do you know you have *two* sons?"

He gulped, tears choking his throat. "How clever is that? An heir and a spare all in one go. Remarkable arranging, I must say! Once you recover, you will solely be mine again for as long as it takes—"

"Shush! People are listening!" Charis poked him in the chest. "Stop making plans for me! Go see your remarkable offspring. They are truly beautiful!"

He did as he was bid, and gazed down at the two infants lying top and tail in a nearby cot. Hmm, they did look splendid. Visions of them running through the grounds as he and Henry once did filled him with the nostalgia of the past. He'd teach them to play cricket…ah, what the hell, that was a long way off, and at this moment he had his beautiful wife safe after her labour and his to adore. What more could a man want?

Acknowledgements

Authors may write in solitary confinement but they never stand alone. They are guarded by a team of people who do their best to produce the work that emerges from an imaginative mind. Their efforts do not go unsung by authors, for without their input no books would ever appear in shops or libraries. So thank you, my dear friends and gallant team at SilverWood, for your stalwart efforts are very much appreciated.